CW00517324

AN AGENT'S DEMISE

Philip G Henley

ONLY THE TRUTH BROKEN

Once we thought war would be fun
A chance to fight to learn whilst young
And then we learned some did not return
Or their bodies broken

Where they stood was wasteland made
The shells and bombs and bullets rained
And then rebuild for their return
But the spirit broken

What of the leader swept away
Who roused the people to the fight
They will fear not a return
They are never broken

Behind the scenes a goal conspires
To seek a path for other means
The cause provided a just return
Only the truth broken

© Philip G Henley 2012

BBC NEWS REPORT

Fresh doubts over Iraq's arsenal

"A leaked US intelligence report has cast fresh doubt on the coalition claims that Iraq had banned weapons which served as justification for going to war. The secret September 2002 Pentagon intelligence report concluded that there was "no reliable information" that Iraq had biological or chemical weapons. It is believed the report was widely circulated in the Bush administration at a time when senior officials were putting the case for military action."

BBC News Report 6 June 2003

THE ORGANISATIONS

The Security Service

MI5, Five, Thames House

Jonathan Braithwaite - Operations

Stephen Carlisle - Controller

Michelle Carrington - Personal Assistant (PA) to Ian Hedges

Sally Carver - Former PA to Ian Hedges

Julian Clarkson - Director General

Ian Hedges - Divisional Policy Director

Gerald Hemmings - Controller

Colin McDowell - Chief Information Officer (CIO)

Ian Shoreditch - Divisional Director Security

Jenny Wallace - Analyst

The Secret Intelligence Service

MI6, SIS, Six, Vauxhall

Jessica Carver - Analyst

George Claridge-Briggs - Divisional Director

Tony Grayson - Lead Analyst

Luke Hargreaves - Internal Affairs

Harriet Hollingsworth - Operations

Bahaarat Ibn Kalid - Agent

Monica Pennywise - Director General

Richard Templeman - PA to Director General

Central Intelligence Agency

CIA, Langley, The Farm

Jamie Adams - Agent

Reach Claremont - Agent

Geoff Hidelwietz - Divisional Director

Casey Richenbach - Former Station chief

Carl Schlemburg - London Station Chief

Beth Schwarz - PA to Station Chief

Special Branch

John Drinkwater - Detective Sergeant (DS)

Dave Grahams - Detective Constable (DC)

Jack Hooper - Detective Inspector (DI)

David Jones - Commander

William Pollard - DC

James Rutledge - DS

Pete Watkins - DC

Metropolitan Police and The Serious Fraud Office

The Met, SFO

Duncan Asquith - Assistant Commissioner

Dan Gibson - Police Constable (PC)

Stewart Hillier - Information Technology (IT) Technician

Liam Jones - PC

Gary Parkinson - Detective Sergeant

Andy Rhodes - Sergeant

Rick Stark - PC

Shelly Stephens - PC

Other Agencies

Elliot Bloomstein - United States of America's (USA) Ambassador to the UK

Sylvia Cardôtte - Agent, Direction Générale de la Sécurité Extérieure (DGSE). The French External Intelligence Service.

Frederick Carmichael - Lieutenant Colonel, The Army

Mark Ellis - Officer, Royal Air Force (RAF) Intelligence

Tom Ferguson - Controller, Canadian SIS

Charles Goodson - Procurement, Ministry of Defence

(MoD)

Andy McLeish - Staff Sergeant, The Army

Jodi Parker - Operations, Defence Intelligence

Celia Romero - Agent, DGSE France

Helena Salbert - Agent, Canadian SIS

Peter Smith - Analyst, Defence Intelligence

CHAPTER ONE

Prologue

The four men had met for the third time in two weeks. They were seated as before around a small table, but no one was drinking alcohol. The first man asked for a progress update.

The second man on his right responded, "The asset is in play and set up; he has already proved himself. I won't trouble you with the details but better than expected."

The third man said, "Good, I should have a mission for you soon, but I need to work on the funding a bit more."

The fourth man said, "Excellent progress, I'll have something for you soon, probably in the New Year."

The first man grunted. "All of this will be pointless unless the politicians can be persuaded to act. No needless bloodletting though, use the asset as sparingly as possible and only for this, no sidelines," he challenged.

"He's my asset. I'll use him as necessary, don't worry he can't be connected. We know the politicians, especially on my side; we have to have something they can't ignore." The Second man again.

The fourth man asserted, "A change of presidency will help."

"We can get something, but it will need verification. It's a matter of pointing others in the right direction, and removing or constraining conflicting evidence," the second man.

"If we have sources coming from multiple locations it will become overwhelming, privately and publicly. The politicians will have to act," the second again.

"Well, the UN can be persuaded as long as the French are on side, the Russians won't be happy, the Chinese will stay quiet. I might need some help with the Canadians. I'll let you know," the third man said.

"It's agreed then," said the first. They all nodded. "Contact codeword will be 'Demise' plus the date."

CHAPTER TWO

Match

"Can it be that it was all so simple then..."

The lyric crackled from the car radio. He smiled. It was not a genuine smile, more a cynical adjustment of the teeth into a grimace. He checked the mirror. The car was still there, three vehicles back, and in the outside lane. The traffic lights turned green. He edged the car forward.

They were definitely onto him. Do not be paranoid, how could they be onto him? He thought that his answers and explanations had been sufficient, but perhaps they were following everyone connected? "Must be costing a fortune in resources," he thought with another grimace into the mirror. There was always the danger that he had misjudged or made a mistake.

He pulled into the nearest space and went to the cash machine. The car following had also stopped, definitely following. Cash, balance check, all normal the money was there. Estate agents and pick up the keys for the new penthouse. Meander down the street into the coffee shop; regular coffee with an almond croissant and a seat in the window. He watched the watchers whilst scanning the paper. Third page news, slowly disappearing as the latest politics or a disaster took its place in the headlines, until the next one. Four now, that they knew about. Each producing more headlines for a suitable period, then slowly disappearing, just like the evidence. No leads, said the paper. So why were they outside? Two of them, not being very discrete. Probably trying to push him into the error that they wanted; create the moment that would make their careers. No chance, no mistakes, he was on a list that was all. Give it time; just stick to the routine and let them get bored. Let the resources run out; until next time.

White, male, six feet, dark hair, shoulder length, wearing... He laughed to himself, as if the clothes would stay the same. Okay he was white, six-one; his off-blond hair should rule him out. It was cut short, easy to wash, no drying, his squad had said when he had first had it cut short. It had been dark then.

Had it started way back then, years ago? No, it was before that. Fate, maybe he had always been fated to do this. Okay, when then? At school when he had started following that girl in the year above, what was her name? Angie, yes Angie, he had followed her around for several weeks despite lessons. She had never caught him, even when he was in her house two streets from his. He was fourteen. '*Memories*,' that was the name of the song. He knew it would be in his head all day now.

So, why the attention from the two in the car? Just checking on him? They were probing, looking for an opening. He understood the methodology.

It was time for the match; the crowd was building on the pavement. He left the shop and walked to the ground. He showed his member's card and entered the Oval at ten forty-five for a day of watching, whilst remembering, in the comfort of the crowd. How had it come to this? He played 'what if' with himself. The 'what ifs' were always more negative. He could not help himself. That was the ultimate answer. Polite applause around the ground a fine piece of play he joined in and then returned to his thoughts.

The two men entered and scanned the row of seats as they walked towards him. Stay calm, concentrate on the match.

"Hello Sir, we just had a couple more questions." The smaller one, with the narrow eyes, Sergeant something, or other.

"How on earth did you track me down here?" Pretend ignorance of their chase, not too confident, relax they know nothing; they're just probing, checking, hoping for a break.

"Did you say you were here on the 15th, Sir?"

"Yes, it was the day-night match."

"What was the result?" The taller one spoke, Detective Constable, DC, Grahams.

"The game was abandoned due to rain, Surrey on the Duckworth Lewis calculation." Duckworth Lewis was a method of calculating needed scores when weather affected cricket matches.

"And what did you do then?"

"I had a drink in the Members' bar, then chatted with a couple of people, and then went home," slight exasperation.

"And what time was that?" Sergeant… Rutledge that was it.

"Left here about eleven, got in about midnight."

"What about before the match what were you doing then?" A proper duo, exchanging questions like a pair of TV Panellists.

"When exactly?"

"Just take us through the day."

They were completely unalike in appearance, but they were merging into a single entity. What was that film? Schwarzenegger and De-Vito as *Twins*? They were almost thinking each other's thoughts, finishing each other's sentences, and merging together as a greater sum of the parts, teamwork. He hadn't been a team player in a long while. He was drifting. He needed to concentrate. One of the other members in the stand asked them to sit down as they were blocking the view. The Sergeant gave him a withering look, but he knew he was attracting attention from the stewards and the other members.

"Is there somewhere quieter we could go?"

"Look Detective Sergeant, I've already told you what I did that day, I'm here to watch the match, perhaps we could meet up at another, more convenient time." He added a compliant smile and pulled his diary from his inside left jacket pocket.

"That's okay Sir, we'll be in touch, if we need to ask any other questions."

They walked off without a backward glance, probably to

resume their watch from elsewhere or more likely to return to another potential target.

The Members' steward came over. "Are you all right Mr. Slater, Sir? Who were those… those, those *Gentlemen*?"

"That, Henry, was the police. Nothing to worry about. I'm sorry they disturbed the other members."

Henry ambled off to fetch him a pre-lunch drink. He returned to the game and his thoughts. What could they have? CCTV maybe, but that would not show much. The taxi driver had dropped him in the frame, a mistake; a careless mistake, too close to a pickup, and a direct route back to the house. He should have done a swap. They would then be looking for another cabbie. Instead, they had him being picked up near the Oval ground, but also near the Vauxhall tube station at the time the girl had disappeared. Careless, he could not be careless again.

CHAPTER THREE

The Twins

Detective Sergeant James Rutledge and Detective Constable David Grahams made a good team. Between them, they had nearly twenty years' experience and three each on this squad working for Detective Inspector Jack Hooper.

"Something's not right about him, Dave."

"I know what you mean, but he's checked out okay, so far."

"He's the right height, shape, colour."

"Different hair though."

"We need to check that alibi and check Mr Slater a bit more. Try to get the taxi driver to be more precise, or get another witness from the tube. You go back to base. I'll stay here."

"What about the girl?"

"Check her movements more, see if anyone else shows up from the tube CCTV, and see where we've got on any other CCTV. There must be some other coverage, another camera? How many have we got on film?"

"On the tube?"

"Yes"

"We had five, two were black, which we've put on the back burner because of the previous description. There's that old bloke Potter, and we're left with two. One might be Slater and then Mr

X."

"Anything from John's team on Mr X?" Detective Sergeant John Drinkwater led the second team working for Hooper.

"Nothing they've passed on, but he looks too short on the CCTV."

"Okay, we'll carry on with Slater."

"Surveillance?"

"Only when we have time, I'll start with that Steward after lunch, I reckon Slater is set for the day."

CHAPTER FOUR
Night On The Town

Four, the paper said, if only they knew. He returned to his diary. The girls plus the others were a lot more than four. He did not bother to add them up. It was odd that the male targets had not attracted attention, and had not been linked in the press. Who had leaked it and why? Proper *missions* as he called them, plus practice runs. All recorded in the diary if you knew the key to unlocking doors and unlocking secrets. His lecturer Professor Reginald Gabbins came to mind; his scruffy tweed jacket and thick glasses; his effortless way with numbers and ciphers. Gabbins wanted to unlock secrets, whereas he wanted to hide them. Gabbins was dead now, and his biggest secret went with him. Could he count that as his *mission* as well? Maybe it was a side mission, successful, but not the main event. Eight years since the first, what did that make him? Monster, madman? They were easy press headlines with which to label him. What would the headlines be like if they really knew? What was it that made him the way he was? Forget it, savour the moment. Plan the next. When? Several weeks at least, out of the country, another research trip should cover it. How long would he need? Perhaps two, or three weeks, maybe a month dependent on the target's actions. His mind raced with anticipation, already beginning the journey to the final climatic ending.

Lunch came and went in a relaxed atmosphere of half remembered acquaintances and discussion of the finer points of the game. The afternoon sped by. He followed the match more closely keeping the deeper, darker thoughts away. Close of play, and wandering back to his car, no sign of the *twins*. He drove back to the house and parked. He changed, and then caught a cab to the Covent Garden area. No tail as far as he could see. Time for some dinner, and then, he thought, maybe a stroll through a couple of nightspots, admiring the women from a distance. Not his next target. No traces, no track, no records, planning practice and execution. Briefings flooded back SMEAC - Situation, Mission, Execution, Any Questions, and Check Understanding. The whole strategy in place of objectives, tactics and missions. Yes, *mission* was the right word.

In the second bar of the evening, she was sitting on a bar stool waiting for someone. She turned expectantly as he walked in the door. The look of disappointment was clearly etched on her face. She reminded him of a previous mission; similar hair, height, and looks. She covered her disappointment with a smile, he smiled back and went to the far end of the bar ordering his large gin and tonic. Whilst he toyed with his drink, he casually watched her via the bar mirror. Nice, his type. The door opened, and she showed that look of disappointment again. She sipped her drink. It was something with coke in a tumbler. The memory of the previous mission interplayed with the reality in the bar. She caught him looking at her in the mirror; he smiled, his winning smile rather than the grimace he used in the car mirror. He waved his glass at her miming the offering of a drink; she shook her head holding up her own nearly full tumbler, half-returning his smile. She checked her watch. Her red blouse was open at the neck a glimpse of cleavage from the second button down. She wore a thin gold chain around her throat, with a small pendant dangling down the blouse; a beige skirt knee length and bare legs with strapped heeled sandals; nice. In the mission, her look alike had been thinner and with longer blonder hair, but there was a striking similarity. They could have been twins. He smiled with the memory of his other twin fascination from the ground earlier. The door opened again; again disappointment. She removed a mobile phone from her small clutch bag, called a number, no reply. He stood to go, his observation over.

"I'll take that drink if you are still offering," she said as he went to pass her on the way out. He stopped and smiled.

"Sure, what would you like?" He called the barman over and

sat down next to her. He noticed her nails. They were medium length with that polish to them. French polish that's what it was called.

"I'm Jess," she said, offering her hand with a bright open smile, soft lipstick.

"Mike," he quickly conjured. Her handshake was firm, not soft, even if her hand was. He did not want to let go.

"Really? I seem to be surrounded by Mikes."

"What would you like my name to be?"

"Oh I don't know, maybe a Tom, a … or a Harry." The last name slurred slightly, she was a bit tipsy and definitely flirting. Her left hand had no rings. She did the flicked hair thing that body language experts claimed was a sure sign of flirting. He had always thought it was just a way of moving hair out of the way. She was flirting.

"Why so many Mikes?" He asked, as their drinks came and he paid the barman. Her smile slipped a little. He'd touched a nerve.

"Oh my brother, my father, my…"

"Boyfriend?" He interrupted.

"No boyfriend, I have a brother and an unreliable one at that." More raw nerves.

"What do you do? No, let me guess, PR or publishing?"

She laughed. That was much better, "No, I'm a spy for a secret foreign power," more flirting.

"Really, I didn't think there were any secret foreign powers left?"

"Only this one, and I'm its top spy."

"Ah, does this mean I'm in imminent danger?"

"Of course, but I'll protect you."

The drinks were almost gone. "Another?" She checked her watch; disappointment on her face. This little interlude was being turned into a warm memory, with no further action.

"No, thank you, I should head home."

"Can I get you a cab?"

"No, I'll walk to the train."

"May I escort you?" He tried to make it sound informal, whilst dressing it up as a formal proposal with a gallant bow.

She laughed, hesitated, considered the options. "Why thank you Sir Michael, I would be honoured." They left the bar; he offered her his arm and she took it. He could smell her perfume. As they moved off towards the station he glanced down, unable to prevent his eyes drawn to the second blouse button. A hint of black underwear, and a swell before he looked up at her. He stopped, and she turned to him. She lifted her mouth up towards his, a kiss, lips slightly parted, a taste of lipstick and the brandy and coke from her drink. She broke off. "That was nice, and now I think…"

He kissed her again, this time holding the back of her head with his right hand whilst his left settled on the waistband of her skirt. Her right hand slid inside his jacket onto his waist and round to the small of his back. "About that cab," she said as they broke lip contact, her hand stayed where it was. He released her head, but lowered his left hand to the swell of her hip. He flagged a passing one.

"Where to?"

"Cranmer Road, number 23."

It could not be; too much of a coincidence. His heart raced, he had to stop this. It was too dangerous. There must not be any connections. He still climbed into the cab next to her. She shuffled close to him, her hand holding his against her knee.

"I shouldn't be doing this," she sighed.

"Why, what are we doing?"

She again leaned into him offering her mouth, and pulling his hand slightly up her leg. He returned her kiss whilst trying to control his racing mind. How to play this, he must stay calm. Think.

When was it, five years ago? No, more like six. He would need to check his dairy to be sure, but not now, not when he could feel her tongue touching his teeth. Her phone rang, and she slowly broke away with a dreamy half smile. She looked at the caller identity number.

She answered "Jess," a long statement from the caller followed, but he couldn't hear. "No, I'm okay, I'm with someone. No one you know." She looked at him and squeezed his hand onto her thigh. "I will, bye." She finished the call.

"Let me guess," he said, "another Mike?"

"You are too good at guessing," she smiled and moved to put her head on his shoulder. She moved his hand higher. He glanced down; he could see most of her thigh now and his hand was beneath her skirt. Her thigh was velvet. What was he doing here? This was crazy. He had to stop this before the situation was compromised, the mission was compromised. The cab turned into the street. It looked familiar. The house looked familiar. The memories were there. The door was a different colour, the windows were different, but it was the same house. He must not go in, but he knew he would. "Would you like to come in for that drink and ..." She stopped with that flirting smile. He paid the cab and followed her up the two steps to the front door. She already had the key out of her small bag. She opened the door, and he entered the target operating area.

"Stop this. Stop it now," he thought.

She closed the door behind him, and then pushed him back against the door. Her kiss was electric. She stepped back from him and, looking directly into his eyes, unbuttoned her blouse so that it hung open. She unbuttoned her skirt, and let it fall kicking off her sandals as she did. Then, she moved in and kissed him again. Just as his hands had begun to explore her back she pulled away and, barefoot, wiggled her way through the first door on the left to the kitchen. He followed into a reorganised open plan lounge with a small round dining table. It was not like before. She was reaching into a cupboard for a bottle and two glasses. The layout was similar, but different, his mind raced to reorganise the layout with his memory. Hallway, kitchen, dining room, lounge, another reception on the other hallway, small bathroom, rear garden door, then the stairs up to the three bedrooms, and another bathroom. The fourth step had creaked.

She poured the drinks and motioned him to sit on the sofa. He did so, shrugging off his jacket. She smiled and sat next to him curling her bare legs under her as she leaned against him for another slower kiss. The drinks were placed on the floor. She stretched out on the sofa like a cat. Her head descended to his lap, and she looked up at him. She pulled his face down for another kiss. The blouse had parted, revealing her torso and black underwear. He brushed the outline of her stomach with the tips of his nails. His fingers followed the outline of her black panties before rising up to cup her breast as he kissed her. She eased herself up and taking his hand pulled him back to the corridor and up the stairs. The fourth step still creaked.

The digital clock was showing 3:30 a.m. when he heard the creak. He felt her leg against his. Her arm was across his stomach and her breathing was deep. He was alert now he had heard the creak. He moved to pull away from her. She rolled away, her spine in outline with her back to him, taking the tangled sheets with her. He rolled off the bed onto the floor sensing the movement outside the bedroom door, which was only half closed. A clink sounded like his trouser belt where it had been discarded earlier. He silently crabbed his way to the wall adjacent to the door. Heart accelerating, adrenaline filling, he slowly rose to his feet in a slight crouch, ready to pounce. How many out there? He strained to hear and discriminate the foot movements, the breathing, any metallic clicks signalling the attack. A stumble from outside of the door and then …

"God damn it Jess," a young man's voice. Another stumble, the bathroom light clicked on, Jess stirred. He started to collect his clothes but had to reach out into the hallway, lit from beneath the bathroom door, to collect his trousers and shirt, where she had stripped them off him. She stirred. In the half-light he could make out her body with the sheet wrapped around her, her left breast above the sheet. Desire rushed in on him.

"Mmmmike," he thought she murmured. He returned to her side, stroked her shoulder, and pulled the sheet to cover her, and reluctantly got up again. He finished collecting his clothes. He heard the bathroom toilet flush and another stumble, before the footsteps went into another bedroom. He heard the slump of someone hitting a bed. Darkness, silence, his friends return. He crept stealthily downstairs, treading over the red blouse and black bra; he avoided the fourth step. He dressed in the lounge where he collected his jacket and checked the pockets; all was well. He found her mobile phone and noted the number. On a piece of paper, he quickly wrote a note.

Jess, I will call, M

He moved towards the front door, smiling to himself as he noted the discarded clothes. More memories to keep. He left the house for the second time.

CHAPTER FIVE

A One Night Stand?

Jess awoke with a small start. She looked at the clock; six-thirty. She realised he had gone and leaned back onto the bed's headboard. Damn, a one night stand, how had she let herself do that? No condoms, what was she thinking? She ached in all the right places and smiled at the memory of him touching her, her touching him, his muscles, his strength. She did not have a number, or a second name. What a smile he has, she reflected. She angered, "Get a grip girl you ought to have more control," she told herself. She got up before her alarm, seeing the wreckage of the room. She showered, picked up her blouse and bra from the hall, and dressed ready for work. Michael's door was closed.

She went downstairs and retrieved her skirt and shoes. Had she really done that, undressed like that in front of him? She must have been drunk, but she knew she had not been that drunk. Why then, what was it about him that had let him bring her home, bring him to her bed? She went into the kitchen diner, remembering the events of the previous evening and saw the note. Relief, joy, concern, flooded through her mind. Not a one night stand. He will call. His handwriting was neat and precise. She smiled. When would he call?

"Hi Jess, what did you get up to last night?" Michael, her brother, wandered into the kitchen area stealing her coffee mug and giving her his best fatherly look, which failed utterly, due to the grin he could not hide. "You seemed to be keen to get undressed?"

"None of your business, and how is the luscious Lucy?"

"Very luscious," he laughed. "Well who is he and, more importantly, where is he?"

"His name is Mike, and he had to go."

"And who or what is Mike?"

"None of your business," she tried to stall.

"Oh Jess, not a one night stand?"

"No, he left me a note. Anyway it's your fault. If you had turned up as arranged, we wouldn't have met."

"I told you on the phone I was detained. I think I fell over his trousers last night."

"Don't change the subject. Lucy wouldn't let you out? Anyway whilst we're questioning certain people's morality what time did you get in last night?"

"After three," her brother sheepishly replied

"Why didn't you stay, or won't she let you?"

"It's not her; it's her flat mates, one of the rules of the house apparently."

The conversation drifted to a close. Jess finished getting ready for work and left at eight thirty for the short trip to the office, waiting for his call. She made a diary entry of their meeting on the central system. Delving into the files of the morning, she found it hard to concentrate. Tony her boss smiled at her, but left her to her own devices, seeing she was busy but looking happy.

CHAPTER SIX

Ask That Again

It took him two hours to get to the house which he used as his main home for the John Slater ID. It was a safe house of sorts, albeit a semi-public one. It is not a real home. He has no *real* home. He had to go to two safe locations before he dared to make the direct route. In an early morning cab, he had checked his diary. It was just under six years ago. Sally Carver, not twins but sisters. Jess would have been 21 or 22 then, and at University. Mike, her brother, was two years younger, also at University. Sally had been alone in the house. No parents, no visitors, solitary and lonely. She had been an easy target. He'd spent two months on reconnaissance for the mission, before deciding the house had to be the target area. Jess could not know, could not possibly suspect, who he might be. Their meeting was a coincidence and nothing more. That did not solve his current entanglement. He showered, smelling her perfume which still lingered on his body. He dried, shaved, and set the alarm for two hours. Rest is a weapon; old training cliché over used by Ludlum in his Bourne series, but still true. He had been awake no more than ten minutes when the doorbell rang. He checked the CCTV coverage. The police twins stood waiting.

"Ah, Mr. Slater you are in."

"Evidently Sergeant, would you like to come in?"

"Thank you Sir, if you have a few minutes?"

"Please come through. Can I get you coffee, tea?"

"No, we're fine thank you."

He gestured for them to take a seat. "What can I do for you officers?" Calm, casual, no hints. Do not give them anything to grip.

"Did you enjoy the game? I hear Andrews played well?"

"Sergeant," more exasperation, "Andrews didn't play, so can we stop the silly 'let's catch you out' questions and get to the point. I do have a job to do you know." Careful, do not push back too hard, they will only suspect more.

"What is it exactly you do, Mr. Slater, or may I call you John?"

"You can call me what you like Sergeant, as I told you before, I trade in shares and bonds as an individual."

"Isn't that a very risky occupation," a slight hesitation before, "John?"

"Only if you don't know what you are doing."

"Could you tell us where you were last night?"

"No, I couldn't."

"Something to hide, Sir?" Back to sir now, careful, but they can't find out about Jess.

"Nothing to hide, I just like to keep my private life, private."

"We are struggling to confirm your whereabouts on the 15th?"

"I'm surprised you're struggling as I have told you where I was."

"Yes, but we seem to have a gap."

"Really, for when?"

"Ten in the evening until midnight."

"And why should that be a problem?"

"That's the nub, you see? That's when Miss Wallace went missing."

"As I told you last time, I don't know a Miss Wallace." He stared them down believing the statement until they both consulted their notebooks.

"Perhaps this picture might remind you." The Sergeant pulled a 10" by 6" photo of the girl. It was her, albeit a younger version. His expression was blank.

"Attractive girl, but I don't know her." That was true; he didn't know her in the way they thought he might.

"Sir, what if I told you, we have you on CCTV on the station platform with Miss Wallace at 10:15 p.m. on the 15th."

"Well, you will have mistaken me for someone else. As you know I was still at the ground in the members bar then."

"It's less than 5 minutes away."

"So is half of London, now I'm sorry to interrupt this conversation, but the market is about to open and I need to earn my keep." He gestured back to the front door.

The twins left. He turned to his screens and made three deals, two sells, one buy, all futures. The sells netted nearly £50,000. He recorded the deals, checked the tax return, paid three bills, and logged off. Ten o'clock, now for Jess.

He called her mobile, no caller ID on his phone.

"Hello this is Jess Carver." She was not tipsy now, not gasping, nor flirting.

"Hello Jess, I said I'd call."

"Hello Mike, I missed you this morning." Her voice was cautious, protective, seeming to sum up the, 'would he call, wouldn't he call, do I want him to call,' situation in just those few words.

"I'm sorry I left early, we didn't discuss if I should stay."

"I think we were otherwise engaged. Did you want to stay?" Back to flirting. He'd passed a test by calling, and another with the tone of the call.

"Can I see you later?" So blunt, so straightforward, and

completely the wrong thing to do, why had he said it?

"When? I mean aren't you at work?"

"I'm free for lunch if you are, does the super power let its spies take lunches?"

"I had too much to drink, but yes I am free for lunch, and the afternoon." Was that an implied offer?

"That would be nice, shall I pick you up from home, or where do you work?"

"Home is fine. I'll see you around one?"

"See you then." He reluctantly disconnected the call. He must be mad. Why was he chasing her when he could easily walk away? 'Something', George Harrison's song, a haunting melody that would be in his mind all day now.

Jess checked with Tony. She could have the afternoon off. It was okay; he would ring if he needed anything.

Two more calls, regardless of the now, he needed to set up his next trip soon. Sunday for flights, hotels, cars; they all needed arranging, and starting with a one way to Rome. Time to move location and hope the twins were not outside. He did not want to have to lose them. He secured the house, double-checking the computer was shut down, and he secured the Smart Card encryption key in his wallet. Even with that, the system would not even boot without the pass phrase written how he wanted it. He had a spare card, but not on him, and no one would find it without his help. He had called a cab from the house. It pulled in. He saw the twins in their car about fifty yards away, in the wing mirror of a parked car, but showed no sign of having seen them. Just for fun he got the cab to reverse direction and go back past them, but he made sure he was looking away when the cab accelerated past. The cab dropped him in Tottenham Court Road. He strolled down the road, apparently window-shopping. Just as the twins pulled into a nearby side street, he reversed direction, and ducked into one of the larger electronics shops.

Slater purchased a small Dictaphone and a pre-pay SIM card. He left the store through an alternate front exit which came out twenty yards further from where he'd last seen the twins. Out of one shop into another, slowly making his way further from their car. If they still had him, they would both be on foot. He walked briskly across the road, through a gap in the traffic, and into another shop. His SIM card count was up to 5. He also had another Dictaphone, and five SIM free phones. All the same make. All purchased via two separate credit cards with different names and variable pins or cash. He now needed time to switch settings and get their batteries charged. Time for a cab ride. First, to ensure he lost the twins. Three shops, two alleyways, a short sprint and a brisk walk and he dived down into Holborn Station. Down into the tube, then back up the alternate stairs, out of the alternate side exit across the road, and up Southampton Row. He hailed a cab and knew he had lost them.

The cab stopped a hundred yards, and two side streets from his destination, which was his 'third' safe house, or rather a safe flat. He used the number pad to get through the main door and into the flat; he had an hour before lunch. The phones were all put on charge, and all settings adjusted. He swapped his current SIM with one of the new phones. He put the other on charge. He checked the other gear. All okay. He collected some cash from the bedroom safe, showered, and changed. He removed the credit cards from his wallet and cut them into pieces before selecting two new ones from the safe. Think, had he given Jess his last name? No. Both new credit cards were in the name M Johnson. Thinking again about how mad this was, he walked two hundred yards before risking a cab, which dropped him off one hundred yards from her house.

"Hi Jess," he said as she opened the door. Another two button open blouse, cream coloured silk, a blue skirt, bare legs, sandals. Her hair was tied back with a velvet black scrunchie. Nice. She smiled.

"Mike, come in."

Three hours later he was ravenous and tired. She lay naked with her head on his chest, forming a T on the dishevelled bed. The sheets were on the floor with their clothes. A thin film of perspiration was evident from her throat to her still erect nipples. Her breathing was slowing back to normal, as was his. She was twirling a strand of her hair with her right hand around her middle finger, while her left hand held his thigh. He was tracing a line from her throat to her breast and back again in slow circles.

"I enjoyed my lunch," she half giggled, "but now I do need to eat!"

"Me too," he said.

They showered together and dressed slowly with the odd interruption before they finally, with a slight crumpled look about them, left the house. It was still light as they strolled off. "Take me somewhere nice," she said. They found an Italian a few minutes' walk away. They ordered, sitting across from each other. Her foot kept accidentally brushing against his calf. Her eyes glittered as she smiled at him. They barely said a word, just stared. The food came, and they ate. She drank some wine, and then provocatively, knowing the waiters were watching her, undid the third button on her blouse. Her bra had not made it back on. She leant forward so that he could see, and held his hand. Her foot travelled up his calf she had kicked off her shoe. "I'm ready for dessert," she said.

Midnight was displayed on the bedside clock, back in the house, back in her bed. She was lying like she had the previous night, with one leg across his. He had slept a good two hours. The bang of the front door brought him fully awake.

"Hey Jess have you got a guy with you again? You're such a slut!"

Jess stirred and sat up. He raised an eyebrow but said nothing. "Michael, don't be a pig," she called back, reaching for a gown on the back of her bedroom door. Her naked body was now covered, but in some way enhanced by the robe. He moved to get up.

"You stay right where I want you, and no leaving before breakfast," she said. She left the room, and he heard whispers and giggles before he got a chance to move.

"I'm the man of the house, and I ought to meet him." Michael burst through the door. He had covered himself with one of the tangled sheets. However, the bedroom evidence was obvious. "God it stinks in here," he laughed. "I'm Michael."

"Mike," he said, and they awkwardly shook hands.

"Fancy a sandwich?" he offered.

"That would be great," he said with some trepidation. Jess was smirking over his shoulder. Michael backed out of the room, and he followed, wrapping the sheet around his waist. They sat in the kitchen eating cheese sandwiches, just chatting. It seemed normal, almost.

Back to bed, Mike found a spare tooth brush. As he returned to the bedroom Jess was already laying there, half-asleep. She had a long T-shirt on which just accentuated everything beneath.

"Make sure you stay for breakfast," she said as she snuggled closer. He promised he would. She fell asleep in his arms.

He awoke with pins and needles in his left arm and the smell of fresh coffee under his nose. Jess was still in the T-shirt holding out a mug of coffee.

"You stayed," she said.

"Well, I'm scared of spies from evil super powers. Who knows what they might do if I don't obey."

She put the coffee down, looked at him, and pulled off the T-Shirt. She pulled back the sheet and examined him as much as he examined her. By the time, they had finished, the coffee was cold and his pins and needles had gone.

CHAPTER SEVEN

Weekend

It was Saturday, so no work, and no Stock Market. They lounged in bed until eleven when Michael knocked on the door, "Anyone for brunch?" he said.

John Slater alias Mike Johnson dressed back in his crumpled clothes, needing a shave despite a shower that took longer than it should have because of some interference from wandering hands. Jess slipped into some jeans and a light sweater. They found a cafe with all day breakfasts open two doors from the Italian of the previous evening. Jess chatted and smiled and squeezed his hand. Michael probed gently but could see his sister's state of mind. He deflected questions by asking his own. Then, family came up. They said that Sally their sister had disappeared. Travelling they thought. Six years ago, but they did not know what to think. The police were not interested until recently, when Sally's disappearance had been linked with the Wallace girl in the papers. The police had thought and had evidence to think, that Sally had gone off with a new friend probably female to Greece and on from there. His trail at work. He changed the subject by asking Michael about his job, which was in software sales. They asked about his. His truthful reply was stocks and bonds.

"Jess is a spy apparently," he quipped. A smack and a knowing look from Jess.

"You're no good, you'll give away all my secrets," she laughed.

"I think I need a change of clothes," he said.

"And a rest," Michael blurted out before he could stop himself.

Jess flushed in embarrassment whilst smiling at them both. "I'll come with you."

"No, that's okay," he said too quickly, "I've got some errands and business to finish." He tried to cover his mistake. Jess looked slightly taken aback but recovered to smile.

"When will I see you then?"

"How about seven thirty? You must have some spying to do before then." He tried to lighten the slightly leaden atmosphere.

"Okay, but I may have to spy on you." He almost stopped in his tracks, but managed to turn with a grin.

***

The route back was tedious but necessary. As he approached his house, the twins were not outside. The main door opened to his key. He sensed the change before he checked any signals. Okay, they had been in. The CCTV showed nothing; stopped and wiped probably. They would not have found the backup, without a very detailed search. He checked the play back via his disk. There they were, in through the front door, an hour after he had lost them in Tottenham Court Road, straight to the CCTV system, the obvious one, and then the rummage around. They had tried to fire up the PC, but could not get past the boot pass phrase without the smart card. Through his drawers, but they had not found the safe, nor the cabinet behind the wardrobe. They had flicked through his desk papers, trying to keep things in place. He noticed the bug placement only on the second scan. After thirty minutes, they had left, resetting the CCTV as they went.

Stock take; re-assess the enemy, adjust plans as necessary. These were not ordinary cops. They were too persistent, and the bug was the clincher. Who then? Special Branch, Five? Who knew? But they were probably Special Branch. They obviously thought they had something. It was time to find out what they knew. He had a couple of hours. First, the bug needed locating. He retrieved the scanner from the cupboard behind the wardrobe. Okay, running on that frequency range, about 50 yards to the receiver, probably a relay in the garden or the street. He had to leave the house to get anything done, leaving the bug in place. He secured the place. He then took several alternate routes before he was sure he had no shadows. He settled into an Internet café and then got to work. With the new mobile he phoned a contact who gave a number that he phoned.

CHAPTER EIGHT

Contacts at Work

Stewart Hillier had been an IT Technician for seven years. Many of his colleagues and superiors were surprised by his lack of ambition given his skills and experience. He explained that he was content in his role as he did not want any extra responsibilities or duties. He spent his spare time playing English Civil War re-enactments, and his evenings, he told everyone, were spent researching his roles. His regular security interviews and checks found no evidence of any illicit activity, and he quite truthfully could answer that he had no involvement with any foreign power. He had been abroad once (Gothenburg on a work's outing), but he had not liked it, and the group who had invited him, had not invited him again. The façade of his life was just that; carefully built up and established as a typical IT geek and loner. He was mostly left to himself in charge of the main servers used by the Special Branch, with some network links to the Security Services, GCHQ as well as the Home Office and various Police Forces. Over the years, Stewart had carefully built up systems administration access to nearly all the systems, whilst performing his duties with diligence; consequently, he had virtually unlimited and untraceable access to all the central databases and electronic case files. He could go anywhere in the building he wanted. He had hacked the building pass control in his first year. Stewart's one problem was money. His pay was standard public sector for his role, but was nowhere near enough to indulge his public hobby let alone his real interest.

He had a penchant for prostitutes, preferably young and in pairs. He liked to service his hobby at least once a week at upmarket hotels, but how could he afford it? Luckily, he knew virtually every villain in London via their intelligence file. From the files, he had selected two contacts and via a very circumspect route had established communications over a period of several months by offering information. From there he had built up a select clientele. They would drop payments into an undeclared (to the taxman and his employers) bank account in Guernsey where he had never been. From there he transferred the money to a false name in a UK account which also allowed a credit card registered to a PO Box that he maintained. He established a line of credit to an escort agency he had found in one of the files, which had then become corrupted and lost. The unofficial services he provided included the provision of copies of case files, and intelligence files, which he could place onto undisclosed disks. Then, he would email via an unofficial Internet link, he had installed in his office, to a file server, again rented and run by his false name. From there, clients could log on via a one off password and user name that he provided on payment of the fee. He would not alter a file or lose data, apart from for the escort agency, which he ensured was not connected to his clientele. He constantly ran scans on the databases to see whether any of his contacts or the agency was tracked, and he had built up his side line up to four times his official earnings.

The call, at the weekend for the case files, regarding the Jenny Wallace investigation, was nothing unusual; however, he did scan the file for his own curiosity as the case had been in the papers. He noted the Security Services involvement in the victims, definitely one file to keep an eye on. It took him fifteen minutes to get into work, ten minutes to find the Special Branch file and a further five minutes to upload. The payment was already in his Guernsey Account (he checked by phone banking), and he released the username and password to the person who phoned. He didn't read the whole file, but thought he recognised the voice on the phone from a previous encounter. He covered the system logs, faked an IT incident to cover his presence, not that anyone checked, and left for home. Thirty minutes later he booked a room at one of the London Hiltons and booked a visit from a blonde, and brunette to arrive in two hours for a special session. Even after escort and hotel expenses, he was nearly ten grand richer. He tidied up changing his 'pay as you go' mobile number and phone and emailing his two primary contacts the change to his phone number. He neither knew nor cared what their number was, nor did he want to find out. As long as the money flowed he was content. He hoped the girls would remember to bring his favourite toys.

CHAPTER NINE

Back to Jess

Mike Johnson, or was he back to John Slater now, reviewed the electronic case file via the username and password. The file had cost him £15,000, but was well worth it. He wanted direct access to the source of the information, probably an IT geek, but had to go through a contact that Hemmings had given him when he first started; another risk which he would have to bypass at some stage. He knew the identity of the contact's real and fake names, but decided to leave that possible route. The money transfer was at possible risk of being traced, but his Swiss account to a Luxembourg account should be safe. Where the money went after that he did not know. Slater was not aware of where the account payment went. He could find out, but that would just get him another bank account somewhere. Rutledge had updated the Special Branch file, which he now read, the previous evening. Henry at the club had let him down, getting his times absolutely correct instead of slightly imprecise and confused, which was how it was supposed to be. Tactics; what to do now? Henry to forget his timings, but that would be tricky and would create more questions, if he disappeared. He could just flow with it; perfect alibis are not perfect; nothing is ever quite that clear. Create some confusion, the fog of war that was what he needed. Detective Sergeant Rutledge needed to be pointed in an alternate direction to get him out of the picture, while he figured out what the hell he was doing with Jess. God, Jess. He had become distracted. What time was it? He needed to move. He needed to think, he needed no distractions, but distractions kept piling up, fate again. Back to Jess this time with a small overnight bag picked up from another safe flat.

"I hope I'm not too presumptuous Miss Spy," he smiled as she opened the door.

"Hmm I'm not sure, but I think I might let you in."

He followed her into the lounge watching the jeans wiggle. She topped off the jeans with a light sweater.

"I wanted to see where you live," she pouted a little.

"But then you'd know all my secrets."

"Exactly," she pulled him down onto the sofa with her. "I thought we could get a take away and chat, Michael's out with his luscious Lucy." He could imagine luscious Lucy, but he was far more interested in Jess right then, especially as somehow her sweater had been removed. "Do you want a starter before the main course?"

"Everything's food with you isn't it?"

His meals seemed to have become very irregular he thought, as they sat wrapped in a blanket whilst eating Chinese and watching an old film on the small TV. She kept accidentally dropping food onto him so that she had to lick it off. She was driving him mad. Every now and then she would ask a question, gentle probing. Where had he been to school, and university? How old was he? What was his favourite colour? When was his birthday? Where did he work? Was he rich? He deflected and nudged her line of attack like a top batsman.

Finally, "You men are all the same always hiding, never opening up." She was cross now or trying to be, slightly sulky and pouting. She stood up in front of him, her arms under her bare breasts one leg slightly forward. Her body almost in silhouette. "Tell me who you are?"

"I'm who you want me to be," he said.

She stamped her foot, "That's not an answer."

"Jess, I'm me, let's just take it one step at a time."

"What is it? Just sex?"

"You know what it is." He realised he couldn't tell her everything. If he started it would all come out and then what; arrest, prison worse? She would never forgive him, how could she; her own sister. "Jess, I'm Mike, I'm very glad to be here right now." He reached for her. They cuddled, caressed, and kissed.

"I'm ready for bed," she said softening her stance, tone, and look. "I'm done with Chinese. I want Anglo-Saxon."

He awoke to sunlight filtering through the partly closed window blind. It was nearly ten on Sunday Morning. Jess was still sleeping beside him. He realised he had to get away right now before it was too late. Yes, it would hurt her, but not as much as if she found out the truth. He dressed as quietly as possible.

"You're leaving," a flat statement. She was propped up on one arm watching him.

"Jess, I…" he struggled to find the right words. "I have to go away for a few weeks on business. Sorry, it was arranged before I met you."

"It's too intense isn't it?" she said, pleading.

"No, that's not it, I just have work." He went to sit on the edge of the bed.

She half shook her head. "When will you be back?"

"I don't know exactly. I'll call you when I know."

"No, you won't!"

"Jess I will." He took her hand.

"I'll call you, if you give me your number."

"I'll give you the hotel number when I get there."

"Where?"

"Rome," it slipped out. Why had he said that?

"When do you go?"

"This evening."

"So, why are you leaving now?"

"I need to get some things sorted before then."

"You're married!"

"Jess, I'm not married, or living with anyone, but I do have to work." She was not satisfied, but the probing stopped. He leaned down and kissed her on the forehead the tip of her nose and finally her lips. She went to pull him down, but he broke away. "In a few days, Jess," he whispered as he left.

CHAPTER TEN

Travels

He took the evening BA flight from Heathrow to Rome in the name of Harris. As Johnson he took a room for two weeks, cash in advance, in the two star Luciani, just off the Via Castro Pretonio, in the city centre near the station. He set the phone to auto forward to his mobile. He then moved to the room at the Four Star Hotel Torino near the Museo Nazionale Romano, which he'd previously booked. He got there via a taxi away from the area, a walk, another taxi back, and a short walk. He settled in making sure the room's safe worked. Four star business hotels only, never five star, too many staff with good memories. He called Jess and gave her the direct dial room number of the Pretonio, she was already distant, annoyed.

"I'm sorry," she said. "I don't want to moan, but I've never felt this way before. There, I've said it now, but I don't want to lie to you, or hold back."

"Jess…" he said.

"Please, I know I'm going too fast, but oh damn, I want you here. I want to tell you here not over the phone, Mike."

"I'll call you tomorrow," he said. She made him promise before he disconnected.

Work, concentrate on the mission. Get your head in the right place. He called the contact number with the second mobile. He entered the access code. The pre-recorded message played back. Situation, Mission, Execution, no questions or check of understanding. Those were his concerns. The message was dated three days ago. He had three months to achieve the mission. First part-payment, was the usual inside stock tip of ten-cent shares on the Bourse. They were expected to rise to two Euros in three months. Completion part was the usual. To the Swiss account. Press one to accept, two to reject. It was that easy. He pressed one as he had done on the previous occasions. If he wanted to wait, he could have hung up and come back to it on another occasion. It was all very 'Mission Impossible', but he was not Tom Cruise, and his missions were not impossible. His insurance broker had once called him during a mission, and he had forgotten to switch a phone to silent; he had almost had to abort. Since then he'd taken no chances during execution, but the unexpected could always get in the way. Jess could turn, was turning, into that distraction.

He switched phones and placed the trade order through a broker, using yet another account number. He had to be careful with the buying. Under the Slater name he ordered one hundred thousand shares, and a further one hundred thousand futures, at eleven cents. His total expenditure was twenty-one thousand Euros, with only twenty-thousand due that week, via his trading account. In three months, the deposit would be worth two hundred thousand. He would sell the futures at the halfway point, clearing nearly another hundred thousand. Commissions and taxes would eat into it, but not bad. He made three other trades, a couple in no hope stocks, just to cover his tracks on the Bourse. Under Johnson, a new stock name, he did a fifty-thousand trade, and one other in some blue chips, and then two on the London exchange, one blue chip, one in the Alternative Investment Market, known as AIM. Stocks picked at random, more covering. It was the most he could spend as a new account. He needed to create a background under the Johnson name for Jess which gave him another idea. Another name and another few stock trades under several different accounts including a French and US identity. Then, he was complete. All told he could clear well over half a million, all legitimate, most declared to tax authorities as legitimate income. He would update the main accounting software for Slater when he got his Internet access sorted. He did not think his controller (if that was what he was) realised he could make so much money from his missions, but they probably were not into stock markets. He bet himself that the twins would be doing the financial checks. He had completed a good trading year even without the two tips this financial year. He would clear well over two million after tax and a further two million through the offshore trading accounts in the Caymans. When he added it all up, he was a very wealthy man. Maybe time to stop. He checked his diary and entered his coded figures. He ordered some food from room service. While he waited he went over his plan for the twins. He had a number to call them if he thought of anything else, another old cliché. He'd call tomorrow, but not from Rome.

***

The great thing about modern travel is that there is lots of it available and on the European continent intercity rail travel. Without checking out, he flew from Rome to Amsterdam, on the morning Air Italia flight, and then took the Thalis under a different name to Paris. Five hours travelling plus an hour of waiting. He had shown his passport in the name of Romonde, one of his French identities, only once in Rome at check in and not since. The phone rang whilst he was half snoozing as they waited at a stop in Brussels. It was Jess.

"You do answer your phone," she sounded annoyed.

"Did you try earlier?"

"Yes, of course."

"I was in meetings."

"How's Rome?"

"Fine, how are you?" Stop her probing.

"When will you be back?"

"A few weeks, like I said."

"I could come out to Rome."

No! How to stop her? "I'll be in the far east by the weekend. I've some more business there." He hated lying to her.

"Oh, I could still come out if you wanted me to?"

"That would be really nice, but I would be busy, but if you can stop from getting bored…" He needed to get her to withdraw the chance to meet up.

"I'd never get the time off anyway."

"You'll call me with the new number in, where is it you're going?"

"Jess I'll call you before that, tonight when I get back to the hotel."

"Okay, I'll speak to you then."

"Bye," he disconnected the call just as the train announcer loudly stated their next destination, Paris.

***

He purchased two French pre-pay phones. From a Paris Internet café, he called the twins, but they were both out. He left a message saying he would call later. He checked the last flight time back to Rome. He had three hours to kill to ensure he called from Paris. He spent the time researching his target. Amazing what you could find out on the Internet. He had used one phone to call the twins, and one to call his contact at the UK's tax collectors, HMRC. While he waited for a credit check and criminal record check on his target he browsed to the secure web site where the target file was accessed. All the general background stuff was there. The checks came through. He got print outs of the web site, managing to avoid the Internet Café attendant's attempts to see what he was doing. Time for the twins.

He called, Sergeant Rutledge answered on the third ring. "Mr. Slater, how pleasant to hear from you. We called for a chat yesterday, but you weren't there."

"That's because I'm here Sergeant, in Paris."

"Is that on stocks and bonds business, Sir?"

"Yes, it is."

"I wish you'd let us know before you left the country."

"I didn't realise I needed to keep you informed of my travel plans."

"Well, what can we do for you, Sir, you did ring us?"

They were tracing the call or trying to; good he was in Paris. They would eventually trace the room he was checked into just outside Charles De Gaulle, CDG, but not until tomorrow.

"I remembered something from the night of the fifteenth."

"In a tube station were you, sir?"

"No Sergeant, I was at the ground, but I did step out to make a couple of calls. One to my broker in New York, and another one to another broker in Taiwan." He had called, but not from the ground. He gave them the details.

"We will check the stockbrokers concerned. When will you be returning to England?"

"I'm not sure yet, probably in a few weeks." He didn't want them waiting for him at the airport, especially as he had left under a different name.

"You will be in Paris all that time?"

"Very unlikely, Sergeant I may well need to go to the States soon."

"Okay sir, we'll be in touch."

CHAPTER ELEVEN
The Suspect

"God, he's a good liar," Rutledge said to Grahams. He had been trying to listen in whilst tracing the call.

"He was in Paris," Grahams said hanging up another extension. "Mobile, no caller ID. We can ask the French, but you know how long that will take."

Detective Inspector Jack Hooper had been in and around Special Branch for nearly twenty years. His unit, and his pride, and joy, was a left-over of the cold war counter espionage teams. Five did that work now and Counter Terrorist was mostly run by the Met. For the last five years, his unit had concentrated on a group of cases concerning odd happenings with various state security personnel. There was no normal case for them because of the discreet nature of the enquiries. The cases ranged from financial inappropriateness (a senior civil service procurement officer using black funds for his own lifestyle, such as race horses and some domineering call girls) to pornographic pictures and potential paedophile links (both in prison on 10 year sentences). His team had investigated and solved one murder (the husband did it) and two blackmails (both undeclared homosexual activities even in these liberal days) in the same period. His hand-picked team was good and worked well together. His only failures so far were an outstanding fraud case (an official in the Procurement Division at the Ministry of Defence was probably complicit in running the fraud) and the disappearance in the last five years of four female members of the Security Services. He suspected that there may be more, but Five had not given him access to any others, or any earlier potential victims. Jonathan Braithwaite, his liaison, had hinted at others including a potential French victim. Victim was not the right word because there were no bodies, just inconclusive disappearance trails.

He had the four files in front of him including the latest girl, Wallace. Rutledge and Drinkwater were both leading the initial teams chasing two different lines. The only facts that were clear, were that she was seen at Oval tube station at ten-fifteen on the 15th. She had gotten on a northbound tube, and not got off anywhere as far as they could tell. Of the twenty plus stations on the Northern Line, eight had no Northern Line platform CCTV working, and of these, four had no tube station CCTV at all, resulting from the pre-planned centralisation of CCTV services to aid counter terrorism. She could have changed at any of these four stations without being seen, and a further twenty stations then added to the complexity of the situation. They had been unable to ascertain why she had been travelling north, when her home was south after leaving a meeting with Six in the first place. Not helped by the obvious holes in the Five case file. What the CCTV did show was Jenny Wallace on the platform with five males. Two black, an old man, a Mr Grainger who turned out to be a friend of the Commissioners, and another male that Rutledge was convinced, for some intuitive reason, was this Slater character, but with no other evidence other than an over enthusiastic cab driver who had picked Slater up from near the Oval at eleven.

Slater was attracting attention because he was almost too clean and the steward at the Oval might have contradicted his timings by a few minutes. Five had nothing on Slater according to their latest email, and the rest of his stuff, credit ratings and so on, had checked out. He was rich, successful, modest, and a bit of a loner. He had been a member at the Oval for three years, his only outward sign of socialising. Rutledge was good, all his team was, and he trusted his judgement. His intuition had put the first nail in the coffin of the Procurement chap. Rutledge supported by Grahams, very promising DC, was almost certain that Slater had deliberately lost them, twice! Grahams was certain he was trained in counter surveillance and had kept saying it to the team. They had done an unofficial house entry and bug plant and gotten absolutely nothing. Now, according to this morning's report, Slater was in Paris as of yesterday and due to go to the States soon.

Hooper had been against the press release about the possible serial killer. He understood the methodology to try to shake the targets to get some action. The release implied there were bodies and evidence connecting the women. The only connection was the one not mentioned, security. He doubted it would work; however, it did give him a cover for the deployment of some additional resources. The forensic team was bored though. He got them chasing down some DNA on the paper files for the fraud case. You never knew your luck. Go back, thought Hooper, was there anything connecting Slater with the previous girls.

Sally Carver a Five analyst (not field they had emphasised a little too much). Five-eight, blonde, good looking, single, lived on her own just outside Vauxhall. Had booked two weeks holiday shortly after another Greece holiday, and disappeared in Greece, or Rome, or God knows where? Five different countries showed up as evidence of potential location. She had allegedly met a girl (that tendency had not shown up before) in Greece and decided to live the traveller life. The typed letter to her boss (name blanked out) but apparently signed by her, said she would be back in a few months. That was six years ago. They needed to DNA test the letter again, just in case. She had a brother and sister, but the parents had died when she was at school. Brother and sister still both living in London. Worth a chat; he would put Drinkwater on that, now that his Mr. Grainger had checked out.

Harriet Hollingsworth, was or had been twenty-eight. She was tall, five-ten, dark hair, model like, tall, thin, and gorgeous in the personnel photo, and a big ballet fan. An analyst in an obscure department of the Foreign Office (more likely Six thought Hooper, but Six were not saying). She had gone missing whilst on a trip (business or pleasure?) to France. The Sûreté had been very helpful and had possibly traced a hire car she might have used to a small Pension, north of Cannes. DNA was inconclusive. There, the French trail went cold although her ATM card had been used back in Paris, and again in Brussels several weeks later, implying she was missing not gone. The French were very keen to help as they suspected who Harriet was, but they wanted to know what Six were up to on an allies' soil; probably a tawdry reconnaissance effort on some nuclear facility, or a counter illegal immigration racket. Who knew? No parents, no siblings, no one left behind. What about Slater? Something to get Rutledge to ask, maybe he would come along just to test the water. According to the report Slater had only been asked about Jenny Wallace.

Jodi Parker disappeared in Morocco whilst on a Club 18-30 holiday. No leads and no support from the Moroccans who were sick of European girls in trouble in an Arab country. They put it down to drugs, drink and sex and that was it, no more resources. They had no idea that she had worked for GCHQ and Defence Intelligence, and they were not telling the Moroccans that. She had been twenty-seven when she disappeared. The similarities were same age group, good looking, solitary background, single and unattached with no parents. Blonde, five feet seven, liked raves (Hooper thought they had finished in the 80s) and club music. Only family connection left was a cousin who claimed not to have seen her for two years before she disappeared. A waste of time, but he had sent one of the teams. No Slater, in fact, the only men involved seemed to have been a group of Swedish twenty-year olds. One of them claimed to have slept with Jodi the night before. He had raised the alarm with the hotel Rep. Time to call the teams in and get an update.

They met in what passed for a briefing room covered in whiteboards and notes. After throwing the junior support team out on a forced coffee break Hooper perched on the end of Rutledge's desk and reviewed the case.

"Slater was in Paris when he phoned," DC Grahams continued, "and his story is checking out apart from the steward's time discrepancy. We've got calls in to the stock exchanges he claimed to have called, but we'll probably have to go through official channels to get formal confirmation."

"Any reason to suspect they won't?" Drinkwater chipped in. "I still don't understand why you two are so suspicious of him. If he was our man, he would've had to grab the girl and get rid of her in what… fifteen or twenty minutes?"

"John, I agree but there is something about him that doesn't feel right."

"I'll come with you next time you interview him, Jim, see if my senses coincide with yours," said Hooper. "John, I want you to pick up the Carver case, go back over it and chat with the brother and sister. The original team gave up too early, because they couldn't get travel funds to check out the locations, let's see what poking around can do."

"Okay Boss, what about the other cases?"

"John take the Hollingsworth case as well. Jim, you and Dave take another look at Jodi Parker. Both of you pull in some of the juniors for the background stuff. I want you," Hooper looked at each of them in turn, "all out talking to the families, neighbours, and friends getting your noses sniffing around. I'm going back to the bosses to try and get something on what, if anything, connects them. There must be something. It's time Five, and the others helped out; if they really want the cases solved."

"Are they just playing games, Boss?" DC Grahams probed.

"Probably, but they don't like airing any dirty laundry let alone letting others in on their games. John, I'm pretty sure Hollingsworth was Six. Give your contacts a buzz and get some unofficial confirmation."

"Will do."

"Right get the juniors back in and chasing. Keep them out of the sensitive stuff, then let's get a beer and catch up at seven." Team morale was essential. His team smiled they would get a break.

CHAPTER TWELVE

Rome

Back to Rome, dumping the pre-pay in a street bin. Back in his room. After a shower, he lay on the bed and thought of Jess. Time to call. "Hi, did I wake you?"

"No, I thought you had forgotten."

"Jess, what are you wearing?"

"My T-shirt."

"Nothing else?"

"I'm in bed, it's lonely."

"I wish I was there."

"I wish you were here as well."

"You could imagine I'm there."

"What are you implying?" He could see her smile.

"Oh just letting my imagination roam from Rome."

She laughed, "You have a very inventive mind."

"Night Jess."

"Night."

Now, he would dream of her half the night. That was not a good idea. He could picture her in that T-Shirt… and out of it.

Jess grabbed her pillow and tried to sleep, but she knew it

was useless. Mike was in her head and not about to let her sleep. She tried to be cross with him, but she kept thinking of him in her bed, in her arms, holding her hand in the restaurant. She could feel the need for him deep in the pit of her stomach. Maybe a cup of tea and a chat with Michael, he was still up; she could hear the TV.

"Hi Sis, can't sleep?"

"No."

"Was that him?"

"Yes that was Mike."

"Short call."

"Thanks that really helps."

"God, you have fallen for him."

"Michael I can't help it, I don't know, there's something about him I can't get him out of my head, and I just want to be with him."

"But you hardly know the guy."

"That's what makes it so maddening; you know I'm not like this so why couldn't I hold back?"

Michael laughed and sang the Madness song "It must be love, love, love."

"I know," she was suddenly serious.

"Hey come on, it's not that serious?"

"Yes, it is." She was on the verge on tears, "There's no point talking to you, you're just another over sexed bloke."

"Me, over sexed? After last weekend?"

"Oh don't remind me, I mean do remind me but, oh you know what I mean. I'm going to bed."

"Jess, I love you dearly, and he did seem like a nice guy."

"Thanks for the support," a hint of cynicism. "He is a nice guy."

"That's what I meant, night Jess."

"Night, I'll see you in the morning."

CHAPTER THIRTEEN

Snoop

Snoop Digger's day had gone from bad to worse. Starting with a missed snatch outside Leicester Square tube, he had to run like hell to avoid some German tourist trying to play the hero. He had gotten a call on the stolen mobile from the club telling him no for the tenth time, and that if he called again they would stick his demo where the sun did not shine. Now, he was sitting in the cell of West End Central police station. He had been caught breaching his ASBO when he got off the tube in Tottenham Court Road. After the arrest and search they had found the two stolen credit cards he'd gotten from the bitches bag on the 15th. He'd meant to dump them after he'd tried and failed a buy in the Virgin Mega-Store. He noticed store security moving in and legged it before he could be taken. Now, he looked down at his lace-less Nikes and pondered how long they would keep him locked up. The cell door opened, and the arresting pig escorted him towards a plain interview room. The pig asked him if he wanted a drink. He asked for an Espresso to wind him up, but the pig just smiled. As he left, two plain clothes men came in and exchanged some whispered words with the cop and then came and sat down opposite. He went to stand up, but the shorter guy shook his head, and his expression made Snoop sit back down.

"Where's my solicita, pig? I know my rights. I ain't sayin' nuffin' till he gets here man."

"Oh dear Devon, that's not very friendly, and we haven't even been introduced."

"Ma names Snoop, shit head. Where's m'coffee?"

"Devon, I'm Detective Inspector Hooper, and this is Detective Sergeant Rutledge. All we want is a friendly chat."

"No chat, man. Why ain't the tape on? You can't talk to me wiv aht the tape runnin'. I knows mine rights."

"Devon why don't you drop the street talk? Your mother won't like it."

"That bitch ain't nuffin' to do wi' mi' ways."

"Devon, let's put this into context for you. You have been caught in breach of your ASBO. That's a virtual automatic 3-6 months prison sentence." An ASBO was an Anti-Social Behaviour Order used by the courts to prevent and deter crime as an alternative to prison or young offender's institutions. "We have you on CCTV from this morning trying to take a nice German lady's handbag. She's already picked you out from a photo parade, and with your record that's another couple of months, and you're sixteen now, so no getting off with Community Service. We have another CCTV of you trying to use stolen credit cards in Virgin, and now you are behaving like a spoilt child when we are being all friendly. You already have a criminal record longer than most hardened criminals twice your age. Why don't you calm down and talk to us?" Hooper gave his best winning smile and waited. With perfect timing, the Police Constable returned with a tray of three coffees. All in Styrofoam cups. Snoop Devon looked stunned as a Starbucks' Espresso was placed before him with some sugars and a stirrer. "Thank you, PC Stark, we'll take it from here." The PC left the room. "Now where were we Devon? Ah yes, the stolen credit cards, how did you get them?"

Snoop/Devon started to deny everything, then he looked at the two officers and stopped. "I found them, din' I."

"Devon you are a known thief with bag snatching a speciality. Where did you get the cards?"

"I didn't touch her, the bag got left when he took her, I just helped myself, honest."

Rutledge tried really hard to stay calm. Hooper gave him a studied look. "Okay Devon let's back up. We need this on tape and, if you help us, we'll try to help you. Deal?"

Snoop knew when he was beaten. "Okay man, deal."

Rutledge leaned forward and started the tape. The officers identified themselves, and then they asked Devon/Snoop to identify himself. They asked him formally if he wanted a solicitor or someone else to be present. He declined, prompted by Rutledge shaking his head. Snoop had been in Oval Station, he had followed the girl onto the platform, and then onto the train. He was one carriage down, but could see her through the doors. Just before the first stop, after they had boarded, a man had approached the girl, touched her arm, and helped her off the train.

"What do you mean, helped her off Devon?" Rutledge interrupted.

"Just that man, she seemed a bit wobbly and he helped her off. They walked off the platform, and that's when I noticed her bag still on the train, so I went and got it."

"What time, Devon?"

"I dunno, after ten suppose."

"Okay, what did the man look like?"

"The light wasn't great man, and he had his back to me."

"Come on Devon, you're as sharp as a tack. You notice things. Tell us about him."

"Okay, dark suit, shoulder length dark hair, white, taller than her, as he was ducking to get out the door."

"Did you see his face?"

"No."

"Are you sure Devon?"

"Yeah I tried, but it was pretty quick, and I wanted to get the bag, so I was watching that."

"You said he touched her arm. What do you mean?"

"Just that man, he seemed to lean in close, touching her arm, then they got up."

"What was in the bag Devon?"

"A purse, one of them flashy ID cards, a pair of tights. I only wanted what was in the purse so I threw the rest away."

"Where?"

"When I got off at Embankment."

"Is this the girl?" Rutledge pulled a print from the unmarked file in front of him.

"Yeah probably, she was pretty good lookin'."

"Thanks, Devon. You keep thinking about the man. Anything you can remember; you tell PC Stark." Hooper called PC Stark back in the room with a few more whispered words.

"Hey man," said Devon to Stark, "can I get another Espresso?"

Hooper and Rutledge raced back to base, almost unable to contain their excitement. They had their first big break.

CHAPTER FOURTEEN
Follow The Target

He left Rome early to set the trail in place. Another flight, another identity. This time French. Out to Athens, then a quick hop north to Sofia, booking a city centre hotel for Celia Romero for a months' time with a cash deposit. Back to Athens, and then onto Amman for an overnight stay, again booking another hotel, and making some tour arrangements with a travel company. Another flight back to Rome, ignoring three messages from Jess, until he returned to his hotel. She just wanted to hear his voice and know his travel plans. He could not call back. He needed time and concentration to prepare the Mission. He needed some activity in the States as well, and a move to the Far East, Taiwan, or Singapore. Okay, take the long way round to the States via Frankfurt to check on the target, and then Taiwan. He checked the flights and booked with the American identity through to LA with a two-day stop over. He would have to return to London before he completed the mission. He would rather avoid London, but he needed to get the UK police off his back, and to make sure Jess stayed happy. He checked out of both Rome hotels and caught the next flight to Frankfurt. Time to take a look at his target. He spent six hours trailing the target in Frankfurt, dropping off and picking up from various regular spots in her routine, as described in her file. Checking for any surveillance on her or counter moves from her. She was another tall thin one, five feet nine with an athlete's figure. Volleyball, he remembered from her file. Her long black hair was tied back in a ponytail with a plain black band. She was more attractive in real life than in her photo from the file. Her work and evening routine complete, he left her entering her apartment in Bornheimer Landstraße and set off for LA, via Taiwan on the overnight flight.

He called Jess before he boarded the flight.

"Hi, how are you?"

"Mike, I was worried when you didn't answer my calls. I left a message on the hotel voicemail."

"No need to worry about me, I've been on the go for days now. I'm heading east."

"Oh, I thought you'd already gone."

"No, tonight to Taiwan. I'm waiting to board."

"Oh."

"Have you been busy with your super power spying?" He again tried to lighten their tense conversation.

"No," and he could imagine her smile, "I'm quite busy though. When will you be back?"

"Hopefully, a few days, before I have to go off again."

"Getting any good tips?" Anything but talk about how much she was missing him.

He hesitated; it was too good an opportunity to back up his credentials as a trader. "Actually yes, try buying some shares in this." He gave her the name of the hot tip on the Bourse Euronext CAC Mid & Small190. "Now remember past performance is no guarantee of future performance. Only spend what you can afford etc. etc."

She laughed. That was better, now he was on his way back to her albeit in a few days. Her mood lightened. "Can I pick you up from the airport?"

"No," he almost blurted out but managed to say, "I might want to surprise you."

"I like surprises," she said, "especially quick ones."

"I thought you were the long and slow type."

She giggled, "Ah, I like all types."

"Really? I didn't know the extent of your needs?"

Suddenly serious, "You know my needs, Mike."

"Jess, I'll be back soon to take care of them." Get the laughter back, leave on a high note. They exchanged more flirtatious comments before, "I'll call you later in the week."

"Bye."

He hung up and boarded his plane, using his Johnson identity, and took his place in business class. He tried to sleep, but kept dreaming of Jess and a silk blouse coming undone.

Jess hung up smiling at the phone call and the flirting which left her with a warm glow in her stomach. Michael came in an hour later with Lucy in tow. She was luscious, five feet six and curves in all the right places. Michael seemed to like bustier girls although Lucy had lasted longer than most. Jess made sure she gave her a welcoming smile, and hello, despite her reservations about Michael's choice in women.

"You look happier," Michael remarked. "You must have spoken with Mike?"

"Yes, he just called on his way to Taiwan."

"He does get around. When is he back?"

"A few more days," she sighed, "but he's given me a hot tip."

"Really? Did it involve staying in bedrooms?"

"Michael, I'm serious. Look, a stock tip in France." She showed him her scribbled note. Lucy looked too. "Should we buy some?"

"I don't know. What else did he say?"

"Nothing more about the tip, just personal stuff."

"Jess, I do believe you're blushing," Michael laughed. "Go on then put some money into your Mike and see what happens. I'll join you for a thousand. It might pay off my student loan. Come on Lucy I need to get my beauty sleep." Lucy raised her eyebrows at Jess, mouthed 'Men,' and followed him from the room with a parting smile.

Jess waited for what she thought was a decent amount of time before heading off to bed. The sounds from Michael's room did not make sleep easier, as she dreamed of Mike.

***

Taiwan was hot and humid and busy. He used the stop over day to enhance the trail for his target, using an Internet Café to book multiple routes to and from Athens, Frankfurt and Sofia. He created on-line banking accounts for her using the ID information in the file in the UK and US. He then deposited cash below the money laundering thresholds into those accounts. He did a couple more minor stock trades under the Johnson name, including another buy in the Bourse tip, already up to twenty-five cents. He hoped Jess had bought early.

He purchased some interesting electronics, fresh on the market in the downtown shopping area. His final business purchase was from a speciality shop that did not advertise. Specialist fingerprint layers for his fingers, and a matching RFID passport for the USA, in the name of Jimmy Heidelbaum. This matched with US military travel orders, and a US Army ID. His main US identity was James Harper. He could get back into the States on any of these. He just had time to get a silk gown for Jess, before he headed back to the airport and the LA flight.

On landing in Los Angeles, as Slater, he transferred to a domestic route under his main US Harper identity, and flew to New York where he entered his rented apartment, a two-bedroom affair, just off Central Park West, with views, if you looked sideways, of the park itself. He made three contact calls, none from the apartment. One to get an update on his target, the second to get an updated case file, and the third to get a UK delivery of some supplies to a post office box he rented. The case file was printed out by a bored attendant who could barely speak English, in an Internet café. He took a roundabout route back to his apartment. Exhausted, he slept for fourteen hours. On awakening, he showered, dressed, and went out to collect breakfast bagels, before returning to the apartment to update himself on the progress of the investigation against him.

Not good. He remembered the thief, but had not really noticed him get on the train. Okay, they still had no better description, but they would keep pushing now they had a witness to the mission execution. The false trails were useless, because they had a disappearance, and she had dropped her bag in the confusion. The train doors had closed before he could get back and retrieve it. Little mistakes compounded by fate. He had missed the boyfriend. How could that have happened so quickly with no exterior signs? He then thought of Jess and realised the timings could be that fast. Sally's name being rechecked was to be expected. As far as he was aware the Press had not come round to her house to hound them, although no one had mentioned the press articles. He could certainly do without a bunch of nosey journalists digging up dirt on the family. He noticed the anti-press release stance of this DI Hooper. They were all Special Branch. Maybe they had advised the press to keep away from the *victim's* families. The fact that Five, Six and Special Branch were all slowly putting things together, did not surprise him. However, it would take a glacial change in operations for them to share the information to crack the case and then see the other successful missions, especially outside the UK. This Hooper was the type who could stitch it all together, if he got the chance. He did not want to have to take action against the team, but attack might be the best form of defence. He would need more supplies for that, and they were the type of supplies that would attract attention from lots of people.

He did not like the Americans hinting to Five that something was awry. His contact in the CIA had disappeared two years ago. He did not have a replacement to give him a heads-up. Something for the future, but it would need a lot of research. With all the counter terror operations going on, it was hard to find real dissatisfaction with which to turn contacts. He contemplated dropping the contact giving him the case file, at least for a while. If they turned, despite the money he paid, then there would be another trail attracting a lot of interest. No more inside track on the police investigation but one less risk. Not yet he decided. He needed to know what was going on; however, expensive that access was. Well, he could afford it. At least it was not Rutledge doing the checking on Sally, but this was getting close. Should he abandon the

London return? No, he needed the supplies just delivered to his flat. Okay, stay away from Jess. Not possible, she was expecting him and, given what had happened to her sister, would raise the alarm if he just disappeared. He did not want to disappear anyway. He was settled into his routine. He had money, and the start of a social life, without paying some call girl to love him, or chasing a one-night stand through the city night life. Okay then, keep the timings simple. Back to London, see Jess, then out again after no more than two days. Avoid Rutledge who wanted to bring him in for more formal questioning. He would avoid the Drinkwater team by arriving after they had questioned Jess and Michael. They still did not know how he had done it, and they had no trace of the girl. Not surprising.

He thought of her now. Under the drug, she had been totally compliant. He had taken her away from the station, placed her in the store, and been back in the members' bar in under thirty minutes. It was luck that the timings had worked out, luck and exceptional planning. She had still been out of it when he had returned the next day. She was out of it for good now. He had made £300k clear on her via three stock tips, all on the NASDAQ. He was still waiting for the final Swiss cash payment. He could not chase it, and there would be some reluctance to pay it until the heat died down. He was only doing this next one so quickly in recompense for the failure of the disappearance. He had seldom dwelt on his missions, a quick lesson learned, and then on to the next. He was not squeamish or psychotic about them either. They were missions. The few minutes of enjoyment were really a mix of professional satisfaction as much as anything else. What Jenny Wallace had told him, had not made much sense. She was really a financial analyst chasing funding streams, unofficially diverted from other budgets. Probably how he got paid. The Dictaphone tape and file were all stored in a London lock up behind three bricks and a small safe. It was his insurance policy. He did not trust his employers. He did not trust anyone.

CHAPTER FIFTEEN

What Happened To Sally?

"Michael Carver? I'm Detective Sergeant Drinkwater, and this is Detective Constable Pollard." They flashed their IDs. "Could we ask you a couple of questions?"

Michael showed them into the lounge, "Is this about Sally? We saw the papers."

Jess rushed out of the kitchen area, "What about Sally?"

"Good morning, Miss Carver," said Drinkwater. He noticed how much she looked like her sister. "No news I'm afraid, we are trying to establish and check the connections between the vic.. I mean the various girls. The papers are a bit premature in their statements."

"So there is no serial killer?" Michael said. "Please come through. Would you like a coffee or tea"

"Coffee would be nice, thank you." They took a seat in the lounge area. After they were settled and Jess had provided a steaming mug of coffee to each of them, Drinkwater continued. "There are some similarities between the cases; however, we have not found any bodies. If we didn't have a couple of witnesses to the last girl's disappearance, we wouldn't be looking for her?"

"But Sally just went whilst she was on holiday, or something, in Greece," Jess exclaimed on the verge of tears. "I'm sorry to get upset, but all the memories and the shock come back."

"That's okay Miss Carver. May I call you Jess? I'm John, and this is Simon."

"Jess is fine," she said.

"Michael?" Drinkwater asked of Michael and received a nod. "And Jess, it's your memories we are after. In your original statements," he said pulling some papers from a portfolio folder, "you strongly raised the point that you didn't believe that Sally had just gone off to Greece without telling you. Why was that?"

"She just wouldn't go like that," exclaimed Michael. "She would have told us. She'd never been to Greece before."

"The evidence shows she went three weeks before her final trip." It was DC Pollard's first comment.

"I don't believe it," exclaimed Michael. "I spoke to her from Uni', and she never said she was in Greece."

"That was to her mobile was it?"

"I thought it was to the house, here, but I couldn't be certain."

"This girl story," Jess interjected, exasperated. "I mean Sally had boyfriends and everything."

"We know Jess," calmed Drinkwater. "You had no suspicion that Sally might like girls?"

"No, none, and I would have known," said Jess. "After Mum and Dad died we were very close, we all were. We spoke every week. It was when she didn't call that I got worried."

"You were at University as well, Jess?"

"Yes, I was at Bristol, and Michael had just started in Durham."

"What do you do now?"

"I'm in software sales," said Michael.

"And I do PR for the Foreign Office," said Jess very quickly.

Drinkwater gave her a look. "Did you meet any of Sally's work colleagues?"

"From the Home Office?" asked Jess.

"Yes, the *Home* Office," Drinkwater over emphasised the home.

"No," said Jess. Michael looked confused with the tone of the exchange.

"We had a letter from a Mr Hedges who said he was her boss, Sally was his PA, saying he understood she had gone off travelling, but that was that," said Michael.

"Sally seemed to have plenty of money. Do you know where she got it from?"

"She had her share of our inheritance, but that's mostly in this house, so that was a bit of a surprise, especially when her accounts were used a few weeks later," Michael again. Jess sat quietly contemplating.

"The accounts are frozen along with everything else until Sally can be declared legally…" Michael stopped as he saw tears in Jess's eyes.

"Well, I think that's all, just one more question. Did Sally ever mention a man around six feet tall with shoulder length dark hair?"

"No, and she would have, if she had met someone."

"Did either of you see anyone like that around the house, before Sally went missing?" They both shook their heads. "Well, thank you for your help today. I'm sorry we don't have any proper news, but we will keep you informed. Here's my contact number if you do think of anything else."

The two policemen left. Michael looked at Jess. "What was that Home Office stuff about, Jess?"

"Sally was in security, not just Home Office, that's why she never spoke about her job."

"And she did to you?" Michael was looking upset.

"I guessed, one time when I went into town with her, she didn't say no when I asked, but she told me not to tell you anything."

"And you, Jess, this Foreign Office stuff, that's not true is it, you work there." He pointed towards Vauxhall.

Jess gave him a look. "I can't talk about it Michael."

"Does Mike know?"

"He thinks I'm in publishing or PR or something."

"But what's the spy stuff about then?"

Jess smiled at the memory. "It's just a running joke. It was funny at the time. Michael, don't be upset about this. We'll never forget Sally, but we have to get over it, us two. Just like we all got over Mum and Dad. I wish it wasn't all being dragged up, but I would like to know what happened."

"Can't your people find out?"

Jess gave Michael a 'don't be silly' look and picked up the phone as it rang, breaking the tense atmosphere. It was Lucy for Michael. Jess took the opportunity to head out the door.

CHAPTER SIXTEEN

Round The World

He took the overnight Air France Flight to CDG as Harper, and then via the train express to Gare du Norde. He took the Eurostar to Waterloo as Romonde. He did not go to the house, but instead went to the new apartment. He made sure there were no signs of any identities around the place which he'd purchased in the name of Slater. He wanted to bring Jess there, but she knew him as Johnson. He needed to assign the apartment to that ID. Via two solicitors he had set it up from the USA. He used the house and one of the flats as correspondence addresses, creating a six-month rental agreement, effective immediately. He picked up his supplies from a post office box, and some tinned food, fresh milk, and bread, before returning to the penthouse. He stopped and had a chat with the doorman, Harvey, by the visitor's entrance, slipping him fifty pounds and introducing himself as Johnson and explaining the rental. They traded some jokes and quips on the state of English cricket. He asked him to look out for his new girlfriend, Jess, and asked him to watch out for some deliveries that he was expecting. He returned to the penthouse. He used a cupboard in the spare bedroom to store the supplies. He locked the door to the cupboard. He put his US identity documents into the safe, and spent the next hour setting up his backup CCTV. He went out to the nearest computer suppliers and spent a further two hours setting up his various security measures, including the CCTV recording.

***

By seven in the evening, he was hungry for food and Jess.

He called her.

"Hello?" He heard the enquiry in her voice.

"Hi Jess, are you hungry?"

"You're back? Where are you?"

"I'm waiting for you, would you like to come over?"

"Give me half an hour; did you say you were hungry?"

"I thought we could get takeaway"

"Oh did you?" she smiled. "Chinese please, I'll bring desert, where to?" He told her he'd send a cab and where to go. "See you in half an hour," she said as she hung up.

He altered the answer phone to say Mike Johnson was not home. He called Harvey and asked about the nearest Chinese takeaway that delivered. Harvey recommended the restaurant in the next block. He told Harvey that Jess would be there soon and asked him to show her straight up. He ordered the Chinese, twenty minutes for delivery. He then arranged the cab with a credit card payment in the Johnson name. He quickly took a shower, shaved, dressed in a light sweater with no shirt and some chinos with bare feet. He checked the built in cellar for some wine, poured some Shiraz into one of the two glasses. The noise of the city was coming through the half-open balcony window as he waited.

Jess rushed to her room, to quickly change and prepare. She would need work clothes, if she stayed over. Why was she so crazy with him, like a bitch on heat? She did not know why, but she knew she wanted to be. She hesitated for a few seconds, then grabbed a bag and put a work outfit into a small case. She applied light makeup and put toiletries into the bag. She dressed in a summery, three quarter length skirt with a light cream blouse. She grabbed her bag and walked down stairs. As she wrote a note for Michael, he came in laughing with Lucy in tow.

"Hi, where are you off to?"

"Mike called, he's back. I was just leaving you a note."

"You're going to his place?"

"Yes, he invited me over."

"Aren't you the lucky one? Where does he live?"

"He's sending a cab, I'll find out then." A beep from outside The cab was there. "I've got my mobile," she said as she went eagerly to the door.

"Take care Jess, give me a call," Michael said, watching her go out the door to the black cab.

The cab took less than ten minutes to arrive at a block of swish looking apartments in Vauxhall. She went to pay the cab, but the driver said the fare was covered by credit card. She stepped out as a doorman opened her door. He took her bag.

"You must be Jess," he said. "Mr. Johnson, Mike, said you would be coming over."

"Oh hello," she said slightly flustered and impressed. He escorted her to the lifts.

"It's the Penthouse," he said pressing the P on the control panel. "Have a good evening, Miss."

"Thank you," said Jess. The lift pinged to announce its arrival at the top floor. She was almost shaking with anticipation. The doors opened to the smell of Chinese food and the sight of Mike waiting patiently for her. They kissed for what seemed like forever, before he broke off, pulling her inside the apartment and taking her bag without comment. He held her hands at arms' length, whilst he looked her up and down.

"Better and better," he said. Before she could answer, he pulled her close and kissed her. "God I've missed you."

She almost melted right there. He took her hand and led her further into the apartment, closing the penthouse side door of the elevator. She looked out onto the river from the balcony, with the view of Parliament; he gave her a glass of wine, its warm taste matching the taste of his lips. He invited her to the dining table where the Chinese was cooling. "Let's eat," he said. They sat together looking out at the view. They ate the Chinese with just the odd word. She told him about the visit from the police. He asked a couple of polite questions, but it was obvious she did not really want to talk about her sister. She looked at him and thought he looked tired. They finished eating, and the remainder of the bottle went the same way.

"Come and sit here," he said, leading her to a sofa that also looked out at the river, which was darkening with the summer dusk. "I've got something for you." He went off to another room and returned with a gold paper wrapped package. "What's this?" She asked.

"Oh, just a little something I get all my girlfriends," he said as he sat next to her, his arm draped casually on the back of the sofa above her shoulders.

She smacked his leg playfully "You're not nice," she said. She opened the package to reveal a stunning silk gown. "It's lovely, Mike. Thank you."

"You're lovely," he said lowering his arm onto her shoulder and pulling her towards him.

"And you are nice," she whispered kissing him. She pulled herself away from him. "I'd better try it on," she said with a smirk. She stood up in front of him and unbuttoned her blouse. She unhooked her bra, the dimming light from the river casting shadows over the swells of her breasts. She unbuttoned the skirt and let it fall around her ankles, followed by her panties. She moved towards him and he buried his face against her groin seeking out her flesh with his tongue. She gasped at his probing. His hands held her buttocks pulling her close as her hands pulled his head trying to control his touch As she climaxed she collapsed onto his body. She lay there for a few moments before rising and taking the gown slipping it on, before moving towards the balcony outside. He followed her and, standing behind her, wrapped his arms around her. She could feel his excitement pressed against the small of her back. She turned and undid his chinos, pushing them down with his boxers, she lifted one leg and grabbing his penis, pulled him into herself. He almost fell, but reversed the push of her weight back against the balcony rail, forcing himself deeper into her. A few moments and he too climaxed. They slid to the floor in a tangle of his chinos and limbs. After a bit of giggling and caressing, they crawled back inside. She pulled the sweater from him and told him to stay naked. They cleared the room of the Chinese and put the glasses and cutlery into the dishwasher. She still wore the silk robe undone as he padded about the room. He closed the balcony window. She noticed him check the security systems, before taking her hand in his whilst carrying her bag to the bedroom, from where he recovered the parcel.

"I'm presuming you'll stay?" He arched his eyebrows as he spoke.

"Seeing as I'm locked in, I might as well," she said with a throaty catch.

He pushed her against the wall with her hands above her head. "You're my prisoner now," he said.

She laughed as he kissed her. She could taste her own juices mingled with the wine and the Chinese. "Bathroom?" she asked. He nodded to the door leading off from the room. She disentangled from him, scraping a nail down his stomach as she pulled away. She heard him leave the room and then the flush of another toilet in the apartment, probably the opposite door she had seen. The bathroom was luxurious with a full wet room type shower. She finished, flushed, washed her hands then retrieved her bag from the bedroom.

"I'm having a shower," she said. "You better join me."

"Yes, Ma'am," he laughed. In the shower they soaped each other teasing and encouraging.

Later, lying entangled in bed, with their breathing matching in a restful half-sleep, Jess asked, "Are you very rich?"

"I don't know. I suppose I'm rich compared to many, but not super rich."

"This apartment must have cost a fortune."

"I rent it."

"Still," she said, "look at this place, with the views and space in central London." She sat up in bed, the sheet falling from her breasts as she used her arm to dramatically take in the bedroom.

"It's just a place, Jess. Much better with you here."

"Flattery will get you everywhere," she laughed. "When you're ready?" She lifted the sheet to check for progress in the recovery.

"You are wicked. An old man like me? You'll kill me."

"You're not old. I still see signs of life."

They slept until six-thirty. He woke with Jess in his arms with her back to him. He felt his loins stir, and his erection push up between her legs from behind. She murmured and pushed back and down, forcing him up and into her. He held her tightly, running his hands up to her breasts and kissing her neck.

"Harder," she murmured turning her head so that her mouth could find his, whilst holding his hand against her breast. They accelerated their rhythm until they reached the peak. They dozed, linked together, until Jess noticed her watch showing seven thirty. She pulled away and went to the bathroom and shower. She came back to the room and quietly dressed. He watched her with his eyelids half closed. She sat on the end of the bed and brushed her hair. He moved towards her,

"Would you like some breakfast?"

"Just some coffee and toast would be nice."

He got up and pulled some jogging pants on before preparing the breakfast. She came through, ready for work, in a smart navy business suit.

"Very professional," he said with a small whistle.

"More flattery?" She smiled at him. He provided the toast and coffee. "What will you do today?" she asked.

"Catch up on the paperwork, maybe make a few deals."

"Should I sell my shares in, what's their name?"

"Not yet," he laughed. "I'm glad you bought some."

"I've only had shares in trusts before. Michael got some as well. He wants to pay off his student loan. I ought to give him a call. Can you come over tonight, to stay?" She sidled up to him.

"That would be nice. Jess, I'm sorry, but I'm off away again tomorrow evening."

"Oh, for how long?" A slightly pleading voice.

"Just a few days around Europe. I should be back on Saturday."

"Promise?"

"I can't promise, but I certainly want to be back." He raised her chin with his fingers and kissed her very tenderly.

"Oh Mike," she murmured, "I have to go." She pulled away before his hands distracted her.

"Can I get you a cab?"

"No, I can walk," she said. "Come round for seven, okay?"

"I'll be there."

***

Jess left the building carrying her overnight bag, with a smile, and a nod from the doorman, turning down his offer of a cab. She took a leisurely stroll away from the riverside into the small park at Spring Gardens, before checking her watch and making her way back to the river and into the office. Tony her boss was, as usual, already at his desk. He mumbled good morning and returned to his incessant emails. She sat at her desk, logged on to her computer and recorded her meeting with Mike. Tony looked over her shoulder.

"Ah, the mysterious boyfriend is back, is he?"

"He's not mysterious, but yes, he is back."

"Do we need to run a full check on your Mr. Johnson?"

"I hope so. I really hope so."

"Okay stick his details into the system. Do you have a photo?"

"No, but I'll try and get one."

"What have you told him about the job?"

"He thinks I'm in PR or something."

"Have you mentioned the FO?"

"No, it hasn't come up."

"I was going to make a smutty remark," he laughed. "How is the Plato analysis coming on?" He changed the subject with a smile.

Plato was the small department's code name for a historical analysis project. The particular effort was researching activities leading up to the disaster that was the Iraqi dossier. It was being done to try to detect how so many agencies had made the false assumptions regarding weapons of mass destruction before the war. Her work at the moment concerned the disappearance of a French Agent. She had been investigating Iraqi attempts to get hold of European nuclear information, which had led to the belief that the nuclear programme was still under way in Iraq. This hypothesis had been supposedly backed up with the claim from another source that the Iraqis were attempting to buy uranium from Africa. The problem was the French were not sharing anything, and Five were holding back tons of stuff.

"It was ever thus," thought Jess as Tony let her get back to work. She would enter Mike's details for the check later.

CHAPTER SEVENTEEN

How Did I End Up Here?

Slater stood at the balcony of the apartment and savoured the memory of the night before with Jess. After she had left, he cleaned the apartment and then spent an hour in the complex's gymnasium and pool, both in the basement. Now with a cup of coffee in hand he turned his thoughts back to his latest mission. He needed to get back to Frankfurt soon and get the job done. He tried to picture the essential path of the planning in his mind before he committed his notes to his coded diary. There was always a critical time period in a mission. Back in his brief spell in the Army it might have been a patrol or an interrogation. The briefing might have instructed him to advance to contact or ambush. It was the take or the contact. That brief moment of maximum anxiety, fear, and adrenaline rush. The live or die mentality that made you feel alive, and then sick to your stomach as all the chemicals flooded through your system. He had a gift, a total control of his emotions and feelings at that point. It allowed him to operate and react when others faltered. It set him apart from the others then and allowed him to operate now. There were still enemies, non-combatants, neutrals, and all the other labels applied to non-allies. These days he had no allies, he was on his own. His orders could be ignored if he wished. He either accepted or declined the offer.

He remembered from his childhood watching old war movies with their jingoistic terminology and the gung-ho 'here we go' chaps. Later he watched the post-Vietnam American movies, with their peace messages hidden in the horrors committed on the civilian populations. He had not felt inspired by either approach.

He supposed he was amoral. He knew right from wrong, but that did not stop him doing wrong, whether that was speeding in his car on his rare longer drives, or when on his missions. When he was on the mission he knew the contact, and subsequent actions, were in many people's eyes wrong. His mission control did not think they were wrong (they ordered the action), and on the rare occasion like now, when he moralised over what he did, he regretted the losses but still carried on.

On his first ever live mission, he had stayed calm, followed his training and shot dead two Arab guerrillas in Oman, before either had reacted, or anyone else in the team for that matter. His Staff Sergeant, Andy McLeish, had carefully appraised him and waited for him to develop the post action shakes. He merely carried on without a second thought. His commanding officer, Lieutenant Colonel Frederick Carmichael, was pleased with the result, but concerned with his most junior officer's lack of reaction. He did not want to get drunk, laid, or go and cry; he just casually removed the two targets from the living planet and carried on as if it never happened. He did get drunk later, and his men took him to a suitable brothel to celebrate the success; the link between violence and sex was tenuous but still there even if it was just another night out to him. The Medical Officer checked him over but was not allowed the details and could not see a reason for his check.

Three patrols later, in virtually the same circumstances, he had acted again and reacted in the same way. One of his men was injured on that occasion, and he had looked on in almost disdain whilst ordering all the correct action, the same way he had with the enemy. His Staff Sergeant went to see Carmichael behind his back, he found out later, expressing his concerns, but it took five more patrols, and one more incident, before Carmichael acted to stop his brief career. On that occasion the patrol had missed the ambush point, but caught the team as they were leaving the target. They desperately needed to know where they had planted the bomb. One target was dead or nearly dead. The other was slightly wounded and female. He had gotten the information in less than fifteen minutes. He had been completely unaware of his men watching him, as the girl had whimpered and cried before telling all. She was naked and ashamed and covered in small cuts to her arms and thighs. He had then ordered his men to raise the correct alarms and, as they left, he had shot her. When Carmichael had questioned him, he argued that if she had been killed in the action no one would have blinked an eye, but the bomb would have gone off killing tens of civilians. The only difference was the delay in her death, and the consequent saving of those lives. Carmichael could not fault him on his logic, but did not want him in his Unit.

He was sent back to the UK for processing. He was given a pension and asked to leave on medical grounds; a knee injury apparently, as the details of his missions were not allowed to be given to the psychiatrists. He accepted the result in the same way he had accepted everything to do with the Army, and life in general. He briefly nodded and then got on with it. He found himself unemployed but reasonably well off, with his inheritance and an Army pension, and decided to return to University to finish the education he had dropped out of on his father's death. He knew that if he were ever arrested the psychologists would blame his nature on the Army experience, or his father's death, but he knew different.

His first ever serious girlfriend had realised his true nature two minutes after she slapped him round the face. He had been sixteen and desperate to get close to her. Earlier that summer, he had been on the tube with his father and had stood looking down the tops of the office girls, trying to catch a glimpse of their underwear or better. He was tall, dark haired, from his mother's genes, looked at least twenty-one and often caught girls looking at him. One of the girls had noticed, and almost deliberately leaned forward to give him a better look. She was not wearing a bra and the lean allowed him a clear view of her creamy white breasts below a bikini top tan line. She gave him at least twenty-seconds of ogling before leaning back. He licked his lips. As she got off at the next stop, she deliberately bumped into him and squeezed his groin, letting her hardened nipples brush against him as she squeezed past. She gave him a simmering glance over her shoulder as she flounced from the platform. His legs were shaking from the excitement and embarrassment. His father who was half-reading another passenger's paper, had asked him if he was all right. Yes, he was all right.

With the girlfriend, he had started with the same technique

of trying to look down her top. She had caught him watching, so he had asked her out. For some reason she had agreed. After bits of light petting he was desperate to go further. She had been wearing a light strapped top and no bra. She had let him touch her breasts on previous occasions. Today, he had slipped the straps from her shoulders. A major step forward, as they lay on her bed at her home one Sunday afternoon. Her parents were out, and they had the house to themselves. He started to kiss her nipples, and she moaned gently and pulled him up to kiss her. As he did so, he lowered his hands to her jean's waist band. Before she could react he was pulling the jeans off of her. He realised that she was fighting him. He stopped, surprised at her actions, and that's when she slapped him. He had smiled and casually finished pulling the jeans off. She was frightened now, he leaned forward and kissed her on the head and whispered.

"I could take you now, and I can take you anytime I want." He used his forefinger to pull her briefs down away from her waist but not off, exposing her blonde pubic hair and with the back of his finger he brushed between her legs and back up to her belly button. "Anytime I want," he repeated. She began to sob; his body surged with the power of control linked with lust. He fought to control himself, realising he could do anything he wanted, but deliberately resisting the urge so that he could savour the feeling. He left her kneeling facing him. He did not see her again.

He lost his virginity three weeks later with a girl at a party. Carrie Barker had gotten a bit too tipsy at the party on vodka enhanced punch and ended up in one of the spare bedrooms at her best friend's house. They had fumbled with each other's clothes, and the further he went; the more she encouraged him. With his trousers and pants around his knees, she had pulled him into her. It was not her first time and despite his excitement he managed to last. She had ignored him after that, despite him pestering her. Then, he had been sent to boarding school for his A Levels.

***

He was a bit of a loner with no real friends. In his second year of sixth form, he had followed one of the female teachers. He worked out her entire routine. He used the library to study locks, doors, and windows as part of a project on building design. He went to a builder's merchants and purchased several locks and keys. He learnt how to break in. Using his new knowledge with an exact copy of the teacher's home door key to guide him, he broke into her house at three in the morning. He went through the main front door using a dummy key. He was dressed all in black wearing another boy's ski mask. He entered her bedroom. She was lying on her side with her back to the bedroom door. He moved towards her. He took one of the five ropes he had brought for the occasion and tied one end to the bedstead. A noose was at the other end. Silently he walked to the base of the bed and tied two more bits of rope, each with their nooses. Finally, he walked to the far side of the bed and created his fourth noose. He tried to look closely at her face but in the darkened room he could not see clearly. Her breathing was light. She was asleep. Her left hand was stretched out onto the pillow. He very gently looped the noose over her hand. She stirred slightly. He slowly tightened the noose onto her wrist. A duvet covered most of her. He had one arm secured. Now for her other arm and legs. He lifted the duvet from the base of her bed exposing her shins and feet. They were tucked together. Her right leg was slightly higher. He slipped the noose around her foot, pushing the mattress down to avoid too much contact. She was stirring. He rushed to do the left leg and then stumbled as he moved back towards the door and the top of the bed. She rolled onto her back starting to wake. He grabbed her right hand put the noose on it and placed his hand on her mouth as she went to scream. She bucked on the bed, realising she was tied. She tried to bite his gloved hand and shake him loose. He reached for the gag and, only letting go of her mouth to allow an intake of breath, he stuffed the gag into her mouth. Her blue eyes were wide open in panic. He pulled back and went round the bed tightening the ropes so that she could not move as easily.

He stood up and went to the bedside light. Checking the curtains were closed, he switched on the light and took in the scene. She was spread-eagled. Her flimsy night gown had risen up exposing her white briefs and lower abdomen. Her breathing was rushed through her nose; tears had formed in the corner of her eyes. He moved closer and sat on the bed breathing quite hard too. He brushed a tear from her cheek and looked hard at her. She could have seen see his eyes if she had looked, but they were tightly closed. He turned his gaze from her face. Her chest heaved with her breathing. His hand settled onto the top of her gown, and he traced the line up to her shoulder. He wanted to slip it off her shoulder but realised, too late, that it was not practical. He was annoyed with himself at his lack of forethought. Now what? He stopped and thought, whilst checking the bedside clock. It showed three-fifteen.

He left the room and went to the kitchen, where he found a kitchen knife. She was looking at the door, trying to struggle free from the ropes, when he came back in. When she saw the knife, she started to panic. He went over to the bed. She went still, her eyes on the knife. He placed it under her right shoulder strap and pulled upwards the material snapped. He quickly did the same with the left strap. He pulled down the bodice exposing her small pert breasts. He pushed the bodice further down her body. It bunched around her waist. He turned to her briefs and slipped the knife between the waist band and her thigh. They did not cut so easily but after two, or three tugs they broke away. He pulled them from between her legs. Her pubic hair was light fawn in colour, a neat triangle disappearing between her closely clamped thighs. He took his fifth rope and looped it around her knee and then pulled her legs apart before tying the rope off to her left wrist. He sat back on the side of the bed, suddenly exhausted. He scanned her with his eyes from her sweating matted hair to her toes, seeing the blood forming around the ropes where she was trying to break free. She was still now, waiting helplessly for his next move. He put the knife down, took a long last look at her, and left the room. He returned to his own room in the school. It was three forty-five. He fell asleep with the image of her. The police had searched the entire school for the intruder. The teacher never returned. The ski mask had gone back before he had returned to his room. The rest of the clothes were hidden under a loose floorboard in his room until the end of term, when he disposed of them in a bonfire for his father. He had gotten away with it, but it was not what he wanted. He knew he would have to find a different way.

The odd meeting with a girl had developed and he had several relationships, but none serious, and none lasting more than a few weeks before he backed away, or they sensed something about him. University started, and the freely available girls and easy relationships came and went, whilst he hid from himself his true nature. During his brief stint in the Army, he supplemented his desires with whores and occasional one night stands, if he got lucky. He also practised his following techniques and was never caught. He could lead a completely normal life, if he kept the other side of his nature under control.

CHAPTER EIGHTEEN

University

His father, Robert Ashley, smiled broadly at his results. He had exceeded his predicted grades, and a place at his father's University, LSE, was guaranteed. His father had ruled out the Sorbonne, where his mother had studied. His father was back from one of his overseas postings, apparently to sit in the Foreign Office Policy Unit, although any talk of his father's work was always limited. His mother was the same before she had died, leaving him with her darker looks and her language skills of French and Arabic. French had been an easy A Level. His father's speciality was Arabic following a five-year stint at the Saudi Embassy. He had enjoyed several years from age seven till ten in the international school, but, speaking and writing fluently in Arabic. This was encouraged by his mother, Monique and father. At home, he rarely spoke English with Arabic and French in constant use. His other 'A' Level subjects had been Mathematics, Physics, and History. He particularly enjoyed anything to do with codes and code breaking. He read lots of technology and technical manuals, as he loved figuring out how things worked, especially locks, keys, cameras, and the new computers. After his mother had died when he was eleven, he had spent more time in boarding schools when his father was off somewhere around the world. He had no grandparents or other family and was an only child.

So to University where he would study Mathematics and Cryptology. His parents had been reasonably well off, and he had learned how to budget and handle money from an early age. When his mother died he had a trust fund as his inheritance, which came to him at eighteen. He had invested, with his father's guidance, into stocks and shares, helped by some of his father's friends who worked in the city. He had travelled extensively and felt no need for a gap year like many of his fellow students. He expected he would follow his father into the Foreign Office, although his main tutor, Gabbins, felt he was well suited to academia. He continued to hone his following skills, taking great pride in tracking a particular tutor or student, or even a stranger on the street. He regularly followed women without taking any action. He had a steady supply of girls given his good looks and evident money, so his darker side stayed in check just as a fantasy.

In the final term of his second year, Gabbins had called him in via a message to his digs. He sat him down and told him that his father had died that morning at the Foreign Office, from a suspected heart attack. He was stunned and lost. Gabbins told him that he was clear to depart University, to visit family if he wanted, not realising that he had no family. He took a train to the family house and only returned to University to collect his belongings from his digs. He sold the family house, investing in more stocks and shares and a small car. He decided to join the army, dropping out of university. He was nearly twenty and flew through the Sandhurst training. He deliberately stayed just below the high flyers, not wanting to attract attention, socialised as necessary, and on graduation, joined his unit just in time to deploy as a Second Lieutenant to Oman. His Arabic skills were noted on his file, along with his father's Foreign Office connections.

CHAPTER NINETEEN

Recruited

The Army over, he returned to university to complete his degree with a three-year gap. Gabbins again was his tutor and had persuaded the university to readmit him for his final year. He also recommended him to a friend of a friend who was able to get some details of his brief Army career.

Gerald Hemmings was a hard bitten, seen it all, done it all, Five Controller. He reviewed his new potential player's file with the distaste he normally reserved for only his ex-wife and her new husband. There were three parts to Graham Ashley's file. His background, his formal records and the comments of the recommending *Fisher.* The Fisher in this case was Gabbins, a lecturer in Mathematics at the LSE. Gabbins was his tutor and thought he had a very good prospect, even though he fundamentally did not like his student. Gabbins was a successful Fisher with three other successful entrants, as well as several other good referrals. Ashley's academic record was outstanding before and since the Army. He was multilingual due to a French Algerian mother and a diplomat father specialising in Arabia but with postings all over the world. He smelled of MI6 but that would be hard to uncover on his side of the Thames, especially as he had been 'dead' for several years. Ashley was therefore, an orphan with no other family. He was an apparent healthy heterosexual, private income he discovered via the financial check. In other words, ideal material. He was due to graduate the following month, equal top in his class and probably in the top five in the country. He was being actively chased by the Foreign Office (his father's connections) and several leading city firms, which he showed every intention of joining. Okay, he was good. The military file referred to operations in Oman after the usual basic and professional training summaries. He wanted more on the Oman stuff, which would mean a visit to Carmichael to get the real story.

Two weeks later, after the interview with Carmichael, Hemmings had two issues. Firstly, Ashley could not be allowed formally into the service. He had been fascinated by Carmichael's concerns. Hemmings was not appalled by the coldness of Ashley's nature or actions, he had met and dealt with far worse. Secondly, and informally, how could he recruit him for the black operations he wanted him for? He was concerned about the hook he could use to get Ashley on board. Nearly all Black Ops, the few that existed these days, were done by ex-Special Forces or via blinds to criminal elements. Hemmings controlled a range of agents and his main current operation was counter IRA. They had one suspect bomber under surveillance. Hemmings dare not wait for the bomber to move, or worse carry out an atrocity which would potentially derail the peace process. Hemmings could remove the problem himself, but that might attract attention. It would be much better if the target just disappeared. Hemmings decided to remove the file and talk to Hedges, his control, and start the process of hiding Ashley, before he even knew he needed to be hidden. Ian Hedges agreed with the decision of Hemmings. Hedges had previously had two black operators during his career, both now dead following their mistakes and an identity leak from the controller, also now removed from the service.

"Hemmings, I agree. He'll do, if you can get him to join." Hedges had said in his clipped Old Etonian accent. "I want him deep and set up a completely obscure contact method. Talk to technology to get something in place. This is the last time his name is mentioned. When he leaves University I want Ashley to disappear. I know he wants a job in the city. We can help, but not as Ashley. I don't want to know his new name or names. I want him out of sight. I'll set up the finance through Switzerland via one of the European aid budgets. See how he does with the bomber, then we'll think of something else for him."

As usual, Hemmings barely got a word in once Hedges

moved. Only one problem, what would be the hook? It looked like he would have to make that up as he went along.

***

Hemmings bumped into Ashley the evening before his graduation. He apologised and asked to buy him a drink. Ashley was in the process of following, for the third time, a mousy haired stand-offish fellow graduate, who he was tempted to re-enact an instance from his past. Ashley looked at Hemmings and decided the girl could wait. He knew where she lived after all. Hemmings said he was a recruiter for a Government organisation who would like to offer him an unusual career. Ashley had heard about security service approaches. They were a bit of a joke in the bars and talking shops, and here he was getting one.

"Are you Five or Six?" Ashley casually asked.

"You're quick," said Hemmings without answering. That was the entire hook he had needed. Just a little bit of intrigue. The rest was easy. Ashley was to graduate, then take a holiday. Two months later, via several discreet training courses, he was to return to the UK and become John Slater, amongst others. Slater had joined one of the leading stock traders. He was already making an impact in that career.

The bomber was suspected of carrying out another mission in Belfast, but had lost his tail in the backstreets of Dublin. Hemmings needed action.

***

Ashley's original medium length dark hair had been cut short and dyed; he had been given different contact lenses and taught disguise and various surveillance and counter surveillance methods. His instructors all reported that he was a very gifted natural. He looked very different from his army days. His university tutors, and fellow students would not recognise him. None of his five tutors knew his real name or even his new name. He went through his courses on his own, except for two team exercises where his Army experience meant an easy demonstration of his capabilities in the moors of Scotland. Hemmings met with Ashley/ Slater and outlined the brief. He gave him three contacts that might supply the weapons and other logistics, and the names of four other contacts. He allowed him to write them in a five-year diary he always seemed to carry, when he saw the gibberish they were written as in the diary. The Cryptography had paid off. Finally, he gave him the bomber's photo, address, and name, Liam O'Hara. Hemmings made it clear what he wanted.

"Do you want any other information?" Ashley/Slater interrupted.

"He has to disappear but..." Hemmings was tempted. Could he break the IRA cell? "The prime mission is the target. Anything else is secondary."

"Okay, when?"

"As soon as possible, call me on this number when you're complete. Look, if you have any concerns, John," he deliberately used his new identity, "say now. I need to know you are committed?"

"He's a terrorist, I've dealt with them before," said Slater.

"Other targets might not be so clear cut, and we won't be able to tell you as much as I have this time."

"I understand."

That was it. Slater left. Two weeks later the bomber disappeared whilst out shopping in Regent Street. His surveillance team apologised for losing him, and said they had a vague feeling someone else was watching him, but nothing definite.

CHAPTER TWENTY

The Bomber Wanders Off

Liam O'Hara was short, very thin, and wore his hair close cropped. He wore thick *John Lennon* glasses to counter his myopia. He had been born into the IRA, both his father, and grandfather had been members, along with various family members. His mother had grown up in a safe house used for meetings as the troubles had started. She now lived with his grandmother outside Cork. His father had been hit by the Ulster Defence Force, one of the loyalist paramilitary cells, when he was fourteen. Now nearly forty, he hated the British and most other people, especially the traitors who had sold out for the so-called peace process. He was a bomb maker of high repute in what was left of the proper IRA, not those bastards that had sold out. Now, he had to be called Real IRA or Continuity IRA. He had twenty-five successful bombings to his name, most recently a turncoat Garda member who had been in the IRA, as well as passing on information on British agents operating in Ireland. Then, he had sold out with the peace process, claiming to have been a double all along and handing over several IRA contacts to his Garda colleagues, and probably the British as well.

His little present on his front drive had put a stop to that. Liam had been unable to resist the chance to get revenge, although his prime target was to be a repeat of the Conservative Party Conference hit of 1984. He had a way of getting to their forthcoming conference that autumn. He had diverted himself, to the annoyance of his cell leadership, to get the Garda man, but was back in the safe house in Finchley. The bomb was nearly ready. Getting it to the target was not his problem. Only he knew where the bomb was in preparation. His leader, Shaun knew where the safe house was, but Liam did not know where he was. He had a mobile contact number from a pre-paid phone. Liam spent most of his time reading, and wondering why his appearance did not get him any girls. Once a month he would treat himself to a whore, before his funds ran out. In the good old days, he had a steady supply of girls laid on from the cause. He had money as well, but then the US donations had dried up. The take from armed robberies and protection rackets had also slowed. They could have gone into drugs for funding, but Shaun had refused, as too many noses were in that area. This particular Saturday, Liam was playing one of his favourite games; roam busy shopping centres, imagining he was dropping a bomb off. As usual, it was very busy on Oxford Street as he turned into Regent Street. He felt the sharp stab in his arm and someone grabbing him, but it was too crowded to turn. He felt dizzy and unsteady on his feet, like he was drunk. A man was helping him into a store and then out into a car, or was it a cab? He couldn't focus. He just stumbled and was held up by this man, whom he could not see. He passed out.

Slater had read half a dozen articles on a new drug that the police were concerned about, Rohypnol. He went back to one of the contacts Hemmings had given him. Five hundred pounds lighter, and another odd contact made; he had five doses. He had used one on Liam.

Liam came to in what looked like a garage. There was an inspection pit, he noted, below his tied feet. He could barely move his head, realising it was strapped down as well. He tried to speak, but a gag was between his teeth. His head spun with his attempted movements. The pain at his wrists and ankles added to his discomfort. A shadow crossed his eyes.

"Hello, Liam," said John Slater.

Slater had used £1,500 to rent three garages from three separate advertisements in local papers in London, each with inspection pits. All paid for in cash with no questions asked. The garages were near industrial incinerators. Slater had come up with his disposal method. He had researched some different possibilities. He wanted no evidence at all.

Liam gasped. Who was the bastard Brit' and what did he want? Liam realised he was naked. The man had a knife which he showed to Liam.

"Now Liam, I'm going to ask some questions and you are going to reply. Just so that we are clear, I'll encourage you to answer using this," he waived the knife. "If I think you're lying or holding anything back, then, I'm sorry, it's going to get very painful. Like this."

The man calmly stuck the knife into Liam's bicep. He tried to scream against the gag.

After a few moments, the man took out a Dictaphone. "Now, I'll remove the gag if you'll talk."

Liam nodded but as soon as the gag was removed he screamed. "Fuck off, you'll get nothing from me you British Bastard."

The gag was back on, and the other bicep was stabbed, and a small nick on his stomach.

"Ready to talk?" the man asked.

Taking Liam's look as a 'no', the man lifted Liam's penis and cut off an exposed testicle. Liam passed out. When he came round, he began to talk. Two hours later, with only a couple of knife movements, he was exhausted, nauseous, and the man seemed satisfied.

"What now?" He asked him.

"This," Slater replied, raising a syringe, and plunging the needle directly into his chest. Liam felt an overwhelming warmth and growing blackness with an ecstatic feeling. He felt his heart stop, but no pain. The darkness kept coming until he was gone.

***

Two days later Hemmings got his call from Slater. They met four hours later.

"Well?" Hemmings asked in the saloon bar of a West End pub.

"Mission success," Slater calmly reported. "He has a factory at this address, a store at this address, and he has two contacts in the Met." He passed over a small folder. He was wearing a glove which he took off after passing the folder. Hemmings approved of the precaution. He did not check the file in the pub.

"Mr. O'Hara?" He quietly asked.

"Will not be troubling anyone again," replied Slater. Hemmings was stunned, he congratulated Slater, confirmed his payment, and told him he would be in touch in a few weeks.

***

His boss, Hedges, had been equally impressed. He had given Special Branch the factory and store, but not the Met contacts. They would be his to turn via some favour-inducing time with the anti-terrorist commissioner. The Director General or DG, was very pleased. Now Ashley, or whatever his new name was, could prove most useful in another matter. Hemmings was not cleared for any of it, but he was the conduit to Ashley. Tricky, but Hemmings was a team player. He would understand. He would need the contact stuff; where was it in the file? The file told him about the answerphone and the stock tips. Very clever, he liked the idea. Hemmings and the technology people were to be congratulated. He knew others would like to use his new black player. He jotted down the details in his personal file. The others would pay more with the side issues of information provided or obtained. All to be done via this contact process that used a series of voicemail numbers and options to release or confirm information including mission success and payment details. On his next meeting with Hemmings he asked, "Do we need any physical contact with him?"

Hemmings had replied "No Sir, we could do everything through the phone and via the Internet file transfer, or whatever it's called. Send the file, upload I mean, then issue a password and username for access, and attach the various elements to the menu options. The file is hosted with an overseas service provider as an encrypted electronic file. It's accessed via a site identifier, which only the asset will have and is different from the one you upload to. I created the two sites not IT, so they do not have any of the details. He has the download site, then, when he answers voicemail, he presses to get the access. Everything deletes behind it or becomes available, depending on the option selected. For example, he only gets access to the payment details after a successful mission, or you can split before and after. He can say no to the request, in which case all the details get deleted. I've got the key steps that IT set up, and then I've added my notes, except the download link for him, which he has. He can upload reports, and so on, for you to get, once he presses success."

Hedges had not understood a word of the explanation. The IT people seemed to speak a different language. "Emergency contact?" he asked.

"Nothing in place, but you could offer another option. But that would mean at least telephone contact if you wanted him deep and clear."

"Yes, I did. Can he report failure?"

"No, not really, just the target would stay alive." Hemmings was blunt. "Do you have any missions for him?" Hemmings probed.

"No, nothing at the moment," Hedges lied. Hedges liked the contact methodology, although he did not really understand how it worked. Still, Hemmings could help for the next mission, without having to know the identity or anything about the target. "Okay, set that up. I do not want any links back to you. Does he have enough other contacts to get covers, and so on?"

"Yes, Sir, for the UK anyway. I was thinking about giving him some leads elsewhere."

"Hmm, give him something in Brussels, Rome and the Far East. That should get him going. Don't let the Cousins or Vauxhall get a sniff, but we could do with some entries across the pond."

"I'll set up the leads but, after that it's up to him. We won't know whether he uses them or not. Are you sure you want him that far out of control?" Hemmings rarely questioned his superior and hesitated to even raise the matter.

"I understand your concerns, but we need complete deniability. Have one last meeting with him to complete the arrangements, then cover your tracks internal and external. I will take care of the internal files. Its time Ashley completely disappeared."

***

Hemmings met with Slater in a café on New Oxford Street. Slater did not like the tone of the meeting; neither did Hemmings. Hemmings insisted that there would be more missions and that everything was fine. Slater's well-developed paranoia, sensed the cut off and misunderstood it as a threat. Who knew about him, how safe was he? He had only met Hemmings; he asked Hemmings outright who had told him about him at university. Hemmings hesitated before hinting, but not confirming Gabbins. Slater left the café looking unhappy. He considered his options as he waited for Hemmings to leave. He started trailing him more out of habit then plan. While he thought what to do, his instincts took over.

Hemmings sensed a tail but was unable to spot it. He never considered Slater until he felt the knife in his side. He passed out; when he came to he was in a small cold garage. He was still bleeding profusely. It was then he saw Slater.

"Help me," he gasped.

Slater looked at him and asked, "Who else knows about me?"

"No one but me and my boss," said Hemmings, realising the helplessness of his situation.

"Who is he?"

"His name is Hedges."

"No one else?" Slater moved closer.

"Only I know your new identity. No one else, not even Hedges." He felt weak. He saw the blood pooling by his waist. "You must help me, I'm dying."

"Yes, you are," stated Slater as he left the garage through a side door.

Hemmings tried to cry out and move but couldn't. He passed out before the end came.

Slater left the garage. He would return in the morning to dispose of his contact. He checked that he had no blood on his city suit. He walked two hundred yards before hailing a cab, which took him to the office. That day he made three million dollars for his company, and about thirty-thousand in bonuses for himself. He decided he would go on his own. He resigned that afternoon, and by midnight he had dumped Hemmings in a skip in the East End, making it look like a robbery, and set up his own Stocks and Bonds trading company.

That weekend he went to his old university. He followed Gabbins for most of Saturday. That night, Gabbins died in a house fire. Back in a house, owned in the Slater name, in one of London's Victoria Streets, he used his new-found free time to consider his future. He had already accumulated healthy cash reserves in the Slater name, including the paid-for house in his company's name. He had a new Swiss account with £50,000 in. He had several other identities, which he needed to establish and create activity for. This would be a full time job for several weeks. He had the Far East and Rome contacts to use from the last meeting with Hemmings, along with a lead in the USA.

He still had his stocks and shares as Ashley, hidden by Hemmings for him, but still accessible should he ever want to go back to Ashley. They were steadily accumulating under the management of an exclusive wealth team at Coutts and were well over half a million pounds, thanks to his father's estate sales. He had even had a premium bond big prize drop into that. He got a six monthly account statement into a Post Office box he had rented for that purpose, which again had been set up by Hemmings.

Slater went out and purchased, for cash, two of the new pre-pay mobile phones. He bought a new computer and set himself up at the house. He needed another place to operate, and so found two flats for rent in London. By the time he had finished, his reserves were down to less than twenty-thousand. He had money to live for another few months, but not how he wanted to live. He needed another mission. Hemmings had explained the contact procedure. He considered whether he could safely risk it. There had been nothing in the papers about Hemmings' death.

Hedges checked the police file again; a mugging gone wrong is what the police said. There was no evidence to disagree. Hedges closed the file. Shame, he thought. Dammed good agent. He knew that Carlisle could take on the Hemmings cases, but not his black player. Carlisle was too squeamish for that. Hedges smiled. He realised that he had an untraceable operation in place, for use as his own asset. All he had to do was create the funding routes to pay for the missions. That was easy at his level. Especially if some of his other colleagues, around the world, wanted to chip in. He only hoped that Ashley did not completely disappear. He had kept Hemmings death out of the papers, as was usual for operatives. There would be a small memorial service for his colleagues, but no other recognition. Hemmings' will had explicitly ruled out money for his ex-wife, and had he donated the money in his estate to homes for fallen women. Hedges smiled. Hemmings knew all about them. "Let's see whether we can get contact with Ashley," he thought. Hedges did not have time to read that a low scale Fisher called Gabbins had also died, in a house fire blamed on an electrical fault.

CHAPTER TWENTY-ONE
Sylvia

Hedges had a potential target. A French DGSE agent, Sylvia Cardôtte who was digging too deeply into the UK's nuclear capabilities. The DGSE, or *Direction Générale de la Sécurité Extérieure*, is the French external intelligence agency. He suspected her of working for the Iraqi Intelligence. It was time to find out, with an added benefit of removing a so called ally from the field. He called the contact number and gave the contact details. He found a suitable tip on the AIM Exchange. A small defence company that was about receive a Security Service contract, or they would do, once the evaluation committee was advised of the need. This would be swiftly followed by a takeover from one of his old school friends; he was on the board of one of the defence big boys. Overall, there was a chance of a two to three hundred percent gain. He arranged the secondary payment through a diverted agriculture aid budget to Niger, two hundred thousand. He struggled with getting the electronic file. First, he had to get it uploaded, whatever that meant? Frustrated, he called in his secretary. A bright young thing called Sally Carver. Sally showed him what needed to be done to upload the file, once she had called to ensure that the IT Security people would let it happen. Now, he had to wait.

Slater waited over a week before he dared to check the contact line. He was surprised that there was a contact message for him. Not Hemmings, but still a message. Must be this Hedges that Hemmings had named. He checked the stock whilst he was still on the phone, only eighteen pence. He pressed to accept before he realised what he was committed to. He quickly accessed the file via the website with an access code passed over the phone. He realised he must not do that. He disconnected from the file. A new internet café was open in Holborn. He would go there and read the details. In the meantime, he used eighteen thousand pounds of his remaining money to buy shares in the tip. He now owned nearly 1% of the company. He would have to be careful. Any more than that and it would attract attention from the Stock Exchange.

He printed out the file from the Internet café, which was packed with tourists making email contact home. The Internet was booming. Whoever was the contact sounded public school on the phone message. He printed out the photo. He took the printed-out file to a small park near the British Museum, and in the late summer sunshine, swiftly flicked through it. He could not believe his luck. She looked very similar to the school teacher. This would be quick. He needed the money, but he had to do it right and not like the teacher. He picked up his target at Paddington Station when she got off a train from Reading. He followed her to a flat just outside Finsbury Park. She stopped a couple of times to check for tails, but she was obviously confident she was in a safe environment. Now, he knew where the flat was he could pick up her tail at will. This he did on three successive days.

In between times, he checked on his shares business. Internet stocks were bubbling up. He traded some in to release some more cash as operating expenses. He cleared five thousand; it would have to do. For the Real IRA Bomber, Liam, he had come up with his disposal method. He had initially researched several different measures. He wanted no evidence at all. He considered half a dozen different possibilities before settling on two potential methods, which he had then narrowed to one, the incinerator. He started setting up a disappearance trail for the target. As her assistant, he booked two plane tickets in her name. One was from Heathrow to Paris, and one from Gatwick to Athens. He booked a separate flight for himself to Rome. All flights departed the day after his take. The contact file said that she did a weekly run to Reading, where she met someone from the UK Atomic Weapons Establishment at Aldermaston. She made her contact at a drop the following day with the Embassy Press Attaché. During the three days, he saw no sign of any other drop, but he could have missed it. The timetable was set for after her next contact meet. He watched her off the train and followed her home. He had been in the house during the day and set up a small surveillance camera in the light fitting in the hall. He saw the break-in checks on the other doors to the house and left them untouched. He did not dare go through them. He had left his car parked one hundred yards away. She came into the house. He saw her on the camera from the safety of the car. She took off a light jacket and checked the lounge, kitchen, and bathroom doors for signs of entry. She seemed satisfied and entered the lounge. He dare not stay too much longer in the car, for fear of attracting attention from a nosey neighbour. He drove away and came back 45 minutes later. The road was filling up, so he found it hard to park. As he cruised down the road he saw from the monitor, the target in a dressing gown go from the kitchen to the lounge. He left and went to one of the safe flats where he slept soundly for nearly ten hours.

He was on foot the following afternoon when she left the house. He tailed her to the Tube and followed her as she met the Attaché. The meeting lasted thirty minutes, during which time he spotted two other surveillance personnel. It was unclear who they were watching, the target or the Attaché. As she left, the two watchers stayed with the Attaché. He spent a further thirty minutes checking she was not being followed. As she came out of a small boutique, he grabbed her arm, injecting her with the Rohypnol. She stumbled. He pushed her back against a wall whilst kissing her hard. Any passer-by who bothered to watch would see a couple having an ardent kiss. He checked around for CCTV cameras. They were clear. From inside his jacket pocket, he produced a long blonde wig; he positioned it over her short bobbed brown hair. He also gave her some tinted glasses. She had been carrying her light coat. He put it on her over her light blouse. It matched her light blue trousers. He then hailed a cab. The cab driver, thinking that she was drunk and looking sympathetic, told him to make sure she did not throw up. The cab took them both to a house in the next street to the garage in Park Avenue. He paid the driver with a generous tip. He made a play of getting the house keys out and walking her to the door. He pushed the key into the lock, praying there was no one at home. The driver pulled slowly away. He waited till the driver had gone and then helped his target back around the corner and into the garage. He had made it. No one had seen them come in. The driver would think nothing of a drunken passenger being taken home.

Two hours later the girl was slowly coming out of the drugged stupor. She was tied, standing up to an A frame over the garage inspection trench. She was gagged but otherwise unhurt. He had removed the coat wig and glasses. She looked around her, not panicking, trying to clear her head. He held a water bottle. Her eyes pleaded for a sip, but he gave her nothing.

"Hello Sylvia," he said, "I'm John, and I'm going to be asking you a few questions. Now, we can do this quietly without the gag, or if you make a fuss, with it. What would you like?" He spoke in French. "Will you be a good girl?" She nodded, "Good."

He removed her gag.

"What do you want?"

"Everything Sylvia, everything. Let's get you more comfortable." She looked confused, until he raised the knife, then fear entered her eyes. He used the knife to slice through her blouse. He then flicked the blade through the front element of her bra between the cups

"Bastard!" She exclaimed.

"Oh, Sylvia, that's not very nice." He pushed the two cups of the bra away from her body exposing her breasts to the cool garage air.

"You are sick pervert I think," Sylvia said. "Why you do this?"

He hushed her with a wave of the knife blade near her face. "Tell me, Sylvia, when you lie to your control and sleep with your Iraqi friends, do you look as beautiful as you do now?"

"What are you talking about? Why are you doing this?" He stood closer to her and pushed the knife into the wood of the A frame. He lowered his hands to the waist of her trousers brushing her nipples with the back of his hands as he did so. He unbuttoned her trousers and pulled the zip down. He peeled back the waist band and slid the trousers over her hips where the spread of her legs prevented further progress beyond the tops of her thighs

"Pervert, bastard," she said in rough Arabic. She spat at him but missed. He pushed the gag back into her mouth.

"I told you to behave, Sylvia," he replied, in flawless Arabic which his mother had taught him along with her native French. He removed the knife from the wood waived it across her eyes. He slightly cut the underside of her arm which was tied to the top of the frame. Tears sprang into her eyes. He lowered the knife to the waistband of her light blue briefs. He quickly cut them and pulled them away, exposing her dark pubic hair. He used the knife to slice through the trousers. "Designer I see," he commented. He used the knife to cut the blouse away from her arms and then pulled the cut bra completely clear. Naked, she began to shiver and to sob. The trickle of blood from her upper arm was slowing. He went to the side of the garage and retrieved a dark blue holder, which he carried back to the A frame. From the holdall he took out a black plastic bin liner. He carefully put all her clothes into the bag. "Now Sylvia, are you in the mood to talk?" She slowly nodded, her eyes burning into him. He removed the gag for the second time. "Who do you work for Sylvia?" He asked in English standing facing her.

"I am a reporter for La Monde."

"Sylvia, Sylvia," he sighed exasperated. He reached up with the knife and cut her other arm in the same place; she gasped.

"Please don't."

"Sylvia, I don't want to have to hurt you," he stroked her right breast with his left hand. "I'd much prefer it if we were friends." He lowered the hand between her legs. He removed his hand. "Now, who do you work for?" Nothing. She shook her head. "You're very brave, Sylvia, so you need more persuasion." Another nick, she almost feinted. He stroked her other breast and ran his hand downward to her hip before using the knife to cut her thigh "You can tell me."

She sobbed and then "D, G, S, E," she stuttered.

He put his hand back roughly pressing against her. He forced his mouth onto her mouth. "That's better Sylvia but not quite true, is it?" He said pulling back; he moved the knife towards her stomach.

"Iraq, Iraq," she sobbed. The rest came easily. By the time he knew everything, there were multiple nicks from the knife on her stretched arms, and two on her thighs. He took out a medical kit and dabbed disinfectant on all the cuts. She raised her head from its position, lolling against her chest. He had used a Dictaphone as she told all. He stopped it each time he asked a question so that his voice was not on tape.

"What now?" she croaked.

"Don't worry, Sylvia." He gave her a sip of water.

He took another injection from the bag. He kissed her gently on the lips. As he injected her with a large dose of pure heroin into the upper swell of her thigh, he whispered, "Goodbye Sylvia." Before she could say anything, her eyes closed, her breathing slowed, and finally, after about a minute, it stopped. He cut her down from the A frame and carefully folded her cooling body into first a large plastic bag, and then into a packing crate marked with medical waste stickers. He sealed the crate and manoeuvred it towards the garage door. He took the bag with her clothes and placed it near the crate. He went back to the holdall and retrieved a clean set of clothes for himself. He stripped and re-dressed in the new clothes, placing his with Sylvia's in the bin liner. He waited a few more minutes for darkness, before leaving the garage. He took the tube and retrieved a pre-positioned, rented, plain, white van. It was one of thousands seen every day on the streets of London. He returned to the garage and with some difficulty, loaded the crate into the van followed by the bin liner. He dismantled the A frame and left it in the inspection pit for disposal the following day.

He drove the van to the Polkacrest Clinical Waste facility in Edmonton. Using a false ID, he entered the site and unloaded the crate into the facility. He signed on behalf of one of the local hospitals. They would do a standard delivery two days later. He watched the crate enter the conveyor belt down into the incinerator. His last site of the crate was going between the hanging plastic strips of the safety curtain. He disposed of the plastic bin liner in the non-clinical waste area of the same site. He left the facility and drove to the van rental drop off point just outside Heathrow. It was an almost exact copy of how he had disposed of Liam. Via the

Piccadilly line, he returned to his house, via another cab ride. He was in bed asleep by one in the morning. The following morning he had cleaned and cleared the garage, giving it a coat of paint and a steam clean of the floor. He did some minor repairs, phoned the letting agents, and asked them to put it back on the market.

The next day he called the contact number and requested an email address to which he would send a report. Two days later he checked the number and had an email address read out to him. He sent a report via an internet café to that address. Two days later he had an additional one hundred thousand in his Swiss account. He left the shares to continue their upward spiral for another month, before cashing in and clearing two pounds a share. He reinvested half the money back in at two pounds and spent the rest on others shares. His own company now held shares to the value of half a million, and he had money in Switzerland, which he needed to access. Using a new identity, he applied for some credit cards from one of two flats he rented. He booked a flight to the Caribbean. It was time to take a break and use some offshore banking.

***

Hedges was very pleased with the report confirming the Iraqi double agent operation. He noted SC in his personal address book. He reported to his colleagues the removal of the agent. The French would investigate what had happened, but would not look too hard as they would not want Five to know they were running an agent in the UK. The Aldermaston employee was made redundant shortly after following a careful conversation via the Ministry of Defence, MoD. The French Ambassador was informed quietly a few weeks later that the Press Attaché should go home as the press were about to leak the fact that he was really DGSE. His colleagues were very impressed with this new asset.

CHAPTER TWENTY-TWO

Helena

Hedges was very pleased that everything had gone so well. He had diverted the funds for the project and repaid them using the same stock tip he had passed on. This was a win as far as he was concerned. The report from Ashley had exceeded his expectations and confirmed everything he had suspected.

Several months later he had a regular lunchtime meeting with his Canadian counterpart. The Canadian, Tom Ferguson, had also gained from the stock tip and had asked for Hedges' help in a delicate matter.

Ferguson had a problem. An agent of his, Helena Salbert, was nosing around into illegal stock trades. This was bad enough, but she was investigating alleged illegal payments from various US defence industry companies to members of the Canadian executive. She had reported these activities to him, and he had assured her they would be investigated. Ferguson had discreetly asked the CIA to report on her activities whilst in the USA, rather than the FBI. He did not want her arrested; he wanted to know what she had found out and then silence her. Ferguson wanted her investigation stopped and wondered if Hedges could help. Could Hedges help? Of course he could. Ferguson handed Salbert's CIA surveillance file with Agent names removed by the CIA, he said, to Hedges. He then provided Hedges with other personal details all in a plain blue folder. They quickly discussed finance and Hedges asked for a suitable tip on the US exchanges to fund the operation. Ferguson would have to get back to him. The main payment would be one-hundred thousand pounds on completion. Two days later Ferguson passed two tips through, both on the NASDAQ, both volatile small technology defence companies that were about to get some good news.

Hedges had asked Sally Carver to scan in the file, and now he needed Sally's help again to upload the file to the secure web site. Sally was concerned about the source of the file; she could read CIA on the papers as well. She was further concerned about the movement of classified information to the file transfer site. Hedges re-assured her, but noted her disapproving look. She would have to wait. He then left the messages on the phone.

***

Slater was becoming concerned. He was checking the message service virtually every day. It had been four months since the mission. He had spent the time building the shares business, but this left money a bit tight unless he imported money via the Caribbean from the Swiss account. This was complicated by the need to get other identities funded. He did come up with the idea of using his other identities as fellow shareholders in the trading companies he used to hold the shares, but he needed to keep them separate. As Slater, he met with tax advisers, lawyers, and accountants, keeping the degree of respectability he needed. He had tried out a few bars, had a couple of first dates and had slept with two whores. He was edgy and needed a Mission. In early February, he called the message service and got the Mission details. He immediately invested in futures in the stock tips, gambling over one hundred thousand pounds in the Slater identity. He used three other identities to buy actual shares with a total cost of fifty-thousand. He accessed the file from an internet café, downloading the PDF to a disk before deleting his tracks.

Helena Salbert lived on the US Canadian border close to Montreal. He booked himself a flight as Slater to New York for the following day. He contacted a real estate agent and using the name of James Harper, a new US identity, booked some appointments to see some property he wanted to rent the next day. The telephone message had provided the numbers of two potential contacts in the USA he might want to use. On arrival in New York, he checked in as Slater into the Times Square Hilton and went out and purchased two cell phones on two different networks under the Harper identity. He rented a further cell phone under Slater. He called the contact from one of the Harper phones and the real estate agent with the other. He gave his requirements to the contact and confirmed his appointments with the second. Two days later he had all the equipment he needed, two more identities, various bank accounts with cash deposits, and an apartment, for three months initially, just off Central Park West, rented in the Harper name.

He checked out of the Hilton, hired a car with one of the new identities, David Simmons, drove across the Canadian border as Slater, to log his leaving the US with US immigration, and stayed half a day admiring the scenery and researching in a Montreal library, before re-entering the US using the Simmons hire car identity and eventually getting to his new apartment. He rested and planned his take, fixing the plan with as many details as possible.

He used the contact to get a US passport in the name of Helena Simmons, now his wife using the picture from the file. Three days later he had the identity. He checked the stock position. It had already doubled. He traded in half the futures, releasing his initial investment. He needed some more cash for all the identities. One in particular, that of an FBI agent, he left in a safe deposit box. He also used the released cash to extend the rent on the apartment for another twenty-one months, giving himself an operating base for two years.

It was time for some closer surveillance and then action on the target. He moved to a forward operating base. He checked into a dismal truck stop motel just outside Montreal. He picked up her trail and followed her at different times until he established a regular pattern. She only used counter surveillance on three trips that she made across the border back to the US. There she spent her time following different officials from Canada whilst they had meetings with various executives of US Companies in hotel rooms. He checked out her limited social life, which consisted of telephone calls to various girlfriends, but no men. She played squash according to her file with one former colleague, but not regularly. He estimated he would have three weeks clear after the next squash game. He waited. Two days later he followed her to a squash game using the hire car to follow her cab. He waited outside as she played. Now, it was time. She came out of the centre and waved farewell to her friend. A light drizzle fell, darkening the whole scene. As she walked towards the taxi rank he walked quickly to her side. As she turned to see him, he injected her with a large shot of Rohypnol into the neck. She started to scream then partially collapsed as the drug quickly took effect. He quickly supported her and moved her towards his car. He placed her in the passenger seat checking for any witnesses in the gloom. No one was watching. The friend had re-entered the centre.

The car park was virtually empty, and the taxi rank was hidden behind a wall which she had not cleared before he grabbed her. She murmured something in her half sleep. He made sure her safety belt was secured and then tilted the seat back; she gave the appearance of sleeping. He took her bag and put the false passport in, removing her other IDs and storing in the glove compartment. He drove for the border. The crossing was quiet when he joined the two car queue north of Champlain. He showed their passports, and the guard noted and checked the sleeping woman beside him. With a nod, he waived them through without a word.

He drove for the two hours he needed to reach a pre-rented holiday cabin outside Willsboro on route 22 on the shore of Lake Champlain. There was no one around in the dark when he arrived and helped the target into the cabin. He lay her down on a sofa. She was still almost unconscious; but showing signs of coming to. He quickly went back out to the car and collected his bag. He came back into the cabin. He pulled her up off the sofa. She murmured, but he held her up, and she relaxed into his grip. He took her through into the bedroom. He needed to move quickly now. He pulled off her shoes and sports socks. He undid and dragged down her jeans, leaving a small thong which covered virtually nothing. He struggled and eventually pulled off her sweatshirt and t-shirt leaving her pale blue non-matching bra. He grabbed the four pre-positioned ropes he had placed before and tied her spread-eagled to the bed which had been stripped down to a plain sheet over a plastic cover. She was coming around quickly now.

"What are you doing?" The words slurred from her mouth. He quickly gagged her, having to force her mouth open by holding her nose until she gasped. She tried to bite him as he did so, but he managed to complete the task. Now gagged and bound she calmly evaluated her position. Looking at him, she was memorising every detail about him whilst he sat in a bedside chair and drank from a bottle of water. Sweat was on his forehead below his short hair. He wore a light green polo shirt and chords despite the coolness of the year and the cabin. As she watched he stood and removed his shoes and socks and took off the polo shirt, revealing a well-muscled torso with a slight sprinkling of hair on the chest. He looked at her and smiled.

"Bonjour Helena" he said. His accent was not quite right, not French, not Canadian, she thought. She pulled against the bindings and tried to spit out the gag. "Now Helena, if you promise not to make a song and dance, I'll take the gag off, but you have to promise." He had spoken in English and the accent was mid-Atlantic, but mostly English. She nodded at him. She needed information to make her escape. Stay calm, and she would get an opportunity. She felt the chill from her lack of clothes, which she had only just noticed. He walked towards her and removed the gag. Take command, they had told her during her counter-interrogation, take the initiative. Maybe this was one of those stupid tests that were sometimes placed upon officers. It was a very realistic one, if that was what this was.

"Who are you and what do you want? Where am I?" She rushed out the questions in a slowly loudening voice, giving away her near panicked state of mind. Calm, she told herself. Get calm. If this was a rapist then... She struggled to think. What did rapists do? She did not know. A test, no the sexual angle was wrong. Who was this and why?

"Helena, Helena, ssshh now, you'll disturb the neighbours," he smiled. The nearest occupied lodge was well over half a mile away and with the wind bringing an early spring rain storm in, no one would have heard her, even if they had been outside the cabin window.

"What do you want, whatever your name is?"

"You can call me David if you wish, I'm glad we're getting along so well."

"What do you want?" She asked again.

"You Helena, all of you." The panic began to rise in her again. He was a rapist then. He moved towards her and bent down to retrieve a knife from a bag by the side of the bedroom door.

"No," she said, "don't." He used the knife to cut her bra between the two straps and then the tip of the blade to flick each cup off her breast. They were small, with very dark nipples, which hardened in the cool cabin air. He lent down and licked one of them.

"Pig," she said straining at the ropes. Rape, well she could live through that. Get a chance, get untied, then she could fight.

"Helena," he said lifting his head, "we were getting on so well." He took the knife and snapped the lace edges of her thong. He pulled the remains up through her thighs, exposing a partially shaved patch of dark pubic hair. She tensed and tried to look at his eyes. He ran his hand over her stomach placing his fingers into the dark hair. He sat by her side. "Now Helena, you and I are going to have a little talk."

"What about?" she said, on the verge of total panic. Talk, what talk? She had been expecting rape, now he had stopped. He couldn't know whom she was, what she did for a living. Yet, her suspicions had been aroused. She thought she was tailed the last time she had been south of the border. She had followed an aide to the Defence Secretary as he went to a meeting with an American holding company. The meeting at the company HQ was not in the Aide's diary, she had discovered. Why hide it? She had begun digging after two separate statements from policy makers had turned anti-Iraq. Why? She saw much of the raw intelligence and the change did not make sense? Not another war. Helena hated wars.

"Well, let's just see where the evening takes us. Can I get you a drink, some wine, or whisky?"

She shook her head, "Get on with it."

"Okay," he said. He stood and undid his chords.

"No," she said, "not that."

"Not what, Helena, I thought you were being friendly?"

"Please," she said. Talk, not rape. But the threat was there.

It took him a little over an hour to ask his questions. He did not have to use the knife at all, just the odd touch of her body. She was shivering with cold and fear when he finally nodded at one of her sobbed answers. Then, he stood up and went to the bag. He withdrew another syringe and went back to her side.

"No," she sobbed. "I'll do anything you want, anything." Get some more time; get him to give her the chance she needed. Not just talk she realised, and not rape. The talk confirmed it; all about her investigation and suspicions. He had recorded it on a Dictaphone. He must be CIA she thought, but the accent was wrong. She realised she had no chance.

"Helena, I've already got everything I want," he said as he injected the heroin into her chest. A minute later she was gone. He sighed and untied her body. From the holdall, he took a large plastic bag. He placed her inside. He took her clothes and the bed sheets and placed them in another bag. He carried her body outside and down to the small dock, stopping to put his shirt back on, and a small wind-cheater. He placed her body in the bottom of the small boat and covered it with the tarpaulin. He then returned to the cabin. He collected the bag with her clothes and the sheet and placed it in the boot of the car. He then returned to the other bedroom, showered and slept for seven hours.

He awoke at dawn and, putting on his fishing gear, he went back to the boat checking on the small engine. Accompanied by some trout fishing gear, he steered the small boat out into the lake, heading south away from the cabins. He motored about half a mile out, and cast out the fishing rod, keeping an eye out for other boats and fishermen. Nothing, but it was early and mid-week, the weather was fairly dank, and a light drizzle reduced the visibility further.

He pulled back the tarpaulin. He made sure the plastic bag had a large enough slit in it for it to sink. He started tying off the bricks he had placed in several smaller bags and attaching them to the plastic bag and her limbs encased in plastic. He took two of the brick bags and with some effort lowered them over the side. The boat leaned alarmingly with the weight. He readjusted his position to counter the potential capsize. Now the tricky bit. He manoeuvred the big plastic bag onto the stern of the boat. He was just about to let it go when the boat tipped vertical and flipped him, his gear and the bags into the freezing cold lake. He swallowed freezing cold water in shock and swirled underwater, tangled with one of the ropes and bags as it slipped the down into the four hundred feet depths.

He fought to extract himself from the ropes, losing orientation in the cold and the dark water. He finally disentangled himself running out of breath and pushed for what he thought was the surface. He broke through water, but into darkness. He had come up under the capsized boat. He gulped in air desperately, and then ducked under the hull to the outside of the keel. He gripped the side of the hull and with all his might flipped the boat back upright. The boat settled back down and after several minutes, or was it only seconds, he managed to drag himself back on board, panting. The fishing tackle was floating a few yards away. All the other equipment on the boat was gone, along with the body and brick bags. He moved back to the stern and checked the engine. It started on the second try; he gave a silent prayer to Honda and turned the boat for the shore, shivering in the strengthening breeze. Thirty minutes later he was back in the cabin. The shivering had stopped. A bad sign. He quickly stripped and got into the shower, using the cold water to bring his body slowly back to warmth before turning on the hot.

Several hours later he left the cabin, handing back the keys, and claiming a business call for the abbreviated stay. He still paid for the full week with cash. He drove back to New York, dropping off the hire car and returning to his apartment. His ID still needed drying out fully from the lake. He used a new computer to type up his report. He saved it to a disk and went downtown to a public library. He used the public access terminal to upload the file with his report; mission complete.

***

Hedges reviewed the report that he had to get Sally to download for him. Damned computers. He could not get the hang of them. He stopped Sally seeing the main report, but she could not help noticing the file name, HS, the same file name that she had saved that personnel file with. The one she had uploaded a few weeks before. Hedges thanked her, but her curiosity did not go unnoticed. Hedges used the secure phone to call Canada and Ferguson. Ferguson thanked him for the report and confirmed the payment would be made to the two accounts in Switzerland. Well, it was only right that Hedges had earned some commission. Still Ashley, or whatever he was called now, would have fifty-thousand to play with, plus the stock tips. HS was in his personal diary.

***

Two weeks later Slater cashed in the options. He cleared nearly one hundred thousand dollars and was happy to see the balance in Switzerland, which he passed through the Caymans and split amongst various accounts throughout the world. With internet banking, he did not have to move from the London house.

CHAPTER TWENTY-THREE

Correct The Viewpoint

Peter Smith had been with the Defence Intelligence Agency for five years following his Army career. He had specialised in Weapons of Mass Destruction, normally shortened to WMD, in Iraq, Iran, and occasionally Libya. WMD covered biological, nuclear, and chemical weapons. Iraq in particular had used chemical weapons internally against the Kurds in Halabja in 1988 and throughout the Iran Iraq war from 1980 to 1988. Smith had been on inspection teams, undercover with the UN, following the first Gulf War in 1991. He had overseen the destruction of several groups of munitions before Iraqi intelligence had blown his cover with the UN. Back in the UK he continued his analysis, relying on third party and other intelligence sources. He was preparing a report for the Ministry and the Intelligence Services on the current status of Iraq's WMD capabilities, based on his contacts still in the UN inspection teams and his extensive knowledge of Iraq from his own visits. He had argued with his civil service superiors at their assertion that Iraq was not only capable of using WMDs, but actively that it was actively pursuing an increasing capability. He felt that he was a lone voice in ridiculing some of the assertions.

Peter Smith's passion outside his work was his love of camping and fishing. His wife hated it and never went after he had persuaded her to go for their first anniversary. Every couple of months he would take a small tent and his fishing gear and hike off either in the Lakes in North West England, the moors in the Southwest or his favourite place in the world, the Scottish Cairngorms and lochs in the north of Scotland. His wife would be spending his Army Pension on some Spa treatment at an overpriced hotel. He had found a spot to camp in the late spring weather on the banks of a small loch. Some late snow was on the top of the mountains, but today was bright and clear. Once he was packed up he would walk to a loch outflow and try for some trout. He had packed his tent and been loading it into his backpack when the man approached him, smiling. Always happy to chat with a fellow walker he greeted him. The needle in his arm had barely gone in before he felt dizzy. He felt even dizzier despite the very cold water of the Loch. He could not focus as the water filled his lungs, and he went down.

***

Hedges noted the brief report and mission success. Another troubling loose-end trying to deny the presence of WMD in Iraq. He could not have that, now the dossier was being prepared and Bush junior wanted his own war. Smith's draft report would disappear. Payment authorised to the asset. PS went into his diary.

***

Bahaarat Ibn Kalid had proved to be a very difficult target. As a member of the Ba'ath Party and therefore part of the Iraqi ruling elite, he was open to occasional surveillance to ensure his loyalty, especially when he returned home to report to a deputy to the Iraqi foreign minister. The majority of his time he spent moving between different Iraqi embassies around, primarily Western Europe, but, regularly other Middle Eastern capitals where he was watched by virtually every security service in the World. Officially, he was a trade delegate and since the Kuwait invasion, and subsequent sanctions, his primary role had been to try to continue trade, or to get round sanctions on behalf of the Iraqi regime. Unbeknown to his watchers he had been recruited by SIS in the late 1970's. He would drop information in several contact points around the world except London. He travelled there regularly and had been educated in England at Stowe, before returning to England for his degree, where he had been recruited by a female French Algerian working for the British. His controllers met with him on occasional trade missions but always outside London. Kalid was watched by the Security Service when he was in London, but they had no idea of his real identity.

Slater decided that Dubai was a good location after spending six weeks following Kalid very discretely around the world. He saw lots of other watchers during his journeys and presumed he was seen by other watchers as well. Dubai, he thought, was his best bet. Firstly, there seemed to be fewer watchers there, and secondly Slater could blend in using his fluent Arabic, skin tone and a Dubai identity he had created. Slater also had a contact pass phrase to approach the target. There was a deadline for the mission. Kalid was supposed to hand over an internal Iraqi report on the progress of the restructuring WMD programme to his controller. Slater was to replace the report in the drop with one from the file which told a different tale. The new report would have the correct provenance via a trusted source. It was a complex mission needing careful timing. Slater had met Kalid in the lobby of a hotel, used the pass phrase, and agreed to meet later, when Kalid would hand over the report directly to Slater, rather than the normal drop. Not normal procedure, but this had happened before. Kalid had been very careful going to the meet, as he always was. He entered the hotel room and was unconscious before he had put two steps through the door. After Slater's interrogation, Slater had again drugged him. He was then dressed. Before Slater killed him with two bullets, one to the heart and one to the head. Kalid was left sprawled across the bed. The implication to all watchers was that one of the watching teams had removed Kalid. They could argue amongst themselves who it was.

Slater had taken, read, and then destroyed the real report, relieved that he did not have to dispose of the body. He did not understand much of what the report said. His written Arabic could not cover the technical information contained in the report, but it was clear that Iraq, although keen to re-start its WMD programmes, was not having much success and had not attained any weaponised capability. He used the information from Kalid to drop the fake report into the dead drop, where it was retrieved as usual by Kalid's current controller, and his third in his long career. Two days later, the controller notified Vauxhall that Kalid had been found dead. The authenticity of the file from the drop was not questioned.

***

Hedges noted the report and mission success. They could not have sources contradicting the agreed policy, casting aspersions on the agreed approach. Easy cover as well, Saddam was increasing his counter intelligence operations. Payment authorised. BIK went into his diary. Hedges was very pleased, as were his colleagues. The policy was almost complete. The politicians would have to act with irrefutable proof of Iraq's intentions and WMD capabilities. Hedges finished an internal policy document, exaggerating Iraq's attempts to get WMD information. This went to the DG with a strong memorandum imploring action before they succeeded and threatened the UK.

CHAPTER TWENTY-FOUR

Are We Getting Anywhere?

Michael Johnson left his Vauxhall apartment, after setting up various security checks. This included a hidden motion sensitive CCTV feeding his smart-card protected computer via a hidden hard disk array. The penthouse was safe and transferred effectively away from the Slater ID, with only a couple of lawyers knowing that it had ever been his.

With a nod to Harvey, and a knowing wink in return, he strolled across to Spring Gardens in the warm July sunshine, carrying a small overnight bag. He spent a few minutes on a bench updating his diary before picking up a cab that took him north to one of his safe flats. He logged on remotely via a secure web site to his main house's CCTV. All appeared fine, but he couldn't access the internal systems from outside. He would love to go and check, but he did not want to bump into any waiting Special Branch types. He was pleased their visit to see Jess, and Michael had completed. Now, he would not accidentally run into them when he was there. As far as Special Branch was concerned, Slater was still away, and he wanted it to stay that way. He updated his target information with a bit more research from a contact in Berlin. They thought his French ID was that of a left wing reporter digging the dirt on the counter terror measures now in use across Europe. He then grabbed a couple of hours of sleep; if he knew Jess, he would need it.

***

DI Hooper called the two teams into his office for the

sensitive update briefing before he briefed the wider team. Drinkwater confirmed what they had suspected - that Hollingsworth had been Six, but no more information was forthcoming, although he was still digging. Pollard read back the notes from the meeting with Jess and Michael Carver, Drinkwater added.

"Jessica Carver is Six by the way"

"With a missing sister in Five?" DC Grahams asked.

"She didn't confirm it, the sister that is, but I think she knew. The sister Jessica is certain her sister didn't go off travelling."

"I don't think any of us believe that do we?" Hooper stated, looking around the table. He received shakes of the head from his four team members.

"Nothing more on Jodi Parker, and no connections to Slater for any of them. Of course, we haven't checked any alibis as Mr Slater is still out of the country." Rutledge sounded frustrated. "Our star witness, Snoop, wouldn't last five minutes in a witness box anyway, before his endless lying gave him away."

"Slater was in Paris checked into one of the airport hotels apparently," DC Grahams added.

"And now?" Drinkwater asked.

"Said he was going to the States, but who knows. He could be anywhere."

"Okay, let's go see what the teams have turned up." Hooper led them into the main work area. Hooper updated the rest of the team on the investigation progress, or rather the lack of it. He threw it open to the floor. A young female PC, Shelly he thought she was called, raised her hand from the back of the room.

"Yes, Shelly isn't it?"

"Yes, Sir," her smile lit up her otherwise plain face.

"Well, what do you have Shelly?" He gave her an encouraging smile.

"Sir, back at Hendon…" There were groans around the room. "I did a project on money laundering techniques and identity creation."

Hooper held up his hand to stop Drinkwater interrupting. "Go on Shelly."

"Sir, I've been on the team looking into John Slater and he, well, he doesn't exist before 1998." Tentative and nervous, but she had their attention now.

"What do you mean?" Hooper leaned forward.

"Well, Sir, Slater would be twenty-one or twenty-two then, and yet he doesn't seem to have had a bank account, or I should say there is no trace of one. Then, he suddenly pops onto the horizon and within a few months he's running his own business and shifting tens of thousands of pounds around the globe."

"He does do stocks and bonds and so on in the city," Hooper said, gently encouraging.

"I know Sir, that's what makes it difficult, but he gambled big time, twice in a few months, and made nearly three hundred thousand pounds that he declared. I think he made more out of the country. There were several other big trades in the same stocks around the same time. The payments went all over the place, the USA, Caribbean, Switzerland," she faltered.

"What about pay and bonuses?" DC Grahams chipped in.

"The Inland Revenue had records of a big bonus of thirty odd thousand just before he left the brokers, but he spent that in a similar way, and then he made two big trades with funds from what looks like Switzerland." Shelly faltered again. "Since then he has money going all over the world and back, including the Caymans and so on." She stopped and looked up expectantly.

"Shelly, this is excellent work." That smile was back. "Dave, go over the details with Shelly, but this looks very interesting; even if he's not our man for the girls. Something is not right. Okay, Jim, he's your man. Get some more people on this. Let's start really digging into Mr. Slater. Get some full time surveillance on his house and alert the airports. I want a word with him as soon as he's back. Get a photo and go back to the other girls. See if we can get lucky." Hooper felt the same gut feeling that Rutledge had.

***

Michael Johnson was less than a mile away from the Special Branch Team. He had dressed and showered and put together an overnight bag. He left the flat and headed for the tube. He followed a roundabout route before exiting at Oxford Circus and hailing a cab, certain that no one was following, before heading for Jess. The cab dropped him off one hundred yards and two streets away. He walked casually to the house, checking for watchers and seeing none. He rang the bell. Michael opened the door.

"Hi Mike," he said, "good to see you again. Jess is just changing."

He showed him into the lounge area leaving his bag in the hall. He heard the creak of the fourth step, and then Jess was in his arms.

"Hi," she said after a long kiss. She turned to her brother, "Open some wine Michael. Is Lucy not here yet?"

"Orders and questions," laughed Michael. "Lucy will be here any minute, and you need to stir the sauce."

Jess broke away from Mike and went into the kitchen area, checking various pans whilst asking Mike what he had done that day. A few minutes later and the bell went, and Lucy arrived. Mike surveyed the girl. Luscious was the right description. They had dinner together, sharing bottles of wine and much laughter as Lucy and Jess took turns teasing Michael. Finally, Mike became the victim of the lighthearted questioning.

"How do you get your tips?" Lucy asked.

"That's the secret," he replied, then continued. "I meet with various companies and other traders, read various press reports and check companies out."

"Jess was telling me earlier about your apartment on the river," said Michael.

"It is rented, and I have just moved in, but it is nice."

"I should think so," said Michael. "Maybe I could afford one, one day, if I keep following your tips."

"Stocks can go up and down so be careful," said Mike.

"Should we sell yet?" Michael asked.

"No," said Jess before Mike could say anything, "Mike told me to hang on yesterday."

The conversation moved on to travel. Jess said that Mike was off to Europe again the following day. They all helped clear the dishes, and then both couples took their separate leave to bed. In Jess's bedroom, they undressed each other before sliding naked under the covers. They made love slowly before drifting off to sleep.

He awoke to find Jess dressed and sitting with a cup of coffee on the end of the bed.

"I have to go to work," she said. "When are you leaving?" She added sadly.

"Evening flight to Paris," he said, "and then all over."

"Will you be back for the weekend?"

"I'll try," he said.

She told him there was toast waiting downstairs and to let himself out. Michael and Lucy had already left. She got up and smiled, but there were tears in the corners of her eyes as she left the house.

"I'll call you tonight," he said to her retreating back.

Mike dressed and had left the house before ten. He took a circuitous route back to a safe flat and from there, equipped with cash, electronics, and identity documents, he returned to the penthouse. He took the Heathrow Express from Paddington and caught an early evening Air France flight to Paris as Pierre Romonde. He checked into the CDG Hilton under the same identity. He set up the phone to forward to one of his French mobiles. He then left the hotel and caught the late flight to Berlin. He found another airport Hilton, checked in using an American identity, and then called Jess from his mobile, giving her the Paris hotel number. He asked her to come out and meet him in Paris. She agreed she would take the Friday evening Eurostar; he'd meet her at Gare Du Nord. He booked a room at the Central Hilton in the name of Johnson. He had two days to complete his latest mission. The following morning he was in Frankfurt.

CHAPTER TWENTY-FIVE

Plato Pieces

Jess was busy, and the call from Mike had cheered her up. She had found two odd links in her research. One a change in the Canadian position on Iraq in May 1999, which was unexplained, and also a lack of further reports from the French agent. She followed some of the paper sources but kept coming up with dead ends. Opening a heavily censored *Five* file, she was stunned to discover her sister's distinctive handwriting, although her name was blacked out. Jess burst out crying just as Tony walked up to her desk.

"Jess whatever is the matter?"

"It's Sally," she blurted out between sobs.

"What do you mean?"

She showed him the file. "This is Sally's writing," she explained calming down.

"Oh Jess, what a shock, but you knew Sally worked for Five?"

"I know, but it was just in this context. It scared me."

"How come?"

"You know the French agent that reported on the nuclear capability?" Jess was back in control now.

"Yes."

"I don't understand why her reports just stop, when she obviously has good contacts into Iraq, and then this sudden change of policy in Canada which shows no signs leading up to it in the public reports. Now Sally's writing a request for the same reports and then she disappears. And then there's this, which I was about to bring you." Jess had found an internal memorandum from the Foreign Office asking where their contact Harriet Hollingsworth had gone to. Hollingsworth was working on Iraqi Weapons of Mass Destruction, WMD, specialising in Iraqi attempts to obtain French nuclear technologies. "The thing is," said Jess continuing, "Hollingsworth is one of the other girls, with Sally in the Police investigation."

"Are you sure?"

"Yes, Michael and I had a visit from the team investigating the latest girl, Jenny Wallace, and they have linked her to Sally, Hollingsworth and another girl. Jodi Parker I think her name is."

"Jess, I need to stop you there. Are you saying the police are hunting a serial killer or something, and that Sally is one of the victims, like they said in the paper?"

"I don't know if it's a serial killer because no one has been found, including Sally, but they seemed to think they are all linked in some way." Jess was struggling with tears again. Six years and it was still raw just beneath the surface.

"And what do you think the link is?"

"I don't know, but..." She hesitated.

"Go on, Jess, this is what we recruited you for. To making links."

"Oh I'm just guessing, but we have a French agent who suddenly stops then, Sally and this Harriet, but I don't know about the others so it may be coincidence."

"What if I told you that Jenny Wallace was Five, worked on the counter Iraq desk. Not for general release by the way, but I went to a couple of courses with her, I don't know about the Parker girl though."

"Oh my God."

"Jess, write it up, I'll sign it. I don't want your name on it at all because of the link to Sally. I don't like this one little bit, and I doubt most coincidences." Tony had turned pale. "I'm taking this upstairs. Have you got the names of the police, CID were they?"

"They were plain clothes, but I think they may be Special Branch. I think they guessed about me being in the Service. I didn't say anything though."

"That's okay. Look, Jess, we may not be able to discover what happened to your sister. It's been six years, and I need your mind on this project, but if there is a link we may have something to go on. What does your new beau know?"

Jess was thrown a bit by the change of tack. "He's invited me to Paris for the weekend, if that's okay. I'll fill in the overseas form," she said distractedly. "He knows Sally went missing. I mean it was all in the papers. We discussed it once, but he doesn't know what I do. He thinks I'm in PR."

"Fine for Paris. He must be serious Jess?"

"Yes," she did not hesitate, and she knew it from the depth of her heart. "Yes, I'm in love with him. It sounds silly and childish I know, but that's what it is."

"That's good," Tony smiled. "Okay, you write it up, keep it simple, a couple of bulleted pages should do, provide the corroboration as appendices. Get onto vetting and see if you can track down Jodi Parker, and link her into anything on Iraq. As for your new friend, you need to check with vetting before you say anything, which gives you a nice excuse to talk to them."

Tony Grayson instinctively knew that Jess was onto something. Up until five years previously, when his cover was deliberately blown in Beirut by the Israelis, he had been a field agent for fifteen years around the Middle East. He had been horrified by the Iraq war and the misuse of intelligence in its lead up. He had been given the Plato project to keep him quiet initially, and then, as the political storm mounted, he had been given more access, as the Six politicians tried to cover their backsides from the blame culture. He called upstairs and went up to see his department head, another former field agent who at least understood instinct.

He was shown straight into the office of George Claridge-Briggs. Claridge-Briggs was old school Etonian and Cambridge. Thirty years in the FO with over twenty as an undercover Six operative in various embassy staffs around the world. Even the CIA had not known he was an agent until he returned to head office and turned up at liaison meetings. Claridge-Briggs had known Michael Carver, Jess' father, and had followed the sisters' University careers, but missed out to Hedges over at Five for Sally Carver.

"Sir," started Tony Grayson. Claridge-Briggs was very formal. "I think the Plato team may have unearthed something."

"Well, Mr. Grayson, what is it?"

"I reported last week on the sudden drop off in activity from the unnamed French Agent."

"Yes, a bit unusual that?"

"Well, Sir, it's got a bit more unusual. You'll have read the speculation about the missing girls in the papers?"

"Yes, of course, I knew Sally Carver, Jessica's sister as well."

"Yes, Sir, Jenny Wallace is also one of them. She is, was, Five, on counter Iraq."

"Really?" Claridge-Briggs mused and sat forward behind his desk, evidently deeply concerned.

"And Harriet Hollingsworth is another potential victim."

"Didn't know her, but heard about her, very attractive apparently. So you think the killings, if that is what they are; disappearances then, are connected to Iraq?"

"As usual sir, you have it."

"Supporting evidence?"

"Limited. I'm having a report drafted. Sir, Jess is doing the drafting. She found the connections, but I don't think her name should be on the report."

"Anthony..." It was only the second or third time that Claridge-Briggs had ever addressed him by his first name. "Good thinking, keep her away from it officially, do some track covering with other Plato areas. What about the other girl, name escapes me?"

"Parker, sir"

"That's it."

"Jess is checking with vetting to see if she has a background."

"Her excuse?"

"She is chasing up a boyfriend check."

"The rich broker?"

"Yes, Sir," Grayson smiled, "she seems smitten."

"That would be good news. I hope he checks out. Hmm..." he hesitated a moment. "I am going to sniff around and talk to a few folks, see whether I can find out where our police friends are in all this."

"Jess thinks Special Branch are investigating."

"Really, she does take after her father. She would have been good in the field, but she does the analysis very well."

"Yes Sir," Grayson agreed

Grayson left and Claridge-Briggs thought over his next actions. Logically he should give Hedges over at Five a call, but he had never liked him and he did not trust him. No, not Hedges, instead there was the Commander of Special Branch, David Jones. He had met him on a couple of social occasions. He could also check with his Five friends to see if they knew who the Five liaison was. Thirty minutes later he had found out, via one of the counter-terrorist contacts he had in Five, that the liaison was called Jonathon Braithwaite. Time for a friendly chat. He gave him a call and, within five minutes, had himself invited to an off the record meeting with Special Branch.

They met in a pub for a drink that evening, just off the Bayswater Road. Claridge-Briggs started the discussion after the usual introductions, with no names, and job titles, and the three pints of best bitter were sitting in front of them untouched at a small alcove table.

"This is off the record, and I will deny this meeting took place, for the record and your tape Hooper."

Hooper looked suitably chastised, both that he'd been caught, and that the Six contact had known his name. Hooper had Pollard with a directional microphone at the far end of the bar as back up, so made a big play of switching the Dictaphone off.

"Oh and please tell your pet at the bar to spend more time with his family," Claridge-Briggs continued in the same pleasant vane.

Hooper, further chastised, waved Pollard to leave. "I'm sorry," he mumbled.

"I would have been disappointed if you hadn't tried," smiled Claridge-Briggs. "Now to business; I understand you are leading the investigation into the disappearance and possible murder of four girls, all intelligence operatives, is that correct?"

"Yes, Sir" Hooper slipped into the deferential mode without thinking. "Although we have not had it confirmed that they were all in intelligence, Harriet Hollingsworth..."

"Was in Six, Jodi Parker was GCHQ DI," vetting had confirmed that afternoon. "Sally Carver and Jenny Wallace were both Five." Claridge-Briggs looked at Jonathan Braithwaite who was staying very quiet, but who gave a slight nod.

"We had presumed as much, but obviously we do not know of any other connection other than the obvious female, white, late twenties early thirties and attractive professionals similarities. We have no bodies, and we would not be any the wiser if Jenny Wallace hadn't disappeared on CCTV." Hooper decided that frankness was the only way with this Six man, whatever his name was. "We have one man with a slightly dodgy alibi who may match a description. He doesn't appear to have a past, before 1998. He may have nothing to do with it, but something smells wrong. Apart from that, we are re-checking with families and friends trying to get a break."

"Thank you for your honesty, Detective Inspector," Claridge-Briggs interjected. "I have two pieces of information that may help your investigation. Firstly, I need a favour and an assurance from you."

"I'll try to accommodate it Sir, but if it impinges on the investigation I may not be able to keep that assurance."

"Thank you again, I expected nothing less. May I call you Jack?"

"Yes, Sir," Hooper was again amazed at his deferential nature.

"The assurance is that you do not re-interview Michael or Jessica Carver?"

Hooper was surprised. He started and then stopped saying something.

"If you have questions for them I will arrange for them to be answered as quickly as possible, but no interviews, unless of course you suspect Michael?"

"No, not at all. I won't ask why, Sir, and I think we can accommodate that request."

"Good, now for the information. Firstly, the connection is Iraq, and secondly, we think there may be another victim. I have no name, but we believe a French Agent might have disappeared in 1998. My analyst believes that the agent may also be a she. We have a request in across the channel for a name and so on, but it may take a while."

Hooper was shocked by the abruptness of these critical pieces of information. He also had a good idea who the analyst was; again he started to say something but stopped as Braithwaite finally said something.

"Can I share this with my people?"

"Yes, leaving my assurance out if you would."

"Yes, Jenny Wallace, well, I didn't believe the trail. As soon as I saw it I alerted the investigation to start with."

"You wouldn't be the mystery boyfriend then Sir?" Hooper probed.

"No, that was just more cover for one of the planned meetings with an undercover agent, working on...well we won't go into that."

"The undercover agent has an alibi I presume?" Hooper was annoyed that his Five liaison wasn't helping.

"It's a she," he casually lied. "Which is all I'll tell you, and yes, she does."

The meeting broke up and Claridge-Briggs disappeared before Hooper could get Pollard back on his trail, leaving an email address for a contact. Hooper collected Pollard and called the team in for an evening briefing.

Braithwaite almost ran back to Thames House. Hooper had nailed it. He had been having an affair with Jenny for two years; carefully, hidden from prying eyes, especially that bastard Hedges who always seemed to have a pretty bright PA as he prowled the corridors of power. Come to think of it Sally Carver had worked for him? Jenny had been an analyst doing some research on Iraq WMD failures and now the revelations from Six, another smooth bastard but at least that one was talking. It smacked of Hedges. He had a shady reputation with all his casual hints of black operations. Braithwaite had been around long enough to know when an operation smelled of cover ups, and the news of the Iraq connection to the other girls just made the smell worse. So Sally's sister was Six, he had not known, although it appeared Hooper had guessed. He had to be careful with Hooper. If he uncovered his affair with Jenny, he would be out on his ear and his pension with it. Unreported affairs were a big no. His wife would throw him out as well; a double whammy. So what could he do? He was determined to get the killer of Jenny. He was sure she was gone now. A casual meeting with Hedges, where he could probe might help, but he was a wily fox and would wriggle without giving up. Maybe, if he let slip to Hooper that Hedges was the boss of Sally Carver and, effectively Jenny's boss as well. Yes that might set a few trails running, but would mean having Hooper probing away. No not yet, a dig around the paper trail first might help.

***

Hooper was on a mission, the news from Six had confirmed

a connection and the thought of another potential victim added to his determination. Whilst he waited for the rest of the team to join Pollard and himself, he mused on the likely situation. First, could he trust the Six contact? Probably not completely, but why would they hide anything when they seemed to be after the same result as his team. They were protecting Jessica Carver that was clear. He did not like having to stay away, but he could understand the anxiety on their part. Secondly, the Iraq connection was big, but at least it was a connection; thirdly, the French agent. Maybe a few other leads would appear about that, but in the meantime they could search the databases. When the Special Branch team was ready, he updated them on the latest developments.

"We can search the computer for missing French women. We might get something," offered Dave Grahams.

"We'll be lucky, but we need some," replied Rutledge. "The financial checks on Slater are still very odd, as PC Stephens, Shelley, said. We have checked back; his birth certificate and so on check out, just nothing from birth to twenty-two. He may have legally changed his name, but we'll need a more time and more luck to persuade those records to be opened."

"We are trying to get to see one of the directors of the company who first employed him, but they are playing hard to get, especially as the director concerned has retired," added Grahams.

"He's not back then?" Drinkwater asked.

"Not as far as we know, we have an alarm on his house and a discrete all-ports, but nothing."

"Any luck with his photo?" Hooper asked. There was a hesitant silence and a look around the team, "You're not telling me we don't have a photo of our main suspect?" Hooper's voice betrayed his annoyance.

"No, Sir," admitted Rutledge, "it's my error and we'll get one as soon as he's back."

"Nothing to be done then," Hooper acknowledged the error and the admission. No point dwelling, he thought. "Jim, keep digging with the stocks company. Threaten the FSA if they keep playing up." Keep the team motivated. "John, you'll have to keep away from Sally Carver's sister and brother, but you can still sniff around. Any questions route them to me. The fact that she is Six stays in this room, okay?" He got nods from the four subordinates. "We've got one sister disappeared, and I don't want another. As for the Iraq connection I would rather keep that in here as well; not for the wider team, yet."

CHAPTER TWENTY-SIX

Celia

Pierre Romonde was tailing his latest target. Celia Romero was shopping in the Taunus-Zentrum centre in Central Frankfurt. She was in a small, fashionable clothes boutique, while he waited across the corridor pretending to window shop in a crockery store. He was dressed to make him appear shorter and fatter, further enhanced by a grey wig and thick glasses. He was slightly crouching and stooped, and, at first glance, people would think he was a fifty plus German business man. Celia came out of the shop. He knew she had the afternoon and the rest of the week off all from her file. She was planning a few days at home redecorating. His trail would imply a last minute trip to Athens or Bulgaria. She was heading for the car park. It was time. As she had unlocked her car door, he was beside her and had injected the Rohypnol into the base of her neck. As she had stumbled, with a grunt, he eased her into the car seat. He quickly went round to the other side and opened the passenger's door. He checked up and looked around. The nearest other person was a young mother fighting to get a toddler into a rear child's seat. He leaned in and pulled Celia across into the passenger seat, strapping her in and pulling her skirt which had ridden up back to her knees. She murmured again, but otherwise she was quiet. He shut the door and returned to the driver's side, wiping the sweat, caused by the humid car park atmosphere, from his brow. He took her dropped bags and placed them on the back seat of the two-door Golf. He rummaged through her handbag for her keys before realising they were in the car door. He quickly retrieved them, adjusted the driving position and left the car park.

Four hours later he was in a disused garage outside Brussels. The car was at the back of the thirty feet long dilapidated building. Celia was tied naked to the table. Her long dark hair was hanging down to the side of her head, which was raised by a small cushion. The gag was held in place with a bondage tie to keep her head still.

"Hello, Celia," he said in French as she opened her eyes and focused on, first him, then her predicament. She tested her bindings with the ropes on her limbs, the strap across her head and another strap across her waist. She could barely move. She grunted. "Celia, I will remove the gag if you will cooperate; blink once if you agree," she blinked once. "Good girl," he removed the gag. She coughed and spluttered. He gave her a sip of water. "Now Celia, I'm going to ask you some questions."

"What do you want, pervert?" She asked in French

"Now be nice, Celia," he said. "Just tell me everything you know."

It took three hours and a couple of nicks with a hunting knife before she told the tape everything to do with the investigation into misuse of EU payments, and then the second injection, into the heart with pure heroin. His usual sense of elation and power was missing. Instead, he felt tired and dirty, and the morality of his actions was eating away at him. Disposal of her body was trickier, but the nearby incinerator was less than twenty minutes away. The car was more difficult, requiring a change of plates and a cash sale with a back street trader, after a full clean and valet. He made the late Thalis to Paris and was back in his hotel by midnight.

The following morning he sent his report in, and then checked out as Romonde, before checking into the Arc De Triomphe, Hilton as Michael Johnson. He took a leisurely stroll around town before returning to his room for some sleep to await Jess' train. He checked the stock on the Bourse as Slater, sold the futures at ninety-one cents, clearing seventy-thousand Euros after tax and commissions, and spread some of the money around into other stocks. He deliberately bought some poor performing stocks, and ones he had no confidence in, to complete a proper trading picture. He researched some tips on the NASDAQ in the US and the AIM in London and put twenty-thousand dollars and twenty-thousand pounds into a total of five stocks. All of these were set with immediate sell, with a plus ten cents or minus five cents for the US Stocks, and a plus ten pence minus five pence for the UK stocks. He did not want profit. He wanted activity. As Johnson, he sold half the shares and left the other half to accumulate further. Finally, he phoned the contact number. He received confirmation of the planned payment to the Swiss account. He stopped and considered his position. There was no doubt that the police were on a trail and may find him through sheer persistence. He needed to go back as Slater to face down some questioning. He would want a lawyer for that. One who only knew him as Slater, and one he could trust. Then, it would be time for Slater to disappear, including his Oval membership; maybe a couple of years out of the country? He had the New York apartment and the penthouse in Vauxhall, neither under the Slater name. How about a nice villa in the Caribbean? A topic of conversation for Jess he mused.

CHAPTER TWENTY-SEVEN

Weekend In Paris

Jess was on the train, having got away slightly early, after Tony had reassured her. This had involved a visit from Claridge-Briggs himself. The shock of seeing her sister's handwriting had dwindled and turned to a determination to get to the bottom of it. What she was beginning to believe was, well she wasn't sure what it was. Some sort of conspiracy? Vetting had come back on Mike with their usual no negatives, rather than a positive. She knew that this weekend she would tell Mike about it, well as much as she could. She spent the journey trying to figure out what she could, or could not say. What did she really know about this man who had burst into her life? She knew one thing; she had completely fallen for him. She smiled to herself as she remembered how brazen she was with him. He only had to look at her and she was turned on. Her smile had attracted the attention of the fat grey businessman sitting opposite. She hid her face behind her half read copy of a fashion magazine discouraging any further eye contact. She refused the complimentary meal but did have a glass of wine, which was surprisingly good. She refused a second when the businessman offered.

She arrived at Gare Du Nord wearing a front buttoned down pastel dress and strappy sandals. She walked off the platform towing a small case. As she exited immigration, Mike was there smiling at her, with his casual jacket and slacks, his arms were folded and he was wearing light sunglasses. She hugged and kissed him. He effortlessly picked up her bag, and they went to get a cab. She held onto his arm and pulled him close. In the cab, he stroked her arm and rested his hand on her bare knee, where the buttons finished from her dress. The Paris evening was sultry as they reached the hotel, despite the attempts of the Paris traffic to kill them. She held his hand in the lift to their very nice room. As the dusk descended, he carried her bag into their hotel room. He shut the door and, just as he had been about to speak, she put her fingers to his lips hushing him. She closed the gap between them and, looking into his eyes, undid his trouser belt and zip, pushing the slacks and his boxers down his thighs. She pushed him back on the bed and, with barely a second to remove her underwear, climbed onto him. She stayed still for nearly a minute before beginning a slow grind which ended with them both hot, sticky, and sated. They lay next to each other, her dress was now all undone. His jacket was on the floor. His shirt damp from sweat was undone but still on. His trousers were looped around one ankle

"That was very nice," he said smiling at her. "Have you eaten?" he asked stroking her thigh.

"I just have," she giggled. "Order room service. We can have a bath while we wait."

They undressed properly and put on a complimentary white hotel robe. Room service would be half an hour. He ran the bath, adding some of the bubble bath she produced from her bag. They both got in the bath. She sat leaning with her back to him, his arm around her waist, sloshing the water up to her breasts as he nuzzled her neck.

"Mike, I have to tell you something," she started. The room buzzer sounded indicating their food had arrived. Mike climbed out of the bath and went and dealt with the delivery. When he returned to the bathroom she was out of the bath in her robe, tidying her hair in the mirror.

"I was going to scrub your back," he said, rubbing her shoulders through the robe.

"Just my back?" she said to his reflection in the mirror.

They left the bathroom and went and sat where the waiter had laid out the room service. The Merlot was open on the table. Through the window, they could just make out the hum of the

Paris traffic and see the Arc. They started to eat the beef bourgeon.

"You were going to tell me something?" He encouraged.

"Mike I want to tell you, but I'm scared that I'll spoil this..." She looked around. "Us..." she looked at him pleadingly, "If I do."

"Jess," he said, "you know I love you, and I've never said that to anyone before." He took her hands and leaned across the small table to kiss them.

She felt herself welling up with the sheer romanticism and joy of the moment. "I love you," she said, fighting to control her tears.

"What is it you want to tell me about? A husband, another man, another girl?" He smiled lightning the tense mood.

"In your dreams," she laughed and gave him a playful tap on his thigh. "And no one else either, I just need to tell you about something... my work."

"Oh the PR stuff, or the Super Spy stuff?" he put on a poor impression of Sean Connery as James Bond.

"The spy stuff," she said, quietly taking a gulp of wine.

He was on alert, his mind racing to understand the implications of what she was saying. At the same time, he kept his face impassive. He felt his hand tightening with the tension on the knife. He forced himself to let go of the cutlery and casually take a sip of his drink. "What do you mean?" His voice had become icy cool.

"I work for the security service as an analyst, not in the field. Just paperwork." She was looking down at her plate as she started, then looked up as she finished the statement. "Mike, I didn't mean to mislead you. I... we, ... I mean, I'm not allowed to just say what I do. I had to get permission first, and they have to run some checks first."

"On me? You've had me checked out have you?"

"Mike, it's not like that, please don't be angry. I've wanted to tell you almost since that first night, but I couldn't. I need to tell you about Sally as well." She was rushing her words, on the verge of crying.

"What about Sally?" Cold voice staring at her, fighting to control his hands.

"Mike, please. This is very difficult for me. I shouldn't be telling you this, but I want you to know. I want to share this with you."

"Go on," warmer, but no encouragement from his eyes.

She reached for his hand. "Please," she said. "Michael and I told you that Sally had gone missing, and then there was that silly paper story about some sort of serial killer. I discovered at work..."

"In the Security Service?" he interjected sarcastically.

"...At work," she emphasised, "I found a link between Sally, she was Security Service as well, and another girl who was also missing. All connected by Iraq."

"You were both spies? What about Michael? Is he a spy as well?"

"Don't be silly. Not Michael, and I'm not a spy. I'm just a low grade analyst who wants to tell the man I love everything about me, but I'm frightened. I'm frightened by what I've found out, and now I've annoyed you. I'm frightened that I'll scare you away."

"Jess, I don't know what to say?"

"Don't say anything yet, please. Just hold me and tell me you still love me." She got up from the table and crouched by his side. She put her arms around him.

He put an arm, reluctantly at first, around her shoulders, and then pulled her up and onto his lap. "Jess, I do love you." He knew it was true, but that did not solve the problem. The problem could wait for now. He tilted her tear-streaked face up towards him and kissed her eyes, nose, and finally her mouth.

"Make love to me," she said.

She tasted of red wine, the food, and her lipstick. Her perfume drowned him as he lifted her onto the bed. He undid her robe, pushing it away from her body as he kissed her shoulders, her breasts, pulling her nipples into his mouth with his teeth. He kissed the undersides of her breasts and down onto her stomach, circling her belly button with his tongue, further down onto her hips, and finally she dragged his head between her legs, forcing him onto her. She cried out as she came with his tongue probing the soft folds of her sex. She pulled him back up, her body pulling him into her as he reached her face. Wrapping her legs tight around him and then grasping his buttocks, forcing him deep within her until he climaxed.

They lay still and gasping for air. They took turns in the bathroom. She went first, and when he returned to the bedroom, she had tidied the bed and was under a single sheet waiting for him. She pulled back the sheet and, as he lay down, she snuggled in close to him. They slept.

She awoke in the early hours. Mike was not by her side, and before she could begin to panic, she saw him sipping a drink standing by the window. He had been standing thinking for the best part of an hour when he heard Jess stir behind him. He had almost packed and gone half a dozen times to distance himself, disconnect himself from the mission of six years ago. If he had gone, it would raise more questions for Jess. She would try to find him, maybe even alerting her bosses and the Special Branch. If he stayed he kept Jess, for now. He might even get more information. He mulled over the various merits of leaving or staying. His other alternative of removing Jess had wafted across his mind and been dismissed. He might be cold and calculating on a mission, but Jess was not a mission. He sensed her approaching him from the bed. So he would stay whilst planning to leave. He turned as Jess reached him.

"I thought you'd gone," she said taking and sipping the drink, malt whisky from the room bar.

"I'm still here, I'm not going anywhere."

"Oh yes you are..." The flirting tone was back as she led him back to the bed.

They spent the next day wandering from café to café just enjoying the warm sunshine and watching people. They had risen in the late morning and left the hotel to find breakfast in a small café near Notre Dame. They had talked around subjects. He asked her about a place in the Caribbean. She had been to Barbados. He showed her some printouts for villas for sale that he had found on the Internet in the Turks and Caicos. Jess looked at the prices.

"I thought you weren't rich?" She was smiling not accusing. "One and a half million dollars sounds rich to me!"

"It's a good investment, Jess, just like the shares."

"Would you live there or rent it out?"

"Live probably."

"But you've just moved into the apartment in Vauxhall?"

"I'll still need a London base."

"Where does that leave us?" she asked quietly.

"Come with me," he said squeezing her hand.

"My job might not like that."

"You can join the investment business, be my partner?"

"I know nothing about shares," she said, "and anyway I want to find out what happened to Sally."

"Do you think you ever will?"

"I don't know, but I have to try."

"After that, come with me, join me, please."

"Yes," said Jess, "I'd like that."

They walked and talked, kissed, and caressed their way around the sites of Paris. The weather changed, and early evening they returned to the hotel. They made love, showered, went out for dinner, and looked at the sights at night cleaned by the rain. Back in their room, he undressed her by the street lights filtering through the room curtains. He stroked her and kissed her and told her he loved her. They made love slowly and gently. Afterwards they lay just holding fingertips as their bodies cooled.

"What about tomorrow?" she asked. "Will you come back with me?"

"No, I need to finish off a few things here, I should be back mid-week"

"Okay, I can wait that long, as long as I don't have to wait that long for anything else!"

"I might need a few moments."

"Let's see if I can speed things up," she said dropping her head to his groin.

***

Jess left on the midday Eurostar back to London. After dropping her off at Gare Du Nord, he checked out of the Hilton. He moved to a CDG airport hotel with his American identity and onto a morning flight to JFK. He needed to return to the UK as John Slater from the USA. He had been researching lawyers. Someone who would be very difficult for the police to push around. He contacted the solicitor Carolyn O' Butu, specially chosen for her civil liberty stances, but without any publicity hungry side. Being black and female would help as well. The last thing he wanted was a press scrum because someone was in custody over the missing girl's story. He explained to her the situation. He did not embellish the story, but he did say that he expected to be arrested as soon as he returned to the UK, either at the airport, or at his house.

Before boarding his flight, he posted his Michael Johnson identity documents, credit cards, and so on back to one of the flats. He removed all trace of Michael Johnson or any other identity. He moved money from the UK to Switzerland and the Caymans and instructed a real estate agent in the Turks and Caicos to begin the process of acquiring a three bedroom private villa. He said he would see it in the next few weeks, but wanted all the paperwork prepared in advance. The agent suggested a possible alternative, which he accepted as a good choice if the first one fell through.

CHAPTER TWENTY-EIGHT
I Think I Need A Lawyer

He saw the immigration man press the concealed button; just a slight flex of the arm muscle. He had arrived at Manchester via the overnight flight from Chicago. He had slept surprisingly well on the flight. He waited patiently whilst the immigration official asked a couple of daft questions allowing the time his colleagues needed to be in position. He cleared customs with just a small suitcase. He headed for the domestic flight to London. He saw the tail duck back behind a pillar as he rode down an escalator. An hour later he was leaving Heathrow on the Paddington Express. He called Carolyn O' Butu from a pay phone, advising her of his return. From Paddington, he took a cab to his house. He noted the too neat pile of mail just inside the door. He put his bag in the bedroom and had put some coffee on whilst trying to get the jet lag and travel weariness out of his system with some exercises. He had been in the house less than an hour when the doorbell rang. The twins stood smiling on the doorstep.

"Detectives, how are you?" He said coolly.

"Mr. Slater, we need you to answer some more questions," said Detective Sergeant Rutledge.

"Well, you had better come in," said Slater opening the door and waving them inside.

"We'd prefer it if you came down to the station, Sir," said Detective Constable Grahams.

"Oh, am I in trouble? Am I being arrested, do I need a

solicitor?"

"No, you're not being arrested, at present," Rutledge casually threatened, "but we would like to put our questions more formally and on the record."

"Oh I see, well I think my solicitor should be there then. I'll get my jacket and switch my coffee off."

"If you insist on your solicitor, maybe we could give him a call?"

"Thank you, Detective Grahams, but I can call whilst I get my jacket."

They followed him into the house, but did not look around, concealing their previous search by their lack of interest. Slater called O'Butu, and after asking which station they were going to, agreed to meet there.

An hour later he was sitting in an interview room in Paddington station with a truly awful cup of machine coffee, when Caroline O'Butu was shown in. She was five feet five, with a smart dark business suit and rimless glasses and carried a smart leather case. They shook hands. He told her what had happened. She asked him whether they had asked any questions yet. He replied only about his journey back from the States. As he finished, Rutledge entered the room, with a slightly surprised look on his face at the sight of Slater's lawyer. He was accompanied by another man who Rutledge introduced as Detective Inspector Hooper. Caroline introduced herself, and immediately asked Hooper which branch of the police they were with. Hooper smiled, nodded at the tactic from the lawyer, and said, "Special Branch."She raised her eyebrows but said nothing. They all sat down and introduced themselves for the tape and video. Caroline again took the initiative and asked.

"Is my client under caution?"

"No, Miss O'Butu, he is here at our request, but voluntarily, to help us in our enquiries into the disappearance of Jenny Wallace." Rutledge smiled with a hint of condescension.

"I believe my client has already given a full account of his whereabouts on the night in question and provided support for this. Unless you have some evidence that contradicts his account, I fail to see why he is here."

Hooper smiled, obviously enjoying the sparring and then said, "Miss O'Butu, Mr. Slater is here to re-confirm his previous answers on the record, but also so that we can ask some new question about some of the other girls who, you will recall, have been luridly linked by the press. Now, if you wouldn't mind, we would like to ask Mr. Slater these questions." O'Butu smiled back, and gave a slight nod to Hooper.

"Mr. Slater, what time did you leave the Oval on the night?" Rutledge began.

"As I said previously Sergeant..." The questions began, going over the same old ground. Virtually the same questions, including the phone calls to New York, providing the confirmation that they had checked with his stockbrokers. Then came the questions about the other girls. Did he know them, where had he been at a particular time? He was shown photographs of each of the girls. He shook his head at each one. He did not avoid eye contact or rush into a no. For two of the dates Slater had been out of the country. He yawned a little theatrically as he answered.

"I'm sure you could check that with immigration, Detectives," said O'Butu, shuffling her notes. "I think my client has been very patient with you, but I think that is enough. As you know he has a business to run, and has only just returned from a long business trip, but perhaps you could tell me why Special Branch is investigating the disappearance of these girls?"

"I'm afraid we are not at liberty to disclose that, but they are connected." Hooper replied

"Not a serial killer then?" she pressed.

"As I said, they are connected and we are treating the disappearances as suspicious," said Hooper.

"One last question, Mr. Slater," said Rutledge. "Have you ever changed your name?"

Very careful now, "What a strange question? No, I haven't." He had never changed his name, just used different ones.

"What has that to do with the girls?" O'Butu asked.

"We were doing some background checks on Mr Slater as you would expect, and we can't seem to find any trace of him before 1998?"

"Are you investigating my client for other things, Detective?"

"Would your client just answer our question, Mr. Slater?"

He stayed calm, the cold calculating mind back to the fore. "I don't know why you can't find me. I was at the LSE prior to that. I suggest you look a bit harder," he said, a bit too forcefully as he was standing up. "Now, if you don't mind, I need to check the market before it closes."

Slater and the lawyer left. She regarded him with a degree of suspicion as they parted.

"That was not a good finish, Mr. Slater, and why didn't you give a straight answer?"

"I'm sorry, I'm just tired and I'd had enough. They have been on my back for weeks, no matter what I say."

"Don't be surprised if they come back for more. If there is something else they may have on you, you need to tell me first?" She looked at him accusingly. He shook his head. "Give me a call if they do, and be prepared for another round."

She left in a cab, and he took another back home, noticing two watchers halfway down his street. He needed some sleep and organising, and then Slater would have to disappear.

Hooper was comparing notes with Rutledge back in the office with freshly printed photos of Slater on the desk.

"Okay," said Hooper, "I can see why you suspect him, way too calm and collected and with a shirty lawyer as well, but do we have any evidence for the girls? If his out of the country story checks out, we'll have nothing apart from a fifteen-minute discrepancy with the Steward. We can't go to the CPS with that!"

"How about a warrant and turn over his house?"

"Only if we want Miss O'Butu on our backs with the Independent Police Complaints Commission for harassment. He may be up to his neck in dodgy money laundering or some such, but we are chasing the girls. Pass his details onto the Yard and let's see what else turns up. Check out the LSE for pre 1998; get one of the juniors to do that. Keep the surveillance on him for a couple of days and the bug going, but we need something more solid."

***

Once back at the house, Slater played the stockbroker until the market closed, then switched to the New York Exchange. He needed to move without being watched. He needed to become Johnson again, and he needed to clear the house of all the hidden treasures. Most of all, he needed to see and contact Jess. He booked a flight out as Slater to Paris for the next morning. He was sure the Special Branch had an alert out for him now, but he doubted they would follow him abroad. He finished dealing, ordered in a curry, and then had an early night. He missed Jess, but could not risk a call with the bug in the house.

The following morning he transferred his computer data to three portable, encrypted USB sticks, before wiping the hard drive with specialist software. He removed all his identity equipment from the cupboard behind the wardrobe and emptied the safe of the cash £10,000, $5,000 and €2,000 in large denomination notes. He spread the money around his two bags, along with the other disguise items. He placed the sticks into envelopes, addressed one to the USA apartment, one to a safe flat and the third to the penthouse. He placed them in his jacket pocket and then called a cab for the airport. He needed his Johnson identity to meet Jess, but needed to get back in the country first, which he would do as a Frenchman that evening. He watched the tail follow him to Heathrow and easily lost him in the busy terminal. The Special Branch team would have to hunt through CCTV to find him. He posted the items from the airport. He left one of his bags in a left luggage locker, sure that his watchers would still be trying to find him in the busy terminal. His jobs completed, he waited for his flight in the business lounge. Ten hours later he was back in the UK via Gatwick under his French identity, which became Johnson picking up the documents sent from the USA, after he reached the safe flat. He then travelled to his penthouse, calling Jess. She was annoyed he had not called; he placated her with the offer of dinner and the theatre.

Thirty minutes later Jess arrived. After a long hug, and a slightly cool kiss that got warmer, she said, "I was worried about you. I wanted to call and talk, but you won't give me your number."

"I'm sorry I didn't call, but I was travelling again to the States and back. I'm here now." Another kiss, much warmer. He allowed his hands to travel down the buttoned dress she had worn in Paris. She stopped him, "I thought we were going for dinner and a show?"

Much warmer now, and she did not move his hands. They ate in Covent Garden and then watched a lively musical. She held his hand on her thigh throughout the show and in the cab back to the penthouse. In the lift, she pushed him away and started to unbutton her dress. It was completely undone by the time they entered the apartment. He quelled the alarm as she walked in. When he looked back the dress was on the arm of the sofa along with her cream bra. She was walking towards the bedroom. She stopped and removed her panties. She turned and leaned against the bedroom door. He picked up her dress and neatly folded it, before placing it on the sofa seat whilst never taking his eyes off her. He removed his jacket and shirt. His other clothes followed, folding them all neatly next to her dress. He walked towards her, she turned to enter the bedroom, but he caught her arm. He held her against the cool wall of the corridor and kissed her. She responded. He then stopped and turned her around pushing her face first against the wall. He bent his knees and took her from behind spreading her legs with his knees, until she submitted, gave into his demands, thrusting back onto him as he penetrated.

"On the bed," she said.

He virtually carried her onto the bed. Kneeling down, he re-entered her. She buried her face into a pillow to stifle her own gasps of delight as she climaxed. He moved off her, lying unspent by her side as she calmed. She lifted a knee over him and pulled him back inside herself, thrusting down and pulling his hands onto her breasts. She squeezed and ground her pelvis down until he could finally take no more. In the last few seconds, she pinned his arms over his head and kissed him.

They lay together with her collapsed on top of him. Both of them were breathing hard.

"Bastard," she said at last rolling off of him. "It's a good job I love you."

"I told you I missed you," he said stroking her neck and breast and then running his fingers down between her legs. She held his hand there, wrapping herself around it.

"More later," she said with a smile. She pulled herself away and went into the bathroom. He dozed whilst she showered and when she returned, took his turn. Back in the bedroom she was already asleep when he joined her.

The following morning, another weekend, he awoke to the smell of toast and coffee. Jess was holding both under his nose. She wore the silk robe he had bought her. Her hair was tied back.

"You slept well," she said.

"It's all that travelling. It wears you out," he joked. She sat on the bed with him and fed him toast, but resisted any pulls down.

"I need to go home and change."

"I'll come with you."

"Okay."

They left the penthouse twenty minutes later and took a cab back to Jess's. Once back at her place, he showed her the picture of the Turks and Caicos place.

"Very nice," she commented, "but aren't you rushing that."

"I seem to be in that sort of mood." She blushed at his response.

"This is different," she said, "you don't strike me as that impulsive."

"I'm not normally, but something seems to have changed my behaviour."

He pulled her close for a kiss, but she pulled back with her serious face on. "When will you go there?"

"It depends on a few things, in particular you."

"No pressure, then."

"No, but I understand about your need to find answers to Sally."

"What about Sally?" Michael said, entering the kitchen where Jess and Mike were sat.

Jess ignored the question by saying, "Mike is moving to the Caribbean."

"Really? Is this a sudden need to get away from my sister?" He joked. Jess hit him on his arm, a smile returning to her lips.

"No," Mike smiled, "I've been thinking about it for a while."

"I suppose the rich have that luxury. By the way, is it time to cash in the shares?"

"Probably. They have done pretty well, but they have a little way to go yet." He used his best stockbroker voice. He did not want them to push too hard.

"I've noticed."

"Have you, Michael?" Jess said. "I haven't been watching."

"Nearly trebled in value so far as I make it. Is that unusual for you?" Michael quizzed.

"I win some and lose some."

"If you are going to the Caribbean you win more than lose?"

"Yes, I do, I suppose. Anyone want dinner?" Time to change the subject.

Lucy joined them as they returned to the Italian. Later that night, in bed with Jess, he again avoided questions. Finally Jess, exasperated, knelt astride him, threatening to tickle him unless he talked.

"Okay, I give in," he said.

"Parents, family?"

"My mother died when I was eleven, and my father died when I was at university. I was in the army for a while. I have no brothers, or sisters, and my Grandparents are all gone as well."

"I'm sorry that must be hard."

"You lost your parents, as well as Sally," he said. He realised his mistake. Had she told him about her parents? He could not remember. Jess did not seem to notice. She kissed him and rolled off him.

Snuggling down she said, "We are both orphans then."

"Yes," he replied. They both slept.

CHAPTER TWENTY-NINE

Investigate The Investigators

Braithwaite paced around his office. He smelt something bad in all this. How far could he dig; he wanted a complete look at the Special Branch files. He knew Claridge-Briggs was onto something, which could uncover his affair if he did not control that information. If he dug around in Five, on Iraq, Hedges would notice, unless he could set him running as well. He wanted answers to Jenny and the wider issue of the girls. Why only girls? If Iraq was the connection, there were plenty of men involved, but it could not be coincidence. There had to be more than girls if this was not a coincidence serial killer. Serial killers were rare in the first place. Four British girls, all either in or connected to the security services. All connected to Iraq in some way, and then the French girl.

He had picked up some legacy IRA responsibilities the previous month, whereas his main area was other crack-pots like animal liberation who still thought that blowing up scientists was good for their cause. He hummed to himself, out loud he realised. Starting to talk to himself, not a good sign. Hedges had been involved with counter IRA, what was the name of the lead man. He had died, if he recalled correctly. Mugging or something; is there a connection there? Maybe he could review what Hedges was up to as part of one of his new responsibilities. Maybe he would rattle his cage a bit and see what was shaken out. He was mixing his metaphors now. He arranged a meeting for that afternoon. Next, Claridge-Briggs. He called him. He knew who and what he was, even if Special Branch did not.

"Braithwaite, how are you?" Claridge-Briggs said, after they were connected by respective secretaries. They agreed to meet on Westminster Bridge within the hour. The summer was being spoilt by a warm front and drizzle, upsetting the tourists gazing at Parliament. They met in the middle on the West pavement, but strolled south.

"What can I do for you?" Claridge-Briggs asked.

"I was having an affair with Jenny Wallace," said Braithwaite.

"Ah I thought there had to be something, hence, the immediate concern at her disappearance. Just a fling or something more long term?"

"Long term, but not reported. She was supposed to be coming to see me that night."

"I see. That explains her heading away from home. You have my sympathies. Do Special Branch know yet?"

"No, and I would rather they didn't."

"Yes, you wouldn't want that in any report"

"No that would not be helpful. A couple of other things you may already know," he offered.

"Go on."

"There is another connection on my side of the Thames." He hesitated, Oh well in for a penny in for a pound. "The connection between Jenny Wallace and Sally Carver is Hedges. I presume Jessica Carver is one of yours?" He quickly added his own question after the revelation.

"Hmm interesting, Hedges eh? In the interests of this cooperation, yes, Jessica is one of mine, and I don't want her name raised further than being the sister of Sally. She is on the Plato team by the way and picked up some of the connections. Quite a shock for the girl."

"I knew the father slightly and by reputation," said Braithwaite.

"Yes, I did know him personally. Hedges, I don't know him that well but I can't say I like what I have seen." He decided to be indiscreet. "Too full of himself and always hinting at stuff." He studied Braithwaite's reaction.

"In the interests of cooperation, I couldn't agree more, but I still fail to see how he can be involved with disappearing girls. He was up to his neck in the dossier, but he seems to have a rising star again. I'm seeing him this afternoon."

"Are you really? Setting some rabbits running are you? It would be good to know what his reaction is."

"There is another thing, but it goes back to the nature of the case." He hesitated again. "I don't understand the Iraq connection if it's just girls?"

"Yes, that is odd, if it is connected? Any indication on your side that it might not be?"

"I don't think anybody has actually looked, but one more Hedges connection. Does the name Hemmings mean anything to you?"

"Name rings a bell, but I can't recall why?"

"He was Hedges' number two but was killed in a mugging a few years back."

Claridge-Briggs contemplated the new information. "I don't believe in coincidences, do you want me to forward this to our Branch friends, see what they can stir up?"

"Yes, I would do myself, but I don't want my side of the Thames to know about a link just yet. I intend to casually raise this with Hedges and see what happens."

"Good idea, I appreciate your confiding in me. I'll let you know how Hooper and his team are doing."

They separated, agreeing to meet again, and Braithwaite returned to Thames House. He had time for a quick sandwich at his desk before the Hedges meeting, two floors away and along the corridor. He arrived on time.

"Jonathan, what a pleasant surprise," said Hedges as he rose from his desk offering his hand. He had been shown in by Hedges' latest bright young thing, Michelle. "Can I offer you tea, coffee, something stronger?"

"No, I'm fine thank you."

Hedges topped up his own coffee from a machine behind his desk. "Well, what can I do for you?"

"Two things to tell you about actually."

"I'm intrigued?" Hedges exclaimed.

"First, Special Branch believes that the missing girls in the papers are connected. Sally Carver was one of yours wasn't she?"

Hedges sat up straighter, the only visible sign he gave. "Yes, she was my PA. Went off travelling apparently."

"Special Branch doesn't believe that at all."

"Hmm," Hedges could only manage, noncommittally, but clearly very interested. He tried to hide it. "And the other matter?"

"IRA is now in my remit, and I wanted to take a look at the cell that was operating a few years ago. Your man Hemmings was in charge wasn't he?" Hedges sat even straighter in his chair.

"Hemmings, yes but that was years ago. Why would you be looking there?"

"Had some HUMINT on the players," Braithwaite lied. HUMINT was Human intelligence.

"Really, didn't see that in the weekly briefing?" Hedges was senior enough to be on the distribution list.

"Not in there yet, just wanted to get some confirmation before raising anything, but I'll need your say so on a couple of the files."

"Oh that won't be a problem," said Hedges, although clearly, from his body language, it would be. "I'll set you up."

"Thanks." He got up to go. "Oh, one more thing, are you involved in Plato at all?"

Hedges appeared to be going white. "Plato? What is that?"

"Oh, just something running around across the river," Braithwaite replied. "I wondered if you had heard about it. Thanks for the meeting," he said leaving the office. Hedges was lying. He knew what Plato was. Braithwaite knew he had rattled Hedges with Sally, Hemmings, and Plato, all in one conversation. He had not mentioned Iraq, but Plato was near enough. Nor had he mentioned the other girls. "Well," Braithwaite thought, "what rabbits would now run, and from where?" Braithwaite also knew Hedges reported to the DG, Julian Clarkson, and was virtually out on his own and very pally with various other agencies across the pond and in Europe. Now, he would have to wait for Hemmings' file access. He expected a long wait so he arranged a request with the DG directly; he set that running as well.

Hedges sat for a considerable while, despite two requests from Michelle for further meetings, which he had her cancel. "What was Braithwaite up to?" He did not believe in coincidences either. He had not been aware that Special Branch was on the case of the girls; an added complication. He knew the commander, but if he asked about the case without being told about it in a briefing, he would expose his connection. Special Branch had not interviewed him about Sally. Surely, they would come and see him. He had told the police that he knew nothing when she was reported missing, which was true up to a very limited point. Now, the connections had been reopened because of this Wallace girl. Wallace had been snooping around on funding and payments to foreign bank accounts. At least the report on her showed that her involvement with Plato was limited to sending some position papers. Hedges had provided papers as well; one had been his very pro-Iraq war, regardless of WMD. He had kept it out of the Hutton Inquiry but, now Vauxhall had it.

Braithwaite's name was in the asset Ashley's report as well, why he could not recall, just a name Wallace had mentioned. Nothing to do with Plato or Iraq or her fund investigations. Ashley had not asked further, why would he? Not in his brief. Were Braithwaite and Wallace connected? Not that he knew of, and Braithwaite had not mentioned her. Did this mean he was in Plato's sights as well? That was water under the bridge, he had survived the post Iraq cull, but what if Plato's remit was wider. Again, he could not ask, not even the DG, without arising suspicion. Why had that damn asset failed to get the Wallace girl to disappear? He could not ask him except via the web site, and he had gotten the main report as usual. Since Sally, he had done his own uploads. It was getting harder, due to IT restrictions, to get the information out and copied. He would have to close the mission down or change the contact method. He did not like this turn of events one bit. How to proceed? He had dinner planned with the DG, Julian Clarkson, and the nearly new CIA Station chief tonight. He would have to come up with a plan.

***

DI Hooper was just leaving the office when he took the call from Claridge-Briggs.

"I have a name for you that links two of the girls. Hedges in Thames House," said Claridge-Briggs.

"Which girls?"

"Carver and Wallace."

"I see," which he did not, "but can you tell me anything else?"

"Not at this stage, but I have been considering the lack of male victims if the connection is really Iraq. You may wish to take a look at some male victims if it's not a serial killer, and coincidence of course."

"Do you have anyone in mind, as I haven't seen any missing male reports?"

"I am investigating at my side, but one name is worth a look from a few years back. Hemmings from Thames House, but please keep me informed." Claridge-Briggs hung up and immediately called Grayson. He needed some extra precautions. "Mr. Grayson, please put an access flag on Jessica and Plato. Let's see if anyone is paying too much attention, especially our friends across the river." Grayson had agreed, and he had hung up.

Hooper thought the trouble with secret services is just that, the secret tended to come before service. It was one for the team to help decipher. Hedges, he had heard that name before. He ran through his memory, Hemmings, that was it. Security Service chap who was killed in a mugging gone wrong. It had briefly crossed his desk years ago because of the Security Service involvement. Hedges was his boss. No evidence to suggest anything other than a robbery. He had left it with the Met, but he could not recall any outcome. Coincidence, that was unlikely. He called in the senior team.

"This is getting even more complicated and linked, and likely to get messy. Keep all notes on this part off the system. We don't want to spook any spooks unnecessarily," he told them. "Now where are we on Slater and the rest?"

"Shelly, I mean PC Stephens has checked with LSE, no Slater on the books and nothing computerised from them. Staff are all different, so the photo went nowhere."

"Do we even know what Slater's degree is in? We could try the tutors again with his photo."

"Another question we failed to ask," said Drinkwater exasperated. "On a better note, we have turned up the stockbrokers' director's name, but he lives in the Algarve. I don't suppose we can swing a budget to go see him, he won't talk on the phone."

"I'll see what I can do. What about the money side?" Hooper asked.

"With the main team, but SFO are interested on insider trading and getting one over on the FSA if they can," said Rutledge. SFO was the Serious Fraud Office in the Metropolitan Police and the FSA was the Financial Services Authority. "They are all over those types of incidents at the moment, if they can spare the resources."

"Not sure we can influence the SFO resource budget," said Hooper. "Okay, keep pressing, but let's not get too fixated on Slater as he could be dirty for other reasons. Where is he by the way?"

"We think France again, but he could be anywhere frankly, and if we push too hard that lawyer will be all over us," said Drinkwater.

Hooper discussed Hemmings. There was a general agreement on it being worth a look. He raised Hedges' name but kept the fact that Hemmings worked for Hedges to himself. He asked the team to check the Met. Police Report on the mugging.

"Anything on our potential French Connection?"

"Three possible matches who fit the timeline. We're waiting for photos and background," Drinkwater continued. "We're waiting for the French to confirm, or more likely not."

"Okay," said Hooper, "tomorrow, let's interview other victim statements again. Go back to Sally Carver. I know we have to keep clear of the brother and sister, but what about the boss, Hedges. His statement is very thin." He dismissed the team for an overnight break. He felt that some progress had been made, but not necessarily solving the disappearances or murders. If that was what they were?

CHAPTER THIRTY

Hedges

Hedges had enjoyed a good dinner with the DG and Carl Schlemburg, the Central Intelligence Agency, CIA, Station Chief. The company and food were excellent, and then Schlemburg had offered him a ride home as well, saving on the hassle of a cab. In the US Embassy official car, Schlemburg had given the *Demise* and date code, which was a surprise to Hedges.

"There's a lot of chatter in my neck of the woods about the police linking various girls together."

"Understandable," Hedges had replied, "but nothing for anyone to concern themselves with. The asset is completely clear separate and untraceable. Iraq caused a lot of bad feeling on this side of the pond, and some people won't let it drop."

"Still, it's messy, with the take being seen."

"Yes, that was unfortunate, but she has gone. The debrief from her was satisfactory. She was getting close to one of the funding streams, so had to be stopped."

"Good, I may need some action on my side of the pond soon. I'll let you know, but I don't want any police sniffing around."

"Let me know the details. I'll take care of the police. The contact is clear and running, and ready for his next job. He has already completed another job since the Wallace girl by the way."

"That's good to know," said Schlemburg.

Hedges had imparted that information as further reassurance to the CIA, but Hedges had no idea where Ashley was, what he looked like, what he was doing, or if he was ready for his next job. He had never spoken with him and his photo was seven years old, before Army training. The details on Ashley were in his personal safe at home, not in the office along with all the debrief reports printed out, and deleted from the central systems. He doubted he would recognise him even if he were sitting next to him. Schlemburg did not need to know that. They parted with a promise to stay in touch.

The following morning Hedges paced his office and had cancelled his regular monthly budget meeting. Hedges realised he needed to get in better control of the asset, Ashley, or whatever he was called these days. Maybe a meeting, but that might not be safe. Unbidden, he thought of Hemmings. His mugging had been after the IRA bomber had disappeared, a real success that one, with enough hints up the command chain to promote his own career. Was the mugging correct; the police had not questioned the assumption? Had Special Branch reviewed it? Is that why Braithwaite had raised Hemmings? The DG had nodded and winked at the disappearance of the IRA man, but had not pressed on where the information about the bomb factory and safe house had come from. The DG had basked in the glow of success with the Permanent Secretary at the Home Office. The politicians did not care; they had some nice TV headlines. Hemmings, why was Braithwaite digging there? He did not believe for one minute Braithwaite had another asset in play. He had dropped that in as a connection to provoke a response. He checked the Hemmings file. Nothing in there apart from the IRA reports, and the bomber getting lost by his Watchers, oh yes, there it was, the Watchers had suspected another tail. Had that been Ashley? Nothing in Hemmings' file about Ashley, or an off the book asset. Who else had been looking at Hemmings' file? He checked the log. Braithwaite, but he had not given authority. The DG had approved access that morning. Damn he had been hoping to delay that and if Braithwaite checked the logs he would now see that he had seen it. Well, Braithwaite had nothing, nothing but suspicion.

He checked his private diary, which listed as addresses the initials of the targets Ashley had been given. Except for the debrief folders in his private safe at home there was no other record. The initials would mean nothing to anyone, but spread in the list were SC, JW, JP, and HH, tying in with the missing girls' case. The first initials were LO, Liam O'Hara the un-missed bomber from a long line of Irish militants. He wondered what Special Branch knew? How could he get the file without raising suspicions? Perhaps the CIA could help, and if they were caught, well that would set another diversion running and deflect their attention. He called Michelle to call Schlemburg to set up a meeting. So quickly after their car chat, but it had to be done.

Michelle knocked on his door and said, "I have Special Branch on hold. They are asking for a meeting to talk about Sally Carver. I hadn't realised she worked here."

"Before your time, Michelle, nothing to concern yourself about. Book them in for Friday if you can." Today was Tuesday. Could he get their file before then? Michelle hung back for a second and then asked,

"Morning or afternoon?"

"Afternoon."

"I thought you were going away this weekend and wanted Friday afternoon clear? You have time on Wednesday and Thursday." Michelle looked confused as she knew he had very little in his diary.

"Something is coming up which I can't put in the diary, I'll brief you later. I'll see them before I go, say 14:00."

"Okay, Mr. Hedges." She left the room, and he heard her pick up the phone and speak to a Detective Rutledge, before his door finally swung closed.

Michelle knocked and came back in. "That's all set and the Embassy said that Mr. Schlemburg will see you at your home at 18:30. I have those budget figures for you that you missed this morning, if you want them?"

"Thank you, please bring them through, and we'll go over them together." Drown her in mundane important tasks and she would not have time to speculate about Sally. The trouble with pretty bright girls was they were bright he thought.

CHAPTER THIRTY-ONE

Are We Making Progress?

Rutledge was unimpressed. Despite pushing, he could not get an appointment with Hedges before Friday. He reported to Hooper.

"I'm not surprised. He will try to delay whilst trying to find out what we are up to. Give the troops a quick word on confidentiality, especially the junior ones. Any news on the Hemmings case and what has happened to Slater? I have to see the CPS later about the procurement fraud case; it seems my misuse of the DNA resources has paid off. Our main suspect has his DNA all over the letter to the brokers."

"That's good news; I'll get the team in for an update later when you get back; the full team, or just the chosen few?"

"Full team I think, let's see if any more of them have some bright ideas. By the way, our Five liaison has just sent this over, it's a heavily redacted Hemmings file, but worth looking at. Not for the Juniors, and not on the system either James, I have a strong sense we are being watched." Hooper departed for the CPS office, the DNA evidence would give them a conviction unless the suspect decided to testify against others. They would need to arrest to find out.

The full team was assembled and waiting when Hooper arrived back. "Updates people, victims first," he ordered.

Rutledge started, "We have reviewed the Hemmings file. On the surface, a clear mugging, wallet and mobile taken, never found, or traced. Single knife wound to stomach; he died from blood loss. Now the interesting part that separates from a run of the mill mugging; he was not killed on the site, or anywhere in the immediate area. They tried blood dogs to trace, and nothing. And then, our golden girl, Shelly found something." Rutledge smiled.

Shelly said, "There were two witness statements of possible people in the area; one from a café owner shutting up shop, and one from a street girl. Both said that the only thing they had seen was a plain white van coming out of alley where the skip was. No number plate or anything, but the girl said it was a man in a city suit driving. She thought he was stopping to pick her up. It's all vague with the only description, apart from the suit, as long dark hair and dark complexion. The thing that triggered my mind was that's the same description as our bag thief gave."

Drinkwater chimed in, "We are trying to trace the girl. We also showed Slater's picture to Snoop, he calls himself, but all we got was a could be but, not sure."

"I'm less convinced by Slater as our man for this, but anything more on his past or finances?" Hooper asked.

Grahams stood up, "We have taken the photo to the University. No joy with the admin staff, but we are trawling through the ID card records. The photos are all small. Could we get some forensic support to rapid scan them?"

"Set that up, James," said Hooper. "Finance?"

Shelly responded, "The SFO had a small file on Slater, mainly for a big trade he made early on. Apparently, he bought into a small defence stock and made a fortune when it got a big contract a few weeks later. The SFO was alerted because of the foreign funds that were going into the shares of a sensitive company, but didn't pursue it because a lot of the holders sold when they made their money. At one point Slater may have had 1% of the company. That's below the regulation notification. He sold nearly all his shares within a couple of months, just below their peak, when they were bought by one of the bigger players. He probably had futures in them as well, but that's harder to trace."

"Shelly, excellent work again," he noticed the warm smile

Drinkwater gave her, "but this, again, looks like Slater is dirty for money, and not for the girls, unless we have something else?" Hooper questioned the team with his look. "Parker, Hollingsworth?"

"The Parker girl is a dead end, the Swedish potential boyfriend was killed in a car crash three years ago," responded Rutledge.

"Hollingsworth still waiting for Vauxhall to pull their finger out," said Drinkwater.

"Okay, I'll try and put some pressure on," said Hooper. One for his new friend he thought. "Anything from France or French girls?"

Drinkwater again, "I hadn't realised the number that get reported missing, but I have three names that are possible because they have no background. Before anyone asks, I'm running them past a Sûreté contact this evening."

"Okay, anything else?" Hooper asked.

Grahams raised his hand then hesitated before saying, "Sir, about Slater." He paused for the team groans.

"Go on," said Hooper.

"We have no history on him before 1998. He says he was at the LSE, but we don't know what he studied, and his name is not on the records. He has a lot of money, even before he left the stockbrokers, where he had only been for less than 12 months. I'll have more on that tomorrow, if it's still all right to see his old boss in Portugal. This smacks of cover up. That's what I'm getting at, slowly I know."

The team had snickered as Dave Grahams went off on his favourite subject of spies everywhere.

"Settle down," said Hooper. "So what do you think, Dave, spy or witness protection?"

"Spy, he's too obvious for witness and too rich." More half pulled laughs.

"Let Dave make his case. Go on Dave," Hooper

encouraged.

"No history, lots of travel, and the biggest thing, he runs counter surveillance and lost us twice. Once is lucky, twice he's professional, then he lost Watkins in Heathrow." Grahams turned and looked at Watkins. "I know Watkins is a new boy," more laughs, "but he's pretty good on the tracking jobs. It's too many times. I think his house is rigged as well, possible entry detection checks on doors, papers very neat and precise. The CCTV is too obvious and the alarm easy. Our bug has got nothing." Rutledge coughed to interrupt. The team was not supposed to know about illegal entries and bugs. Grahams realised his mistake, but continued, "Anyway, he is too smart by half; how did he get that lawyer set up when we hadn't even pulled him in? She was waiting for him to be arrested. Where is he? He's been gone out of his house for days again."

The team looked at Hooper, as Grahams came to the end of his rant. "Dave thanks, and team forget you heard about the house." He gave them all a look. "Okay, so let's work on the presumption he is a spy. For whom, and for what would be the obvious questions? But our job, may I remind everyone, is to find out who killed the girls. That's if they are dead. If we add Hemmings to the list, the serial killer motive for girls is gone."

"Boss," said Rutledge, "I think we need to share some information with the team about the girls. They have nearly all guessed or rumoured stuff anyway."

"You're right, James. The girls are all connected with the security services, and all have had some involvement with Iraq." There were nods around the room. "That does not, and I repeat does not, get in the press, or put on reports. Let the press continue the serial killer speculation, they have other news to worry about anyway, and we have dropped from sight. No links to Hemmings either. Dave, who is going with you to Portugal?"

"I am boss," said Drinkwater.

"Good, Dave and John in my office; the rest of you, see you tomorrow."

"Here goes," thought Grahams, "rollicking again."

"Dave," said Hooper once the door was closed, "sometimes

I could strangle you, but you have changed my mind on Slater. Are you sure about the counter surveillance?"

"Sorry boss, I got carried away, but yes, he definitely dropped us," Grahams said sheepishly with a look from Drinkwater.

"John," Hooper continued, ignoring the apology, "get the SFO to raise a warrant investigating illegal trades. That will keep noses out of our investigation and not in our file. James can attend low key on our behalf. He can take one of the Met support to help with searching. If Slater is a spook... Who knows what he knows, or who will tell him? Okay, are you set for your trip tomorrow? Let's see if we can rule Slater in or out by tomorrow evening." They left for the evening.

CHAPTER THIRTY-TWO

Schlemburg

Hedges met with Carl Schlemburg as arranged. Once he had settled him into his small library with a large malt, he told him what he wanted.

"I wouldn't mind seeing that file for myself," Carl replied. Hedges was not happy with that, but there was no way round the problem whilst keeping Schlemburg out of it. "I think we have someone who can help," Carl continued enigmatically, as expected.

"How soon, it is very urgent?" Hedges did not mean to appear so eager.

"A day or two," said Schlemburg. He reached into his bag and pulled a thin folder out. "This is one for your asset, also very urgent. No report needed, we know what he knows, but it needs to be soon, and it needs to be a clear accident, no disappearance to be investigated." He passed the file over. "The file has movements, address and so on. How soon do you think?"

"I'll set it up," Hedges responded. "As for time, tricky. I can press, but we normally give him a few weeks."

"Normally, eh? How many has this guy done?"

"That would be telling, but he has been fairly busy over the last couple of years."

"Did he do the Canadian girl?"

"Who would that be?" Hedges lied.

"Okay, I understand. I have to go. The Ambassador thinks I should give him a report. Make sure the target is in the next two weeks, preferably sooner." Schlemburg left Hedges with a shake of the hand and a smile.

Hedges checked the file. A member of Congress, and not a low profile one. The stock tip and payment matched the high profile. Well, this would test Ashley if he accepted the job. He had no way of forcing him except via verbal message, which he may not check for a few days. He did not want to let Schlemburg know that, but it could be a problem. He could set it up if he could upload the file now. How? He did not have a scanner at home. It would have to wait until the morning when he could get Michelle to help.

***

Stewart Hillier was basking in the afterglow of one of his special nights. The girls had left thirty minutes ago, and he had just showered and was planning on getting some sleep. The knock on the door surprised him. He thought that maybe one of the girls had forgotten something. He pulled on a hotel complimentary robe. He opened the door without checking the peep hole. Two men stood outside the door. He went to close it, but one was already coming inside. They were both bigger than him.

"What are you doing? I'll call the manager, get out," he stammered.

"Now Stewart that is not very friendly," said one of the men with an American accent. "All we want is a little chat, nothing to worry about. We could have interrupted you earlier," he continued, "but we want to be friends. We need your help. Now, let's sit down and have a few words."

The other man, and the speaker, both came fully into the room. Stewart's fear was evident, but he backed off to the bed where he sat down. One of the men checked the bathroom, whilst the other turned the small table's chair around and sat down. The other man went and stood by the hotel room door, still saying nothing. They both wore suits and almost identical light coats. Stewart swallowed hard.

"What do you want?" Stewart asked.

"Stewart, we understand you provide various files on request."

"I don't know what you are talking about."

"Stewart, let's cut the crap. We know you do, and you know that we know you do. Now, we want a particular file."

"What do I get?" Stewart asked, giving in.

The man by the door started to step forward until the sitting man raised his hand. "Stewart, there is no reason why your normal arrangement should not apply. Your contact has given the details, and we are happy to pay the normal amount, plus a bonus for speedy work. We do need the speedy work, hence, our choice of meeting you instead of your normal call. Now, can you help us tonight?"

"Tonight? Yes, that's possible but I was going to stay here."

"Sorry," he said but clearly did not mean it, "but it is very urgent. This is the file we want."

It was the Jenny Wallace Special Branch file. "That won't be difficult," he thought, but he said nothing. He would not even need a new upload. He was uploading the file every eight to twelve hours on a retainer since the first request. He knew that file was going to be interesting when he first was asked for it, but he could have done without the personal visit. Stewart replied, "It will take me a couple of hours to find it and upload it; is tomorrow morning okay, say by 10 O'clock." Stewart tried to buy some time.

His guest considered the timing. "No, Stewart, phone us on this number before eight with the access name and code. You'll have your money then. We'll call you every hour for a progress report. We may have some more work for you as well."

Stewart's fear returned, "Don't worry," the man continued, "we like your work and we'll revert to normal contact methods in future. Now, you better get dressed and moving."

They stayed and watched him dress and then leave his room. He had pre-paid the room on his false account. They must have known everything. He did not like it, but could not change anything now. They saw him into a cab, and then Stewart was alone on his way back to his flat. He had told them he needed some things from his home. It was a lie, but it gave him more time to think. He calmed himself down. He spent 30 minutes at his home before grabbing his office keys and heading into work. He checked in with the duty desk and got a smile from one of the duty guards. "Systems playing up again," he explained.

He got a rueful smile and sympathetic comment of, "Bloody computers," in return.

He went up to his office. The two men had been outside when he went in. They had made sure he had seem them. The office was not deserted. There was always something going on behind various doors, even if it were two in the morning. He entered his domain, ran his normal system checks, no flags, then checked the latest version of the case file. It had not changed since he had last updated it, when he left for his evening of fun. So he could simply pass on the same access details, and he would be done. Stewart hesitated. The original contact had paid him well, and with no issues for the regular access to the file. He knew he had provided information before, based on his voice, but could not recall what. He set up an alternate user name and password for the file. He had not properly browsed it before.

He noted the suspect Slater and the follow-ups, including his photo. He would recognise the man. "Rich bastard," he noted from the file. He could certainly pay me. That was it! He probably was paying him. He checked the mobile number listed for Slater. He would not know it, as the contact had only ever called him. His contact mobile rang. It was them doing their hourly check. He told them he was making progress, but had not found the file yet. They urged him to hurry. Back to the file. If it was Slater, he thought a warning would be in order. What could he say? He quickly typed a text file, which he then added to the contact's file upload asking him to call him urgently. It was approaching three in the morning. Where had the time gone? He was delaying. He read the whole file. Then copied the main file, without the text file, to the site, and gave access to the user name and account. Just after three, the mobile went again. He pretended a system issue with a new firewall. Again he was urged on. He said it would be thirty minutes or so. He waited twenty before he contacted them. He gave them the site

URL, user name, and password.

"That was very good, Stewart," the man said. "Your money is on its way. We'll be in touch." He hung up.

The man, whose name was Claremont, but was normally called Reach, for some obscure training incident, called his boss immediately on his secure phone. He answered on the third ring.

"Carl, it's Reach," he said. "Success, here are the details." He waited whilst his boss grabbed a pen and paper. He passed the details over.

"Cover?" Carl questioned.

"All okay, the contact passed us on with barely a murmur, cost £2,000. The inside man is an IT Tech at Scotland Yard. He could be very useful, if expensive, in future. I'll write up the details in the morning. It only took longer because we had to wait for two girls to leave his room."

"Two?" Schlemburg laughed. "I wouldn't have the energy. Still, well done, I'll see you later." Carl hung up. "Now for the file and to see what the trouble is about," he thought. He got up. His wife had barely moved. No change there he thought, imagining the two girls. He left the bedroom and dressed. He then called for his car.

Carl Schlemburg was an Agency man of twenty years' experience. London would probably be his final posting before obscurity into a Langley policy unit with some made-up title. He had been in the field for three quarters of that time and had buried too many colleagues and enemies. He did not like the black elements, but accepted them as a necessary part of his role, and they had always been a part of his operational tasks. The file he had passed to Hedges yesterday was probably the last straw. He had objected in principal to the request from Deputy Director Hidelwietz, but the impact to the Agency if action were not taken was too great. Despite his cynicism, he was still a patriot, and whatever the fiasco of Iraq had cost his country, it would cost more if people dug up matters that were properly buried. Over the last few years, he had become embroiled in this operation, if that was what it could be called. Firstly, assessing the risks to the CIA and, by implication, the USA and then, because of his involvement with getting the Canadian girl taken care of, he had prepared a file for Ferguson in Canadian SIS. That was before he knew the full scope of the operation and the implications. His pension fund was being topped up, although, like any operative involved in the black side, he had fund sources. It was 04:30 when he left for the Embassy. By the time he had gotten to his office, persuaded IT Security to allow him access to the unofficial URL, downloaded, and then read the file, it was nearly 06:30. He called Reach, asking him to come in immediately. He needed more eyes on the file. After Reach had arrived, he let him read the print outs whilst he ordered in some coffee and breakfast. He had drunk too much with the Ambassador the previous evening, whilst deflecting as many questions as possible.

"Well?" He asked Reach after he had sat back. The print outs were scattered over the desk between them.

"Good team on the case; they are connecting dots as you would expect. I'm not sure about Slater," he said jabbing at his photo. "He is probably insider trading, but there is not much more. I could run some checks back home with Homeland and Quantico?"

"Not sure I want them involved at this stage," Carl replied. He would not want any flags raised whilst the mission was in progress. He had not realised one of the girls had worked for Hedges, not surprising he was twitchy.

"There are several loose ends though," Reach continued with no comment on Carl's statement. He was too long in the game to ask why the checks should not go ahead.

"What do you mean?"

"Unaccounted for meetings with no notes and no follow up on the file."

"Where?"

"See here, they report they will have a meeting with a Five liaison, not named, but no notes of the meeting. Also, they make a jump to Iraq, but where did that come from. They are keeping stuff out of the report."

"I see what you mean, which means they are probably closer to some of this than the report implies. I may have to talk to Hedges again. How are your contacts in Thames House?"

"Getting better now we have stopped grabbing people off London streets. I can have a word, but what do I ask?"

"I understand the problem. Let's keep this quiet unless there is a special contact you can trust? I see Braithwaite's name here reporting the Wallace girl. Do you know him?"

"Met him once or twice, I think he has the internal Animal crackpots and IRA brief now. Last time was six months or so ago. I'd have to check when exactly. As long as we continue to block funding streams for the IRA, or letting them know about arms purchases, not much involvement."

"See if you can have a chat, as they say over here. He probably knows more, but let's not tilt our hand unless he can offer us something back."

"He will question why we are asking?"

Schlemburg considered what he could tell Reach to pass on to Braithwaite. Careful now, must not expose his own involvement. "Claim a question from the Canadians about their missing analyst that they raised a while back. The details are on the system and offer some info on IRA if we have anything. What about your IT man?" He finished changing the subject.

"Stewart Hillier, seven years in post, usual background before. Weakness for pairs of prostitutes and money, of course. Into English Civil War re-enactment, whatever that is? Loner, no great social skills but, very clever technically. He set up his whole system and contacted the criminal elements we tapped into. We used Scarecrow." He gave the code name of an organised crime leader who had helped the Agency for a fee for several years. "Great potential asset, he's been making a small fortune in his role. Complete access to Special Branch and a few other databases. He will cost, but I would recommend leaving him in post."

"Agreed, stick him on the books and when this is done we'll get him some detailed training. We'll want to know everything he has leaked out and to whom as well. If necessary, we'll have to pull him in. English Civil War doesn't exactly go with pairs of working girls." Carl shook his head at the world. They broke from the meeting. Carl collected, then duplicated the file. It was not even nine o'clock; too early and too keen for Hedges. He could wait till lunchtime. He needed more sleep. Instead, he stretched as his PA arrived. She made no comment on the breakfast remains. She cleared them away, and then returned with fresh coffee and a pile of files. Another day began.

Reach went for a walk, leaving the Embassy, crossing Park Lane and wandering into Hyde Park, where he strolled to the Serpentine, avoiding the morning joggers as best he could. He could do with some exercise himself he thought. So what was this all about? The urgency of the contact, the need to talk to Five. No contact back to resources in the USA. Something was going on, but he was out of the loop. Schlemburg was relatively new in London and they had been getting on reasonably well, despite his previous boss Casey Richenbach's warnings to be careful around Schlemburg. The Ambassador, Elliot Bloomstein, had asked him about Carl only yesterday, when they had met in a corridor in Grosvenor Square, the US Embassy. The Hedges character, he had met twice. Did not like him at all; Casey had warned him about him as well. He would give Casey a call once the time zone suited, but now for Five. He called his main contact in Five for counter Islamic terrorism, and asked him to get Braithwaite to call and he did so twenty-minutes later. He asked for a meeting to discuss some Irish issues. They set it up for that afternoon. He returned to the Embassy to dig up something on the IRA that he could give as an excuse for the meeting and look up the Canadian thing. He wondered, "What was that all about?"

CHAPTER THIRTY-THREE

Scarecrow

Scarecrow was in reality, Frank Coalfield. Coalfield had started his criminal career as getaway driver for his uncle who fancied himself as a hardened armed bank robber, until he got caught coming out of a National Westminster branch in Enfield to face a police cordon who had been tipped off. By pure luck Frank had been going round the block whilst the gang had their allotted five minutes in the branch. He had been held up by an old lady crossing a street; before he could get there the gang had walked into the trap. Frank had carried on driving. Frank then made his name by giving the grass who had tipped off the Police, a haircut that started at his neck. He rose rapidly via drugs, protectionism and prostitution to be an area boss in North East London. Frank had decided that armed robbery, although a good reputation builder, too easily went wrong.

He had come to the attention of Special Branch following some unproven drug dealing with the IRA. He had an almost clean record, listing only a minor possession charge, for which he was fined, and some speeding tickets. Stewart Hillier had come to him and they now had a fruitful business together. Coalfield had distanced himself from the day to day criminal activities. To his prosperous neighbours, he was something in shipping and import/export. He lived in a five bedroomed town house in Chiswick, well away from his North London business.

He charged the contacts for Stewart Hillier a twenty percent introduction fee. A nice side-line, but really petty change against his current cocaine operation, which netted him nearly five million a year in his overseas accounts. Enough to pay for his third wife who was twenty-five years his junior, and turning into a real bitch with her holiday and shopping demands, and the maintenance on his one ex-wife. She lived quietly in the South of France. His two teenage children attended suitably expensive private schools, and both being encouraged to take law at University. The new wife was supplemented by a steady stream of new girls from one of his business interests which were growing. He imported East European girls who he enjoyed breaking in before setting them up in one of his outlets. He was having to deal with the growing Albanian, Russian, and Croatian threat to his business, but was hoping to come to a suitable arrangement with the Russians which would solve a territory squabble.

He used Stewart Hillier himself to check on opponents and any sign of police interest in himself. He paid off two Metropolitan Police Inspectors and always paid the taxman on time. One of his other contacts, and not as expensive as Hillier, was a wealth inspector in HMRC investigations branch. He paid him, but his real hold was his penchant for young boys, another one of Coalfield's sidelines. The photos of that were in a safety deposit box.

CHAPTER THIRTY-FOUR

Time To Run?

Michael awoke alone and, for the first time in his life, unhappy with that fact. He heard noise from downstairs, the creak of the fourth step again, and then Jess came into the bedroom with a tray, wearing the long T-Shirt, and a smile.

"I missed you," he said.

"That's sweet," she replied, smiling and placing a piece of toast in his mouth before he could reply. "I've been thinking about your proposal."

He coughed and thought, "Proposal, I haven't proposed." She smiled with the extra smirk he had come to love, probably reading his mind.

"I meant your proposal to take me away from all this to a luxury Caribbean Island." She swept her arms around the room as she spoke, before he grabbed her arm.

"Would you like another proposal?" He smiled back at her.

"What's that?" Smiling, and raising her eyebrows.

"That young ladies be taken over a knee and spanked." He pulled her across his knees, but instead of a spanking he caressed her thighs and then pulled her back to him with a kiss. She pulled back.

"I have work," she said. "Will I see you later? I could come to yours?"

"That would be great, sixish OK? We can go out for dinner."

"Don't you ever cook?"

"Not if I can help it."

Jessica dressed, avoiding his grabs and kissed him before leaving. He had the house to himself, but did not explore. He dressed. He cleared the kitchen by loading and putting on the dishwasher. Then, he checked the doors before letting himself out. He walked around the streets for a while. He did not want to work whilst he thought how to get himself out of this mess with Jess. He found himself across the street from Jess in Vauxhall. He pondered what she was doing and saying in her search for Sally's killer… him. This was mad. He speeded up his walk back to his apartment block. Once in the Penthouse he tidied. He would have to arrange a cleaner to come in, or spend more time tidying. He did not even have a vacuum. Perhaps the doorman would know someone. He logged onto the secure site, more by habit, and checked how Special branch was doing. He found the text file.

"I have some very important extra information for you, please call this number as soon as you get this"

He read the note again. Extortion? How? He was paying the man extra for the continuing access. He did not know his name or vice versa. So what was the point? It had to be something else. If he called it could be traced if someone were onto him. As far as Special Branch had been concerned, he was out of the country as Slater. He needed to be gone soon, but then there was Jess. As a habit, he checked the contact voicemail. There was Hedges with an urgent mission that had to be completed as soon as possible. Damn! He did not want another job, he was sick of them, and sick of himself for doing them. He had a bright new light shining in his life, which he wanted more than anything, Jess. How could he do a mission when he felt like this, with Special Branch on his tail? He did not press one or two on the menu options. He just hung up. He had never pressed two. Slater did not know who or where the target was. He would only get that information if he pressed one, then accessed the target file; he did not like the urgent message either. They had never asked for an urgent mission. His mind was racing.

He was confused for the first time in his life. Stay calm, he told himself. Think things through. Deal with the actions one at a time whilst keeping your plan flexible. Contingency planning is fine, but plan first. First, the Special Branch file and text file. He checked the number. He went to his safe and removed a pre-pay phone; he had charged it before switching it off and storing it. He now took it out. Phone locations could be traced. He changed and, carrying a bag with some equipment, he left.

He stopped only to organise a cleaner with the doorman, Harvey. He knew one of course. They had spare keys for all the apartments in the security office. He put the security system code into an envelope and left it with the building manager for the cleaner. Mrs. Koswchz they said. She already did a couple of other apartments. She would be in that afternoon. He was not happy about letting someone he did not know in, but he had to appear normal for Jess. He grabbed a passing cab and headed north of the river. He settled on St. James Park. It was warm and pleasant in the late summer sunshine. There were a few tourists about, but he found an empty bench in the early afternoon sunshine. He called the number.

"Hello?"

"You asked me to call."

"Ah, I hoped it would be you."

"If you want more money, I'm sorry but no."

"No, it's not that, I wanted to warn you that's all."

"Warn me about what, and why would you warn me?"

"We have done some good business, and I don't want to lose any customers." Stewart felt that this was not going well.

There was a silence, his contact contemplating, was it Slater? How could he ask? Then, the man said, "What do you want to warn me about?"

He quickly spurted it out. "Other people are looking at that file, unofficially as well."

"Are they? Who?" A cautious tone.

"I don't know who exactly, but they were American and very keen to get the information Mr. Sla..." He stopped himself.

"What did you say?"

"Nothing, just they were American and came to see me last night to get me to do the file. They knew who I was and everything." He let out the last in a whine. He was Slater the response had given it away.

"Okay, please update the file. If you discover anything else, please put a note on the file. I'll send a bonus for your time."

"Thank you," Stewart blurted, but the line was already dead.

Stewart Hillier should have been pleased. He had passed on the warning, confirmed his suspicion, well probably confirmed it, and earned a bonus. The American's money was already in his account. So why did he feel exposed? The Americans had found him. He speculated who had told. How much money did he have saved? Not even £100,000. The flat would sell for more, but that would take weeks. He did not want to run anyway. He liked his jobs. All of them. He liked the girls even more, but they were a very expensive hobby. He would have to stick with it, but he had a premonition that this was not over yet.

Slater had not missed the name drop or the reason for it. So someone knew he was checking the investigation. He needed to read the file properly to see how close they were. He needed to decide on the mission. He needed to plan to see the new property. He needed a break; he needed to close this whole thing down. He did not need the money, never had really, so was he doing it just for the adrenaline rush, the perversion with the girls, love of country? He laughed. He was doing it because he could. Some egotistical mind game he was playing with humanity. He did not want that anymore. He checked his bag he had come prepared to force a meeting. The bag had a simple wig, a light jacket, a Gloch 9 mm, and one of his passports, all just in case. He put the mobile into the bag, switching it off. He checked to see whether anyone was paying him attention, but nothing, he had been on the call for less than sixty-seconds. Possible trace, but not to get anyone there, and then a crowded area full of tourists. He took extra measures before going to his safe flat, just in case. He did not like being hunted. He dropped the bag and put away the equipment in the safe. He then took a roundabout route to the Penthouse in time for Jess to arrive.

Slater needed to close the possibility that the contact would expose him, but that would mean exposing himself to the intermediary, another risk. Slater did not know who it was he had just spoken to. He just had the number to call. He had been given the intermediary contact by Hemmings. Frank Coalfield, a member of organised crime he recalled, so he would be security aware. A job for tomorrow. Time some doors were closed, permanently and their risks with them. Slater felt better having made one decision. The intermediary would lead Slater to the IT Contact, whoever he was, and he would have to decide what action he needed to take. The urgent mission would have to wait, but he would make some preliminary enquiries and set ups; another job for tomorrow.

The cleaner was just leaving as he arrived. They had a brief chat. He paid her in advance and said he would set up an account and get some cleaning stuff in the flat. Jess arrived early just as he was finishing his chat, and before he had been in the apartment. He had wanted to change and prepare for her. She carried an overnight bag he was pleased to see. They said hello's and goodbye's to Mrs. Koswchz who was Bulgarian or something and went up to the apartment.

"You're not annoyed I came early, are you?" Jess asked.

"Not at all, I just wanted to change before you got here and finish sorting out the flat, but I'm glad you are here."

"We'll have more time to talk and..." She was in his arms then in his bed. They washed dressed and went out to a restaurant in Soho, missing the theatre crowd. A cab back and more bed. He lay exhausted by his efforts. She had collected a glass of water from the kitchen and was getting back into bed. He stole the glass. "Hey that was mine," she exclaimed. He passed it back. She climbed back into the bed.

"No, T-Shirt I see," he commentated.

"Don't think I need it here, anyway I want you to see me, even on that first night, I don't think I have ever been so... what's the right word... Forward." Her voice was soft, silky, and close.

"How about brazen, verging on slutty."

She playfully slapped him. "Don't you like my being brazen and slutty?" She sat up exposing her breasts.

"Yes, please," he said realising he had a bit of energy left.

Mike was up before Jess and this time he brought her breakfast in bed.

"You'll get crumbs everywhere, and Mrs. Koswchz won't like it," said Jess.

"I'll take my chances. Now where are those crumbs?" he said, lifting the sheet.

"Behave," she said, pushing the sheet back down and his hands away. They lay quietly together. "You're going off travelling again aren't you?" she asked tentatively.

"Yes, soon, more business, and the Caribbean this time."

"Sounds nice."

"Look Jess, why don't you join me to look for houses out there, do you have any holiday you can take?"

"I have some left, I could ask. I'm sure Tony wouldn't mind. God, look at the time," said Jess, "I have to go." She leaped from the bed and rushed to the bathroom. She quickly showered and then came out with just the towel. Grabbing her overnight bag she went and dressed. Skirt and blouse this time. She caught him smiling at her from the bed. "Can I see you tonight?"

"I'll pick you up, is eight all right?"

"Why so late?"

"I have a lot to do today," he said.

"That's why you are still in bed I suppose," she laughed. "I'll see you later." She gave him a kiss and left before he could pull her back onto the bed.

CHAPTER THIRTY-FIVE

Get The File

Hedges had waited all morning for something, before he got an email from Schlemburg, telling him he was couriering the file over to him. He had faced a difficult couple of hours trying to get the mission file scanned in. Michele had asked lots of questions about the file's classification, and he unfortunately had to speak harshly to her before she had finally explained the process of scan to a file, then collect the file with a code, then upload the file. He thought she had heard him set up the message for Ashley to collect. She was becoming troublesome, just like one of her predecessors, but he could not get rid of her as well. He called her in and made up some baloney about the Americans and assets he was running. She seemed placated but not convinced. He did not need another problem. It personally had cost him to remove Sally Carver with no report. He had raided his own funds to pay Ashley and wheedle a stock tip from Charles Goodson, a procurement contact to whom he now owed a favour. He hated owing favours. The price had been cheaper than others, but no comment from Ashley; he had carried out the mission as expected.

He checked to see whether there was a response to the voicemail. Urgent he had said, but he had no idea when Ashley would pick up the voicemail. Michelle came into the office with a sealed envelope from Schlemburg. No, he did not want it scanned in. He would store it in his safe he told her; more unhappiness in her expression. The Special Branch file was what he had waited for. He read it quickly. They had nothing as far as he could tell. He could run the Slater chap through the system, but that would raise a note that he had run the name. Special Branch had done some checks already and got nothing. He noticed the 1998 reference and the planned meeting with himself. Hooper and Drinkwater would come. He read the interview with the Carver brother and sister. They did not know anything. He had sent a polite letter during the first investigation. He knew nothing about the trail Ashley had created, other than what he had learned then, and now in the file.

Why were they going to see the stockbroker? It was a waste of time. Slater was the wrong man. Then, he saw the photo. He stared hard, could it be him, Ashley? He looked closely at the photocopied enlargement. The only photo he had of Ashley was from his army days, in the file, safely hidden in his safe at home. He could not remember it. It was not something he had looked at for years. Working hypothesis; it was Ashley, in which case his operation could be blown at any moment. If it were not Ashley, then it did not matter. But if it was? The stockbroker could open this all up if he told the detectives that Ashley was the original name. He did not know; did not want to know, how Hemmings had set it up, or which stockbrokers Hemmings had got Ashley to join under his new identity. Was that Slater, when was that? Late nineties he recalled, but when? The Hemmings file at home on Ashley had very few details. He had asked Hemmings not to tell him. He had been so eager for the asset to be live and hidden. Then, Hemmings was dead, and he had an untraceable asset. He had to get home and see the Hemmings file, and soon. He noted the change in the file. Some details missing. He surmised, as had the Americans, that not everything was in the file. Five liaison, that had to be Braithwaite he realised, but where were the notes of the meeting? He would have to see. Braithwaite was becoming problematical. Hedges knew there were not just girl victims. Braithwaite may have to join them, but how would he fund it. He would have to have a word with Procurement again. His address book had the list of victims' initials. The serial killer angle was good camouflage of course. Special Branch knew nothing of the overseas missions. The French girl, Sylvia Cardôtte, had been a traitor anyway.

He put in a call to Schlemburg. While he waited, he checked the voicemail; nothing. Michelle put the call though. He made sure she could hear as he started the conversation.

"Carl, old chap," too good fellow well met, but the performance was for Michelle, "thank you for the file. I have passed it onto the contact we discussed. No, no confirmation yet, I may have neglected to mention it can take time as it is not easy for him to make contact. Yes, I appreciate the urgency; I will let you know as soon as I can. The second file you sent, seems to be missing some of the usual elements. Oh, you had noticed that as well. Has your source misplaced some of the data?" He thought that maybe the American's were withholding material. They normally did. "I see; do you presume they may be closer than we suspected?"

Then Schlemburg asked, "One of the targets listed, was that a mistake clearly connected to you?"

Hedges almost blurted out Sally's name in his shock at being questioned. What did Schlemburg know and how much, he thought? Michelle was still listening. He had to be very careful what he said. He lowered his voice and wished that he had not left the door ajar. "That particular target was troublesome, but dealt with at the time, yes it was close to home, but as long as the serial killer theory holds, then there will be nothing to investigate." He then raised his voice again. "I appreciate the concern, Carl, but I think we are all okay. Yes, I'll be in touch." Damn Americans. Michelle reminded him of his planned meeting with the DG in five minutes. Damn budget again. The Hemmings file would have to wait. He locked the Special Branch file away with his own notes.

***

Schlemburg managed not to slam down the phone. Reach walked back into his office, reporting on his meeting with Braithwaite. Had he heard the conversation? His reference to Sally Carver had been earlier. He covered himself with his anger at Hedges. "Asshole, supercilious, pompous, asshole," said Schlemburg, explaining he had spoken with Hedges and that Hedges had questioned the file content. "Did Hillier hold stuff back do you think?"

"No, the file was missing something, but not by removal. Hedges has just spotted what we did, but Hedges presumed we had withheld information. I can check if you want?"

"No, don't bother. What about Braithwaite?"

"That's why I'm here."

Reach had met with Braithwaite at a cafe between Thames House and the Tate Britain gallery. After a shake of hands, they got down to business in a small cubicle away from prying eyes.

"You have some information for me?" Braithwaite asked.

"Yes, and I hope you have some for me"

"Really?" Braithwaite was intrigued. Reach passed over his snippet on fund collecting by Continuity IRA in Boston, including the names being used.

"That's very helpful, and in return?"

"We have had some comm's traffic on analysts going missing, which we think is tied to these girls going missing in the papers." Reach decided to go all out. "We think they are connected, and as we know that you are Five's Special Branch liaison, we thought you could tell us more?"

Braithwaite was stunned, he had to be careful, and he certainly did not want any flags raised by the Americans, which would come down from high. What could he tell them? "Yes, I am aware of the case and there does seem, on the surface, to be a connection, but nothing definite. It is perfectly possible the cases are not connected, or that the other three girls did just go off somewhere. The last case, Wallace, seems more likely to be abduction though." He felt himself stumble in his speech as he remembered Jenny. He recovered, hoping the American had not noticed. "Special Branch is investigating because of the girls' background, not the actual background itself. They have a potential suspect, but very little hard evidence, and what they do have, is not conclusive. Do you have more information?"

Reach knew he was not telling the whole story, and he noticed the stumble over Wallace. What did that mean? He had confirmed the investigation. If he revealed more, Brathwaite would know they had a leak. If he said no more, then Braithwaite would wonder about the fuss and why the meeting. "Confidentially," he said, "we believe a Canadian analyst can be added to the list."

"What, in the UK?" Braithwaite asked.

"No, in Canada. Her name was or is, Helena Salbert, in Canadian SIS." Claremont had seen the request from the Canadians on the system.

"When was this?"

"A couple of years ago. I'll see if I can send the report."

"That would be helpful. In return then, we think there is an Iraq connection, and we have a possible male victim." He gave Hemmings' name. That was not in the report. The so called 'Special Relationship' was occasionally special. They agreed to keep in touch.

After he relayed the meeting detail to Schlemburg, they discussed options.

"Okay, let's just see what happens. Hedges has what he wanted, but he appears to be protecting something, what we don't know." Carl did, but he was not going to tell Reach. "Anyway we have plenty of other things on." Reach, effectively dismissed, left the office.

***

Reach Claremont did not like this at all. Yesterday, getting the Special Branch file was essential; today, take our time. He left the building and put in the call to his old boss, Casey Richenbach. He passed over the names of Hedges, Hemmings, the girls, and John Slater. His former boss was intrigued.

"You said Hedges and Schlemburg have been meeting, are you sure it wasn't just about this?"

"Casey, I'm not certain but there was something else going on. Beth told me that a file had been taken from Schlemburg's safe, copied and taken to a meeting with Hedges. The copy had not returned and showed as issued to MI5 on the register." Beth was Schlemburg's PA, and had also been Casey's.

"Never liked Hedges when I was over there. What's your gut feel, Reach?" His former boss asked pointedly.

"Hedges is dirty and connected to the disappearances, and I don't mean just by his PA being one of the victims. Do you want me to dig, I'll need some top cover if you do?"

"Yes, I will dig at this end as well. I'll get the Ambassador to set up something with you. I'll relay with him and send you anything on the names. Let's keep Carl out of this for the time being, and Reach..."

"Yeah, I know, watch my back."

"Good man, and keep an eye on Beth as well. I'll try to get something overnight, whilst the limeys get their beauty sleep."

He hung up. Reach needed some sleep, with the Hillier action he was worn out.

***

Hedges returned from his meeting with the DG and the Finance Director. No increase in budget. He could not get any funding for his special operations ideas. All the new money was going into counter Islamic fundamentalist operations, which was not his speciality. Maybe Six would lose their Plato funding. That would take a weight off his mind. The DG had briefed him on Plato during one of their one to one sessions. Six had requested some files and when he asked the DG why, the DG had briefed him, but he did not know where they were going with it. Did Braithwaite know more? Why had he raised it? He had been reeling from the Sally and Hemmings bits, then casually dropping Plato into it? Did Braithwaite know he knew of it? Too much double guessing. He needed more information. He could search the databases for references to Plato. It was not unusual for the security services to share information, but normally not historical files, especially policy position papers. He would get Michelle to look into Plato on his behalf.

If his actions were being tracked, then it was at least one step away. Braithwaite was Special Branch liaison as well. What else had he told them? Who else had they been meeting with? Braithwaite? As he was liaison, why was his name not listed; that was unusual, was someone else there? Hedges was a political animal rather than a field operative making his way up the hierarchy of the Security Service, but he was not without skills and intelligence. Working hypothesis, he noted on his desk jotter accidentally. There was a liaison meeting, and someone else was there with Braithwaite who had ensured that no notes were taken of the meeting. Who could that be? Plato? So assume Six were there. Who would that be? He had few friends at the Secret Intelligence Service to ask. The clear out after the Iraq debacle had removed some of his contacts. He replaced the file, keeping the photo copy of Slater's photo, which he folded and placed in his inside jacket pocket. He needed to get home and check the main file. He asked Michelle to research Plato for him, giving her as few details as he could; she gave him a quizzical or was it suspicious, look? He told her he had a private appointment that he had just recalled before leaving for home. He left.

CHAPTER THIRTY-SIX

Michelle

Michelle Carrington had been in the Security Service for nearly five years after Graduating from Durham. She had begun her career as an analyst on the Russian desk but became bored. She had seen an internal advertisement for a PA vacancy and had applied. Michelle had not been short of admirers at University, and she had a few relationships, but nothing serious. She was a tall, slim, brunette with a steady Royal Air Force boyfriend, Mark Ellis. They had been together nearly two years. Mark was currently deployed in Berlin, in the Attaché's department. They were in the process of moving in together. He had sort of proposed, but nothing definite. She was eagerly awaiting his next London leave when she was sure he would ask her properly; especially now that he had notice of his promotion and return to the UK, to work in the Defence Intelligence Agency in the Ministry of Defence in Whitehall.

They had met on an advanced Russian language course at an army base, where they had been the only two single trainees. She had gone on the advanced Russian course, really to keep her hand in, and her language skills up to speed. At the end of week two, after a Russian drinking game in the Officers' Mess bar, they had gone back to her room with the remainder of a bottle of Stolichnaya, as the other trainees had headed home for the weekend. They had started with another toast that had led to him removing his jacket and tie. She had removed her blouse, to show team spirit, and Détente, she said. She had then removed her bra, when he offered to pour vodka on her to check if the taste were the same. They had spent most of the weekend exploiting various positions, with and without Vodka, whilst trying to find out the correct Russian words for the activities they engaged in; not something that was easy to find out from the Russian instructors or dictionaries, but they tried. They met up as frequently as they could. He knew she was Home Office and after three months, she received permission to formally tell him she was in the Security Service, which he had already guessed by that stage.

The PA work was certainly more interesting, even if her second boss, Hedges, was not easy to work for. She did not trust him at all. In the canteen, after she got the Hedges job, she had noticed that colleagues had become more distant. She did not get invited out by other staff anymore, maybe because she was no longer available in the single's market, but that was not it. She had worked for Hedges for nearly a year. When she told him of her relationship, as she was required to do on her appointment to his staff, he had seemed disappointed, and became a bit more stand-offish. She had put his treatment down to her more working class background from Leeds, instead of the traditional Home Counties set. That background seemed to dominate the upper echelons of the Security Service.

Hedges was a senior director, and a direct report into the DG. She appreciated his position, and on nearly everything he did, demonstrated he was a stickler for correct records and paperwork. Except, now and then, he would get a file that seemed to be off the books. She only knew because of his complete aversion to information technology. He hated email and reading anything on his screen. She had to constantly help him with anything related to technology. The scanning that morning had just been another example. Why had he not just given her the file and she could have done it in a couple of minutes? Then there was the couriered file from the US Embassy. That used to be normal, she was told by the mail office, but in the days of email why had it not come across electronically? Why was it in Hedges office safe and not returned and logged in the registry? Why was that not scanned in? Then there was the phone call farce about the file. Hedges had deliberately let her hear the call, well his side of most of it. Why? He never normally let her hear his calls.

She went into his office to clear his coffee up. She was

picking up a cup and saucer, and about to brush off the crumbs from one of the Fortnum and Mason biscuits that he insisted on, when she saw the notes on his ink pad, written in his familiar precise handwriting. He must have missed the file he normally wrote on. Plato, Braithwaite, Hooper, Iraq, Special Branch and Photo were all noted in a list, with Braithwaite underlined. She remembered the meeting that Hedges had held with Braithwaite. She had not been asked to take minutes, not unusual, but they were in different departments, which was unusual. Hedges had been flustered after that meeting. Then there was the deliberate delay in the Special Branch meeting, set now for Friday, and the urgent meeting with the CIA held off site. Michelle did not know what to think.

She cleared the room. Sat down back at her desk and did a Plato keyword search. She received hundreds of hits. There were multiple World War II operations. One was a reference to the Greek Philosopher and his library information, and one was a reference to a SIS file from her own department. There was a link back to Hedges noting a policy paper that had been transferred to the Plato Team in Vauxhall. The email went for the attention of Tony Grayson. There was a receipt back from a Jessica Carver on his behalf, thanking her for the prompt sending of the file. She typed into the system… Braithwaite. She got his internal contact details. She typed in Hooper. She got contact details for Scotland Yard and a reference to Braithwaite. She typed Hedges and Braithwaite and got a reference to Hemmings.

She typed Hemmings and got the file with deceased marked on it, and a pointer back to Braithwaite for access to Hemmings' files, with permission from the DG. She had shown Hedges how to get the Hemmings case files off the system only a few days ago. That was all right then, and that would explain the discussion with Braithwaite. After that meeting though, Hedges had also asked for Sally Carver's file. Sally Carver had been one of her predecessors. Sally Carver. What had she just read? Where was it? She retraced her steps. There, it was… Jessica Carver on the read receipt; coincidental name? Possible, Carver was not an uncommon name. "Slowly now," she told herself, "don't jump to conclusions." She typed in Jessica Carver and got her contact details in Vauxhall. Sally's name had been in the press and that was why Special Branch,

Hooper and someone else were coming in, rechecking in relation to the Wallace girl. She was on the staff. She tried to remember. That rang a bell now as well. She pulled up the Jenny Wallace file, and looked at the access log. Hedges' name was in the list a few weeks before Wallace went missing. Michelle had no access to Jenny's file details, but Hedges would have, at his Security level. She could see the personal details, but nothing on what work she was doing. She did not need to know those details. Why would Hedges have looked at her file? She was a different area as well.

She checked Sally Carver's name in the database. She got her personal record. When had she disappeared? She scrolled though the data. She had gone to Greece, according to the report in the paper, hints of a Lesbian affair, the press liked that angle. Michelle could see her vetting reports and that sexuality was not even implied in there. There would be no reason these days for Sally to hide such a preference. No mention of contact reports of a new friend. Hang on... That was not right. The copy of the police report in the file stated, that Sally had gone on holiday to Greece a few weeks before she had disappeared there. That could not be right. She had all her leave remaining according to the Human Resource record, and no mention of a holiday in Greece, or of a contact report of a new friend. After some fiddling with the computer diary settings, Michele was able to see the time period when Sally was supposedly on holiday. There were meetings, and minutes of meetings which Sally had to have recorded, given Hedges' inability to move a mouse! There was a copy of a brief statement from Hedges given to the Police. Nothing about the contradiction in timings was in the statement. Why had Hedges not reported that? This did not make sense. It was clear that Hedges knew she had not been in Greece, unless she was listed in a mission file that Michelle did not have access to. That could not be true, because who would have acted for Hedges as PA if Sally were operational, which she could not be. There were no references to operational code names in Sally's file at all. No different PA logged in the details for Hedges. Hedges had deliberately, it appeared, not told the police about the contradiction. Why? Michelle was nervous now.

Who could she talk about this with? Her previous PA assignment had been with the deputy of internal vetting who had been seconded from Special Branch. He was now Head of Special Branch, David Jones. She had enjoyed working for him, especially when he had encouraged her to go on the Russian course. They privately had met up a few times, including a dinner party with Mark at the Jones' house. David had looked very pleased for her. They exchanged occasional emails to keep in touch. Could she talk to him about this? Not straight away but how about Braithwaite? But, he may be involved as well. She could not just raise suspicions. Vetting? It was not really their scene. Internal Security who did they report to? The DG of course, but Hedges was not in the chain of command. If she went to them it would be instantly formal, and if she were wrong, Hedges would destroy her career. It was getting late. She could sleep on it, maybe that was the best thing to do. She began to pack up for the evening, still undecided, when the phone went. It was an external secure line, but outside the building. She answered with her name and department MI number.

"Miss Carrington, my name is Tony Grayson. I am calling in regard to you accessing a file on one of my staff. I wanted to know why you were looking it up?"

Michelle, was on her guard. What could she say? Who was on his staff? That could only be Jessica Carver. That was the connection with him and the file she had looked up. "I was checking something," she noncommittally answered.

"What exactly, Miss Carrington? Is that on behalf of your superior?" He probed.

"No, not for him," she replied un-guardedly, regretting her statement as soon as she said it. "I was trying to check if she was related to one of my predecessors, that's all."

"I appreciate that Miss Carrington, especially given the press speculation, but why are you checking Jessica Carver's name specifically?"

"Is she related?" she probed. She noticed the hesitation before he replied, and the change in tone.

"They are sisters," he confirmed. She could find that out from the papers if she spoke to the press. Urgently, he followed up, "Does your superior, Mr. Hedges, know that?"

"No, and I have no intention of telling him," she followed up. She made a rapid decision, "Look, could we meet up. I think there is more we should discuss."

"Like what, Miss Carrington?"

"That's just it. I am not sure, but if I said, Plato, missing girls, Hemmings and Special Branch would that be enough?"

Grayson was cautious but very interested. "Have you spoken to anyone else about this, Miss Carrington?"

"Why?" She was now nervous. Had she just made a mistake? Perhaps this man, Grayson was part of it, whatever it was?

"Miss Carrington, is there anyone you trust you could tell on your side of the river?"

That was a more reassuring answer, "There is someone at Special Branch, I know."

"Who is that, if I may ask?"

"David Jones, the Commander, I used to be his PA when he was here."

"That would be a good person to talk to," said Grayson, relieved. "Perhaps you could get him to join us for a meeting as soon as you can?"

They agreed to meet that evening. She used her personal mobile to call David Jones. She got through to his PA, and after some pleading, he interrupted his meeting with one of his senior investigators, DI Hooper. Jones took the call with Hooper still in the office. He was about to update him on progress.

"Slow down, Michelle," he said. "Sally Carver and Jessica Carver, you say. Okay, when are you meeting this Grayson? Yes, I'll be there. I'll bring someone with me. Michelle..."

"Yes?"

"Does your boss know any of this?"

"No, and he has already gone from the office, I'm on my own, David?" She almost broke down.

"Okay, Michelle, try and stay calm. I want you to stay at the office until one of my team gets there. Detective Inspector Hooper will meet you in reception in thirty minutes."

Jones turned to Hooper. He was staring incredulously at his boss. "I think you may have your break. I want you to go and pick up Michelle Carrington from reception at Thames House, keep her under wraps until this meeting with Grayson this evening at the Hilton in Park Lane. I'll meet you there. Before you ask, she was my PA at Five, when I had my secondment there. We have stayed as friends." He saw his expression. "You're too suspicious, Jack, really, friends. I'm hoping I'll get to go to her wedding, if her boyfriend ever gets round to proposing. Now get over there."

"Grayson," Jones mused, he did not know him. Time for liaison with Five though. He knew and trusted Braithwaite. Hooper would call him. Braithwaite would want to come along as well. Michelle was going to be surrounded. He definitely needed to be there to reassure her.

Braithwaite called Claridge-Briggs. He had already been told by Grayson. Claridge-Briggs was already across the river at the Foreign Office, so he said he would meet him there. Grayson called the hotel and booked a small conference room, as instructed by Briggs. It was going to be an interesting evening. Grayson went to see Jessica, but she had already gone for the evening.

***

Hooper was pacing in the reception area when he saw a tall slim brunette exit the internal security barrier. The receptionist pointed her in Hooper's direction. The girl was clearly very nervous. Not surprising given the sudden turn of events. He introduced himself, showing his ID Card.

"One moment, Detective Inspector," she said. She took out her phone. "Hi darling," she said, "hopefully nothing, but I wanted to let you know that I am with a Detective Inspector Hooper from Special Branch this evening, going to the Hilton Hotel on Park Lane for a meeting with a Tony Grayson. No, I can't tell you more. No, don't be worried, I'm sure it will all be fine. I'll call you at eight. Yes, I love you too." She hung up and turned to the Inspector.

"I appreciate your concern, Miss Carrington."

"Please call me Michelle."

"Michelle," he gave his best reassuring smile, "I'm sure there is no need to be concerned."

"So why did David send a Detective Inspector here at a moment's notice?"

"Good point, Michelle, let's get a cab to the meeting and we can discuss it on the way there, okay?"

They left the foyer, grabbed a cab fifty yards away, but said nothing as the cabbie complained about the traffic, the cricket, and the government, before dropping them at the reception to the Hilton. The doorman let them out. Hooper paid the fare, grabbing a receipt, and they went in. Sitting in the lobby was Claridge-Briggs, with whom, he presumed, was Tony Grayson. They stood. They were just being introduced when Braithwaite walked in. Michelle shrank back despite Braithwaite's smile, and she was turning to leave when David Jones arrived. She went straight to him, and he gave her a hug before turning back to the team.

"I have a room booked," said Claridge-Briggs. "Why don't we adjourn there, away from prying eyes?"

They went to the conference area and found the room. David Jones held back with Michelle, quietly reassuring her, especially about the attendance of Braithwaite. Once they were all in the room, and the hotel staff had stopped putting out tea, coffee, and water, and had left the room, Claridge-Briggs started.

"I think a round of introductions, and roles is necessary. Without holding back this time." He nodded at Hooper. He smiled and nodded back. After everyone had said who and what, Claridge-Briggs turned to Michelle with the same smile he used with Jessica. "Miss Carrington, Michelle, I think you may have caused this meeting by flagging a file today. In the interests of all here, that file was for Jessica Carver, a precaution I put in place with Tony here," he nodded in Grayson's direction, "after our last meeting. Mr Braithwaite and I have been comparing notes in the background, Detective Inspector, sharing what we can along the way. Good to see you again, David. I hadn't realised you had a connection back to Thames House. Perhaps we should hand over to Michelle to tell us what she has found." He inclined his head towards her. She looked bewildered.

"Start from the start, Michelle," said David Jones.

Michelle explained what she had uncovered.

"Hedges," said David Jones.

"Yes," said Hooper, Grayson and Braithwaite together. Claridge-Briggs laced his hands behind his back and looked at the men before turning his eye to Michelle. He placed his hands back on the small conference table and gave her his best smile.

"Michelle, can you take us through today's activity again please, and please comment on Mr. Hedges demeanour during this process."

"Yes, but I need to phone my boyfriend, I promised I would call him by eight it's now five past."

"I'll have a word with Mark as well if you would like," said David Jones.

She popped out of the room with Jones to make the call.

"Clever girl," said Briggs, "we seem to have several of them and I don't want to lose anymore. Whilst she is out of the room, any progress Jack?"

It was Jack now, thought Hooper before he replied. "Hemmings looks like another victim, the mugging was a good cover, but the forensics don't add up." He had just finished the explanation of blood and moved bodies when the others returned into the room.

Michelle still looked upset. David Jones shook his head at Hooper and mouthed "later" at him.

Michelle took her seat and commenced her story. "It started a while back, but this morning, Mr. Hedges was in before me, which is not normal. He was pacing and then swearing at his computer terminal. I don't think he realised I was there straight away, I've never heard him swear before. I asked him what was wrong, and he said he needed to get a file scanned. I offered to do it for him, but he said I wasn't cleared for it. I said that he could only scan up to Secret UK Eyes A onto the main system, and asked him what classification the file was. He said he would need to upload the file to an external site. He has done that before, and I have to get IT Security permission to open the firewall for him. They always need written authorisation that the file is not classified and so on. He said that no one was to see the file, so I explained how to scan-in into the secure share and retrieve with a secure passcode and then upload. He then needed IT to explain to him how they could not see the file and how he can delete it afterwards. I am sure they were concerned as well, but I thought Mr. Hedges would move the electronic file to his secure area, once scanned. Mr Hedges is very senior, so we all just tried to help. Eventually, about ten o'clock, he got the file scanned, and then I think he uploaded it, as he had a call from IT around that time."

She continued, "Then I had a call from the mail room to say they had a couriered file from the US Embassy marked for Mr. Hedges eyes only. I collected the file in an envelope and took it up to him. He virtually snatched it from my hands. When I asked him if I should log it in he said, no, that he would deal with it. It's been a long time since we had a hard copy file come in, and the procedure should be to scan it onto the system. I forgot to say that every half hour or so he would ring an external number. I don't know what the number is, I'm sorry. He then made a big thing of talking to the US Embassy, Carl Schlemburg, about the file. He made sure I could hear what he said. He spoke about a mission. It was urgent, he said, and no contact yet, and that the file seemed to be missing something, or something like that. Then there was a reference to being closer than expected. He cleared his files away into his office safe, and I reminded him of a meeting with the DG. When he came back, he went straight into his office. Then, he announced he was leaving for a personal appointment, which wasn't in his diary. I went into his office to clear his coffee cups and that's when I saw the notes on the desk."

"Was he still agitated when he left?" Briggs asked.

"Yes, very, and no 'good evening' or anything when he left. He is normally very polite."

"And then you started your search?" Braithwaite asked this

time.

"Yes, and look where that has got me."

"That's okay, Michelle," said Hooper. "If the Commander agrees, I think you should stay here tonight, out of sight and call in sick tomorrow, whilst we try to figure a plan out. He does not suspect you as far as you know?"

"I don't think so, but he knows I'm suspicious over the last couple of weeks. Is that what happened to Sally Carver?"

"We don't know, Michelle," said Jones, "and it's not worth speculating. I agree with Jack, let's get you settled with some room service for food. You can call Mark again, and we'll continue this amongst ourselves. If you think of anything else, give me a call, you have my number. For the rest of us, I suggest a short break and then we should order in some food."

They reconvened twenty minutes later, as the hotel staff had delivered some hot buffet food and some wine. "My treat," explained Claridge-Briggs before continuing, "as I have already said, Jessica Carver is one of my staff, working directly for Tony here, she is on the Plato team, John." He nodded to Braithwaite. "Plato is something to do with Iraq," he explained for the benefit of the others. "Jessica and her brother never believed Sally went off travelling. She also discovered that Sally was involved, as she came across her handwriting on a report from Hedges. I can now confirm that we have a Canadian angle as well, and the name of the French agent you have been looking for is Sylvia Cardôtte. She was investigating Iraqi nuclear ambitions when she disappeared."

"I have another name for you from across the Pond," said Braithwaite. He also gave an account of his meeting with Reach Claremont.

"What's his game?" Briggs asked. "I thought he was number two to Schlemburg?"

"He is," said Braithwaite, "but he was digging as well, trying to get some information on the connections. I gave him the Hemmings name. I got the feeling, I don't know, but I got the feeling he already knew what I told him about the investigation, apart from Hemmings. He claimed the meeting was for him to give me some IRA info'. I think he wanted to know what was happening in the investigation."

"I'm just going to give someone a call," said Claridge-Briggs. "Grayson, why don't you fill our colleagues in on where Plato is going. You have my authority to brief our friends in Special Branch." He left the room.

Whilst he was out, Grayson reluctantly outlined the investigation. When he had finished, Hooper said. "So we have a Six investigation into a Six debacle that cost countless lives and now a Six investigation into how the policy came about. What about Hutton?" Lord Hutton had carried out a very limited inquiry into how a dossier had been produced, which was used as evidence to justify going to war with Iraq. "Now, we have a series of potential murders that may be covering up that position, or helping it get created in the first place." Hooper was angry, as Briggs returned.

"I appreciate your anger," said Grayson "but not all of us in Vauxhall held that view on Iraq. Some of us have been trying to uncover what happened, hence, Plato."

Briggs who had been gone for over thirty minutes, continued, "I concur with Tony, there are a lot of people in high places who want Iraq buried, especially their role in it. Hedges is one of several. He wrote a very embarrassing paper on Iraqi activity in the UK trying to get hold of WMD information; all supposition, and no facts. That was not shared with Hutton because it was from Five who, of course, had nothing to do with that damned dossier."

Hooper calmed down, "All right, I apologise for implying you were all responsible, but what now?"

"I have just spoken with the American Ambassador," he casually dropped into the conversation. "He had just had a call from the former Station Chief who raised several issues with him. Claremont is working for the Ambassador directly now. The Ambassador is concerned that Schlemburg is up to something off of the official radar. Claremont has also told the Ambassador that they had obtained the case file on the missing girls. The

Ambassador did not ask how, probably best not to."

Jones and Hooper looked stunned. Jones said, "Could that be the file that went to Hedges?"

"Probably, but Claremont told the Ambassador that they felt some things were missing, like Hemmings' name for example." Briggs explained. "Claremont also told him that Schlemburg was not sharing everything, and that he had a meeting with Hedges on Tuesday evening. Schlemburg's driver confirmed that he called in on Hedges."

David Jones said, glancing at his watch, "It's getting late, we need to take some action to protect Michelle, and I think we should also protect Jessica Carver. I'll need to arrange some extra support. Jack, get a couple of the team watching Michelle for tonight, and send two more to Jessica Carver's house, discretely overtime authorised. We then need a plan for Hedges, and or, Schlemburg. Can we rely on the Ambassador's man to watch his boss?" He thought how ridiculous that sounded.

"I have the Ambassador's assurance, but if it impacts on American interests, that won't count for much. They won't want anything public connecting them to those missing girls."

"Jessica Carver may not be at her home. She has a new boyfriend who she is probably with," said Grayson. "I don't have his address, but he has checked out okay on vetting."

"She is probably safe there then. We'll provide cover for her from tomorrow morning when she is in work."

"Jon," said Briggs to Braithwaite, "what about internal security? Can you go to them, we could do with some hard facts about file transfers and so on?"

"Yes, I think they are okay. They tend to keep themselves to themselves, apart from briefing the DG and his Divisional head, but I'd rather come in from that level. They would have to report upwards any requests for IT logs anyway."

Briggs looked around the room before saying, "And the DG, are he and Hedges close?"

Braithwaite was uncomfortable discussing his Service in

front of Special Branch, let alone Claridge-Briggs and Grayson. His unease was accentuated by the level and seniority of those they were discussing. Nevertheless, Braithwaite chose to reply, "They are on friendly terms, but I cannot believe my Director General knows anything about this."

"No, I think he is clear," agreed Claridge-Briggs. "I need to take this to my own leadership as well. They will not be happy, to say the least. Very well," continued Claridge-Briggs, "let's reconvene in Scotland Yard after lunch tomorrow, if that is okay with you, David?"

"Yes, that's fine I'll sort a room out."

CHAPTER THIRTY-SEVEN

Thursday Vauxhall

It was just before nine on a bright September morning when Jess breezed into her Vauxhall office. Mike's Vauxhall apartment was really close as a commute. Tony, as usual, was already there. She had grabbed a coffee on route for him as well.

"Someone is full of the joys of spring in late summer. Your broker, I presume?" he said forcing a smile. Actually, Tony Grayson had been waiting for her to come in. He had checked for her at her house late the previous evening, but only got voicemail and the same on her mobile when he had finally found her number. Now, he did not want to alarm her. Special Branch could and would, protect her.

Jessica did not notice his tone. "Tony, he's so nice. He wants me to go away with him; can I take a week, I have two weeks on my allowance?"

When Jess smiled, Grayson wanted to do anything he could for her. The rest could wait "Well you have bribed me with coffee. When do you want to go, and what about the investigation?"

"Soon, I'll let you know dates. I'll have the interim report on funding connections and potential changes to the dossier ready by close of play this evening. As for the rest of Plato, there's nothing pressing. It's only the Sally stuff, and you told me the Gods above are dealing with it."

"Yes, they are. I saw Briggs yesterday. He was concerned about you, but he is investigating." What could he tell her? "He wants answers as well. Okay, let me know when you want to go, perhaps after this evening, and you can have ten days." Maybe it would be best if she were safely away with her broker boyfriend, out of reach for a while.

She walked up to him and gave him a kiss on the cheek. It was Christmas the last time she had done that; he would treasure that just as long.

"Thank you, you're a star."

"Now get back to work," he playfully threatened.

"Yes Sir, three bags full Sir."

He stirred his coffee; with Jess away maybe he and Claridge-Briggs could make more progress by rattling more cages. He went up to see him. He told him that Jess wanted some time away with her boyfriend, and that he had not told her about the previous evening's events. He had not left messages on the voicemail. Claridge-Briggs also thought it was a good idea to get her away. He asked Grayson to accompany him to an urgent meeting with the Head of the Secret Intelligence Service that he had managed to get that morning. They went up to the office together.

Dame Monica Pennywise had been in post only five months, most of which had been spent dealing with personnel appointments following the restructuring of the Service. She was short, greying, and slightly plump or so she thought of herself. She also knew that her nickname was Moneypenny during her previous tenures in the Service, but she had not heard that since she had returned this time as Head. Claridge-Briggs had known her for years, and for a brief spell more intimately, especially when she had been in the field, until her cover had been blown in East Germany. She had turned to analysis and then spells outside the Service before returning to steady the ship. She had been intrigued by George Claridge-Briggs' meeting request, as they had a scheduled get-together planned for Friday with a Plato update. They were both due to be guests that weekend at a social gathering with a mutual acquaintance in the Treasury. She had asked her PA to move some meetings around to clear a thirty-minute slot.

Claridge-Briggs arrived with Tony Grayson in tow. What

could this be? "George, Tony, what brings you to my door so urgently?" Her PA, Richard Templeman, was about to leave them, having shown them in, with checks for tea or coffee all declined, when Claridge-Briggs requested he stay to take a formal note of the meeting. She motioned them all to sit at the small conference room table, towards the back of her office. "Now I'm even more intrigued George, what is it?"

"Director," Claridge-Briggs had begun, this was much more formal than their normal discussions, and this raised her concern level even further, "I need to update you on some side issues from Plato that have become critical." He went on to outline the situation, which with questions, meant her PA had to rearrange her morning, cancelling two further meetings. By the time he had completely briefed her, and she had gone back over some elements, it was nearly lunchtime and her morning was blown. More importantly, she was very concerned.

"Your girl, Tony," she said turning to Grayson. "How concerned are you for her safety?" Grayson told her of the Special Branch plan for protective surveillance and Jessica Carver's plan for a holiday. "Are Jessica and Sally Carver, Mike Carver's children?" she asked.

"Yes," said Briggs, "at the moment we do not believe that Hedges knows that Jessica is one of ours. The Special Branch file only shows her as a sibling of Sally, along with their younger brother."

"I remember them as children," said Monica. "Mike was a good man, my controller for a few years." She reminisced for a few seconds, before turning to the rest of the team. "You were absolutely right to bring this to me, George. I don't know what Hedges is up to, or has been up to, and anything formal on him will have to go through Thames House internal. If Braithwaite is briefing Shoreditch today, I may give him a call after I brief the Cabinet Secretary." Shoreditch was the divisional head in Five, responsible for internal security. "This could get very messy. I presume that this is just us four, this side of the river?"

"So far we have us, Braithwaite, Michelle Carrington, and the Special Branch senior team, and not all of them have the complete picture. Jack Hooper does not pass on everything to his senior team, let alone the regular police who are supporting him. So we have this fairly tight. The Americans know some of it, plus they have the Special Branch main file, but Hooper has already kept most of the story out of that. They may know more than they are saying of course, and Schlemburg is not to be trusted, judging by what the Ambassador said."

"Will Special Branch want to make arrests?"

"I would expect them to. The Detective Inspector running the case, Jack Hooper, will be on the look-out for cover ups. David Jones is a more political animal, but he will not let this go under the carpet either. There is also the danger of the Americans, or someone else, leaking it if they thought it was in their own interests. Elliot Bloomstein the Ambassador, will only go so far, but I think that will be limited to avoiding getting in the quagmire with us. Will you talk to Clarkson?" Clarkson was the current head of the Security Service, Monica Pennywise's counterpart across the river, and Hedges' direct superior.

"I want to talk to the perm' sec' first and Shoreditch, then I'll decide. Richard, please set up the calls as soon as possible. You'll have to clear out my diary as well. That will upset HR and finance, no doubt. I have the PM this evening for my routine chat. Can you both update me at 17:30?" She got nods from Briggs and Grayson. "If you need some more resources, use our internal affairs as well, you have my authority to brief them on the risk issues but keep them out of Plato for now. Only what they need. Richard, send a mail to Hargreaves please. I'll think about what we could tell our French and Canadian colleagues as well, but for the time being let's not ask. Make sure Special Branch don't either. If they leak it, then we'll have no hope of controlling the situation. The French, in particular, would love to drag us through the mire on Iraq again. For Jessica, she can go on leave from this evening. If necessary, we can safe house her, although that would alarm her. On further thought, let's not. We don't want to raise a flag over the river. We would have to use one of their houses, if we stayed in London. Is she going abroad with this boyfriend?"

"I think so," replied Grayson. "He is a bit of a globe trotter.

She mentioned something about the Caribbean."

"Nice and safe, away from it all. What about her brother, what does he do?"

"He's in software sales, so not on the inside. I can't see that he is a threat to Hedges, or at risk, but we can leave Special Branch and their team to watch him once Jessica is safely away. As long as Hedges does not know Jessica is with us, then her risk is lower. Hedges' PA is more concerning."

"All right, make sure we have contact details for both Michael Carver, and especially Jessica when she travels with this boyfriend. As for Hedges' PA, I think Special Branch and Jonathan Braithwaite should have that covered. Please check with them if they need our assistance. Have I missed anything?"

"One more, Director, and this is not for the record." He looked at Richard who glanced up from his notes. "Braithwaite was having an unreported long term affair with Jenny Wallace. Braithwaite told me, but Special Branch does not know, and I agreed with Jon we would try to keep it that way."

"I understand. That explains him raising the alert when she went missing. Anything else we should do?" She received shakes of the heads from Grayson and Briggs. "And George…"

"Yes, Director."

"Thank you for giving me something operational to do, I miss that buzz. I'll see you back here at five thirty."

CHAPTER THIRTY-EIGHT

Thursday Thames House

Hedges was just as agitated as the previous day, as he arrived at Thames House. Reception told him that Michelle Carrington had called in sick and therefore had not unlocked his office, so he had to sign for his keys. "Good," he thought, "I won't have to deal with her today; I can concentrate on the matter at hand." Hedges had compared the photocopied picture of Slater from the Special Branch file to the Graham Ashley photo at home. There were similarities. He would rate it at only sixty percent probability if it were not for the coincidence, which raised it to near certainty. Slater was Ashley. I need to close that off. He had re-read Ashley's file, then destroyed the notes on the introduction to the stockbroker and the photo. Afterwards, he realised that the photo had come from the army and would therefore still be in the MoD personnel files, if someone got that close.

If Special Branch got the name from the stockbroker in Portugal, they would eventually get the Ashley name. He could not do anything about that except warn Slater, if he could contact him. He had checked the voicemail contact for the mission five times, including twice that morning. He had to make contact. He recorded a revised message from his outside line, with a request to leave a contact number, and he mentioned the name Ashley as a code word on the voicemail. Reluctantly, he had requested IT to show him how to add a third option to the first menu on the voicemail. The voicemail now stated:

"Press *one* to accept, *two* to reject, or *three* for Ashley message," in his clipped tones. Option one would then play back the Username and password. Option two, would delete them. Option three, provided his mobile number as a contact.

Hedges then tried to concentrate on his normal work whilst checking the voicemail every thirty minutes or so. Mid-morning, he had a call via the central telephone exchange, due to Michelle's absence, from Carl Schlemburg. After going to secure, Schlemburg asked him, if the mission was accepted yet. Hedges had to tell him, "No." Schlemburg was now agitated.

"Why not, surely you have made contact?"

"That's not how it works," explained Hedges. He decided to explain the contact method.

"Unorthodox, but I see how that could keep distance from the asset," said Schlemburg. "So you don't know who this guy actually is then?"

"No," Hedges lied. "It was set up that way right from the start. The only person who did know was my former deputy, and he's gone."

"Well, you better hope he gets on this mission soon, for all our sakes," threatened Schlemburg. "Our mutual friends need action."

Hedges was even further on edge. How much did Schlemburg really know? "What's that supposed to mean? The method of working has been going on for years. Just because you have an urgent need does not mean I should threaten the future of the entire operation."

"Let me make it clear then," continued Schlemburg. "If this mission does not happen in the timeline needed, then other action will follow. Get on with it, Hedges, or face the consequences." Schlemburg hung up.

Hedges was furious and was about to respond when he realised the line was dead. "Fuck the Americans," he said out loud. "How dare they?" he thought. "This was my operation, and very successful it has been for everyone so far. Where was Ashley?" He used his outside line to check the voicemail again.

John Braithwaite and the Head of IT for the Security Service, or CIO, Chief Information Officer, Colin McDowell, sat in the bowels of Thames House, and put down their respective headphones, along with Ian Shoreditch. McDowell decided it was a good time to get a coffee for his guests. He went and encouraged two more technicians to go and check some logs further away from Braithwaite and Shoreditch.

"Is that enough?" Braithwaite asked.

"Nearly," said Shoreditch, "once we have the logs of the file uploads. I'll be having a word with the IT team once this is over. Unauthorised file uploads and firewall openings. I know our new CIO has only been in post a couple of weeks," he glanced toward him at the far end of the IT room, "so he'll be clean, but his Head of IT Security is already in an interview room explaining himself, and justifying why this was not reported."

"I'm not worried about him; it's Hedges I want."

"It's not as clear cut for him. He didn't fail to report the unauthorised access. In fact, he asked IT for help; they actually helped set up the method in the first place; however, the phone call from the US Embassy is not good. No operations or missions are logged on the system for Hedges since his IRA responsibility days, and he had no assets logged. He's in policy after all, not active field."

They had been through that overnight and this morning, before ensuring all the necessary people were in place before Hedges arrived at Thames House that morning. They were also now monitoring Hedges home phone, and a bug team would be in his house as they sat and listened. Braithwaite was ignoring calls from the DG, which had started as soon as Shoreditch had told the DG he had an issue to deal with and mentioned Braithwaite. Braithwaite did not want to brief the DG until he had solid facts. What they had so far was at least ten unofficial file uploads and a lot of phone calls to a voicemail number. They had listened to the message as well and were listening into the number, waiting to see who else called. They listened again after Hedges had asked the IT Technician they had been sitting next to, to set up an Option Three on the Voicemail message, requesting a contact. The voicemail gave them an username and password but no URL. The file upload went to a File Transfer Protocol, FTP, site, but they did not have the file, and they could not download it back, as the system was upload only. Which web site in the whole of the Internet accessed the FTP site would take time, and if it was an overseas web site, getting that information would be virtually impossible. The voicemail system had a setup configuration, so they could see how many options there were, but only by listening to the options could they hear content. If they pressed the wrong option or interfered with the system they were concerned they would lose the data. Hedges had deleted the file after he had uploaded it. They were waiting for an engineer from the phone system to make contact, but he would not be cleared for any of the data. They were trying disk recovery systems with the IT team, but a safe delete was designed to be exactly that. They had then searched the database for an Ashley code word mission. There was nothing on the main system. They had to get McDowell to authorise a search in some other areas and systems, which again had drawn a blank.

Braithwaite had tried to call Claridge-Briggs with an update, but was told he was incommunicado; after digging and explaining the urgency of the matter, he was referred to a PA in the Director's Office, where he managed to find out Briggs was with the Director. After backtracking with the PA, asking for Grayson this time, he ended up in the same spot. So Vauxhall were briefing senior management, as they said they would. He then called Hooper, informing him that they may wish to make an arrest at some stage, but they wanted Hedges to run for a bit to see whether they could find out about this mission, and who the asset was. Braithwaite told them he would update them that afternoon when they met up. Hooper offered some surveillance assets if needed, but Braithwaite said that would not be needed now Shoreditch was on the case.

Braithwaite had not told Shoreditch everything, but he definitely wanted to come to the afternoon session, when he would learn everything. He also checked with Hooper on how Michelle Carrington was, to find out that her boyfriend had flown in overnight and they were both in the Hilton hotel room. One of Hooper's team was trying to persuade her boyfriend not to drag in MoD Security and the Defence Intelligence Agency, especially when Jodi Parker's name had been mentioned. Braithwaite agreed that should not happen, but her boyfriend would have to be placated. Hooper said that David Jones was on his way over. There were a lot of meetings being cancelled at the moment, Braithwaite thought.

CHAPTER THIRTY-NINE

Thursday Slater

After Jess had left, Michael Johnson moved into action. He assessed what he wanted to do. First the IT Contact. He needed to get to him and take him out, along with his lead to him. Then set up some travel as Michael, for himself and Jess; could she go with him tomorrow or tonight even, if he could get flights? He needed to call her. He would shut up the apartment for a while. He could always come back into the country as someone else; it was only the doorman, the security office, and the cleaner who knew him as Michael Johnson. Although the original name on the apartment was John Slater, it was actually owned by one of his offshore companies. He had visited a show-house apartment as Slater and put his name down to purchase the apartment, but that was in a different block. The main house Slater used was clear as well, owned by a different company. Slater declared the beneficial income on his tax return. The two *safe* flats he had were both in different names, purchased through different corporations, and leased.

The car Slater used was again owned by a different company, but the Special Branch detectives had tailed him in that car, so it could not be used. Easy steps first. He called Jess, and she agreed to ask if she could go that evening, but what if she could not go? Would that waste the tickets? He told her not to worry he would ensure flexible tickets. He then booked tickets for that evening, or the following day on hold waiting for final confirmation. His travel company was used to flexible account booking for a variety of different people. They suggested, given the uncertainty of his arrangements, using their special executive jet arrangements. He had done that once before. It was expensive, but very flexible. He booked them into the Regent Palms from the following day, then cancelled the flights and put the jet on standby. Eight and a half hours of indulgence that would save any airport watchers and Jess was worth it. He smiled.

Now for the contacts; the address for the organised crime intermediary contact, Frank Coalfield was, unbelievably, in the phone book; so much for security measures. Frank lived in South London and whilst travelling to Chiswick by train, he considered the urgent voicemail. He had already decided to decline. He had done enough. He would call the number after he had seen Frank Coalfield. The Chiswick address was on a quiet side street. He got off the train at Chiswick station. The house was a five-minute walk away. He had collected his bag from one of the safe flats. He was already disguised. The Gloch was in an inside pocket, protected from the disappointing weather by a reversible dark blue jacket. He walked past the house twice, seeing no sign of life except a downstairs light. He decided to take the direct route; he rang the bell. A pretty woman of perhaps twenty-five answered the door.

"I'm sorry to disturb you, but is Frank in?" he asked pleasantly.

"Yes, probably," she replied with a sulk. "I think he's in the library down there on the right." She turned and walked up the elegant stairs, with barely a glance over her shoulder. The target's daughter or maybe a maid? She was wearing a wedding ring, so, a young wife he guessed. She would have to wait, or he would have to use a separate dose.

Slater closed the front door quietly behind him. He quickly moved down the corridor. As he got to the door, she had indicated. It started to open. He pressed himself against the hall wall. A man came out of the door. He sank the injection into his neck before he had time to react and pivoted into the room with his gun drawn. The room was empty. He quickly checked his victim. Getting his wallet from his jacket pocket, he found a driving license in the name of Frank Coalfield. He reached into his own coat and retrieved some nylon rope. He tied up Frank in a sitting position and then tied him to the heavy oak desk in the centre of the room;

now the girl. He walked out of the room quickly and checked the other downstairs rooms. They were empty. He locked the rear door onto the private garden. He could hear faint music coming from an upstairs room.

He went up the stairs; he checked each room on the landing. The music was coming from an end room, the door to which was partly open. He approached the door; he could just make out the girl in her underwear sitting at a dressing table mirror applying makeup. He was through the door and had injected her neck before she had time to turn her head. He held her up as she passed into unconsciousness. He carried her downstairs and into the study, where he tied her next to Frank. He now needed them to come round. He had used only half the normal dose. He got some plastic bin liners from the kitchen and manoeuvred them under their bodies.

The girl was wearing a matching floral bra and pantie set which he removed. She had good body, but there was no time to admire it as it was nearly midday. He struggled to strip Frank, but eventually they were both naked. The library window overlooked the garden so there was plenty of light. He searched the downstairs and found a wall safe which was open. The safe contained £10,000 in cash, a bag of Cocaine and the passports. The passport photographs, confirmed Mr and Mrs Coalfield lay tied naked to the desk. He found Frank's mobile on the desk and scanned through the contacts, but what name was he looking for? There was a groan from the desk floor. He was running out of time. He went back to the kitchen and collected a bowl of water and threw it at the faces of his captives. Frank stirred and glanced around. Slater pulled up a chair and sat looking at him. Frank focused.

"Who the fuck are you and what are you doing in my house?"

"Don't waste your breath, Frank," answered Slater. The girl was stirring. He quickly gagged her before she screamed. The girl's eyes got wider as she looked at her predicament. Her face reddened as she realised her nudity, then Frank's.

"What do you want?" Frank said. "I have money, just leave us be."

"Information, Frank, and your complete co-operation. Who is the contact who provides the police information?"

Frank almost smiled, "Is that all, well he is popular. I would have told you without all this hassle."

"Just get on with it, Frank." Frank told him. He then asked him who else had asked. That took longer and involved a couple of snicks with the knife before he revealed it was the CIA. Slater wanted to ask more and, once upon a time, would have enjoyed a few minutes with the girl, but he did not have time.

He reached inside his jacket and pulled out the case holding his syringes. Before Frank could say anything, he injected half the dose into his chest. He hoped it would be enough. He injected the other half into the girl. He waited, as their breathing slowed, and then stopped. Now for cover. He left the girl tied but, after untying Frank, used his hand on the knife to stick it into her chest. Some minor bleeding which he extended to two other knife wounds. It was getting messy in the room. He partially redressed Frank, then sat him in the chair opposite the girl. He took the cocaine from the safe and opened it near Frank, placing some in his nostrils and on his fingers. He then put the cocaine packet in Frank's pocket. It was the best he could do. A post-mortem would uncover the truth once they were found.

He checked the room and the house for CCTV. He found the system and deleted the last three days' worth of recording, implying the system was not working. He then broke the main video feed to the recorder by breaking the cable at the F-type plug. It was not one of the systems with offsite recording. He rechecked everything. He carefully left the house, checking the street was clear before he went. He heard the phone ringing in the study before he left. Now for Hillier, Scotland Yard IT; what an excellent contact, but one that would have to go. Now to get to him. It would have to be that evening. He had told Jess it would be eight before he picked her up. The timings were getting difficult if they left that evening and that was if she could get away. Okay, plane tomorrow morning. If they used the jet they could go at any time, provided he could get a crew in flying hours, but would that look suspicious on top of extravagant. He needed confirmation that she could go. He would get an updated Special Branch file as part of the routine he had established with Hillier, but that would not help him. He had Hillier's name, place of work, and a contact number, but he did not know what he looked like. He needed his home address.

CHAPTER FORTY

Thursday SFO raid

Gary Parkinson was the Detective Sergeant in the Serious Fraud Office, SFO, assigned to serve the warrant on Slater's home. Rutledge joined him at the morning briefing, where his presence was deliberately ignored in the team's planning. Rutledge was joined by PC Liam Jones from the Met's support team to the missing girls' inquiry. The SFO was supported by a small team of uniformed staff from the Met. They descended on Slater's house at 6:30 a.m. No one responded to the doorbell, as expected, and the Met support team forced entry. The alarm did not go off, which was a surprise, until they searched the house. The SFO bagged the desktop computer for forensic analysis back at base. Wandering around the house officially this time, Rutledge had the sense that the bird had flown. There were some clothes in one of the bedroom wardrobes, but not many. The fridge was empty, apart from some sauce bottles. The freezer had some meals-for-one, but neither the fridge nor freezer had fruit, vegetables, milk or bread. On the second pass, one of the Met. team found a hidden cupboard behind a wardrobe in the second bedroom. It was empty except for four video feed lines that clearly had gone to a second CCTV system, now missing.

Rutledge had discreetly removed the bug from Slater's study as soon as he had got in the building, to avoid any more difficult questions from the SFO. The safe was found in the cupboard under the stairs. It was a good one and would take some serious work to get into, until PC Jones suggested a 0000 PIN code as a test. The safe opened with nothing inside. Rutledge returned to the study and checked the landline voicemail. There were three messages. One from Drinkwater requesting a call, one from a cleaning company asking when it would be convenient to call in, and one from the solicitor, Ms O'Butu, requesting a call back. The answer machine model would allow remote access with a PIN code that was set up. There was no way of knowing whether Slater had collected his messages. Slater's "I'm sorry I'm not here, please leave a message" recording included no name to identify the recipient.

There was a commotion at the front door. A cleaning company was trying to get in, claiming a booking from Slater. Well, that message had got through. One of the PCs was dispatched to collect a statement, for what use it would do. There was nothing personal in the study or the house. Rutledge could not recall seeing any before, in either of his visits. This was a waste of time. The only hope might be the computer.

"Not much hope," said Parkinson adding to Rutledge's depression. "He has smart card based security, 128Bit probably, with a pass phrase code access. Given the state of the house, I would bet that it's wiped clean anyway. Chances are virtually zero that we'll get anything out of it. We are making progress with some Internet banking tracks, but I wouldn't hold your breath. He may be moving money around, but tying a particular transaction to insider trading will be a long process, and frankly we have bigger fish to fry. He has enough failed stock tips as well to suggest legitimate trading, and punts on high risk stocks. Any decent lawyer will tear a case like that apart, which reminds me, I better call his lawyer to inform her of our warrant before she finds out from Slater. I presume he is still out of the country"

"Is he money laundering or something?" Rutledge asked, already guessing he would be disappointed.

"Very probably, just as he is probably insider dealing, but knowing, and proving are very different things. I wouldn't like to try with the CPS on what we have, or are likely to get."

"Thanks anyway," said Rutledge, feeling disappointed.

"One word of advice though," Parkinson continued, "my experience of chasing these guys is that they have lots of accounts and lots of companies through which these funds are traded and hidden. The companies are nearly all registered in fun places, from the Channel Islands to the Caymans with Panama, Switzerland, and Luxembourg adding to the mix. This house is owned by one company, which is owned by another. Slater has beneficial use, in tax terms, of the house via another trading company, which probably owns shares in the others. This is tax avoidance, but it's not illegal. He has stayed under the radar, but is probably worth millions. My bet would be that he has several identities as well, which will be hidden in the ownership of these companies."

"But won't those identities all be illegal?"

"Not necessarily, you would need to speak to the new identity team doing IT fraud for details. Some tax havens will happily grant a passport and residential status to someone who deposits money in an account. No questions asked. Add illegal identities and this guy could have dozens of legitimate and illegitimate identities, all of which will check out without a serious look."

Rutledge thanked the team and left with PC Jones to go back to base, calling Hooper on the way with the bad or at best no news. As far as any of them were aware, Slater was not in the country, not using that identity anyway. Hooper concurred with Rutledge's analysis and the advice from the SFO detective. Slater was out of the country, or using a different identity. That's if he was in the country. The CPS was calling Hooper about his Procurement guy, probably another SFO case in the end, but they needed to bring him in. Rutledge's call had come just as he was going to arrest and charge Charles Goodson, a senior procurement officer in the Ministry of Defence. He could do without the extra activity after the previous evening, and he wanted to be back on the case as soon as possible. David Jones had understood and asked that he processed Goodson as soon as possible, including the risk of bail-jumping if they arrested, charged, and bailed. Hooper would have to rush everything to get back in time for the afternoon meeting and already half the morning was gone, as he drove towards the Ministry. He had pre-alerted MoD security.

CHAPTER FORTY-ONE

Thursday Portugal

By the time Detective Sergeant Drinkwater and Detective Constable Grahams had gotten through Portuguese customs, and collected their hire car, it was late morning in Portugal. It took them forty minutes to get to Andrew McKinnsley's villa, which was on a gated estate with a golf course on one side and views of the ocean on the other. The stockbroking business had treated McKinnsley well. As they drew up, a uniformed maid opened the imposing front door. She apologised in broken English, saying that Mr McKinnsley was late returning from the hospital, but they could wait on the terrace by the pool. Would they like coffee or tea? Mrs. McKinnsley had prepared a light lunch as well, which would be served when they returned. Drinkwater and Grahams strolled out and admired the stunning view down to the azure blue of the Atlantic in the distance. They chatted about football and cricket whilst they waited for McKinnsley to return.

Drinkwater had set up the protection for Carrington and Carver following a call from Hooper, and really wanted to be back in London, but they needed this information to close off the Slater line of enquiry. The wait was the best part of forty-five minutes, causing a deepening frustration. Eventually, they heard a discussion at the front door and an attractive woman in her sixties walked onto the terrace, holding out her hand.

"Marjorie McKinnsley," She introduced herself in a Home Counties accent. "I'm sorry we weren't at home when you arrived. We were delayed at the hospital. My husband, Andrew, is suffering from Parkinson's and had a bit of a turn this morning. He'll be down shortly. He should have explained his illness on the phone, but he doesn't like telling anyone. Please be prepared, he is frail and easily tires these days. I see Maria has given you coffee. I'll get lunch arranged."

Maria came back and escorted them to the elegant outdoor dining table, shaded from the sun on another part of the terrace. They had just sat down when Mrs. McKinnsley returned, this time with what they presumed was her husband and a stout looking nurse. Mr. McKinnsley had a stand, and a drip connected to his left arm. He attempted a wave and beckoned them back to their seats. Introductions again and then Maria returned with a selection of salads and other dishes for their lunch. "We don't have many visitors these days," Mrs. McKinnsley explained, whilst encouraging them to help themselves to the food. Mr. McKinnsley tried to speak, then stopped. His attempt to pick up a knife and fork failed due to the shaking. His wife gave him a mouthful of food. "Please go ahead and ask, I may have to translate as poor Andrew's speech is suffering today."

Drinkwater put on his most sympathetic voice before explaining, "We would like to ask you about one of your recruits in the late nineties, John Slater, do you remember him?"

"I've got Parkinson's not Alzheimer's," stuttered Andrew McKinnsley.

"Now, Andrew," said Mrs McKinnsley, "don't take it out on these officers who have come all this way, at your insistence I might add."

"Hmph," announced Mr McKinnsley. "Yes, I remember him." He tried to get a drink from a glass of water, but had to let the nurse help him this time. "He was a real star, made us a small fortune. Shame he left when he did, would have easily made partner. He should have stayed, much better than my awful son-in law. He can't spot a good deal when it hits him in the face. Waste of air that one!"

"Andrew, the officers don't need to know about Tom," Marjorie interrupted.

"Yes, well," he continued, "handsome chap, would have made a good catch for Stella, ex-Army you know."

No, they did not know. "Could you tell us how he came to join your company, Mr McKinnsley?" Drinkwater asked.

"Ah that's the secret really; I thought chaps like you would know. He was recommended to us by some of your secret squirrel types in London. They do like their games, those chaps. We had helped out before of course, and happy to do so for Queen and country." Drinkwater and Grahams had both stopped eating. They were hanging onto McKinnsley's every word.

"Don't rush him," thought Drinkwater.

"Yes, all secret stuff. Chap from Thames House popped in had a call from Roger, asking me to meet him, showed me Slater's file, and said how much it would help if we could place him. Showed me his photo and I thought I recognised the chap. Reminded me of a former school friend, but he was called Slater you see, so no connection. Anyway, said we would give him a chance on the floor, and he was excellent. Duck to water really, fluent French I recall, very helpful dealing with the Bourse. Had a First-class honours in Maths from LSE, so we knew he would be good at numbers."

He laughed and then tried to eat some more food. Drinkwater was desperate to press home questions, but he did not want to lose the co-operation and flow of information. Grahams was trying to get better sound for the concealed tape recorder, without being obvious. Who was Roger? Who did he remind him of? He wanted to get a word in. McKinnsley was continuing anyway, "Made an absolute killing on one trade for us, and promptly resigned. Well, we tried to persuade him to stay, but he was arrogant and ambitious like the young are. Hard as nails by the way, we had one of those team building things and he walked through it with barely a sweat. Army training I suppose. Gave his teammates a really hard time when they didn't try hard enough. A bit cold I suppose. Should have pushed Stella on him, much better than that idiot Tom." He trailed off, looking tired.

Drinkwater went for the killer question. "Did he, was he, I

mean did he use a different name?"

"Different name? No, he was John Slater," he paused. The nurse tried to get another mouthful of food into him. He pushed her away, almost causing the drip stand to topple. After things had calmed down, with some fussing from his wife, he seemed to regain energy. "Robert Ashley that was it, looked like him. I told Roger as well. Both gone of course. Told Roger not to get that young wife, you should investigate that. Heart attack my arse, she bumped him off."

"Roger was Andrew's chairman at the time," interrupted Marjorie. "There was nothing suspicious about his death, so stop your slanderous tone, Andrew. I'm sorry detectives," she said, "he can drift off sometimes."

"Anyway what is Slater up to? Has he been doing some dodgy dealing I expect?" McKinnsley continued, with barely a pause for breath.

"We are just doing some background checks," explained Drinkwater. "You said he had army training. Do you know which regiment?"

"No, sorry, always get confused about those things. Didn't join myself, university of course, that's where I met Robert and that lovely wife of his. What was her name? Something French, no can't have been at university, she was French you see. Died. Terrible tragedy, they had a son. Whatever happened to him? Can't recall." He lapsed into silence and his head nodded down.

"There, he's managed to exhaust himself now," said his wife. "I'm afraid he'll sleep for a few hours now."

"Did you know John Slater at all Mrs McKinnsley?" Drinkwater asked, almost in desperation.

"I heard his name, and I think he came to one of our social events, but I could not be sure. Andrew did speak of him, especially when he resigned. Andrew was quite cross, so why he speaks so favourably of him now I have no idea. I'm sorry detectives, but I need to take my husband up to his bed so that he can rest properly. I'm sorry we couldn't be more helpful." She asked Maria to show them out. They shook hands, and they thanked her for her time and hoped her husband would recover, although they all knew there was little chance of that.

"Poor bugger," said Grahams once they were in the car on the way back to the airport. "He's not all there. I'm not sure if he helped at all. I was losing track at one point."

"I know what you mean," replied Drinkwater.

He called Hooper whilst Grahams drove. "We did get confirmation that he was set up by Five, not that it will help much, unless Five give up some information, and I have seen no sign of that," he reported. "We have one other name mentioned, but a real long shot, hardly worth bothering with - Robert Ashley, whom Slater apparently looks like. Possible French connection to his wife as well. Well, we could check, but I don't see how or for what purpose. With the girls, I mean. Oh yes, Maths First-class Honours at LSE that should narrow it down." Hooper was quizzing him back. "Yes, I know, but follow that through boss. If Slater is Five, so what? Does that make him a killer? We still don't have anything with the other girls. Okay," he went on to one of Hooper's comments, "yes we'll be back this evening." He hung up the call

"What's the problem?" Grahams asked.

"They are making progress, but won't discuss it on an open line; we'll have to wait till we return. I don't know what they have found."

Marjorie McKinnsley watched the detectives go; she knew exactly who John Slater was; Graham Ashley. She still missed her dear friend, Monique Ashley, wife of Robert Ashley in the Foreign Office. The Ashley's had been a lovely couple, and Graham was such a bright child. After Monique's death, they had only been in irregular contact. Graham had gone around the world with his father in between various boarding schools. They had slowly lost touch with Robert Ashley until she heard about his death, at his desk for God's sake. He hated desks. She had seen Graham at the funeral, tall handsome with his mother's complexion, looking lost but determined. She heard he was at the L.S.E. Later, at the post funeral drinks, she found out he was quitting university to join the army.

She implicitly understood the need for secrecy. Her brother George was still on that side. He had known the Ashleys too, not that she would say anything to him, as they had not spoken in years. She had recognised Graham Ashley as soon as she had seen him on his first company social. She had a quick word with Roger, with whom, for years, she had maintained an on-off affair, unbeknown to Andrew. Roger said not to say anything as it was part of his cover. Now these plods were digging into the past. Well, luckily that had ended, thanks to her husband's illness. Had the plods noted the Robert Ashley name? She had tried to divert attention. She hated to see Andrew like this. He had once been so virile. She loved her husband and had refused to leave him for Roger, despite his requests over the years. The affair had finally ceased after Roger had found and married, his unsuitable bride. Stella, her daughter, now married to that idiot Tom, would have been a fantastic match for the Ashley's only child. She blamed Andrew; he had introduced Stella to Tom. Tom was then the next bright thing at the brokers and from a hereditary peerage family. Cocaine ruined that, and ruined him and Stella with it. Families, she thought. She went upstairs to see whether her husband was settled. He had only three months to live.

CHAPTER FORTY-TWO

Thursday Afternoon Progress Meeting

Braithwaite, Jones, Grayson and Claridge-Briggs reconvened at Scotland Yard at 14:00. Jones explained that Hooper was delayed on another case, but would be there as soon as possible. Braithwaite introduced Shoreditch. Whilst they had waited for Hooper's arrival, Shoreditch was briefed on the wider aspects of the case. Each agency took a turn in setting out what had happened since the previous evening. The main briefing was from Braithwaite, and then Shoreditch, outlining the measures taken to monitor Hedges. The monitoring was continuing with two members of Shoreditch's team listening in to phone calls and watching his computer transactions. His house was now phone tapped and bugged. His home Internet connection was also monitored. If he left the building, he would be followed.

Jack Hooper, accompanied by Detective Constable Pete Watkins, had arrested Charles Goodson and he had been taken discretely from the MoD to Westminster, with the help of MoD Police. Goodson had protested his innocence all the way in. He was booked in by the Custody Sergeant and put straight into an interview room. He had not asked for any legal representation. Hooper just wanted to get on with it. He entered the interview room with Pete Watkins. After identifying names for the tape and video, Hooper formally cautioned Goodson. He confirmed that he did not want legal representation. Goodson's bluster had gone, and he was now looking shocked and wary. He was a slim, wiry man of medium height with twenty-five years experience in MoD procurement. Hooper hoped this would not take long.

Hooper outlined the case against Goodson, that he had diverted funds to several offshore accounts and that the awarding of several defence contracts had leaked, leading to share speculation, and that he was the source of that leak. He told him that Goodson's DNA had been found on several documents found at a bank, and a stockbroker's. Goodson had grown paler as he sat and listened with no comment. He looked near to tears when he said. "Have you cleared this with him?"

"With whom?" Watkins replied, confused. He was trying to get up to speed on the case, after Hooper had grabbed him that morning in the absence of Rutledge who had been on the case. Watkins had been trying to get further with the missing French agent, whilst reviewing the CCTV from Heathrow, to see where Slater had gone.

"The one who ordered me to do it. Hedges - have you got him as well. I'm not taking the hit for all this. I did what I was told to do in the national interest, I'll have you know." He sat straighter in the chair, and some authority came into his tone.

Hooper was open mouthed with surprise; Watkins was about to speak, when Hooper held his hand up to cut him off. "Mr Goodson, in your defence, are you saying that you carried out these actions, which you are now admitting, on the instructions of someone else?"

"Exactly, Detective Inspector," he started confidently now. "I was following instructions from Ian Hedges at Thames House; I think he is Policy Director these days. He sent me written instructions and requested certain information on procurement awards. I have only been supporting the National interest in helping my colleagues at Thames House. I have not done anything wrong. Yes, it breaks the strict procurement rules, but that is of minor consequence when I have been helping the Security Services get what they need. Surely, you can see that and we can forget these silly allegations."

Hooper was stunned; he sat back in his chair and contemplated what to ask next. Goodson was a pompous so and so, and clearly guilty, by his own admission, of breaking the procurement rules, several anti-corruption laws and the Official Secrets Act, but he was claiming some sort of operational mission and instruction from Hedges. "Do you have a list of all the incidents that this Hedges has asked you to provide?"

"Of course, it's on my system in the office."

"Did you notify your superiors of these requests and instructions?" Hooper asked.

"Well, no, not exactly, they weren't cleared to know of course. Hedges told me they had been briefed separately, but I was not to discuss it with them." Goodson was back to his almost tearful demeanour, as he realised the implications of what he had just said.

"Mr Goodson," said Hooper in his most authoritative voice, "I must remind you that you are still under caution. I must also tell you that your statements have implied that you are implicated in two, very serious, further charges, namely, conspiracy to commit murder and kidnapping." Goodson looked stunned now. Hooper continued "I shall now suspend this interview. DC Watkins will take you back to the Custody Sergeant where you will be reprocessed. I strongly advise you to get legal representation. Or we can provide it for you. I am now formally adjourning this interview at 14:35." Hooper stood and beckoned Watkins out with him. A Met Police PC went into the room to watch the prisoner.

"Jesus Christ, boss," said Watkins. "What now?"

"I can't believe it Pete, but this whole case gets weirder and weirder. Okay, you re-book him in and wait for a solicitor to arrive. Don't re-interview until I can get Rutledge over here. He should be finished with the house visit write up, but you and he need to prepare the interview before you go in. Not a word to anyone outside the team about the Hedges connection. I need to get back to the Yard, I'm already late, and I need to update our colleagues. What a mess this is turning into!" Hooper left Watkins with the tasks and rushed back to the Yard.

It was gone three o'clock by the time he entered the meeting. He was introduced to Shoreditch, and the members present updated him on the progress against Hedges. Hooper had asked for a word outside the room with Commander Jones. He authorised him to tell the team what had happened. The members in the room were equally shocked. Hooper then said, "We now have evidence from Goodson that Hedges has been carrying out illegal stock trades, and influencing procurement decisions. I expect we will get times and dates that will link to your file uploads as well Ian and Jon?" He looked at Shoreditch and Braithwaite respectively. "I can also inform you that, with the SFO, we carried out a search of our suspect's house. There is still nothing to link him with the girls, and, in at least two cases, very strong alibis that he was overseas at the time they went missing. I had a call from Portugal giving me very little, and no positive identity on that suspect. Again, the evidence against him points to insider trading and, potentially money laundering, but nothing else except for the key element that Thames House placed him in the firm. I know you ran Slater's name Jon, as we did, but we still don't have a former name." Hooper had forgotten the Ashley name mentioned by Drinkwater, in all the excitement of the Goodson break.

Claridge-Briggs had been unusually quiet during the other updates and then Hooper's statements. "My assessment, Jack," he said, "is that you have uncovered Hedges funding stream, or at least part of it. I am going to take a leap here, but bare with me. Jon and I are both aware that Hedges has hinted for years that he could organise covert operations." Braithwaite nodded in agreement. "I think we all dismissed his innuendos as part of his character, but perhaps he has been running a black operation all this time." Hooper went to interrupt, but Claridge-Briggs pressed on, "I know you don't like that idea Jack, but they do happen in both our Services." He again looked at Shoreditch and Braithwaite. "Nevertheless, I think it highly likely that this Slater character is an asset. Your own team, Jack, has said that he ran counter-surveillance effectively, so I think we should take it as a working assumption that Slater is involved, either in the money side or more directly. If we had more time, I would suggest a trawl through the army exit records for the time period. We can of course do that, but knowing how slow they were to digitise records, we may end up going through filing cabinets for days, and they would not like us doing that. I appreciate, David and Jack, that your primary concern is to catch this killer, and I would normally concur, but I think that

Hedges should be our focus. He is the national security threat as I see it. I know my Director would concur. I have to brief her at five thirty by the way." The rest of the room's occupants considered Claridge-Briggs statement.

After a discussion of options, they planned their response. David Jones agreed to try to persuade Michelle Carrington to act normally the following day. Hooper and Drinkwater would interview Hedges, as planned, on Friday afternoon. If necessary, they would arrest him then, but they all agreed they wanted the files. Braithwaite and Shoreditch would continue to monitor the voicemail phone line. They agreed to keep Goodson under wraps at Westminster station and the press well away. They were winding up the meeting when Braithwaite mentioned the Americans. This stopped discussion for a moment.

"I can go back to Claremont," Braithwaite stated, "but I have to give him something if I do. He may have something in return, but that will depend on what he is allowed to say." They all turned to Claridge-Briggs again.

"I have had nothing further from the Ambassador, but once the Directors act and brief the Permanent Secretaries we can expect it to go up the political chain. My Director is probably talking to yours as we speak." Briggs indicated Shoreditch and Braithwaite. "I think we should keep the cousins out of it as far as possible unless they come to us. I would love to know what the other file from Schlemburg to Hedges was. My assumption is that it's another target, but who and where I don't know; as it has come from the CIA, I suspect it's an American. On further thought Jon, I will tell the Ambassador that we suspect an American target, and that the file has been uploaded. We can warn him further if the voicemail is triggered. What was the codeword again? Ashley or something, whatever that means?"

Hooper who had started to drift onto the endless task list he had to complete, shot up straight. Everyone noticed his move. "What was it you said?" Hooper had missed the Braithwaite briefing on the voicemail system.

"The codeword on the voicemail system," Shoreditch explained how it worked, and what they had heard again for

Hooper's benefit. "From what I understand, the option selections trigger further options. We dare not trigger a number in case we lose some of the information. The technical people tell me it's perfectly possible to set up automatic deletes and adjust the numbers." Shoreditch was not going to tell the outsiders present that the system had been set up by the Security Service's IT department in the first place, for Hemmings. The IT Security Manager had admitted that in his interview.

"And the codeword for option three is Ashley?"

"Yes, what of it?"

Hooper was referring to his notebook. "My team in Portugal were told that Slater reminded Andrew McKinnsley of a Robert Ashley, but they dismissed it as an old man's ramblings."

"Andrew McKinnsley, you said?" Claridge-Briggs asked, looking ashen faced.

"Yes, do you know him?" Hooper's penetrating stare was aimed directly at Briggs.

Briggs quickly recovered his composure. "I don't think so," he lied, "I just thought I recognised the name." Of course, he recognised his brother-in-law's name, as he did the name Robert Ashley. He had to get out of here and assess what was going on.

Hooper realised he was lying, but kept his silence, whilst giving his commander a hard look. David Jones recognised the look and entered the discussion. "Well, we have another name to check on in our respective systems. Ashley, Robert Ashley," he said.

"I better go and see my Director with Ian," said Braithwaite. "He has been chasing me all day, and now he will have had a call from Vauxhall without knowing what is happening. I'll have to placate him and make sure he doesn't warn Hedges, if they are as close as we suspect?"

"Yes, I need to get back to base as well," said Claridge-Briggs, desperate to get away from Hooper's penetrating look. "We need to get Jessica Carver away with her boyfriend, and then brief my Director." He said it all so smoothly, he almost believed it himself. He stood up, followed by Tony Grayson.

Within a couple of minutes, David Jones was alone with Jack Hooper. "Out with it Jack," said Jones.

Jack Hooper had known David Jones a long time. "Our friend Claridge-Briggs not only knows who Andrew McKinnsley is, but also recognised the Robert Ashley name. I think this has just got messier."

"I agree, Jack, but we can chase down the Ashley name ourselves. Hedges remains the focus… and protecting Michelle. I think the Carver girl will be safe with her boyfriend. I'm not happy with letting Michelle back into Thames House with Hedges."

"I know, but I don't think Hedges is a physical threat to her, inside Thames House, anyway. Braithwaite and Shoreditch are watching him closely, and she might discover more, being in the office."

"Will her boyfriend let her do it?"

"I think so, as long as we keep him in the loop. He had calmed down this morning when I saw him. Okay, actions… Jack, get back to Westminster, and oversee that interrogation. It needs your understanding of the entire case, especially in nailing Hedges. I'll brief your team here on your behalf. If you take Rutledge with you, send Watkins back, I'll make sure Drinkwater and Grahams are back here as soon as they are off the plane. They'll enjoy a blue light M4 trip. Let's get together at eight." They both left to their respective tasks.

Commander Jones asked Pollard to run the searches on the Ashley name. He then checked with the team and got them busy updating surveillance logs for the protection team on Carver, and checked in with the team at the Hilton. He authorised them to escort Michelle and Mark back to Michelle's flat, and to stay with them there. He would love to have a look at Hedges, but Braithwaite and Shoreditch were covering the main suspect. Jones shook his head. He would have to brief the Commissioner soon, and knowing his adversity to political fallout, then the Home Secretary would know, or at least the Permanent Secretary at the Home Office. If the Crown Prosecution Service were involved with defence lawyers then it was bound to leak out. He rang the Commissioner's office requesting an urgent appointment for the following morning.

CHAPTER FORTY-THREE

Thursday Hillier

Stewart Hillier was in the process of uploading the Special Branch file before he left work for the evening, when he noticed a bunch of access logs going on. He backed out and monitored the systems of the team. He saw several keyword searches going on. Pollard was the main user. Hillier had met him; he was virtually illiterate when it came to Boolean logic searches. He had provided support before, when he had found himself helping the Service Desk, one day. Not his favourite past time. Like many IT professionals, he considered end users as mostly incompetent. Well, at least Pollard had learnt how to click on the advanced search and had run a search across two of the databases for *Robert* and *Ashley*. The only response was a reference to a paper vetting file. The reference had FCO in its designation. "Interesting," thought Hillier. He was taking a keen interest in the Special Branch investigation for his own protection. He also noted the written instructions going on the file reference surveillance for Carrington and Carver. "Who was Carrington?" he thought. What with the Americans and Slater, he was sure that was his name, checking the file, he would be stupid not to check what was happening. He decided to wait and see what else Pollard did. If necessary, he would amend Slater's extra file as well. That would earn him a bonus. "As I'm here, I'll just check my other logs," he thought.

A big red flag against his contact Frank Coalfield, reported dead, possible murder. Stewart went cold and started shaking like he had in the hotel room. He looked over his shoulder, but he was alone in his part of the office, as normal. He opened the report, scanning it as fast as possible. Found with his wife it said. A possible burglary gone wrong, possible gang action, possible murder suicide, and possible accidental death, he read. The investigating team from the Met. were still trying to piece it together. They were reported as found only a couple of hours ago, an anonymous tip off it seemed. Forensics and the senior officer investigation would barely have begun. Calm down he thought; Frank Coalfield had lots of enemies this could easily be coincidence. What if it was not? He contradicted himself, then who? Stewart immediately suspected the Americans, after all they had come to see him from Frank. Did that mean he was at risk? That was not what the American had said. They wanted to continue working with him, had something changed? If not the Americans, then who? The only link was Slater, but how would he and why would he kill Frank? No, it was probably nothing to do with him. He would check the file again in the morning.

Now what would he tell Slater. He checked the Special Branch File again. Portugal was noted alongside McKinnsley and the Robert Ashley name with FCO as a reference. Hillier did not understand the significance. Slater's house had been raided, he read. Rutledge had been on the system writing his report. Hillier decided that was enough and uploaded the file for Slater. He decided not to add anything about Frank; he would wait to see what that investigation turned up. He covered his tracks by deleting his log activity, replacing the real log with an edited version removing his access. He then prepared to shut down his systems for the evening, when Reception gave him a call. He finished shutting down, and collecting his coat, he left the office.

***

Reach Claremont had taken the urgent call from Jamie Adams, the agent who had accompanied him to see Stewart Hillier. He had been due to meet Scarecrow that morning at his house. It was unusual to meet at asset's houses, but it had been working like that for several years. Scarecrow was providing information on Eastern European gangs operating on people trafficking. Jamie had gone to the house, rang the bell, and knocked on the door to no avail. He thought he could hear music coming from upstairs. Suspicious, he had gone to the rear entrance through their yard and seen, through the rear window, a naked leg in the study. He had broken in via the back door smashing a small pane of glass and found Scarecrow and a naked Mrs Coalfield dead in the study. Jamie had checked the house, searched the study taken the two mobile phones he found and left the way he had come in. He had called Reach as soon as he was clear, by two streets, of the house and back in his car. He was shaken, but as a former New York cop he was not unfamiliar with dead bodies. Reach asked him what he thought.

"First glance it's been made to look like a murder suicide, but there isn't enough blood from the girl. It looks like a hit to me; she was still tied up. He probably had been as well, then moved to create the set up. I checked out the place, nothing taken, so no burglary unless they were disturbed. I have grabbed their mobiles and checked the safe. Nothing to connect us apart from his emergency contact number on his phone. I'll bring both phones in just in case. The CCTV system was broken, think that was done at the time as well, when we spoke to Frank earlier this week he didn't say it wasn't working. So, I think it's a hit but who by? Could be a cast of hundreds."

Reach was unhappy with the loss of an asset, he told Jamie to phone-in to the police, anonymously, the murder, or whatever. He would have to check the Police did not investigate and find a CIA connection somehow. Stewart Hillier, now codenamed internally by the computer, Thunderbird, could help with that. He would need to contact him. He needed to tell Schlemburg about the loss of Scarecrow, but the Ambassador was expecting him now that Casey Richenbach and he had talked. Schlemburg would have to wait. He was expecting a mail from Richenbach, with the results of searches that he would do. Casey had agreed to search, after Carl had said no. He checked his mail, yes, there it was. Slater was a regular traveller to the USA, mostly New York. He was noted in the financial systems as a shareholder in a Stockbroking company. He traded on Wall Street, in the Dow Jones, and the NASDAQ in Chicago. He filed taxes as needed. One of his connected companies appeared to own an apartment at an upmarket address, in New York, near Central Park, but Slater seemed to use hotels. The apartment was used by the company, but no details of who, or whom that might be. Slater had left New York for Manchester a couple of weeks ago. That tied in with the Special Branch File, and

Slater was apparently still out of the country, according to Braithwaite. Reach thought Slater was into financial misdeeds, but did not see why Special Branch was still interested in him for the girls, but of course he knew they were not telling everything. Hemmings had not been in the file. Perhaps they needed a new copy? Another one for Thunderbird, maybe another visit to help set up the contact, now that he was to be an official asset. Now for the Ambassador, he walked out of his office into the corridor, just as he heard Schlemburg open the internal door between their offices. A lucky escape for now. He hurried around the corridor and up the stairs to towards the Ambassador.

***

Carl Schlemburg was getting more concerned by the hour. Nothing from Hedges, about the mission, two emails requesting an update from Hidelwietz and Reach now nearly always out of reach, stupid nickname he thought. Where had he gone again? He stared at Reach's empty desk. He was sure he had heard him speaking with someone a few minutes ago. He went back into his office closing the internal door and straight out to his PA.

"Have you seen Reach?" He asked Beth Schwartz.

"No," she had replied.

"Can you try to track him down please? I need to see him."

"Yes, Sir," she said.

He went back into his office and closed the door. Beth was uncomfortable lying to her Station Chief, but she did not particularly like him, and anyway, Reach, who she did like, if he would bother to take notice, had gone to his appointment with the Ambassador. Reach had asked some pointed questions about Carl Schlemburg only the other day, and she had told him about the hard copy file signed out by Schlemburg, as going to MI5. There had also been the file that had been printed out that had gone hard copy by courier, after Reach and Schlemburg's breakfast meeting. That was a police file which she then had scanned in and assigned to the new Thunderbird asset. Reach knew what he was doing, she would cover so far, but she was not comfortable lying to her boss, no matter how much she disliked him. She considered saying something to him, but decided to wait till Reach returned, maybe he would finally notice she wanted him to take her out.

***

Elliot Bloomstein was distinctly unhappy. He liked getting regular reports from the Station Chief that Schlemburg seemed reluctant to provide. He had not had that problem with Casey Richenbach, Schlemburg's predecessor. Now he was waiting for a conference call from him. He liked and respected Reach as well. He was unhappy with the turn of events that had meant George Claridge-Briggs, had called him, the previous evening. George and he had known each other for years. He had not realised George was in MI6 until after George had turned up at a liaison meeting, and his name was suddenly flagged. He was a clever fox that was for sure. As far as anyone had been aware, George had been Diplomatic Corp in the UK Foreign office and removed from all the shenanigans of intelligence work. That meant he was a damned good field agent, and Elliot had been interviewed about their relationship, to try to discover what George had really been up to. Elliot had spent time in and around the US State Department, as well as spells at the National Security Agency, before landing the plumb ambassador role two years before. He hoped he would survive the change in Presidency, as he loved the London life. He updated Reach on his call from Claridge-Briggs the night before, without giving out his name.

"Sir," said Reach when the Ambassador finished, "I only know about one file going to Hedges at Thames House, and that was the Special Branch one. That came from our new asset Thunderbird. Beth told me about another file signed out on Tuesday evening. She has not seen that file and neither have I. That's not impossible, but very unusual these days. Everything goes electronically now. I don't know for sure, but I doubt Casey failed to share anything with me during his tenure. That file did not come in electronically by the way, well not through our systems anyway."

The intercom buzzed, and the Ambassador's aide put the call from Casey Richenbach through. The Ambassador put him on speaker. After the pleasantries were exchanged, they got down to business. "I'm digging this side of the pond," said Richenbach, "I've already sent through the searches on Slater and Hemmings that we have uncovered so far, but I am far more worried about this file that Carl has apparently given to Hedges. There is no record here of a file being sent, but and here's the bad news, that search was flagged by Carl's former boss Geoff Hidelwietz. He's now a Divisional Director, and he asked me first thing what I was looking for, and to keep out of London business, now I'm no longer there. I told him I would. Like hell, I will, I'm even more suspicious now. I've reported to the Head of Internal Security that something is amiss. No details, but that ball will start rolling pretty soon. He will probably send an investigation team in, just in case, anyway. Anything from your end, Ambassador or from you Reach?"

The Ambassador and Reach updated Casey Richenbach including the conversation with Claridge-Briggs, which meant that Reach now knew.

"George is onto this is he? Well, he's a smart cookie but he can play the politics. I suggest you keep him onside by sharing what you can. Reach, this new asset, I'd give him up to the Brits if I were you, they are going to find out sooner or later that you guys got the Special Branch file, and they will hunt him down anyway. Better you control it. I'd give him to Braithwaite, and he'll probably give you something in return, like he did with Hemmings yesterday. Have you got a cover story for Schlemburg worked out?" They discussed how they would cover the Ambassador meeting with Reach without Schlemburg's knowledge. "How about that incident 18 months ago with the rendition; you could claim that the Foreign Office is asking questions again. Reach you were there as were you Mr. Ambassador, that's a good excuse, claim you're writing a report for the State Department, also gives you a reason to talk to Beth. Haven't you asked her out yet Reach?" When Casey Richenbach was talking, no one else could get a word in.

With some relief following Casey's last comment to the tense state of affairs, Elliot Bloomstein agreed with Richenbach, as did Reach. They finished the call. Reach then discussed the Scarecrow loss. The Ambassador did not know who Scarecrow was so Reach had to update him about that, and then the link, from Scarecrow to Thunderbird. The Ambassador did not like that turn of affairs, he felt his relationship with the UK could go sour at any moment, with all sorts of follow on issues for Iraq and Afghanistan. He had to attend a meeting with a Trade delegation, so they parted with a promise to get back together the following morning.

Reach returned to the office; Beth stopped him. "Carl's furious and wants to know where you've been, I didn't tell him you were with the Ambassador." Reach quickly told her in a whisper what the cover was. He leaned in close, and before he knew it, had kissed her. He pulled back embarrassed by his actions.

Beth blushed but beamed, "Now that has taken a while, and you can take me out for a drink after work to explain yourself," she continued her smile, then leaned over and kissed him back, checking Carl's door was still closed. "Now, you better get in there and explain yourself."

Reach smiled, went to say something, then shrugged. He took a deep breath and knocked on the door. "Where the hell have you been?" exploded Schlemburg. Reach explained he had been with the Ambassador and started with the explanation before Richenbach interrupted him. "Never mind that, the Ambassador may have to wait for his report, we need to get an updated report from Thunderbird as soon as possible."

"For Hedges?" Reach asked deliberately making sure his pocket recorder was running.

"No, well, we might have to give it to him, is there a problem with that," probed Schlemburg sensing something behind Reach's question.

"There might be," said Reach before explaining by telling Carl about Scarecrow's demise. He did not tell him of the plan to break Thunderbird to Braithwaite.

"Shit, that's all we need. What does Jamie think, what do you think is it connected to this or a coincidence?"

"Best guess at this stage is coincidence, he had plenty of enemies, but coincidence at this stage..." Reach tailed off.

"Yes, I agree," said Schlemburg appearing calmer. "We want that file updated, what about Braithwaite, will he tell you more?"

"Possibly, he gave us Hemmings yesterday so who knows, but I do need something for him. I could send the Canadian's file over, I haven't done that yet."

Carl was not happy about the file going over, but he needed something to trade, and Reach had already promised it. "Okay, let me review and redact some bits first. I'll get Beth to send it to him. Was she covering for you earlier?"

"No, why should she do that?"

"She said she didn't know where you were, which she should do. You two seem pally are you together?"

Reach coughed, "Not yet, but I'm hopeful," he explained.

"Make sure she knows where you are in future."

"Okay," a hint of sarcasm in his voice.

Schlemburg caught the tone and gave his deputy a hard look. What did Reach know? This was getting difficult to balance. He decided to play friendly, "I think that a visit to Thunderbird would be helpful to get a new copy of the file and set up a proper contact procedure."

Reach could not say that they had told Braithwaite so he would have to go along with a visit. "Okay, when, tonight?"

"Yes, unless you have other plans?"

"No, that's OK, Beth and I are going for a drink from work, I'll grab Jamie and go from there."

"That's all then."

Reach nodded and took the internal door to his office. This was getting too complicated. It was already nearly five. He had no idea if Thunderbird would be home or out on one of his liaisons. They had followed him from his home last time. They had the contact mobile number and had Scarecrow's phone to call him on, Jamie's report on the phones listed the contacts; Thunderbird was there as SH, plain as day. The phones were now off, and batteries removed. They did not want anyone tracing them. Jamie had done that immediately he left the house. They had been on briefly in the basement's secure electronic Faraday cage whilst they were copied. Two phones, from a murder scene, showing up inside the American Embassy, would not be good, but now for Braithwaite.

Jon Braithwaite took the call sitting waiting outside the Director's office with Shoreditch, feeling like a naughty schoolboy waiting to see the headmaster. Having been rushed in, to see the Director, he was now deliberately keeping them waiting. "Mr. Claremont, how nice to hear from you," answered Braithwaite. "How can I help you?" Braithwaite stayed silent whilst Reach told him about Thunderbird, not the code name, but the contact. "That's very interesting, Mr. Claremont."

"Reach please," said Reach.

"Reach it is, and I'm Jon, short for Jonathan." What could Braithwaite tell him in return? Very careful now, "We have a potential codeword Ashley, just that no connection," said Braithwaite. "No nothing else at the moment," said Braithwaite the call finished with again a promise to stay in touch.

Ian Shoreditch was giving him a hard stare, "It's okay Ian, that was our cousins with some interesting developments."

Just then the Director opened his door, "You two in here now," he said, with no greeting and a very annoyed tone. This would be fun thought Braithwaite.

Julian Clarkson put on his reading glasses purely so he could look over the top of them. He thought they made him look intellectual. Braithwaite thought they made him squint. The Director launched into what he considered to be a rollicking, about keeping him informed, and avoiding him and calls from Vauxhall, as well as the Permanent secretary, he ended with "What the fuck is going on?"

Braithwaite was about to speak when Ian Shoreditch stepped in. "Director," he said, "I need to ask you a few questions before we brief you. I must warn you that should I not be satisfied by your answers you may become the focus of this investigation, necessitating a call to Special Branch. They are fully in the picture."

My word, thought Braithwaite that is getting on the front foot; he looked at Shoreditch with renewed esteem. The Director spluttered, "How dare you Shoreditch, I'll have your position for that, what do you mean the focus of your investigation explain yourself, or you'll both be out."

"Would you prefer I called Special Branch?" Shoreditch threatened.

The Director stopped to think, "Okay, but this explanation better be good."

"As I said Director, I need you to answer a few questions first. How well do you know Ian Hedges?"

Julian Clarkson had understood from the calls from across the river, and the Home Office's Permanent Secretary, that the issue was about Hedges, so he was partially prepared. "I've known him for years, good man on the policy side, not so great operationally. We meet socially occasionally, most recently the other evening when we had dinner. Should be seeing him this weekend, as well as our routine meetings on policy, budget, and so on. I can't believe he's involved in anything disreputable. So what is he supposed to have done?"

"Does the codeword *Ashley* mean anything to you, Director?" Braithwaite asked ignoring the Director's question.

"No, why should it?" The Director looked confused and concerned now, his earlier temper dissipating.

"Is Hedges running any live operations using that codeword, or any other that would not be on the system?" Shoreditch followed the line of questioning.

"Ian? Of course not. He had some success with counter IRA a few years back, but that was mostly Hemmings, poor chap. Since then he has done policy, nothing operational. He sees the weekly briefings, but he has no funding for operations, and no assets assigned apart from his PA, and the research analyst department. Please tell me what this is all about?"

Shoreditch and Braithwaite did, by the time they were finished it was nearly 7p.m. Shoreditch had also reluctantly explained that the phone message system had been set up by their own IT Department, they agreed that they would not reveal that piece of the puzzle. The Director had needed several explanations, before he understood how the contact voicemail system worked, he had then broken off, to try to speak with Monica Pennywise, in Vauxhall. She was not to be interrupted according to the switchboard. Braithwaite explained she was probably with Claridge-Briggs. Braithwaite passed on what he had learned from the CIA and suggested a call to David Jones, before their planned meeting. The Director put in the call and put it on speaker. He was now fully involved with the operation. His anger replaced by a determination to get to the bottom of what his service, via Hedges, had been up to. If he did not see this through he would have to resign immediately. He might survive for a planned retirement, if he dealt with this properly? No mention of the IT Departments complicities in setting up and sending the files. Special Branch and the Metropolitan Police needed to know about the IT leak.

***

Commander Jones took the call, he was waiting for Hooper to return from his interrogation of Goodson and then the 20:00 planned meeting. He was trying to get some food when the call came through. "Director, Ian, Jon, what can I do for you?"

"Commander, David, if I may? Ian and Jon have fully briefed me now. We can review when I should have been told at a later date, but Jon has some pressing news for you, go ahead Jon."

"David, the CIA has told us that they have a copy of your case files so you were right to keep some things out of it. More importantly they got it via one of your IT Technicians, Stewart Hillier. They have assured me he is a new source, but he supplied them with the file for a fee."

David Jones held his anger in check, as he had done on many occasions during his life as a policeman. Hillier, he thought he knew him, he had probably fixed his PC, he thought. "That's disturbing news," he finally said controlling his voice. "I'll need to take some immediate action, I'll update you, Jon and Ian when you come over." He ended the call. What now, where was Hillier, he would arrest him himself. He looked at the time. He left his office and went to the team room. Drinkwater was back with Grahams from Portugal. They were busy telling the team about the Villa in Portugal and how nice it was. Pollard was still there as well. Drinkwater broke off when he noticed the Commander.

"Commander, I'm afraid the boss isn't back from Westminster yet, can we help?"

"Yes, John, and you Dave, please come with me." The rest of the team were about to return to their work when the Commander continued, "The rest of you please put nothing else on the system, in fact, please log off immediately. I'll update you as soon as I can." He walked out of the room with the two detectives, then in the corridor, Drinkwater noticed the concern on his face.

"What is it Sir?"

"We have a serious security leak which I need closed off now." He explained about Hillier.

"Oh shit," exclaimed Grahams. "He'll be gone for the night now. Who else can we get?"

They called the Met Police CIO. He called his main IT Manager and they were both on their way back into the office, but would not arrive for at least an hour. The CIO commuted and was on his express train out of London, for Reading. He would have to get off at the first stop Slough, then get a train back, then a tube or taxi across from Paddington. The IT Manager would be quicker. Commander Jones also called the Duty Commander who would in turn call the Commissioner. Having planned to meet him the following day he guessed he would see him that evening, when he returned to the office. "Impact?" David Jones asked Drinkwater and Grahams.

"Too soon to say, Sir," said Drinkwater, "and not just on this case. If he leaked this out, what else has he leaked out? I hate to think. These IT guys have access all over the place. I'm too stunned to say at the moment. Does DI Hooper know yet?"

"No, I'm waiting, like you, for him to get back from Westminster. Is any of that on the system yet?"

"No, we are a bit behind, we haven't put our stuff on yet, only the outline we gave the boss by phone, I think Pollard put something on about that."

"Please check and brief the rest of the team. Everything from now on, until we get it cleared, onto paper only. We have a liaison meeting due in at eight. I need some answers by then." Drinkwater and Grahams returned to the team. David Jones made his way to see the duty Assistant Commissioner. It was just after

19:00.

CHAPTER FORTY-FOUR

Claridge-Briggs

George Claridge-Briggs had said nothing in the cab back to Vauxhall. He needed to think. The traffic was awful, and it was nearly five by the time they got in the office.

"Tony, make sure Jessica is clear on leave, and that you have her contact details. The Special Branch protection team can watch her until she leaves with her boyfriend; Johnson isn't it? I need to make some calls, and I'll see you at the Director's office at five thirty."

They had parted. What to do now? Ashley and then his sister and brother-in-law, the McKinnsley's, suddenly this case had turned personal, and back to him. He would have to call Marjorie. Five years at least since they had spoken. What did she know or realise? He checked his private address book and called her from his office. He would have to be quick. The maid, Maria, he recalled her name, answered and said she would get Mrs. McKinnsley for him. George contemplated what he would say.

"George," a very curt answer, no how are you. That was to be expected.

"Marjorie, I'm sorry to call you, and I appreciate, we have not been in touch."

"What do you want, George. Andrew doesn't have much time left and I'd rather not waste it on you?"

"I'm sorry, Marjorie, for you and Andrew, but I need some

information."

"What is it?" Marjorie could guess, but she was not going to give up that easily. George had treated Stella, and Tom appallingly at their wedding. She had not forgiven him, and nor had Andrew.

"I believe you had a visit today from two members of Special Branch, asking about a man called Slater. I wanted to know what you told them?"

"I have no time for your games, George. Andrew mentioned Robert Ashley, but John Slater is his son, Graham. I knew that as soon as he joined the firm, when Roger introduced him. That was as a favour to your friends across the river, and no, we did not tell Special Branch that. Monique was a lovely woman, as you know, and the fact that her son is busy serving the nation, well, Robert would be very proud of him, may they both rest in peace."

"Marjorie, thank you for not saying more. Look I know things have been difficult between us since the wedding, but I would like to see you and Andrew before…" He broke off.

Marjorie hesitated, she was angry with him, but he was her brother, and she missed his wit and company. "Yes, Andrew and I would like that, come whenever you can." She hung up, tears in her eyes. Marjorie recalled that lovely day, when was it 1982?

***

Robert and Monique Ashley were throwing a ball for their son, in the back garden of Marjorie's house, as she stood watching at the kitchen window. The young boy had his father's facial expressions, but his mother's skin tone and hair colour. Monique saw her watching and waived for her to come and join them. She held up her hand indicating five minutes. Roger smacked her behind as he passed through into the garden carrying a tray of drinks. She gave him a smile and a warning to behave. Andrew stood at the barbecue, burning the food, looking hot and calling for a beer. Roger gave him one, and they stood chatting for a while. Other guests were arriving, and Stella, behaving all grown up, was showing them in. Monica had just arrived with George in tow, deep in conversation over a glass of bubbly. Michael Carver was talking to his two girls, Sally and Jessica, whilst Helen changed Michael

Junior, their youngest, upstairs. It was a glorious summer's afternoon, which drifted by with conversation, wine, and watching the children play.

Robert Ashley said that he was off to Libya next week, which caused a frown on Monique's face and a stare from Monica. George, handed her a glass, he was back on leave from Greece or was it Italy. She could never keep up, and she doubted he was really in those places. More likely Iran, she hoped not, Iraq, or some equally awful part of the planet. Marjorie did not share her brother's enthusiasm for the Middle East.

There were the Hollingbrooks from next door, snooty as ever, she thought. The village did not accept you unless you were at least third generation. A few more of Andrew's colleagues stood discussing the state of the markets, with all the turmoil in Iran. Their wives and girlfriends stood, with and without children, around the terrace, whilst Stella continued to play hostess, by carrying glasses back to the kitchen. Marjorie had drunk too much wine and had flirted outrageously with Roger and Robert, much to Andrew's disgust. He had joined in on market talk with some of the young traders, as they kowtowed to their boss and the Chairman. The other wives looked bored, whilst giving envious glances at her home. Yes, you too can have this, if you let your husband work eighteen hours a day, whilst you have an affair with his boss, she thought. Monique called her over. Graham Ashley stood at her side, and he told her about his latest love, a secret code book that his grandfather had bought him, and how he was busy creating new codes to keep his secrets. She laughed with him after she asked him what secrets he wanted to hide. Big ones, he had replied. His mother kissed his forehead and told him to go and play tennis with the other boys, and maybe he could be the next McEnroe or Borg. They had been at the final.

"He's lovely, Monique," Monica said joining them.

"So is Stella," she had said smiling at Marjorie with her lovely accent. The three women basked in the setting sunshine.

"The M&Ms," said George, arriving at Monica's side laughing at the running joke amongst the men. "Plotting something, no doubt." He put an arm around Monique as well. He still carried a flame for her, she thought. Someone had found *A Perfect Day* and was playing it on the Hi-Fi. Yes, she thought… a perfect day. Monique held her hand as they watched Stella and Graham trying to get a turn on the tennis court. The wine flowed, the sun slowly set, and no one shouted at anyone, not even Andrew.

Marjorie turned from her reminiscence, the phone dead in her hand. She replaced the receiver and went to climb back up the stairs to her dying husband.

***

"Now what?" Claridge-Briggs thought, time for the Director, but what can I tell her? This cannot go across the river. It would ruin him. Could Graham Ashley really be the killer? He recalled the child. He had attended the funeral of his father as well and remembered the boy growing up from his occasional social meetings with the parents. Marjorie had been close to Monique. "Be honest with yourself," he thought he had been close to Monique, very close at one point before the boy was born. When was that? Before Monica, Marjorie was with Roger, as well; he had known about her affair. Poor Andrew, more interested in making his millions than in taking care of his sister.

He recalled that Ashley had gone in the army, and he thought, he had heard, that he had left. How could he find out without letting Five and Special Branch in on the secret? If he did, Robert Ashley, his wife and the Service would all get dragged into the mud. It looked like Hedges had set up the black operation and Ashley the asset. That was what it looked like. Monica, the Director, had known Robert Ashley, how well he did not know, but Robert must have reported to someone in the Service? Was that Monica, now the Director, for part of it? He checked his watch; he had better go and find out.

He met Grayson outside the Director's office. While they waited to be admitted, Grayson told him that Jessica was going to the Caribbean for at least ten days, leaving either that night or Friday morning. She would have her mobile with her and been told to check in each day. She would send the hotel details through once she had them. She had asked Grayson what was going on. Grayson had tried to placate her, but she was pushing hard. He had promised her a full update when she returned from holiday. She was packing up as he left for the meeting. She had updated the Plato file with some more analysis, which Grayson would have to look at on the Friday morning. It would confirm the budget funding to procurement link in Jessica's analysis.

Richard Templeman came out of the Director's office at exactly five-thirty and admitted them. They sat down and went through the latest state of play. The Director told them of her calls to Shoreditch, Julian Clarkson, and the Permanent Secretary. She expected another round of calls tomorrow. They discussed the case. Monica checked on Jessica's status and was reassured by her imminent departure and the protective surveillance from Special Branch. "Anything else?"

"I wonder if I might have a word, in private, Director?" Claridge-Briggs requested.

Monica checked her watch; she had hoped to make dinner with her husband that night; a rare occurrence. "Thank you Richard and Michael. Richard please go ahead, I'll shut up shop, have my car ready in thirty minutes."

They both left. "George, out with it! You have been fidgeting like a cat on a hot tin roof since you came in. You better have a drink if it's that bad?" she said, noticing his expression. She poured two malts, and they sat in the more comfortable armchairs in her office. "Go on," she encouraged.

"Monica, I don't know quite how to tell you this…" He went on to tell her.

"Robert Ashley," she said. "I was his controller for a while."

"I surmised you were."

"One of the best, just like you in your heyday." The memory of their brief fling flitted across her face. "Didn't you have a fling with Monique as well?" George raised an eyebrow before a slight nod. "What are we going to do? Is Robert's son, Graham, really this John Slater?"

"I think so; they all know each other as children you realise. The Carver children were younger of course?"

"That day at Marjorie's, were they all there? I can't

remember, too much wine."

"Certainly the Ashleys were. I think the Carvers were, we were still..."

"A long time ago, George," Monica said, cutting off that line of thought. "If Ashley, as Slater, has been carrying out operations on behalf of Five, then he's not to blame. He wouldn't know Hedges was unofficial. He'll have to disappear, and I don't mean how his targets have done. I won't tolerate that behaviour whilst I'm Director; if Hedges gives him up though, it will come out along with everything else. I think Hedges does know who he is, at least as Slater and Ashley hence, the codeword on the voicemail. This connection can't come out. You realise we still have assets connected to Robert Ashley and Michael Carver, despite the time that has elapsed. We cannot put those agents, or the information they have provided, at risk by this operation, or whatever Hedges thinks it is. We have no idea about Graham Ashley's current identity, whatever that is, other than John Slater?"

Briggs had not realised Robert Ashley's or Michael Carver's assets were still in place. "No, we can probably unravel it via Hedges and tracing funds, but that could take months, I doubt Hedges knows." Briggs let the Director think it through.

"Hedges clearly wants to make contact for this urgent mission, which we have surmised is for the CIA, well at least part of it, judging from the Ambassador's response. If it does come out, all hell will break loose on both sides of the Atlantic. Hedges is the key. Can we stop this mission do you think?"

"I don't know, Monica; the voicemail had not been accessed as at four o'clock this afternoon, according to Braithwaite, but it could be at any time. We don't know who the target is without questioning Hedges, or Schlemburg. Not that the CIA will ever let us do that. If Ashley, Slater, or whatever his name is now, collects the mission, he will carry it out. If he selects option three he may make contact with Hedges, if Hedges is still in play. If Special Branch arrested Hedges, then we may lose that option. We'll discuss that later this evening. They now have the procurement chap in custody, which will supplement the Plato investigation, and they could arrest Hedges just on that. There are a hell of a lot of 'ifs',

Monica."

"Okay, George, you were right to tell me about Ashley. Let's keep that between us for now. We can't actively prevent it, but we don't have to help either. We just stay blank, no Ashley operation, and only Robert's FCO file, nothing on Michael Carver, senior that is. If Special Branch suspect there is more, they'll have to come through me and I'm not the telling type. One more concern, George."

"Go on," said Briggs.

"We have Hedges and the procurement chap. Who else was Hedges working with? The CIA is clearly involved, but uncovering that will probably be impossible. What about here? Anything you can think of?" Monica's penetrating gaze was levelled at George.

George did not think more digging would be a good idea, but he only said, "Plato would be our best bet. I don't think Hedges has many friends these days this side of the river."

"Keep digging, I have the feeling this could be bigger. Let's see if they can leave Hedges in play until we have the mission details at least, then see if we can get to Graham Ashley, before anyone else does. I'm sure the Americans can protect whoever the target is, if it is an American target? You had better head back across the river. Grayson can head home. I think he needs to be distanced as well."

CHAPTER FORTY-FIVE

Thursday night

Slater had gone straight to Scotland Yard. He kept his distance from the main entrance, but he needed to find Hillier. He decided to risk the bold approach. Keeping his disguise on, he went out and bought a new mobile phone. He packaged it up. He then went to reception with a private delivery for Stewart Hillier. It was nearly five o'clock. Hopefully, he would be leaving work soon. He left reception, but hung around outside watching, whilst faking a phone call. They had phoned Hillier immediately for him to come and collect. Reception had checked that the package was genuine by opening it, before signing a fake receipt Slater had created. The phone was a top model, and the receptionist gave it an envious look before calling Hillier. Ten minutes later a slim man of about thirty had entered reception and been given the package. He had Hillier. Now to follow him home. Hillier left the Yard and headed towards the tube. It was rush hour so he had to follow more closely. Hillier had looked at the phone and scanned around and outside. His eyes had not settled on Slater, but Slater had to be careful. Two stops on the Tube and Hillier changed trains. No counter surveillance, Slater noted, from his position twenty yards away on the tube platform. A little push in the crowded station and Hillier would be in front of the train. Tempting, but still too risky, thought Slater. Three more stops and a five-minute walk to a residential area. Hillier continued to a terraced house on a quiet street. It was just after six.

Hillier opened his front door. Slater was there in an instant, the syringe in Hillier's neck. He helped him through the door. He lowered him into the hall, which immediately, he realised, was the front room as well. He carefully closed the door, pulling the Gloch from an inside pocket. He checked downstairs, kitchen, WC, stairs. No lights, and no sounds from upstairs. He climbed the stairs two at a time, where he found two bedrooms, and a bathroom. The second bedroom was full of computer gear. Back downstairs; he retrieved the phone as it would have his fingerprints. He hadn't been able to wear gloves in the reception area, but he was now. He carried Hillier up to the bedroom. He tied him up, stripping him as he did, with the spare ropes from that morning removed from Frank. He hoped he would come round soon. He went to Hillier's computer. It was on. He moved the mouse and checked his desktop. The browser was minimised. He raised it and got an eyeful of porn. There was a download application running with films, software and music being downloaded and uploaded. For an IT man, he did not apply security to his own system. He left the machine running after a rudimentary file search. Nothing except for a bank log-in text file in a different name, Howard. That was the account Slater had sent the money to. He noted the details log-in and password, and then deleted the file. He left the porn web site and the download application running. He went back to Hillier. He would not have time to dispose of him, so he would follow the same route as he had with Frank. Set up something, after he had some answers. He went and got some water from the bathroom to see if he could speed things up.

***

Reach Claremont had really enjoyed his drink out with Beth. He had stood over her desk at five thirty as she shut down her system and put various files into the wall safe. She stuck her head into Schlemburg's office and said she was off for a drink with Reach, and she had received a grunt in reply. They had walked a few hundred yards northeast until they found a pleasant pub, where he ordered her a glass of wine and a small lager for himself. He explained that he had a job on later. Beth sympathised, and then found herself holding his hand. The pub was filling up with the post work crowd, and they had to lean closer to hear each other speak. They ended up kissing, before a ribald shout of "Get a room, mate," from another drinker, meant they pulled apart, somewhat embarrassed.

"Why didn't you ask me out before?" She asked him. He could not give a proper answer, other than job, time, and he did not think she would be interested. "Are you interested now?"

"You bet," he said. "Look, my meeting won't take long. Why don't you come along, you can wait in the car, then we can carry on?"

"Carry on what?" She asked playfully. "Are you sure that will be okay?"

"I'll call Jamie. He can pick us up and drop us off at your place?" He asked with raised eyebrows. They continued their drinks, chatting about this and that, the lousy British weather, where the summer had suddenly gone. It was replaced that evening by a dull dreary drizzle. He called Jamie. He would pick them up outside the pub in twenty minutes. It would take that long again to get to Hillier's home.

***

The Duty Commander, Assistant Commissioner Duncan Asquith, was already on the case briefing two members on the internal complaints team. Jones did not recognise them as he arrived in the Operations room. "David, how are you?" He asked as he arrived.

"I'm fine sir, but I am very worried about this. I have a critical operation in play, and this leak could impact that, it's very sensitive nationally."

"You can tell me about it in a minute. The Commissioner will be back in about an hour. He was out at Hendon for a dinner." He turned to the two detectives. "Okay, you two get round to Hillier's place and bring him in. I'll send a forensics team behind, but I want him in. Blue light if you need to, damn traffic, get uniform to meet you there. Silent approach though. Don't want him to run. Bring him here. I need him down in IT. Handcuffs and so on, tell him he's under arrest under the Official Secrets Act. That should stir him up, but we need him here so we can start to uncover the damage." The two left. "Now David, you better tell me what you can about what is going on?"

Jones outlined the case and the sensitivity, without providing details. He then explained that he had the liaison meeting at 20:00, which was rapidly approaching. As he finished he had a call from Hooper telling him he was on his way back. He told him he would meet him in the briefing room before the others arrived. The Commander let him go, telling him he would brief the Commissioner and call him if he needed him. The IT damage was potentially huge, affecting all of the Metropolitan Police, Special Branch, Counter Terror, and the other national organisations based out of the Yard. This was a huge issue. They needed to find out what Hillier had leaked, to where and when, and very quickly.

***

Stewart Hillier came round slowly with a wet, slapped face and a drowsy, nauseous feeling; he tried to speak, but realised he was gagged. He looked up; a long haired, swarthy man was looking down at him. Slater! He recognised him from the photo in the file, despite the long hair disguise. He was spread-eagled on the bed and realised he was naked. Fear ran through his veins, and he urinated involuntarily. The man looked at him in distaste. He had a kitchen knife.

"Stewart," he said, "I need to ask you some questions and I need quick answers." He showed him the knife. "I am going to take the gag off but if you make a noise, or shout, you will regret it. Nod if you understand."

Stewart nodded; he recognised the voice from their phone call, confirming it was Slater. That meant Frank and his wife had been got to by Slater as well. "What do you want, I gave you the information you needed? Why are you doing this?" He asked, as the gag came off.

"Ssshh," Slater said. "I need you to answer my questions. If you do so correctly, I'll let you go, how's that?" He asked him about the file, when was it last uploaded. Hillier answered his questions, calming as he did so. Hillier told him about the Ashley search and the visit to Portugal, which had not been reported. As he finished, the doorbell rang. The bedroom was at the back of the house. The computer bedroom was at the front. "Expecting anyone?" Slater asked quietly.

"No," said Hillier.

Slater went to the front bedroom and carefully peered out into dull evening. Two men stood on the doorstep, a car was parked haphazardly near the kerb, with another occupant. He pulled back from the window before they looked up. Time to go. He quickly returned to the back bedroom, pulling the other syringe from his jacket. Hillier barely had time to register before the injection was in. He could not stay to wait to see whether the heroin worked. The doorbell went again. He went down the stairs watching the letterbox to see if they were looking in. He took out his Gloch.

***

Reach and Jamie stood on the doorstep of Hillier's house. Reach had been expecting the police to be there already, but the road was quiet. Maybe Braithwaite had not alerted Special Branch yet. Unlikely, so maybe they were watching. He saw no sign. The house would be difficult to watch without taking over a house across the street. Could they have done that in the time they had? He doubted it. Reach knew this was a waste of time and that Hillier could not get them the file again, unless he could access it from his home. Chances were he would be arrested very soon. Would Hillier try and run if they told him he was blown? Possible, he did not know him well enough. Go through the motions, he told himself, do not alert Hillier with the news that he was blown, just report back to Schlemburg. Jamie rang the doorbell. The house looked empty. He could be out. Reach sensed movement above, but when he looked up he saw nothing, the hairs on the back of his neck prickled. He pulled his service revolver from its holder under his jacket. Jamie rang the bell again and then noticed Reach had pulled his gun. He pulled his as well.

"I think someone is in," said Jamie. He looked through the letterbox. "Armed man, not Hillier!" he shouted, jumping back, and pushing Reach away from the side of the door.

The right side of the door, where Reach had just been standing, now had a large hole around the lock. Before he realised, he had heard the sound of a pistol firing. They stood either side of the door in the correct posture. Just one shot.

Slater had heard the shout, and he had fired at the door instinctively before he had realised he was doing it. He knew he had not hit anyone. That was not the purpose of the shot. He just wanted them to slow down. He needed time to get out the back, unless that was covered as well. He sprinted for the back door. He opened it. His gun raised as he slipped out. He wished it was dark, rather than just dusk; no one was in the back that he could see. There was a small courtyard garden, and a rear wall with a gate in it. He went to the gate, what was outside?

Now what, thought Reach? Leave or go inside, they needed to know what Hillier's status was. "In," he mouthed to Jamie. Jamie nodded. "On three," he whispered. What a cliché but on three, Jamie kicked the door. Reach went in low, gun ready, no target. Jamie dived in over him, rolling to the bottom of the stairs. They both heard the bang of the backdoor slamming. They moved towards the kitchen, checking and covering each other. The door was swinging. They glanced outside. A rear garden gate was open. They turned. With weapons in front, they returned to the stairs. Beth was standing at the door looking petrified.

"I heard the shot," she almost screamed. She saw the guns drawn and gasped.

"Back in the car," shouted Reach, turning to go up the narrow stairs behind Jamie. They crept up the stairs. The light in the house was bad. Reach did not like this one bit. Jamie turned round the stairs landing. They could see both bedrooms and the bathroom. Unless someone was in a cupboard, it was clear. Reach could see the feet of someone on a bed from his low crouch. They covered one bedroom each. The bathroom was between and empty. Jamie stood and holstered his gun.

"No more than a couple of minutes, Reach," he said. "Someone will have called the shot in."

Reach nodded. They went to the back bedroom and looked down on Stewart Hillier. Jamie checked his pulse, it was just there but very weak; Hillier did not appear to be breathing.

Beth had returned to the car. What the hell had happened? She got into the driver's seat. "Just in case," she thought.

***

The 999 emergency services took the phone call from a Mrs. Harmsworth. The report of a shot was not unusual in

London, but would still alert the control room, which was already buzzing with rumours of something happening because of the senior officer activity. Then the location, matched with a current dispatch for uniform support to two detectives. The senior controller quickly assessed the situation, alerting the uniform drivers. They were under a minute away, urging extreme caution, sending an armed support car that was luckily only two minutes further away. Then the detectives. They were at least a further five minutes. Mrs. Harmsworth was kept on the line. She said that she had seen two men enter a house. She thought they were carrying guns when they crossed the road after the shot, and then a woman had run to the house. They asked her to keep talking. The woman had gone back to the car. She couldn't see the number plate. The uniforms had now put the sirens on. Despite the London traffic background hum, you could hear the sirens in the background of the phone call. The duty commander was now listening as well.

***

Reach and Jamie heard the sirens, was it for them? Sirens in London were not unusual. Better not find out.

"Hillier?" Reach asked.

"Gone or going, let's get out of here," said Jamie. They went down the stairs. As they exited the building, a London Metropolitan police car was screeching to a stop behind their car. The policemen were getting out. Reach and Jamie ran for the car, climbed in. Beth had started the engine, and she was pulling away as they got in, the police were getting back in their car. Reach looked over his shoulder at them, failing to notice the car coming the other way.

***

The Armed Response Unit had been on their way back to their patrol point from their second false alarm of the day. The adrenaline rush had been calming down when the call had come in. Lights and siren on, they had diverted towards the street. A shot fired. That was more like it, Sergeant Rhodes thought. Rhodes had been assigned to CO19 for seven years; he had never had to fire his weapon, except on the training ground. CO19, was part of the Central Operations Directorate of the Metropolitan Police, responsible for armed officers. The Heckler & Koch light machine gun was strapped across his chest as he sat in the passenger seat. He briefly touched the stock, as his colleague of three years, PC Gibson drove through the narrow streets; he turned into the road where the call was from. He saw a Met Police car, blue lights flashing, behind another car. As two men entered it, the car pulled out straight at them. The police car started to follow. There was a garbled call on the radio, before PC Gibson slew their car across the street, blocking the road.

***

Mrs. Harmsworth relayed what was happening in vivid detail. She had a grandstand seat at the most exciting thing that had happened to her since she had met the Queen at a Women's Institute meeting during the Silver Jubilee in 1977. She ignored the police controller's urging to be careful, almost leaning out of her window to see where the cars had gone.

***

The three cars had all stopped. Sergeant Rhodes carefully got out of his side and was pointing his Heckler and Koch at the middle car, a Ford Mondeo, he noticed. The three occupants sat still. PC Gibson had rolled out of the driver's door which was closest to the Mondeo and rolled behind one of the parked cars on the street. He was now also pointing his weapon at the car.

The two uniforms had stayed in their car but with doors open. They were on the radio, updating control. Rhodes could hear their commentary coming from the radio on the Armed Response Vehicle's dashboard speaker. He did not take his eyes off the passengers. Woman driver, male passenger, and a male in the back. He needed armed back up. The doors of the car opened. He tensed, ready to shoot, finger flicking the safety off.

***

Reach realised the impossibility of their situation. "Everyone stay calm." He said as much to himself as well as Beth and Jamie. There was no point trying to escape, and he certainly did not want a gun battle on a London street. "Okay, we are going to calmly get out, hands in the open. They will arrest us and it will take a while to sort out, but we will be okay. Give up your gun, Jamie; make sure you tell them where it is. Beth you okay? Sorry about our date."

"You sure know how to show a girl a good time." She tried to smile.

"All right, ready, nice and slow now."

Rhodes watched the three get out of the car. They kept their hands clear and up. "Thank God," Rhodes said out loud. This was going to be okay. He shouted at them to lay face down on the ground and put their hands behind their heads. PC Gibson moved forward, whilst Rhodes covered. Gibson went to the first man and cuffed him. He thought he heard the man say, in an American accent, that he had a gun. He removed a gun from the man's jacket. Gibson then went to the second man. He heard the other man say, again in an American accent, that he had a gun under his left armpit. Gibson removed that, with the word "Gun," again, and then indicated for one of the uniform constables to come forward and cuff the second man. Gibson then went to the woman; she said, clearly in an American accent, that she was unarmed. Another pair of cuffs delivered from the other uniform constable. They had all been searched thoroughly by Gibson. He apologised to the woman, as he checked her just as completely as the men. Another car pulled up, behind the patrol car. Rhodes saw two detectives flash warrant cards. More sirens were inbound, he heard.

Gibson shouted "Clear!"

Rhodes left his cover and approached the three on the ground.

"We claim diplomatic immunity," said the larger of the two men, turning his head up towards him.

Rhodes realised that this was going to be a very long night and he hated to think of the paperwork. He helped each of them into a sitting position against another parked car. The uniforms were trying to keep a gathering crowd back. He picked up the two revolvers from where Gibson had lain them down. He returned to his car and placed each of them in an evidence bag. He then placed them in the boot of his car, before locking the boot. They joined the two issue shotguns and other equipment in the reinforced enclosure. The detectives, he realised had gone to the house of the call. Gibson was guarding the three prisoners. They were saying nothing. He asked him whether he was okay there. Then, he followed the detectives into the house, noting one of the uniforms talking animatedly to an elderly woman who had come out of her house with a phone still in hand. Other cars were arriving, setting up a cordon he noticed. He guessed he was Bronze Commander for now, but not for long he hoped. His radio squawked requesting an update. It was the duty commander no less. He gave a brief situation report going into the house.

"Up here Sergeant," one of the detectives said. He went up the stairs hoping the house was clear; he was back on edge. The lights in the house were on now, although it was not quite dark outside. He saw the body as he entered. One of the detectives was trying CPR on a tied up man on the bed, whilst the other one was talking to control on his mobile phone, getting an ambulance. Rhodes did not think that would help. The man on the bed was already grey and appeared lifeless. The detective shook his head and stopped.

"Even more paperwork," he thought. "Now, we have a murder as well." He radioed the commander.

"Roger Delta 263," said Asquith to Rhodes on the radio. "Handover Bronze Command to detectives on site. Expect relief in five minutes." A Superintendent was on route. "Confirm India Delta of body, over," he transmitted.

"Standby Control," replied Rhodes. He looked at the two detectives.

One of the detectives had recognised the body from the office. "Stewart Hillier," he said, "who we came to arrest."

Rhodes relayed the message.

"Roger, pass onto Bronze to secure area and await forensics. Collect prisoners and bring them to command," he ordered.

"Confirm to command?" Rhodes questioned. That was not normal, but he had never arrested diplomats before, let alone after a shooting and probable murder.

"Confirmed, my authority, over."

"Roger," replied Rhodes. He confirmed Bronze Command to the lead detective. He left the house and spoke to Gibson. They helped the prisoners stand. Rhodes started the arrest caution, but stopped when he got to what he suspected them of. The taller American man seemed vaguely amused at his confusion, so Rhodes said, "Murder." That wiped his smirk. The woman looked horrified; they then walked them to the Armed Response Vehicle. They managed to squeeze all three into the back with the woman in the middle. It would be uncomfortable, especially cuffed, but he was not sympathetic. He called the radio. "Delta 263 on route to the Yard." Gibson manoeuvred the car around and past the now arriving patrol cars and an ambulance that had a wasted journey.

"Where are you taking us?" Reach asked.

Rhodes glanced over his shoulder. "Scotland Yard," he said. "Now, I suggest you keep your right to remain silent." He turned back. Gibson was accelerating and had kept the lights and siren going. Ten minutes at this speed he thought, then what. Scotland Yard was not really an operational police station it was an HQ. Where would he book them in? He could not go through Reception, well they were going to have to. He hoped a TV crew were not outside doing some political piece. Gibson gave him a quizzical look. "Don't ask? I don't understand either."

***

Slater had run a hundred yards, then walked two hundred yards south away from the house. He heard the many sirens. He ducked down a deserted alley. He reversed his jacket, put the wig in an inside pocket and put on a baseball cap. He walked back out of the alley. He found himself on a busier street. It was already seven thirty. Call Jess, head back to the penthouse and out of the country on the plane. He needed Johnson ID and to dump the gun. He finally found a high street and re-orientated himself. He knew where he was now, northwest of Hyde Park. He grabbed a cab on the Bayswater Road and asked to be dropped at Waterloo. He phoned Jess.

"Hi," he said when she answered.

"I'm on holiday," she said excitedly, "but where are you? I thought you were picking me up at eight, are we going tonight?"

"That's great Jess, I'm sorry I'm running late," he calmly said. The cab driver was looking at him in the mirror whilst they waited at lights. "Can you come to the apartment for nine, ready to go?"

"Yes, of course, is everything all right? You sound a bit odd?"

"Long day," he explained. The driver had continued the journey down Constitution Hill. He saw himself in the mirror, blood, but how? He adjusted his position for a better look at his reflection in the driver's glass. It was dark now and the drizzle had turned to rain. Left cheek. Blood dripping onto his jacket. He searched his pockets for a handkerchief and found nothing. He used the baseball cap instead. Not too bad, but it would probably need a stitch.

"You all right mate?" said the cabby. "You need to get that seen to."

"I will at Waterloo, thanks," said Slater. "I'll try not to get any on your seats." Now, the cabby would remember him. Don't worry, there was no connection to anything. No one had seen him, as far as he knew, except for the men at the door, and they would not have got a proper look. Cops, he thought. No, they had not announced themselves. Who then? American accent he realised from the remembered shout. How had he cut himself? He remembered the garden gate. He had banged his face as he forced it open. My DNA will be on it, he thought. No, the blood would be washed away, he realised. The cab arrived at Waterloo, and Slater paid the driver.

"I'd get that stitched if I were you," said the cabby, accepting the cash, and tip. "Need a receipt?" he asked.

"No thanks," said Slater, "I'll pop into the medical centre, or St Thomas' A&E if I need to." The St Thomas Hospital with its Accident and Emergency Department was a few hundred yards from Waterloo railway station. The driver pulled away. Slater entered London's busiest railway station, found the chemist, and paid for some plasters disinfectant, gauze, and Steri-strips. The assistant gave him a look, but took his money. Slater left the station keeping the gauze against his cheek. He joined the line for cabs and took one to his Vauxhall apartment. He arrived at 20:15. Harvey let him in with a cheery wave. Slater did not stop to talk and kept his face covered. He went up to the penthouse. He put the gun, his wig, and his clothes into a bag. He could not leave them in the penthouse if he was traced there. He put that bag into a larger holdall. He called the travel company. They could depart from Farnborough at midnight if that was okay by him. They would send a car straight away. That would be great, he told them; the joys of money. He used the Slater ID to authorise the company payment. They confirmed the passenger names as Johnson and Carver, passports would be checked at Farnborough. Into the bathroom, he cleaned the thin cut. He put two strips together; it was no longer bleeding. He put a thin plaster over the strips. Now, he needed to shower, change and then wait for Jess. He was exhausted, but he forced himself to check the flat. He also wanted to check the Special Branch file after what Stewart Hillier had told him. He had to decide what to do with the mission voicemail. It would be a no, he knew, but not now, he would call from Farnborough, or even wait until the Caribbean. Check everything. He cleared the safe. Spare passports. He had to dump some of this stuff. Cash, he had plenty. He found another bag to pack some spare clothes.

He distributed cash and passports around his bags against the risk of a bag going missing, before he remembered that it would not matter, as the plane was his, he could carry as much as he wanted. There was no baggage handling system losing his luggage to worry about. If they were stopped and searched they would get everything anyway, regardless of the number of bags. He put his Johnson passport and credit cards into a linen jacket. He secured and locked the bags. The gun; what could he do with that? How would he dump it at Farnborough without getting seen? No, he had to hide it but where? He removed it from the bag before re-securing it. He called the lift to his floor. Jess would be here soon. Once the lift came, he wedged the door open. Covering the lift CCTV, he quickly reached up to the top of the lift cabin where there was an access panel. He pushed through, hoping it was not alarmed and climbed up. He placed the Gloch, wiping it down as he did, onto a small ledge in the elevator shaft. He climbed back down; damn he was dirty again, oil from the shaft. He uncovered the lift CCTV, then loaded his bags into the elevator. That would be a good excuse if anyone noticed. He hoped no one had been watching the lift CCTV. He went down with the elevator, pushed the bags out then went back up. He took deep breaths, he was shaking from the adrenaline and, for the first time in his life, scared he would be caught. Breath deep he told himself. He changed his shirt, wiped himself down, and added more deodorant. Calmer now, his heart rate was returning to normal. Okay, final checks. He shut and locked the safe as his door buzzer went.

"Hello, Sir," said Harvey. "I have Miss Carver here, and a car has arrived for you, as well. Shall I send Miss Carver up?"

"No thanks, Harvey. I'll be right down."

He closed the penthouse, switching off the lights. He got in the lift, which was still on his floor and pressed for Ground again. As the lift opened, Jess dressed in jeans and a sweater was talking to a chauffeur. He was taking Jess' bags to the large Mercedes parked at the entrance. Harvey was walking towards the lift to pick up his bags where he had pushed them out. Two men were standing the other side of Jess. Slater moved his hand to his jacket, before he realised his Gloch was in the shaft above. He was about to run, when Jess saw him, as did Harvey. Jess ran over blocking his view of the men. Then, she was in his arms and kissing him. Harvey was saying something about helping him with his bags. The two men were looking embarrassed watching their kissing, but they had made no other move.

Jess pulled back and saw his stare, "Oh don't worry about those two, they are here to look after me until we get away."

"What?" He stammered.

"I'm sorry, I should have told you. If you ever gave me a telephone number," she scolded. "Work has assigned some protection. I'll tell you about it in the car. A bit over the top if you ask me. Chauffeur service as well I see. What have you done to your face?"

"I," he started; then stopped, assessing the situation, so the men were not here for him, but would they recognise him? They had not so far. "I banged into something, it's nothing," he said. He tried to breathe and slow his racing heart.

Jess gave him a squeeze. "You look a bit tired. Are you sure you're all right?"

"Yes, I'm fine."

"We better get going Sir," the chauffeur said.

"Yes, we had," he replied instinctively. They walked past the men.

"Where are you heading to?" One of them asked.

"Farnborough," said the chauffeur, before Johnson could reply. He showed them into the rear of the Mercedes, and shut the door.

"Farnborough?" Jess asked, "Why Farnborough?"

"Private jet," Mike replied absentmindedly.

"Wow, you do know how to treat a girl," she said smiling.

He could see the chauffeur talk to the two men. They returned to their car parked a few yards in front. The chauffeur got back in. They pulled out, followed by the two men in their car. Mike's head was spinning. "Those two?"

"Tony, my boss, is a bit concerned about the investigation into Sally and the other girls, and maybe some men as well, it seems now. Anyway his boss wanted some protection for me just in case. I thought it was silly, but they insisted. He authorised my holiday as well. They think it would be good for me to be out of the way whilst it finishes. Apparently, the police are close to catching someone. It's causing a real stir. Tony and ..." She stopped herself from giving Claridge-Briggs' name, "...his boss have been working all hours and having to brief the top bosses. Anyway as long as I call in once a day, whilst we are away, they will be happy. I told them I thought we were going to Heathrow, and I have ten days. Is that okay?"

"Yes, that's great. I understand. What about Michael, is he all right?"

"They are watching him as well, and our house. Michael should be okay, as he's not in the Service. I don't want to drag all that up again. I promised to call him from the airport. He won't believe this." She looked at the luxury car. "So what have you been up to, how did you do that to you face, tell me about your busy day?" She snuggled close to him after a kiss. If only he could tell her the truth. He began to make something up, whilst the car sped southwest towards the M3 and Farnborough.

***

At Scotland Yard, Braithwaite and Shoreditch were in reception waiting to be collected, when Claridge-Briggs arrived. It was just before eight. They had barely said hello, when the ear splitting siren stopped outside the main entrance. Along with everyone else in Reception, they all looked astounded as two armed officers escorted three handcuffed prisoners into the lobby. Braithwaite was even more astounded when he realised one was Reach. The briefest of nods from Reach. Jack Hooper came jogging in behind.

"What the fuck are you guys doing bringing prisoners here?" he said to the two officers.

"We were told to, and who the hell are you?" asked Sergeant Rhodes.

"Detective Inspector Hooper, now, what's going on?"

"It's all right, Jack," said Commander David Jones. He was walking into reception, accompanied by a uniformed Assistant Commissioner Asquith.

"Take the prisoners to Briefing Room Three," Asquith told Sergeant Rhodes, "I think we need them away from the public gaze."

He replied with a very inquisitive "Yes, Sir."

Hooper joined the others. "That's where we are going, I think?"

Braithwaite leaned towards him, "Jack one of those prisoners is Reach Claremont, my CIA source."

David Jones came over with Asquith. "I think we need to take this upstairs away from reception and prying eyes. This could take some sorting out."

By the time things were sorted out, and they could begin the planned update, a lot had happened. Braithwaite confirmed Claremont's identity. They moved the prisoners to another briefing room, removed handcuffs, but allowed no telephone calls out, despite a repeated Diplomatic immunity call. A different armed guard was brought in to watch the room. Rhodes and Gibson were cleared to make their report, after they moved their car away from the front entrance. Hooper and the others were told about the IT security leak. Hooper updated the team about the Procurement case and the connection to Hedges. Goodson was in a cell in Westminster awaiting further questioning.

Shoreditch checked with his team that no access had occurred to the voicemail, and Hedges had gone home for the evening at 18:00. He was being watched there. Braithwaite went and had a brief word with Claremont. Claremont gave him an edited version. The onsite team at Hillier's house wanted them questioned for the murder of Hillier. Claremont explained they had found Hillier. Beth confirmed the gunshot, as did the statement of Mrs. Harmsworth. Mrs. Harmsworth also claimed to have seen a man going in with Hillier earlier. Claridge-Briggs agreed to call the Ambassador about his staff sitting next door, which he did.

The Metropolitan Police CIO, and IT Manager were going through everything that Stewart Hillier had dealt with, but that would take time. The Commissioner had been held up, but was still on his way in, Asquith left to update him. Claridge-Briggs interrupted his Director's dinner with her husband with a quick update, before returning to the team. Shoreditch did the same with Julian Clarkson. The US Ambassador would personally vouch for Reach, Jamie, and Beth, which the Ambassador was surprised about. Why was she there? He would send a car for them and make them available to give statements the following day. Sergeant Rhodes was again called to retrieve their weapons and return them, which required Asquith himself to give the order, so annoyed was Rhodes. He had walked away shaking his head. Hooper would give his boss a call and try to explain. The team at Hillier's flat reported finding nothing of value, but his computer was on its way to forensics.

The medical examiner could not find a cause of death, but injection was suspected, unless Hillier had suffered a heart attack.

The body was going straight into a post-mortem. Just when they were about to take stock, the Met police CIO reported that one of the last files Hillier had looked at was the Frank and Mrs Coalfield case. That sent another round of questions. Braithwaite went back in with the Americans, but they were not saying anything else. Not saying led Braithwaite to suspect more. Hooper and Braithwaite were then called, along with Jones, to go and brief the Commissioner. Braithwaite then had to get Clarkson to calm down the Commissioner who wanted Hedges dragged from his bed straight away. Asquith had been relieved of Duty Command and assigned to the investigation team, necessitating a further round of introductions and explanations. Eventually, the team gathered back in Briefing Room Three. It was 22:30.

"What a day," commented Braithwaite, "the US Ambassador will pick up our guests in a moment, we'll get statements tomorrow. He promised George." He indicated Claridge-Briggs.

"They all have Diplomatic Immunity anyway, if we try and push it." Hooper took over the briefing. "As I see it, we have an organised crime scumbag, Frank Coalfield, murdered by someone this morning, along with his wife; that incident was called in by an anonymous tipoff. The emergency call recording may or may not disclose an American accent. We then have Stewart Hillier checking that file. It appears Hillier had flags on various files. We have an unauthorised internet link in Hillier's office, and evidence of multiple uploads to an FTP web site. It's in the UK so sometime tomorrow, with a warrant, we may be able to get the transaction logs, and even the files, with a bit of luck."

"Not the same site as Hedges has used by the way," interrupted Shoreditch.

"Sorry, forgot to mention that. That would have been too much to hope for."

"We have the Americans telling us about Hillier, but going there anyway," added Braithwaite. "Claremont wanted to explain that part, but not without the Ambassador's say so, probably not wanting Schlemburg in on the knowledge. I get the feeling that the Ambassador, Claremont and others are playing another game. You might be able to get more George."

"I doubt it; somehow, I can feel US National Interest blocking anymore questions, especially after we arrested three of theirs. That will not get hidden and will not go down well," said Briggs.

"You are probably right, but my guess is that Frank Coalfield and Stewart Hillier are connected, and the Americans knew both," commented Shoreditch.

"If they killed them, this cannot get buried," said Asquith.

"I don't think they are responsible in that sense," said Braithwaite. "They are already in the clear, we think, for Hillier, and they did not fire a shot or try and run away. Adams, the other man, gave a brief description of the man he saw through the letterbox, but it's not worth having, even if it was accurate. All of this will come out slowly over the next few days, but we still have to deal with Hedges. Jack if you go to see him tomorrow, we need to get that file and find out who the target is. Slater looks to be our man, but he has disappeared and looks untraceable. Thanks to Jack's team we have the Ashley connection to match to the Ashley codeword on the voicemail."

Hooper had collected a quick briefing with his team. He watched Claridge-Briggs as he contributed, "Robert Ashley was Foreign Office. Paper file hidden away in the bowels of Whitehall, unless George knows more?" He turned pointedly.

Claridge-Briggs was prepared and was too long in the tooth at the game to be caught out twice in one day. He made a play of referring to his notes. "Robert Ashley, dead more than ten years, Diplomatic Corps, served throughout the Middle East and finally died at his desk in the FCO in the early 90s. His file is not digitised, but we can dig the paper copy out from storage. Wife died several years before him apparently."

"Nothing else?" Hooper probed.

"No, sorry nothing there, no Ashley codeword missions by the way, and I have that straight from the Director."

"Same here," said Braithwaite rescuing the line of questioning without realising it.

"These killings today," said Asquith. "Is this Slater

responsible?"

"Possible," said Jones, "but we have little or no evidence unless Forensics can turn up something. It could just as easily be a Frank Coalfield connection. If Hillier was leaking information to Coalfield, amongst others, as seems likely, we could have a long list of suspects entirely unconnected with Jack's main case."

Braithwaite stepped in. "I appreciate the IT risk that Hillier has exposed for the Police and Special Branch, but the National Security interest still points to Hedges. My guess, for what is worth, is that this was Slater, tidying up, as they say, because like most of you I don't believe in coincidence. If it wasn't Slater, then the Americans may be involved. Not those next door I might add. If it was Slater, then he has probably run and our chances of finding him are slim."

"Would he go after the girls, to continue tidying up as you put it?" asked Briggs.

Hooper stepped in. "Jessica Carver is on the way to the airport escorted by my protection team, by the way. The rich boyfriend is rich enough to hire private jets." Another update from the team before they had convened. "Michelle Carrington is now at home with her boyfriend and an armed guard outside. Remember we need her tomorrow with Hedges, and she needs to be briefed once we have decided what to do." Hooper had not forgotten that Claridge-Briggs was hiding something about Ashley, but he did not know what.

Shoreditch said, "Hedges is still calling the voicemail to check, but as I said, nothing from the team yet. I better check again though." He left to call the Internal Security team.

"I'll have another word with Claremont before he leaves. I suggest a fifteen-minute break to check with teams," said Braithwaite. They all agreed, pulling mobile phones out. Hooper went off to see his team. IT had come in saying it was okay to reconnect to systems. The Special Branch team was all still in the team room updating reports.

Hooper spoke with Drinkwater. The Robert Ashley name had to be connected, but he was not able to add anything. Rutledge was updating the Goodson report and linking back to Hedges. The team would return to the LSE the following day to look for mathematics graduates called Slater, and connections to Ashley. Was that a first or second name, and was it relevant? Hooper still thought he was missing something. They were comparing dates of the file transfers with Goodson's information on Procurement contracts. There was a clear collation, good enough for the prosecutors. Hooper returned to the room. He was updating David Jones and Duncan Asquith when Shoreditch burst back in.

"We have a voicemail access," said Shoreditch. "Option Three selected. Call was from a mobile. We are trying to trace it, but no caller ID, and it seems to be a foreign pre-pay. London area, from a vehicle or train. Nothing to Hedges mobile number though. Option Three asked for the caller to collect the Ashley message and gave Hedges mobile as the contact."

***

They had been travelling over thirty minutes and were passing Twickenham near the start of the M3, when Mike told Jess he needed to make a quick phone call. He pulled out one of his mobiles. He had two on him and another two in his bags. He needed to dump them. He switched it on. Jess was checking out the built in bar and sound system, looking for a radio station playing something holiday like. The music would go nicely with a bottle of Champagne she had found and decided to open herself. Mike dialled the voicemail. He heard all three menu items. He paused and pressed option three. It gave him a mobile number in the same clipped Eton accent. He took out his notebook and wrote the number down in his own code. He switched off the phone.

"Problem?" Jess asked.

"No, not really, I'll call when we get to Farnborough, or later. Nothing urgent," he lied.

"Here's some medicine for your injury," she said, passing a glass of champagne and stroking his injured cheek. "I can be a very attentive nurse," she said slipping her seat belt and putting her jeans clad leg across his.

"Jess you are imposs..." She stopped him with her mouth.

***

"Will Hedges know Option Three has been accessed?" David Jones asked Shoreditch.

"Possibly, but given his reported IT skills, I doubt he knows how to find out," replied Shoreditch. "We have his mobile, and landline tapped, and they are both warranted." He nodded at Deputy Commissioner Asquith and Commander Jones. "If you arrest Hedges, we want evidence as well, even if the Courts won't accept it." The UK did not accept phone tap evidence in court. "I have four people on his flat, I upped that this evening just in case Slater, or whoever, tries to tidy up there as well. He'll be watched all the way into work tomorrow, and we can monitor him all day with Michelle's help."

Braithwaite said, "I've just had a quiet word with Claremont, without the others, as they were leaving. He'll deny that he told me, but what he said is that Schlemburg is out on his own. Schlemburg passed a file to Hedges. They, meaning the Ambassador and Reach Claremont, don't know what was in it, but they suspect a US target. He said the mission was unauthorised, and a major investigation was getting started in the USA. When I asked him about Coalfield being one of theirs, he didn't say anything, but he did nod. They won't admit that officially either."

"Things get more interesting every minute," said Claridge-Briggs. "I may have to give the Ambassador another call. I need to give him time to talk to his team. I'm sure he will cooperate to avoid a major diplomatic incident."

"I'll update the Commissioner after I have had a word with the two CO19 men. They'll have to amend their reports I'm sure," said Asquith.

Claridge-Briggs, Braithwaite and Shoreditch left. They would meet again at Thames House before Hooper and Drinkwater saw Hedges, unless something happened overnight. They were all tired. David Jones spoke with Hooper after they were gone. "Really good work Jack, on Goodson and the team all round, so why are you looking so gloomy, Hillier and the gang leader are not your remit?"

"It's Claridge-Briggs and the damned Spooks in general,

with all their diplomatic incident crap. Briggs is definitely hiding something, probably on Ashley. Did you believe his FCO story?"

"Yes, he is covering something, and no, I don't believe he was telling all of the story. You know what they are like Jack; they won't give up anything unless it's in their interests. My guess is that Robert Ashley was one of theirs, but he's long dead. He was probably a very secret agent, which is why they don't want his background exposed. As for the connection now who knows? Are you sure John and David didn't get anything else, or miss something?"

"They are still writing their trip up. I'll check in a minute. What about Hedges, should I arrest him tomorrow morning or wait till the afternoon?"

"Neither Jack," said Jones. "I know that's not how we want to play it, but we have to let this situation play out. We have to get that mission file. If we have the target identified, then arrest by all means, but I don't want to have to get that from Hedges. He'll probably hang onto that information as long as possible, even if he talks about other stuff. The procurement links alone should put him away with Goodson for a long time, if they all correlate." Jones continued. "I don't understand why Hedges described it as an urgent mission on the voicemail, and that American, Schlemburg, was pushing Hedges hard; still too many unknowns, Jack. We all need some rest. Let's reconvene at 7:30 with some breakfast and catch up then. Send the team home, the uniforms and other Met can collect information for us overnight. Our team can write up in the morning." It was 23:45.

***

Mike and Jess were seated in the executive departure lounge at Farnborough airport. Mike had been there once before, and they were doing a lot of redevelopment. They were sipping another glass of champagne whilst they waited to be called to the jet, which was sitting right outside the lounge window. Mike told Jess he was just going to freshen up. Jess said she would do the same; she hated plane toilets, although she expected the private jet would be a step up from package holiday economy. She also needed to call Michael, her brother. Mike went into the Gents with his bag. The facility was empty. He called the contact number. The phone rang four times.

Hedges had drunk the best part of half a bottle of whisky, after a half bottle of Claret that he had chosen whilst he picked at his dinner. He was dozing in his chair when his mobile rang. He fumbled to find it and then answered, "Hedges," a single word in his clipped tones.

"You asked me to ring option three," said Slater.

"Ah," said Hedges.

The monitoring team went into overdrive. Another mobile, no caller ID, now they needed location, they could get the number eventually with the help of the specialist tracking teams employed by the mobile companies. The recorders were running instantly. One of the team was calling Shoreditch.

"I need you to complete the mission as soon as possible. It's very urgent," continued Hedges.

"What if I don't want to?" Slater said. "And why the need for a contact?"

Hedges gulped. "The police are investigating Wallace, and making connections and you may be targeted. They seem to be close." He almost added Slater, but held back.

"I understand," said Slater, but why the urgency of the mission? He could hear Jess calling, the flight was ready, he had to go.

"Need to know, old chap. Just get it done. It must look like an accident, accept on the voicemail and you can access the file, but get on with it, no more than a week, our cousins are eager for completion."

"I'll consider it." He hung up. He switched off the phone removed the battery and SIM, dumping the SIM in the waste basket in the Gents. He went out the door, passing another bin before the gate where Jess stood waiting; she was hanging up her mobile phone with a hurried goodbye. He dumped the phone, along with a newspaper he had read in the lounge. They walked out to the waiting jet.

***

The tracking team was honing in as the conversation continued. They knew it was south of London straight away, but had three potential masts. It was a foreign homed SIM, said one of the teams, not a UK network. It can jump around between UK networks, especially if it's a low coverage area. The three masts were all in Hampshire. They were narrowing it down when the call ended, and then the phone's signal was cut off. North Hampshire said the team, Aldershot mast, or possibly Farnborough. We'll need a while to push closer. Pay as you go SIM, French we think, not going to be able to trace that easily, even if the French cooperate. The team leader called Shoreditch again.

***

Jess and Mike were sitting in the seats of the jet. A single stewardess had given them yet another glass of Champagne. She then briefed them on safety on the jet and said they would be taking off very shortly. The jet was already taxiing out. They were airborne at midnight and turned westward, routing for the Atlantic. The stewardess asked whether they were hungry and that she had several choices for food, or they could relax on the full flat beds. Jess thought that was an excellent idea. The Stewardess gave her a smile and said she would bring breakfast in before they landed in a little over eight hours. She left them to it. They were not the first passengers on board who wished to join the mile high club, although they were considerably higher than that already. She buzzed the cockpit telling the pilots she would bring a meal through in a couple of hours. She settled down to read her book.

Jess had removed Mike's jacket and undone his shirt. "I need to check you for more injuries," she said, removing her sweater and bra. She sat back on his lap finding the controls that pushed and reclined his seat flat. She did not find any injuries despite a detailed examination.

CHAPTER FORTY-SIX

Friday morning

Michelle Carrington had arrived at Thames House early. Braithwaite met her in reception, along with Ian Shoreditch. She had received a call from David Jones who spoke with her, and her new fiancé, Mark Ellis. Mark had proposed properly, at last, in the flat. He even had a ring, which he explained he had sorted out ready for his next leave. Mark had been persuaded, eventually, that she was well protected and was heading back to Berlin. David had personally promised an update, whilst congratulating them both on taking the plunge at last. Michelle was ecstatic about their engagement, but still deeply concerned and afraid about Hedges. She was, on one level, reassured by the escort, and presence of Special Branch, but on the other hand concerned that they were considered to be needed. It was, therefore, with some trepidation that she collected the office keys. Braithwaite and Shoreditch took her to a small meeting room, where, to add to her trepidation, Julian Clarkson, the DG himself, waited for her. Michelle had seen him around the building and dealt with his PA, but only spoken a greeting before. Julian shook her hand and poured her a cup of tea whilst asking her to take a seat.

"Michelle, thank you for agreeing to take part in this," started Clarkson. "I appreciate that this is not what your role normally involves. I'll let Jon and Ian bring you up-to-date on the investigation and brief you on what is planned for the day. You are aware I know of how serious this could be for the Service. It seems highly likely that Mr. Hedges has been involved in various, unauthorised, activities, and these could seriously impact the

National Interest. I wanted to add my own personal reassurance as to your safety and continued role in the Service. I have been advised by Ian and Jon that I should not be in contact with Mr. Hedges for now; however, if you feel the need to contact me directly, please relay through Ian. I will leave you all to it now, and thank you once again. Without your vigilance, we may not be as far with this investigation as we are now."

Clarkson rose and headed off to what he knew would be a difficult meeting. The COBRA committee was operating, and he would be joining the Metropolitan Police Commissioner, his counterpart in Six, and the Cabinet Secretary. The Prime Minister might well put in an appearance. COBRA stood for Cabinet Office Briefing Room A, but had become the accepted acronym for serious emergency meetings on security or other situations. The membership varied dependent on the situation to be discussed.

Michelle had only interrupted the director with the odd word. His words were reassuring she felt, despite the slightly pompous tone, but once again her concerns were raised because of who said them.

Neither Braithwaite, nor Shoreditch had been home, and at best they had grabbed a few naps during the night, slumped in office chairs. It would be Monday morning before a specialist phone system engineer was available to go through all the voicemail system options. The trained one in the administration software had left the department two years before, and no one had been retrained. Braithwaite and Shoreditch had been in the IT Room trying to uncover logs, whilst the IT specialist team tried to recover files from Hedges' PC in his office. They would have to break that off before Hedges came in, or swap his machine, which might make Hedges more suspicious. They had also been in the investigation room following the voicemail calls the previous night. They were pleased, as the Director had repeated what they had briefed him to say, after he had insisted he spoke with Michelle. They told Michelle what had happened the previous night.

"We now know the call to Hedges was in the North Hampshire area, probably Farnborough, but narrowing it down beyond that will take time," started Shoreditch. "We know that Option Three was selected earlier, and that the contact called

Hedges. Then the message auto-deleted. Hedges and the caller had a brief discussion, but the asset, which may or may not be this Slater, did not accept the new mission and still hasn't."

"In reality, nothing much has changed," continued Braithwaite. "We still do not know who the target is, or what was in the file that Hedges uploaded. I won't go into the evidence that has been collected against him, but the plan is to see what happens. Our Special Branch friends, you know Jack Hooper, will interview Hedges this afternoon about Sally Carver."

"They will use the information you uncovered, but, they will not reveal how they got it," said Shoreditch. "Special Branch wants to build a wider case against Hedges and others, and they have other information. They will be in this morning, and we may want you to search through more information on the system. I'll leave that to you, to discuss that with them."

"In the meantime, Michelle," said Braithwaite, "we want you to act as normally as possible and fulfil your duties. When Special Branch calls you in, you can explain it to Hedges, if you need to, as a routine internal vetting call. Is that all, all right? Jon and I need to get out of here, and you need to be ready in the office as normal." Braithwaite and Shoreditch did not pass on any information about the deaths of the Coalfields and Hillier to Michelle. The Director had been briefed, but told not to mention them either. They were still not formally linked to Slater and Hedges, but the team suspected they were all connected. Michelle had nodded through the explanation; which matched what David Jones had told her.

Michelle went up to the office. Unusually, the door across the corridor was open. Sitting inside was the Special Branch protection team, dressed in overalls, and looking like painters and decorators. They gave her a smile. Again, should she be reassured, or more concerned? She did not think Hedges was a physical threat to her, but what did she really know about him? If he was involved, not if, she corrected herself, then he had ordered the removal of those girls, and Hemmings, and who knows what else he had done, or could do? She braced herself for the day and fussed with mundane things, waiting for Hedges to come in. She went to unlock Hedges' office door and found it already unlocked. She opened the door. The keys had not been signed out by Hedges in

Reception, so who was inside?

The IT disk recovery team had cloned Hedges' desktop PC and were leaving as Michelle entered the office. Not knowing their independent parts in the investigation, she had challenged them. One of the protection officers was there right behind her, as she must have let out a yelp in shock at seeing someone in the office. The IT team also looked shocked as the man in overalls behind Michelle put away a gun. They showed their authority from the CIO, as Shoreditch came scurrying in, just as things might have got difficult. Ian apologised to Michelle for not telling her they would be there. He had only just found out himself in the IT room. The IT team left. Ian again apologised, and despite her shaking, she reassured him she was okay. He left to go across the corridor with the Special Branch man. Breathing a sigh of relief, she cleared the mail that had not been sorted during her absence. She put fresh coffee on in Hedges' office, got out his in-tray ready for him, printing out the emails that she knew he would not read on his screen. She also printed out his day's diary, which included the 14:00 appointment for Detective Inspector Hooper and Detective Sergeant Drinkwater, budget meeting at 10:00 and an Analyst update from the Policy Unit who operated on the floor below at 11:00.

***

Hedges entered Thames House in a brisk walk, but with his mind on Slater/Ashley's call the previous evening. He had gone over it time and time again, before finally falling asleep for a few brief hours. His normal immaculate appearance was marred by two cuts from shaving. One thing had gone right so far, he thought as he took a lift, Michelle was back in, as his office keys were signed out. At least his mail and diary would be sorted. Damn, he thought, I have the Special Branch visit this afternoon. Could he put them off? But that would raise more questions. Well, he could deal with them. I can just repeat what I said about Sally last time in my written statement. Had Schlemburg got an updated file? He was pretty quick last time he thought, but that would mean calling him, not something he relished after their last call. As he walked down his office corridor, he noticed Ian Shoreditch walking down the corridor. What was he doing up here?

"Morning Shoreditch," he said. "How are you?"

"Fine thank you Hedges, how are you?"

"Fine, yes, fine, thank you, what brings you to my neck of the woods?" It was indiscreet to ask anything like that in Thames House, but Hedges was on edge.

"Oh just checking an office across the way from you, might have a move around, must dash, late for a meeting."

Hedges watched Shoreditch turn round a corridor corner. He approached his own office. Sure enough, the door was open, as was the office opposite. What appeared to be a maintenance crew were rearranging furniture and getting ready to paint. He nodded at them and entered his office. Michelle was at her desk.

"Michelle, glad to see you're better, how are you this morning?"

"I'm fine thank you, Mr. Hedges," she replied.

She did not look that fine thought Hedges, a bit pale and shaky. Well, she was in. Hedges was never sick. "Ah good, you have my tray and I can already smell the coffee. What would I do without you?" He removed his coat, hanging it on the stand by the office door. He took the tray and said, "I'll update you in a few minutes, my dear, now the nation's work is never done." He indicated his tray and entered his office, kicking his office door closed.

Michelle breathed. The maintenance man looked at her. She nodded. She was okay.

***

"That was close," Shoreditch reported to Braithwaite. "The IT team scared Michelle and themselves half to death." He explained what had happened. The IT team was telling the same thing to the CIO at the far end of the room. "Then Hedges turned up as I was leaving, trying to find out what I was doing in the corridor. He knows you never ask that."

"He's bound to be suspicious, given the pressure. Anyway, how did he seem?"

"Definitely on edge, he'd cut himself shaving and looked

almost as tired as us."

The phone went, announcing the arrival of Hooper and Drinkwater. It was just after nine o'clock. They convened in a small meeting room just along from IT. They made sure the Special Branch officers had tea or coffee and access to outside lines. They asked the CIO to come in and brief the Special Branch officers on latest progress. Colin McDowell checked something with one of his staff, grabbed the piece of paper, waved at him and hurriedly joined them in the glass walled room.

"Breaking news," he said, after quick introductions. "We have a file, well a partial file I should say, at last." He showed them the piece of paper. McDowell looked very tired and stressed. Not surprising, as he had not been home for two days, let alone the twenty-four hours Braithwaite and Shoreditch had been in the office.

"Peter Smith, who is he?" Hooper asked, reading the name on the paper McDowell handed him. He used the landline to phone the name through to his team. There was no mobile access, or phones allowed in the IT area.

"I've managed to calm the team down after they met your chaps earlier," McDowell continued, which necessitated a further discussion and explanation. "We are tracing the phone still. The SIM was purchased at CDG in Paris. Don't ask how we found that out. It was several months ago and their CCTV only runs for thirty days. Cash, of course. It was not airside, so no boarding card number to tie in."

"What about phone location, anything since last night?" Hooper asked. Shoreditch had called him as soon as the Hedges' call had gone through. "I can send someone to the operators if you need some support?"

Shoreditch replied, "We have narrowed it down to north Hampshire, but the mast there covers quite a big area, so it will take a while to triangulate down from other masts in the region with a weaker signal."

"We now have Hedges' hard drive from his desktop," McDowell revealed. "We will clone his personal PC hard drive as well." McDowell finished his run down. "I have to write the report for you Ian, and the DG now." He looked just as tired, and he left the room to return to his team.

"Whilst Hedges is here today, my team will carry out a full search of his house. When we planted the bugs we didn't have time," Shoreditch added.

"Not a lot so far from the murder victims, Mr. and Mrs. Coalfield and Stewart Hillier, other than confirmation they are suspicious deaths," Hooper added to the team's knowledge. "The preliminary report on Hillier, which we rushed through last night, shows death from a massive Heroin overdose, with a tranquilliser as well." He turned to Drinkwater.

"We have applied pressure on the Coroner to get the post-mortems brought forward on Frank Coalfield and his wife. They should be starting now. That looks like the same method as Hillier, despite the confusion over knife wounds and murder suicide that was evident from the crime scene." Drinkwater showed Braithwaite and Shoreditch one of the scene photos. "Luckily the senior investigating officer realised that there was not enough blood for the knife wound. See here. He pointed to the floor below, next to Coalfield's wife. Toxicology will probably confirm the same as Hillier, but it looks like the same MO. No fingerprints so far, or DNA, but they are still looking. We'll then try and trace the heroin batch, but that probably won't get us far, and will take a while."

"Thanks John," said Hooper looking at Drinkwater. "It looks like…" He looked at Braithwaite, "…that your American friends arrived at the scene as the killer was leaving, or they disturbed him. He fired one shot, 9 mm through the front door. The bullet hit the front garden wall and was lying by the entrance path." More photos were shown of the bullet, then the front door, and the casing by the stairs. "No forensics yet, and no gun found. The man, probably man, exited the building by the back door and garden gate, no footprints and no witnesses there. It was raining and that back alley is dark even in good weather and daylight. We are trawling cabs in the area, but it's London, and the chances are slim without a public appeal, and we have no description other than what we can get from the Americans and our star witness." Hooper told them about Mrs. Harmsworth and her running description to the Police control room. "She's a real gem and says that she saw a man, well possibly a man, going into the house with Hillier about an hour before the shot. She doesn't know Hillier by name, only sight, and that not much. She only saw the back of this other person when she was putting the milk bottles out. She still does that. We have her description, for what it's worth, dark blue jacket, might have been black, no hair colour, no face. She heard the car doors bang when the Americans arrived, so was looking out when the shot was fired. We might get more today, as the officers on the scene were concerned she might have a turn. She's eighty-two by the way. Brilliant running description of the incident, one for all the training files I should think."

"Thanks, Jack," said Jon Braithwaite, "amazing progress considering what has happened overnight. Hedges is upstairs in his office. Michelle Carrington is working next door to him, and we have your team across the corridor as maintenance men, as Michelle and the IT Team found out. Hedges has had no calls so far, unless he has done something whilst we have been in here. He has a couple of meetings planned for this morning and then you chaps at 14:00. I know you are after the killer Jack, but Hedges is a serious risk to national security, so our focus is bound to be on him. Michelle is safe here, and I understand Miss Carver is safely away overseas. Unless we think there is another potential target at immediate risk, we need to focus on Hedges."

Something was gnawing at the back of Hooper's mind, but he could not think what. He was too tired. "The IT issue with Hillier is potentially huge. The Commissioner is over at COBRA with your DG, trying to do a risk assessment. All of the IT team are under investigation in case they are tied into Hillier. First, indications are that he was acting alone, but they have to check. We need the IT team to help with the search, as they know the systems, so they are not being very cooperative when they are hauled off for questioning. My guess is that Hillier did work alone. Forensics are checking his home PC. John and I need to update the rest of our team and close some of the angles. We need a few minutes with Michelle. Can we do that without Hedges knowing? We will be back for the Hedges meeting though." Hooper and Drinkwater stood. They would have to be escorted to the briefing room that Shoreditch had booked for that purpose. Hooper still had the feeling he had missed something. It would have to wait.

"Just before you leave," said Braithwaite, "here is Sally Carver's personal file, well the relevant parts anyway. This shows what Michelle discovered about Sally's leave and should help you with Hedges." He could see Hooper's suspicions about what might be missing. "Jack, everything you need is there, the only stuff missing is on her background and vetting. Just like Michelle she was a PA, not an agent, or analyst, so we are not hiding anything that's important to the case. We are checking her IT records as well, where we still have them. She seems to have been checking up on Hedges from what we have discovered. If you give Michelle your Fraud details, Goodson isn't it, she can trawl through Hedges' files for you without arousing his suspicion. She may even get you more for this afternoon. She wants to help."

Hooper and Drinkwater were escorted to the briefing room. It was just after ten. Shortly after, Michelle arrived with a Special Branch maintenance man following behind. He exchanged a quick word with Hooper and Drinkwater, but stayed outside as they went through Sally's file and the Charles Goodson requirements. Michelle said that she had taken no calls, inside or out, and that Hedges was having a budget meeting. She then escorted them to reception where they departed for Scotland Yard. Michelle then returned to her office, followed discretely by her maintenance man.

***

Schlemburg was furious again with Reach. He had expected a call the previous evening from him with a new username and passcode from Thunderbird, but nothing. He had found Jamie's number, and no word from him either, and no response to the phone call. He had called the duty officer, and there was nothing. Hidelwietz had called at eleven in the evening and asked for an update. He could tell him nothing. He thought about calling Hedges, but decided it could wait till the morning. He had finally decided to go to sleep. His wife had gone to bed hours before with her latest book. He finally slept, then woke late. Now, he was at his office, to find that Beth was not there either, no response from Reach or Jamie. What was going on? He ploughed through his email, fuming, calling Reach every few minutes.

Reach Claremont, Jamie Adams, and Beth Schwarz were

under US Marine guard in the basement of the US Embassy. Two investigators from CIA internal affairs were waiting to speak with them. They had finally returned back to the Embassy by one in the morning where Elliot Bloomstein, still in a dinner jacket, had awaited them. Alerted by Briggs, and then updated by him in a second call, the Ambassador had called the duty controller and ensured that Schlemburg was not told what had happened. After he had been told their story, the Ambassador had made sure they were safe in the basement, apologising for keeping them there. They would have to do an interview with the UK police, but he would not let them out of the Embassy, and he wanted Schlemburg isolated. He had then called Casey Richenbach and then the Secretary of State. Richenbach told him the investigators were on the overnight plane, and he had alerted the CIA Director with as minimal details as possible. Hidelwietz would be arrested the following morning East Coast time. The Secretary had been very forthright. Close the whole thing down, arrest Schlemburg and get the file name, before there was a major diplomatic issue with their allies. The President would have to be briefed. That was something the Secretary of State was not looking forward to. Reach and Briggs had separately urged him to keep Schlemburg in play so that he would not alert Hedges. The Ambassador agreed, but only whilst Washington slept.

***

Michelle Carrington was back at her desk before the budget meeting ended at 10:45. As Hedges came out with the Finance Director, he asked her to put in a call to Schlemburg. Michelle put the call through. As Beth Schwartz was not at her desk, it needed the telephone exchange to make the connection.

"Schlemburg," he answered.

"Morning Carl," said Hedges deciding to try a friendly approach. The listeners were already calling the contact in to their superiors, and ensuring all was recorded.

"I hope you have some news for me?" Schlemburg replied aggressively ignoring the friendly approach.

"I have made contact."

"And?"

"He has not accepted the mission yet, but I am hopeful, and he understands the need for an accident, and the urgency."

"Hopeful doesn't cut it, Hedges."

"I appreciate your desire for an early resolution, but as you are aware, the method of contact and role of the asset does not compel him to comply," Hedges tried to explain.

"I don't give a shit about that, Hedges." Schlemburg was almost shouting at this pompous Brit. "Get this mission going. You know what is at stake and if you can't control your asset, you better hand him over to somebody that can." For the second time, he slammed the phone down on Hedges.

Schlemburg checked the time, too early for Hidelwietz. He sent an email instead. He looked outside his office for Beth. Was she on a day off? Where were Reach and Jamie? He picked up the phone and tried Reach again. Two men were standing at the door. He did not recognise them.

"Carl Schlemburg, please put down your phone and keep your hands in sight." The shorter one said, flashing a CIA ID in the process. Schlemburg realised that his future policy role would not happen. The larger man produced some handcuffs, putting away a pistol in the process, which Carl had barely noticed. The larger one turned him around and handcuffed him, before carrying out a quick search. "Clean," he said to the other. Before they led him away towards the basement, they asked for his safe's combination, and then realised it was open. The shorter one went to the safe and retrieved all the documents, placing them in a plastic carrier he took from his pocket. As they had gone out, another man from the IT and Communications centre came in. The shorter one said, "Full clone and sweep," pointing at Schlemburg's PC.

***

The COBRA meeting had been a tense affair. Claridge-Briggs had accompanied Monica, but he was outside the meeting room. He had nodded to Clarkson as he arrived, already talking to another man who Briggs recognised as the Home Office's Permanent Secretary. The Cabinet Office Secretary had already been in the room. Briggs had briefed his Director on the way over from Vauxhall. Last to arrive was the Metropolitan Police Commissioner who looked decidedly unhappy. Briggs avoided his look. The meeting had been going for thirty minutes, when a stir of activity forecast the arrival of the Prime Minister. He bustled in. A further thirty minutes and the faint sound of indistinctive raised voices from inside the room.

The Prime Minister emerged with a comment to his aide of "Get me the Foreign Secretary," as they walked away without looking at Briggs.

Briggs was then called in. The Commissioner was leaving as well, looking chastened. Clarkson and Monica Pennywise remained in the COBRA Room along with the Permanent Secretary and the Cabinet Office Secretary. Clarkson looked shattered. They all looked grim. Briggs' phone went, amazingly there was a signal this deep below Whitehall. It was Elliot Bloomstein, stating that Schlemburg was about to be arrested following a call from Hedges. No, Hedges was not alerted. Could Briggs pass onto the police that the CIA officers from last night's incident would be interviewed at the embassy that afternoon, and would provide full statements. The COBRA attendees looked at him as he took the call. Clarkson also received a call. Briggs relayed the latest information from the Ambassador. Monica led the response.

"George, as you can imagine the Prime Minister is livid and wants this stopped as soon as possible. If, as you say, the Americans have got Schlemburg, then they may be able to get the target identity, but we still won't have it, or who Hedges' asset is. Attention will focus on Julian's area." Julian Clarkson looked even more uncomfortable. "Plato will have to close down. The Prime Minister has insisted. We can't have any more exposure from that area raising concerns." She gave him a knowing look that meant Ashley's real identity was still secure, at least from this end. "The police are closing down the IT security angle, but it will take months to find out what has gone missing or been passed on. The Prime Minister was really not impressed about that. For us, we wait and see. I expect Special Branch will arrest this afternoon, and the Commissioner will not hold off, given the murder links, the IT risk and the procurement evidence. MoD wants action on that side as well."

Clarkson decided to step in, "I have Braithwaite and Shoreditch monitoring everything Hedges does, and they have just confirmed the Schlemburg call, and that he checked the voicemail again. That was at 10:45, so an hour or so ago. We have Special Branch protective monitoring right outside his office disguised as a maintenance crew. Special Branch will see him at 14:00. Let's hope we get the file before then. The tracking team has narrowed down the mobile call from the asset to Hedges to the North Hampshire area, but we have only two prongs of the triangulation from two masts. We can't nail his position. The earlier call was from near Twickenham, but moving, suggesting a vehicle travelling towards south Hampshire. Whoever Slater now is, he won't be there anyway."

Monica would prefer that they stopped looking, but how to stop it? It was time for Clarkson to be told, but not the Permanent Secretary or the Cabinet Office Secretary. They would be bound to leak the information. They did not need to know. Monica sent George back to Vauxhall to deal with Plato and asked the Perm' Sec' and Cabinet Secretary for a few minutes alone with Clarkson. "Rum deal this," she started, he affirmed it was. "I need to tell you something, but it must not go any further than perhaps Braithwaite, he will understand." And he can be persuaded. She recalled his unauthorised affair with the Wallace girl.

"What is it, Monica?"

"We think we know who Slater is."

"Then, we must tell the police before anyone else is killed," exclaimed Clarkson not liking where this was going.

"There would be serious implications elsewhere. If his true identity were to come out, it would lead back to others, which in turn would seriously jeopardise other current operations. We need to let him go. There is no way he could be prosecuted anyway without all this coming out in the press. I doubt the CPS would go for it, and Slater will have a 'following orders' defence as well, at least for the main targets. I know Braithwaite won't like it, let alone Special Branch, but Braithwaite, as an operations man, and because of his connections, will, I hope, understand."

"I presume you are referring to his affair with Jenny Wallace?"

"You knew?"

"Monica, please give me some credit for running my own ship. I know there were concerns about whether I was involved with Hedges, which I was definitely not. He has risked the whole service with his actions; but I sometimes do know what is going on. How did you find out by the way?"

"Braithwaite told George, hoping that it would stay out of official reports and, with his help, with Special Branch. So far it has."

"I too want to keep it that way. We'll need good people to get us out of this mess, and Braithwaite is one of those good people. I'll try to help hide this Slater character if we can. I may need Shoreditch told as well as David Jones. That won't be easy. I have a confession on our side as well." He told Monica about how the phone system was set up. "I think the sooner this is all closed down the better."

They concluded the meeting. Monica returned to Vauxhall and Clarkson went with his Permanent Secretary to the Home Office, to brief his Secretary of State before the Prime Minister did. Monica updated Richard, her PA, on her return, with the minimum details, but saying that Hedges would probably be arrested that afternoon. She had other issues to deal with and urgently needed an update on some activity in the UK, with national Islamic Fundamentalists visiting Pakistan. Richard left her and called a number he had hoped never to have to use.

***

Hedges had not had time to properly calm down before his analyst team arrived for their hourlong meeting. He was desperate to check the voicemail to see if Ashley had responded, but he had to wait. After an hour of lengthy explanation of threats from emerging economies, a technology update, and a review of the next few weeks of planned work. He was exasperated and rude to the team. They finally left, not understanding what they had done wrong or why their boss was in such a foul mood. Hedges had gone to the door with them and noticed the maintenance team across the corridor again. The finance director had not been helpful with his budget, but could he at least get his office a new lick of paint.

"Michelle?"

"Yes, Mr Hedges," she said looking up from her computer.

"Those maintenance men…"

Michelle was instantly on guard and prepared to flee. "What about them, Sir?"

"Have a word with facilities and see if, when they are finished, they can do my office?"

Michelle relaxed, "Of course."

"I'll grab some lunch from the dining room now. What time are those detectives due?" He knew what time, but he did not want Michelle getting more suspicious, although she had been quiet today, unlike a couple of days ago over that scanned file. "What are you working on?" He said coming around her desk.

Michelle quickly minimised her screen leaving her email up, hopefully, missing the unread mail highlighted from Shoreditch that had just come in. "Just the usual emails and requests for meetings. Are you still planning on leaving early for the weekend?" She tried to cover her tracks.

Hedges backed away, how he hated IT. "Oh that's good, yes the Detectives shouldn't take too long, then I'm off to the country. I'll see you in an hour."

Hedges failed to notice that the two maintenance men had moved into the corridor whilst he was leaning over Michelle. They returned to their office as Hedges departed. Michelle again breathed a sigh of relief. She read Shoreditch's email, thanking her for the confirmation of emails to Charles Goodson and asking her to access the supporting files if they existed. Michelle hoped this would all be over soon. She was not sure her nerves could take it.

***

Hooper and Drinkwater arrived back at Thames House at

13:30. Shoreditch met them and took them back to the IT room. Braithwaite had just taken a call from the Director, which had concerned him, but he had not said anything to Shoreditch, apart from the fact that the Director was with the Home Secretary. He also passed on the direction from COBRA which was to shut down as soon as possible, once they had enough from Hedges.

Hooper was excited, as he had realised the nagging thought was the Portugal information. The son; that was the connection. He had listened to the tape Drinkwater and Grahams had made with Andrew McKinnsley. He relayed the information to Shoreditch and Braithwaite. This appeared to concern Braithwaite. He went to check on a few systems, he said. So they had the son of Robert Ashley, a former Foreign Office diplomat. The son had been in the army before he had joined the Brokers. Hooper realised that, with time, they would have an identity. His uniformed team had also gone to the mobile operators to trace the call, even though Five said they could not get a more accurate fix. He did not expect them to have any more success, and the likelihood would be that Slater would be long gone.

Now for Hedges, he thought. They discussed with Shoreditch what they would ask. Shoreditch gave them a small directional microphone to relay the conversation back to the investigation team. Shoreditch then took them back to Reception so that Michelle could collect them officially.

As Braithwaite returned, McDowell rushed up to him. "The voicemail," he said. "They have a trace."

Braithwaite thanked him and instructed, "Lose that information, Colin, Director's orders." They were not to report the call trace location. "Which option?" He asked. McDowell wanted confirmation from the Director himself before he told him what had been selected and agreed to lose the trace. It was 13:45. Braithwaite called Claridge-Briggs, avoiding Shoreditch, as did McDowell as he returned. After his Claridge-Briggs call, he told Shoreditch that the voicemail had been triggered and what the number was. It was 14:05.

***

Michael Johnson and Jessica Carver had landed at

Providenciales Airport as dawn was breaking. The Stewardess had woken them discretely an hour before with breakfast, which had been gratefully received. Mike was relaxed and had slept soundly after Jessica had finished with her examinations. They had found robes on board, along with a bigger than normal bathroom. After they had woken, they had managed to resist each other, just. They had thanked the crew, getting a smirk in return, cleared customs and immigration in less than twenty minutes, and then a car had driven them to their hotel. They had checked in, and Jess had thrilled at the large penthouse suite and the ocean view. The private butler for their room offered to unpack for them, but Mike refused the offer, tipping him as he left. Finally, they were alone. Jess resisted the urge to drag Mike immediately to bed.

"I need a bath," she said, looking at the large sunken marble bathroom. "Join me?" she said, shedding clothes.

"In a moment, I need to make a couple of calls first." It was a very tempting offer.

She pouted, "As long as that is first, and only a couple of calls." She closed the bathroom door behind her.

Mike had decided what he would do. He took out one of the two mobiles. They had never been used before nor had their pre-pay SIMs. One was UK, and one was French. These were no good. Could he risk the hotel landline? That was easily traceable, so no. He needed an Internet terminal. He left the room, putting the phones back in his bag, and went down to the lobby and was shown through to a terminal. He logged onto a Skype connection, paid via a Johnson credit card from an international number. Then, he rang the voicemail through that. He pressed the number. He logged off, deleted the browser history, and returned to the room. Jess was standing wrapped in a towel; equal parts furious, concerned, but mostly just beautiful. "Where have you been?" She had asked. It took him several minutes to get the towel off of her, and back into the bath, where the question disappeared unnoticed.

CHAPTER FORTY-SEVEN

Friday afternoon

Hooper and Drinkwater were kept waiting outside Hedges' office with Michelle for a few minutes. Hedges playing games they thought. Michelle whispered to them about the Goodson connections that Shoreditch had already forwarded. She rang the intercom again. Hedges had checked the voicemail again on his return from lunch. He had eaten too much then found himself drowsy, he needed to be alert for the detectives. He had dozed off, and only came to with Michelle's first intercom buzz. Now, she was buzzing again. How impertinent, he thought, straightening his tie. He went to his office door.

"Detectives," he said beckoning them in, "sorry to keep you waiting." Hooper and Drinkwater introduced themselves, showing their warrant cards as well. Hedges joined them at his small meeting table. "I understand from the press speculation, and your request through my PA, that you want to clarify some things about Sally Carver." Hedges wanted to take the initiative. "I did provide a written statement at the time, so I am unsure why you feel the need to ask again, but please go ahead."

Hooper was scrutinising Hedges carefully. Smug, self-satisfied bastard, he thought. Okay, let's get him on the back foot.

"Mr. Hedges, in your original statement you said that Miss Carver had gone on leave. Could you please explain why no leave application was submitted?"

Hedges replied, immediately concerned, "I would not

necessarily have signed it or authorised it. The form could have been lost."

"Mr. Hedges, you also did not contradict the statement that she had been on leave to Greece three weeks previously. All overseas travel for staff must be pre-authorised. Did you authorise that leave?"

"I really can't recall, Detective Inspector. It was several years ago, and I can't be held accountable for forms missing on a HR system." He was already crumbling.

"Mr. Hedges, what if I was to tell you that there is no record of Miss Carver applying for, or going on leave, and no record of her travelling out of the country," Drinkwater fired.

"I'm sure it must be some simple mistake, Detectives. As I said, the application could have been lost or not recorded, and she could have been travelling under a different name." How had they got the HR information, he asked himself?

"You do not think it unusual that, for your PA, there is no record of her leave applications, or leaving the country? Why should she use an assumed name to travel? Did you help her with identity documents?" Hooper persisted.

"That's not what I meant; I'm not sure where you are going with this?"

"Do you know Miss Jenny Wallace? She worked here as well we understand?"

"I'm afraid not," Hedges looked and felt more relieved at the sudden change.

"That's odd, she was a researcher assigned to counter Iraq. How about, Harriet Hollingsworth and Jodi Parker?"

"No, I do not know them," Hedges answered truthfully. How did they know what Wallace was working on?

"Do you know *of* them, Mr Hedges?" It was Drinkwater again.

"I have seen their names in the papers of course, but I do not know them."

"Peter Smith?" They had tracked his file via a newspaper report back to MoD.

More hesitation and PS in his diary. "Who? What would that have to do with a serial killer of girls?" Hedges asked.

"Helena Salbert?" Drinkwater showed a photo.

"Who?" Hedges was beginning to panic, how had they got that name? HS in his diary.

"She was a Canadian, missing, believed killed, a few years ago. Gerald Hemmings?" Hooper again.

Hedges almost jumped, "What has he got to do with it?"

"So you know him?"

"My deputy, of course, I knew him." They would know that, this was better ground. His heart rate slowed a little. "He was killed in a mugging a few years ago, very sad." Where were they going with this, he thought?

"We have information to believe that the death of Mr Hemmings' was not a simple mugging and is connected to the girls, as is Peter Smith." Drinkwater said.

Hooper noticed the beads of perspiration on Hedges forehead. He could also feel the vibration of his phone on silent in his shirt pocket.

"I still fail to see the connection," Hedges said his heart rate going back up.

"You do not think it odd that Sally Carver goes missing, after your deputy is killed in a fake mugging, and another connection, Jenny Wallace, has just disappeared in an abduction, and none of that strikes you as a little too much of a coincidence?" Hooper pushed hard.

Hedges spluttered, what could he say? "I don't know what you are implying Inspector, but I really don't like your tone. Now, I have given you more than enough time. I have other duties and appointments to attend to. If you would be so kind." He stood showing, with an outstretched arm, the route to the door.

They knew from Michelle Carrington that he had no further

appointments scheduled. "Is that to see Mr. Charles Goodson on his estate, Sir?" Hooper stuck the question in like a knife. Charles Goodson! How did they know that? Hedges began to panic. "Mr. Goodson has been helping us with our enquiries, so I'm afraid he won't be joining you this weekend," said Hooper.

What enquiries? Hedges wanted to ask, but could not. He had to get out, he must stay calm and get rid of these detectives. "That's disappointing," he managed to say, "but I really must get back to my work."

"You don't seem to be very curious about your friend, Mr. Hedges. Why is that?"

The questions were like needles sliding into his skull, thought Hedges, realising by not asking, that he had made another mistake, like this whole interview. "He's just an acquaintance really, and I wouldn't presume to pry. It's not something we do here?" Good answer he thought.

"You have no connection professionally then?"

"No, why should I?" He answered too quickly. He wanted them gone, not answering his questions. Could they know about his contacts with Goodson, how?

They did not answer, but finally stood. "Well, thank you for your time, Mr Hedges," said Hooper. "We will be in touch."

Hedges felt relief that they were finally going. He walked Hooper toward the office door with Drinkwater. Ian Shoreditch, Jon Braithwaite and the two maintenance men were standing by Michelle's desk.

"There has been a development," Shoreditch said to Hooper. The two maintenance men came and held Hedges' arms, whilst Shoreditch whispered something in Hooper's ear.

"Michelle, Shoreditch old chap, what is going on?" Hedges blurted out not realising he was being handcuffed.

Hooper nodded to Shoreditch .

"Mr. Ian Hedges, I am arresting you on suspicion of conspiracy to commit murder, fraud, breach of the Official Secrets Act and there may be a few more by the time we are done. You do not have to say anything, but it may harm your defence if you do not mention when questioned something which you later rely on in court. Anything you do say may be given in evidence. Do you understand?"

"Yes, but, but, but, what is this, you can't arrest me I'm..."

"Mr. Hedges I strongly advise you to stay silent at this point, before I physically make you." Hooper had come very close. "Get him out of my sight," he said to the two maintenance men.

***

Geoff Hidelwietz took the call. International, he noticed. The British accent gave the codeword *Demise* and that day's date. "I understand," he said after a brief explanation. He immediately phoned another number, "*Demise*" and the date, he said when it was promptly answered; then he stated, "Hedges. Yes, that's him. As soon as possible." He terminated the call. He was returning to his work, in his home study, when he noticed the two men on the CCTV security system, about to knock on his door.

***

The Custody Sergeant heard the alarm from Interview Room Five in Paddington Green Police Station. Hedges was in there, on serious charges, with his solicitor awaiting interview for the second day running. He opened the door, and the solicitor knocked him down, running out. That was not the same man who had come the previous afternoon, he thought, banging his head against the corridor wall. By the time he got up, the solicitor was gone. He looked at the prisoner. He was slumped on the desk. One of the duty PCs came running into the room. "Get him, get the solicitor," he stuttered. The PC reversed direction. The Sergeant checked the prisoner. No pulse. "Oh shit," he said.

***

Hooper answered his mobile whilst writing up reports with Shoreditch and Braithwaite. He had spent the morning at the US Embassy getting delayed statements from Reach Claremont, Jamie Adams, and Beth Schwartz. They would all be returning to the States the following day. Hooper was fuming as the Commissioner and Commander Jones had both told him to stop investigating the Ashley name. The Home Secretary had told them that morning, and it had been confirmed by Clarkson at Thames House, although the implication was that it was Vauxhall making the very firm request. Hooper did not like it one bit. The team had been on their way to the LSE when they were told to return.

Rutledge was going through Hedges' diary, confirming the initials against the file uploads that had been partially retrieved by McDowell's IT team. Schlemburg was no longer in the country he was told. He had the name of the target file passed on via Briggs from the Ambassador. Briggs sat across the table. Hooper was desperate to ask Briggs about the Ashley name, but had been told not even to ask. Drinkwater was bringing in some fresh coffee. Hooper's expletive matched the Custody Sergeant as he told the others.

CHAPTER FORTY-EIGHT

Resignation

Several months later, Jessica Carver, soon to be Johnson, was sitting on the terrace of a Caribbean villa, overlooking the crystal clear waters and enjoying the morning sunshine, whilst sipping coffee. She was dressed, provocatively according to Mike, in a bikini, at least covered by a light wrap designed to prevent their maid getting too embarrassed. She flicked through some photos back from developers, showing her brother and the still luscious Lucy from their visit the previous week. Mike was typing on his laptop, trading away, not that they seemed to need money. The villa was half hers, Mike had told her once they were married. It had been the second one they had visited.

Jessica had returned to the UK briefly from her and Mike's trip, but only to resign, helped by the decision to shut down Plato. Her final Plato analysis showed a link between the disappearances or deaths, the movement of funds illegally and several personnel in the USA and the UK. She did not have it all, especially as she had not seen the links between Goodson and Hedges, but she had enough. She heard about Hedges' death only on her return from holiday. Mike had stayed at the hotel in the Caribbean to work, he said and deal with the house buying. The Director had approved, with regret, her decision to resign, which she allowed to go through with George Claridge-Briggs' recommendation. Tony Grayson was especially sorry to lose an analyst but grateful for his pending promotion and switch to operational, counter fundamentalist analysis. The Plato report was placed in a flagged file vault marked for Director's eyes only.

Jessica had, unusually, visited the Director's office for a farewell chat at the Director's request. She had been there before, but only once. She noticed a new PA. Michelle Carrington had been happy to transfer across the river; she had received personal thanks from Clarkson and offered a choice of roles. No one mentioned her predecessor Richard Templeman who seemed to have left, for sickness reasons, she was told.

The Director had sat with Jessica in the comfortable chairs after Michelle had shown her in. Michelle had recognised her name. Monica had spoken about Sally, and that she had known Jessica's father. She thanked her for the Plato work and apologised for putting her through the scares of the last few weeks. She complimented Jessica on her tan, which led to a discussion about her boyfriend. Jessica had a photo, would Monica like to see it? Monica managed not to say anything when she saw it. Monica would need to speak to George again, urgently.

Two weeks later Jessica had flown back to the Caribbean, only first-class this time. Mike said executive Jets were too expensive and that he had to save up for the house. Now as she sat on the terrace, still not quite believing that she was soon to be married and living a luxury lifestyle, she looked at the platinum engagement ring with its solitaire diamond; she heard the doorbell. The maid was tidying one of the spare bedrooms, so Jessica got up and went to the door.

The man stood in the shadows at the door. He held up a small engagement present. "What a lovely surprise," said Jessica open mouthed. "Please come in, I must introduce you to my fiancé, Mike." She showed him into the cool corridor. "Mike," she shouted "someone you have to meet."

CHAPTER FORTY-NINE
Epilogue

Two men met, around the small dining table, the two empty seats were noticeable. "Not a complete disaster," said the first, "but too close for comfort, shame about the asset and not completing the mission. It will take us a while to find another, I suppose. Hedges got carried away, too many other targets."

"The mission could not be helped and I agree on the other targets, he went too far. We did warn him, but I may have some good news on the asset," said George Claridge-Briggs.

ACKNOWLEDGEMENTS

Research is never easy, so my thanks to DARPA, MIT and Sir Tim Berners-Lee for the invention of the Internet and the World Wide Web plus the cast of thousands, if not millions, who contribute to the content, official and unofficial.

Special thanks to Charlie Bray at The Indietribe for the editing.

http://www.theindietribe.com/

Thank you to Craig for early editing notes and comments, reading the book, and turning his comments around quickly. My special thanks to Russell, Natasha and mostly Lisa for putting up with me as well as reading and commenting on the countless drafts and adjustments. Any mistakes remaining are mine.

OTHER TITLES FROM PHILIP G HENLEY

Phenweb Publishing

Phenweb.co.uk

Twitter ***@philip_g_henley*** and Facebook at ***Phenweb***

The Demise Trilogy

The Complete Demise Trilogy in one Volume

An Agent's Demise

An Agent's Rise

An Agent's Prize

An Agent's Demise

This book!

An Agent's Rise

The sequel to, An Agent's Demise.

The Demise operation was shut down the killer allowed to disappear, but the conspirators have not all been caught and the efforts of MI6 and the CIA to cover up the dirty deeds of the security services only results in more deaths and destructions. Slater returns to tidy up, but how can he reconcile his new life with what he is asked to do.

The newly promoted Detective Chief Inspector Hooper has not forgotten who his target is but there appears to be another assassin on the loose.

An Agent's Prize

The conclusion to the Demise trilogy.

The conspiracy is over the mistakes and cover up are hidden and buried for good. Both sides of the Atlantic can concentrate on the threats from Islamic Terrorism. That is what they all hope. They want to enlist a hidden black asset in the chase, but there are risks to that approach. Meanwhile the FBI is still investigating what really happened. Is the conspiracy really over?

Al Qaeda plan new atrocities and MI6 with Homeland Security will try to stop them. The newlywed Michael Johnson can help but his wife is still recovering from her injuries and she is suspicious of her husband and the authorities. From the streets of San Francisco to the suburban towns of England the terrorists are plotting an outrage.

The Observer Series - Part One - The World of Fives

Read how the story started. In, The World of Fives, we find Cathy an Observer in The Interplanetary Geographic Service observing the planet Fivur as an exceptionally rare convergence of moons and orbits creates massive tidal shifts on the planet's surface. Carlo, a Fivurian, must overcome the impact of the tides on the planet's power system, whilst keeping his love Sello safe. Meanwhile, Cathy tries to persuade her superiors to intervene and save the lives of the planet's humanoid population. If she can save them they will need a new home but Earth factions have different ideas. Meanwhile another intelligent species on the planet, the Sharok, wait to feast on any human or Fivurian who ends up in the water.

The Observer Series - Part Two - Intervention

The continuing story of Cathy Rodriguez, a Senior Observer in The Interplanetary Geographic Service. Cathy is recalled from her Observer duties as she is asked to establish first contact with a new life form. Meanwhile the Conspiracy to prevent humans changing their non-Intervention policy continues to try and kill her. Together with Marta De Jaste, a Senior Investigator, and Tony Briggs her former jailer and security officer, they travel to the chosen planet. On the planet Tullymeade, Karloon Niesta, a disgraced scientific observer, detects a strange anomaly. A discovery that will change his planet forever. In deep space two groups of survivors try and recover from their battle in orbit above the planet Freevur

To The Survivors

An apocalypse threatens human kind. A lethal virus is detected that attacks mankind and mammals. The Government must act, and whilst the authorities struggle to find a cure, they have to plan for the worst. As the disease spreads it is not clear how many will, or will not, survive, nor what the survivors will have to do to live. They will have to cope with their grief and loneliness before they can attempt to rebuild society. They will need to find water, food, shelter, and power and then face the other threats to their survival. If they survive, there may be hope for human kind. If they survive…

The Persuasive Man

A tale of greed, insider trading love and misfortune, spanning the globe as a terminally ill businessman realises his luxurious existence will not help him. He tries to account for his past behaviour, his life, and loves. Ranging from London to Shanghai via New York, Hong Kong, and Dubai, his greed and behaviour alters his business and personal relationships. His persuasive ability brings him success, but at what cost?

Whether he is in his New York apartment, his French Château, or his St Kitts home, he does not know which relationships are real and which are false due to his past behaviour. Now he has to decide what to do with his money and how to say goodbye.

Landscape

She is a PA who dreams of running her own art gallery. He is an IT technician gambling away everything he wants. They meet and fall in love. Their relationship is threatened by endless bets even whilst they share their love of paintings. Years later some dreams are fulfilled others are dashed. Will the former lovers meet again?

Sailing Clear

Missing girls, missing money, missing man, luxury motor yachts and the people chasing them.

An old MI6 undercover mission to prevent terrorists entering the UK via sex trafficking routes went wrong. The undercover agent is assigned to a new role.

A man lost in the shadows manages the hidden

finances of the security services but dreams of a better life sailing the Mediterranean. When he runs off he is hunted, but he may have been killed by an organised crime leader. The police are assigned to find him.

Two sisters run away to Greece from the sexual abuse of their father.

The characters intersect as the hunt commences. Then the security services need to find options to deal with the fallout.

The undercover agent now in her new planning role is assigned to trace the missing financier, but a corrupt cop may give them all away.

Printed in Great Britain
by Amazon